Lessons from an Evil Mind

this is a Stupid Senseless Story

Lessons from an Evil Mind

∞

To Dorothy
May all your dreams
Come true and your
life be filled with joy

Shawna Lynn

SHAWNA LYNN

Library of Congress Control Number:		2010905089
ISBN:	Hardcover	978-1-4500-7529-9
	Softcover	978-1-4500-7528-2
	Ebook	978-1-4500-7530-5

This book was printed in the United States of America.

To order additional copies of this book, contact:
Xlibris Corporation
1-888-795-4274
www.Xlibris.com
Orders@Xlibris.com
76854

Contents

For my family,
Without your love and support I may never have written this story.

Dedication

I would like to dedicate this book to my husband, John, and children, Jeffery, Kamrin, and Cheyenne. I love you all. Thanks for believing in me.

PREFACE

MY LIFE IS something that I have always cherished. But for the past three years is something that I pray will fade.

My body is weak and my soul weaker, and I find myself unsure how much more pain and torture I can take.

Often I wonder what my life would be like if I had allowed someone to be with on my wedding day. Would I be with the one I love? Or has it always been my destiny to live with the evil that now binds me to this dungeon?

All questions that may never be answered.

My body cringes as once again I hear the footsteps of my captor. He is coming closer to the door! As fast as my weakened body will allow, I run to the middle of the room to take my position. This is not an option; you must be sitting on your knees, hands tucked within your lap, and head faced down. If you are not in this position, you will be taught a lesson . . . a lesson you don't want to learn.

His hot breath on my neck indicates that I have broken a rule. My body and mind – now in complete fear; I sit and await the wrath I know he is about to put upon me.

The silence, unnerving, is more then my mind can handle.

Screaming only within myself, I leave my fear unseen, unheard.

CHAPTER 1

The Unknown

AS I ARISE from my afternoon nap, I peek out the window that overlooks the yard. It's a small window, but it's the only window in this dreadful place, and I am happy to have it. At one time, the window was not blocked; however, now the entrance to the window is covered with sharp shards of glass cemented into the concrete around it, allowing only a small dim of light to seep through the grime and filth that layers the glass. I guess this is to ensure I never try to escape again.

With my weakened body, I slowly crawl on top of an old, broken table, so I am able to get a better look outside. I am just tall enough to see over the barricade in front of the window. It looks like a nice day. I try to guess the season. It looks like fall, as I can see a few orange leaves on the ground that have fallen from the tree that sits outside my window. The sun peeks through just enough that a pin size ray of light hits my hand. I move my bruised hand around as I watch the light dance around, causing the multiple colors of my abused skin to stand out from the milky white flesh that remains untouched by his abuse. Oh, how I crave the sunshine and wind on my face and await the day I can feel it once again!

I hear his footsteps above; the feeling of peace and contentment comes to an abrupt end.

I turn with the intention of jumping from the table; the weakened legs of the table buckle beneath it, and I find myself plummeting to the floor.

He is here!

I rise as fast as my sore, bruised legs will allow me and run to the middle of the floor, preparing for the wrath I know he is about to put upon me!

I hear his voice. My skin begins to crawl and my head twirl, making it difficult to think. My heart pounds faster and faster, until it feels like it is going to explode out of my chest. I wonder what will happen to me this time, what sort of punishment I will have to endure. His footsteps come closer to the door, and I become tense. I want to scream, but I cannot.

He is now at the door!

I scream within myself as I hear the handle on the door begin to jiggle.

"Oh no! Oh no!" I yell in my head.

Ignoring the pain of the newfound bruises on my legs, I get into the position that is deemed appropriate when I am to meet my captor. I am to sit in the middle of the floor, on my knees, head down, and hands tucked within my lap. Most importantly, never raise your head until spoken to. This is the norm, and if you aren't in that position when he walks in, you will be severely punished.

The door opens just enough so that the rays from the sun can sneak in. Ensuring that he did not see me do so, I raise my head slightly and let the sunrays hit my pale white cheeks. The warmth feels nice. A brief smile comes across my face, as I am once again reminded of another time, another place. Afraid that he may catch me with my head raised, I close my blue eyes and lower my head slowly, letting my dirty blonde hair shield my face. I hear the door slam behind him, and instantly tears stream down my cheeks.

I know I have to get my crying under control. I want to wipe my eyes, but I know I do not dare move my arms from their present position, so I try to slowly lift my shoulders so that I will be able to rub my eyes on my old, battered, white gown. I know I am not allowed to move unless I am told to, so I stop and let my shoulders rest, praying with all my heart that my actions are left unseen.

Without warning, the room becomes quiet, and I can no longer hear his footsteps. I have to know where he is. I have to be prepared. Never moving my head from its present position, I open my eyes slightly and try to see him through the corner of my saddened eyes. Through my tears, I can see his old, dirty tennis shoes. He is now standing in front of me. The room is eerily silent as he stands there without making a sound. Afraid of what may happen, my heart skips a beat, and I begin to sweat; my muscles begin to tense as every piece of my body yells, "Run, Lue! Run." Knowing I don't dare attempt running, I sit and await the wrath that I know is coming next.

The silence is unnerving, and I begin to fidget. I try not to move, but my body becomes sore and tired in its present position. My hand begins to slip from my lap. Quickly, I try to reposition my hand in hopes that he does not see it move. Unfortunately . . . I am not that lucky. He grabs my hand and begins to squeeze it with such intensity that a bruise instantly takes over my wrist. Pain shoots through my wrist and up my arm, instantly filling my eyes with fresh tears. I begin biting my lip in pain; I can not scream. I look down and can see that I have bitten through my lip, as now blood is dripping onto the floor.

I try to keep my emotions under control, but the pain is too much to handle, and a slight whimper escapes from within me. I am afraid of what he may do next. I sit as still as I possibly can, breathing lightly, ensuring I do not make another sound nor move again, not even in the slightest. The silence continues. I have to know what is happening. Never moving my head, I look over to where I know he is standing. I can see his shoes. I want to look up at him and apologize for moving in such a way that I had broken his rules.

"If he would just look into my blue eyes and see the pain he is causing me, maybe he will let go," a little voice inside me insists.

"No, he won't!" another voice in my head yells. "He loves to see you in pain. He will never release you if you show him your pain! You know that. You're twenty-nine years old. Now quit acting like a baby and do what you know you have to do."

Coming to terms with myself and what needs to be done, I sit and wait, praying that he will release my wrist soon.

A loud growl comes from beside me. Suddenly, with great power, he releases me from within his grasp and throws my hand onto the hard floor. I can hear my knuckles fracture instantly, and once again a pain shoots through my hand and up my arm. Afraid to move my newly broken hand, I let it lay on the floor. I am in excruciating pain and want to scream, but I know if I do, I will suffer painful consequences. I have no other choice but to keep my head pointed toward the ground. I can never show him the pain I am enduring.

Without warning, I find my head being ripped toward him. Suddenly, I am staring at the darkness that keeps me here. He is wearing a mask that hugs his face like a second skin, his true identity never to be seen. I continue to stare, studying his physique as if I am studying a piece of art. Although I have no way of knowing what he truly looks like, something about him I find hypnotizing. I try to look away, but I can't. His eyes look like empty, bottomless holes, the blackness pulls me in further and further until I find myself in a trance.

With a fistful of my dirty, blonde hair, he smiles as he wipes the tears from my cheeks.

"Is something wrong?" he asks in a devilish tone.

I am afraid to say anything, but at the same time, I am afraid not to answer him. Without thinking about what I am about to say, my answer slips out of my mouth.

"Nothing wrong here. Just another day in paradise," I smirk, as he continues to whip my head in every direction.

The entire time those dreadful words are coming out of my mouth, I know what I am saying is wrong. I can't help it. I am in pain and out of patience. I take in a deep breath, roll my eyes, and shake my head in disbelief. What have I done? How could I have let myself slip that way?

I close my eyes in fear and await the punishment I know is coming next.

With a chuckle, my captor releases my hair from his clutches and throws my head back toward the ground. Instantly my muscles burn, feeling as if a hot poker has just been stabbed into the back of my neck. Without thinking, I roll my neck around my shoulders trying to relieve the pain. When I realize what I am doing, I instantly stop. I am now in complete panic. Not only did I speak in a tone that I am sure he deemed inappropriate, I also moved without permission. This is it; I know I will be hurt again. I just don't know how.

"I think, 'it's' going to cry," he says to me, with an evil laugh.

"My name is Lue. I am twenty-nine years old. I live in small town called Swan Valley. I have a mother. I have a father. I have a fiancé, who loves me dearly. His name is Kamrin," I say in a soft whimper. "I am not an *it*. I am a woman."

"I guess with that little bit of information, you are now wanting to know something about me?" he asks in the utmost condescending voice.

As he walks back over to my side, he pauses where my hand lies.

"Let's play a game," he says. "I know how old you are. Now I want you to know a little more about me."

Suddenly, I feel a breeze against my arm as he slams his heel harder and harder onto the ground, each time coming closer to my hand.

"I am going to continue doing this until you guess my age." He laughs. "So you better start guessing quickly; my heel is getting closer."

Laughter fills the room, as with each time the heel of his shoe nick my skin, he laughs. It is as if he thinks it all to be a game . . . a sick game.

"You're thirty-five!" I scream.

"Wrong!" He laughs as he slams his foot down, coming closer to my fingers.

"Forty," I cry.

"Wrong again!" He laughs.

I try and concentrate on his voice, hoping that I will get an indication to how old he is. I have to get the answer right soon, or I will suffer another fracture.

"Twenty-nine!" I scream. "Twenty-nine!"

As quickly as it all began, it is over. Never saying another word, he turns and walks away.

"I guess I got it right," I say within myself. "What a freak!"

A certain sense of relief overcomes me, and I hope that I am safe for now. I peek through the corner of my eyes again and watch as he walks up the stairs toward the door leading out of the "hellhole" I am in. I am safe; my punishment is over. I take in a deep sigh and look over at my arm that still lay on the floor. I am amazed by the bruise that has taken over my entire hand and wrist. I try to move it, but the pain becomes too intense, and my body refuses to try anymore.

I am exhausted from the pain; I need a minute before I try to get up and bandage my hand.

I lie on the ground and look up at the molded ceiling and stare at the chipping paint, imagining they are stars and I am lying in a plush green field.

I begin to cry, and within moments, I cry myself into hysterics. I am tired, lonesome, and all I want is for this torture and pain to end. I just want to be left alone, and if this is the place I am to die, I wish it would happen without my mind or body enduring any more pain.

A sudden burst of laughter echoes throughout the room, causing the room to shake. Startled by the movement of the room and the loud laughter, I leap up and in one movement sit back into a kneeling position. He is back! "Although you won the game, you still need to learn your lesson!" he screams in my ear.

Without warning, he begins to place the heel of his foot onto my newly broken hand, crushing any unbroken bones beneath it. A sudden and agonizing pain overtakes my arm. I scream only within myself. I will not let a sound of pain escape my mouth this time.

"I will not give in to him . . . I will not give him that pleasure," I think to myself.

This angers him more, as he finds it exhilarating to see me in pain. I know that is why he has come back. He has to see more. He has to keep hurting me until I scream. I will not. I can not do it! This is my only way of getting back at him. I have to ensure that I do not show him any emotion at all.

It is a fight against good and evil; he will not give in, nor will I. He continues pressing harder and harder onto my knuckles until he is sure there is not a bone left unbroken. The pain is overwhelming, and I know he is not going to stop this time until I finally apologize and give him the pleasure that he is so desires. Evil will conquer once again.

"I'm sorry. I did not mean to break the rules," I whimper.

"Did you learn your lesson?" the man asks in an ecric tone.

"Yes, sir, I did," I answer in a soft, apologetic voice.

"And what lesson did you learn?" he asks.

"Not to move unless told to," I cry.

"And?" he continues.

"Never to speak to you in such a sarcastic manner," I answer softly.

He must have been satisfied with my answers, because he slowly removes his foot from my hand and walks away. Afraid that he will come back again, I watch him as he walks up the stairs and do not move until I hear the door shut and lock behind him. It is finally over. I have made it through another punishment. Slowly I reach over and pick my hand up with the hand that was still in good shape. I look down at my hand and realize that he has crushed it so badly that not only is it broken, but the skin has busted, causing two of my fingers to bleed.

I rip a piece of cloth from my dirty gown and wrap the two busted fingers as tight as I can. It hurts, but I know it has to be done.

After a few minutes of pressure, the fingers stop bleeding, and I stand up. It has been about ten minutes since my captor has left, so I know that I am safe for the night. Or at least that is what I am hoping for, as usually once he has one of his fits, he does not return until the next day.

"I need to wash these wounds and find something clean to put on them," I think to myself.

I don't have to look long for something to wrap my hand in. I only have one dress and one extra pair of underwear, and I have the dress on. I know it will anger him if I tear my underwear, and he probably will not allow me any others, but I have no other choice. I have used everything else up on cuts I had received in the past. First, I had to use my grandmother's handkerchief that my mom had given me on my wedding day. Then, when that was all used up, I slowly had to tear my extra dress up, piece by piece as my punishments became more severe and more frequent.

I look down at the clean underwear and convince myself that by using them, I will suffer no more than just a slap on the wrist. He will understand what I had to do and why I had to do it.

"I know he will understand . . . he has too," I say softly, as I hold the underwear in my hand.

I stand and debate with myself for a bit longer, as I continue to stare at the only option I have.

"Just do it," a voice inside me demands. "You know you have no other choice."

I bend down and place the underwear under my barefoot and hold it firmly down. Then with my unbroken hand, I begin pulling on them, ultimately ripping my underwear in half.

"I guess there is no turning back now," I say beneath my breath.

I walk over to the bucket of water rations I have for the week and look into the bucket. There is only a small amount of water left. I sigh. I will have to use what I have left to clean my wounds and suffer thirst until he brings me more. Uncertain of what day it is, I am unsure just how long that will be, as time here seems to stand still. I kneel over the bucket for a bit longer. With my unbroken hand, I reach down and take the last drink of water I will have until I didn't know when. I hold it in my mouth for a brief second. I enjoy the cool water against my tongue. I think of a time when I took having water for granite then slowly swallow. The water feels nice as it runs down my dry throat; however, it only clenches my thirst for a brief second.

Tears well within the corner of my eyes. I have to soak my hand. I just hate the thought of having no more water and the pain that awaits me from the cool water once it touches my open wounds. I look down at the bucket and begin crying harder.

It is either take the chance of an infection or have water to drink; either way I am destined to suffer once again. I take in a shallow breath and slowly put my broken hand in the bucket of water and soak it. The pain is overwhelming, causing me to lose my breath. However, as the cool water remains on the broken and busted fingers, my hand becomes numb, and the pain subsides enough that it is bearable.

I hold in any further tears, lay my head on the bucket, and let my hand remain in the water, afraid that once I take it out, it will hurt worse than it had before. I close my eyes and let my mind and soul relax as I take in the silence of the room.

My body relaxes.

Without warning, my head is overcome with the sound of a loud crack. A severe pain overcomes my head. I try to focus on what has happened, but my mind feels lethargic.

"What's wrong with me?" I question myself.

My head begins to hurt more and more, as I try to move it again. I have no choice; I have to know what has happened. What was that sound and where did it come from? I take my hand and pull my sweaty hair back in order to help my head lift from the bucket. Once I am able to hold my head up without the help of my hand, I wipe my eyes and look down. I find it hard to see anything more than a blur, as my eyes seem to be covered with a film of some sort. Woozy, I concentrate on moving my hand. I wipe my eyes again. My arms are weak, and my hand is slippery, causing my hand to slide off my face and slam onto the ground. I look down. To my surprise, my hand is covered in blood. In that instant, I realize that it is not tears that is blurring my vision, but my own blood.

"Maybe blood had gotten on other hand without me knowing it," I think to myself.

I try to focus on my broken hand. It is still in the water and there is no sign that while I had been relaxing that it had fallen out and that the blood had come from it.

"Where is this blood coming from?" I question.

I try to think back. I look at my blood-drenched hand again and suddenly remember that I had taken a drink from that hand earlier, and at that time the hand was clean.

My head becomes dizzier and begins to droop once again. I am no longer able to hold my upright position. I fall forward, slamming my head into the bucket below. Stunned by the sudden movement, I decide it might be best to let my head rest where it lay, as I am too weak to move it again. As I look down, my heart skips a beat, as in front of me is a pool of blood. I watch in shock as more trickles down onto the floor.

"It's coming from my head," I think to myself.

I become panicstricken.

My fingers begin to wander across my head as I try to find out where exactly the blood is coming from. After only a few seconds of searching, I find a deep gash on my head. Instantaneously, a wave of exhaustion overcomes me, and my eyes begin to shut. I try to fight it, but it is of no use. I can no longer keep them open. The room begins to spin faster and faster, until I find myself unable to comprehend anything that is going on around me.

"I can't let myself pass out. This could be a concussion," I think to myself.

Things continue to spin, and my body weakens. My head becomes heavy, and I can no longer hold it in its present position. My arms become like putty and no longer support my body, causing my hand to buckle beneath me. My face slams onto the floor with such great force that my mouth instantly begins to bleed. Fearful of losing too much blood, I take both my hands and endure the pain while I put as much pressure as I possibly can onto my head. Ignoring the blood coming from my mouth and the pain that is shooting through my broken hand, as it all seems minimal at the time compared to the blood-soaked floor beside me, I look up for a moment, and through my teary eyes, I see that he is standing in front of me holding a bloody hammer. I try to reach for him, but my arms are too weak. I try to speak, but my words are too slurred. As I pass out, the last thing I hear is a burst of evil laughter coming from where his uncaring stature stands.

CHAPTER 2

The Face of Evil

THE SMELL OF dirt and rat droppings fills the warm, musky air, causing my senses to burn. Reluctantly, I open my tired eyes and look around. I wonder what time it is or even what day it is. It seems like days since I have seen my captor. I try to lift myself from the bed; however I am quickly reminded of the past days as a slight pain rushes through my fingers and into my arm. I look down at my hand. To my bewilderment, it is nicely bandaged. Sitting for a moment longer, I think back and remember that I never had the chance to bandage it myself. In fact, the last thing I remember . . . I sit for a moment . . . I actually don't remember.

"Did I bandage it?" I ask out loud.

"I don't remember doing so," I answer myself.

Instantly, I become nervous.

"Was the hand so bad that he had no choice but to bandage it himself?" I ask myself.

I become fearful to what could be underneath the bandage, and terrifying images rushes through my head.

"I have to unravel the bandage," I think to myself. "I have to know how bad it is."

As I unravel the bandage, I am amazed. The hand is swollen and bruised; however, my fingers do not seem broken. And although it hurts to move them, I can move them with ease.

"I know they were broken," I say to myself. "They had to have been."

I stare closer, inspecting every inch of my hand. The two busted fingers are now stitched and seem to have some kind of salve on them, leaving only discolored skin where once-broken bones were. I am confused as to why he would hurt me so . . . torture me so . . . then do a good deed like taking care of my busted fingers. It almost seems as if he doesn't want me to die. He always has to bring me to near death and then ensure that I live. It is like I am his own personal torture toy that he has to keep around for his own enjoyment. Whatever his reason is, one thing is for certain – he likes to see me suffer and experience tremendous pain whenever he is around.

Saddened by the thought of living the rest of my life this way, I look toward the area I last remember being. The floor is stained with blood. Another reminder of how truly evil he is and what he had put me through the last day I had seen him. The day that he busted my hand and took a hammer to my head – my fingers begin wandering across my head. To my surprise, there is only a small lump!

I look around for some indication that he has been back. There is nothing, only the bandage that is on my hand. But how long has it been there? Did he bandage my hand after I passed out, or did he come back? How long was I passed out and how did my hand heals so miraculously? All questions I have no answer for. Suddenly, the worst thought of all crosses my mind. Did he do something to me while I was sleeping? Did he touch me in any way that was inappropriate? I could deal with the pain and the games he plays, but if he were to do something to me without my consent, that would be the worst thing in the world to me. I search my entire body for any sign that it had been invaded by an unwelcoming touch. It seems that once again I have been untouched in such a manner, leaving me with the peace I am hoping for.

I search the room some more. I see a glass of milk that was not there before, sitting on my table. After a thorough look at it, I am able to judge how long I had been passed out. The glass of milk looks as if it was a few days old because the milk is completely curdled, and a horrific smell is seeping from within the glass. Although that means that my fear is confirmed and that I had probably suffered some type of concussion. I don't care. In fact, I feel some joy as that means I have not endured any more pain, for the past few days.

Suddenly, I feel weak and hungry. I look throughout the room for any kind of food, anything that I can put into my stomach to stop the hunger that is rapidly growing inside me.

Although he tries to feed me regularly, sometimes I get punished for things I do wrong. There are rules you must follow, and if these rules are not followed, you will either be punished by starvation or pain. He says this will make me the person he desires. I think he is insane. In fact, I know he is.

My head still a little dizzy I find it hard to concentrate, instantly causing my mind to wonder in different directions. I question myself what I had done wrong this time. I know my hand had slipped from my lap, and I had spoken out of tone. But did those minimal mistakes warrant the punishment I had endured? Besides those two small incidents, I know I have learned all the rules, and I try to follow them as much as I can. I admit that at times I do forget, as there are so many rules, and they seem to change with his present mood.

My stomach growls again, indicating that I must find something to eat.

Usually, I keep food hidden for times when he doesn't feed me, but he has begun feeding me less, so there is no food left to save. Therefore, my extra food supply has diminished to nothing, except for a few crackers that I have managed to hide for the day of my escape.

My stomach growls again with such intensity that it can be heard throughout the room. Suddenly, a pain shoots through the middle of my stomach, causing me to crouch over in pain. In that instant, I know I have to find food or eat the crackers I have been saving for so many years. I begin frantically looking in every drawer, under every table, even under some old boxes that lay in a corner, for anything I can eat. I get a glimpse of a wrapper sticking from within the wall. I walk over and see that, in fact, it is my hidden crackers.

"I can't do it," I say to myself.

I have to find something else, as I have come to think of them as my only hope of freedom someday. I know that sounds strange, maybe even absurd. But they are no ordinary crackers. They have a mark on them, a mark that looks like the wings of an angel. I kiss the unwrapped package, put the crackers back in my special hiding place within the crack of the wall, and then continue with my journey.

I search and search until there is not a place left unturned. There is nothing except the curdled milk. Instantly, my stomach and mind begins arguing with each other. My head says to drink it because my body needs the nourishment, whereas, my stomach screams "no" at the thought of drinking something so disgusting. I pick up the glass and look around. I see no other choice except possible starvation or dehydration.

"Wait, there was water in the bucket the other day," I say to myself. "I know that I had put my bloody hand in it, but it is my blood after all. It won't hurt me to drink it."

I decide that I would rather drink the dirty water than the rotten milk. I walk over to the bucket where I had rested my hand days before. A loud sigh escapes from within me. To my dismay, the bucket is turned over and dry which ensures me that my punishment is not over.

Disappointed, I walk back to the table and grab the glass of rotten milk.

"I don't think I can drink this," I think to myself, as I look at the glass of rotten milk. "I guess I will just have to wait and see if and when he comes back. Hopefully, it won't be too much longer."

I put the glass back down.

The inside of my mouth feels like it is fully encased by cotton, so I decide to take a break before I exert myself anymore and my thirst becomes overwhelming. I walk over to the only place I can rest comfortably. Taking into consideration my sore hand, I slowly sit on my bed, ensuring I put no pressure on the two busted fingers and that they touch nothing that will cause the stitches to rip, ultimately causing me more pain.

After resting only for a few moments, my stomach growls again, and my head becomes dizzy. I try and comfort myself by laying my head back and breathing in deeply. It does not work. My head continues to buzz, feeling as if millions of tiny bugs are crawling inside my skull. I know this is the first indication that my blood sugar is too low and that my body is weakening with every moment that passes, as I have experienced this many times before. I have to do something or my strength will crumble to a state that I do not want to be in – a state of vulnerability that will leave me with little or no defense at all. Or worse yet, I will pass out again.

I sit up straight in my bed, reach toward the nightstand, grab the glass of curdled milk, and sigh.

"I have to drink it. I have no choice," I say under my breath.

Reluctantly, I close my eyes, lift the glass to my lips, plug my nose, and drink the chunks of curdled milk as fast as I can. The taste is more intense than I had imagined it would have been, and the chunks of rotten milk feel disgusting in my mouth. Within seconds, my stomach begins to reject it, causing vomit to rise to my throat. I try to keep it down, but my stomach is burning and refuses. Once again, vomit rises up my throat and into my mouth, making the whole ordeal worse. In desperation, I find myself looking around again for something to wash my mouth out with. I know it is pointless, as I have already checked everywhere, but my body and mind are screaming for me to do so.

"OK, concentrate," I tell myself, as I sit back on the bed. "Just think of it as a big glass of cottage cheese."

I sit back and engross in my thoughts of different foods I used to enjoy eating with cottage cheese. Suddenly, my stomach settles, and I am able to relax. However, I know I have to keep my mind occupied, or I will take the chance of my stomach getting upset again.

As I lay my head on my makeshift pillow, my thoughts become jumbled, and I begin thinking of many different things all at once. I don't mind though, as it keeps me from thinking about my stomach and the hunger that is growing inside me once again.

Without warning, a picture flashes in my mind, and all other thoughts are lost. My memories are taking me back to a place . . . a place in the past, which I remember all so well. I am no longer in my dungeon. I am no longer hungry. I am with my fiancé once again, and it is the last day I would ever see his beautiful face.

I think to myself, "How lucky I was to have had him as long as I did!"

Oh, how I have missed his sweet touch and have longed for him every day since I have been gone, wishing I could see his smile once again and what I would do to be in his arms.

He promised that it will be the first day of the rest of our lives together. That we would grow old together. Who would have thought that some stranger would have taken it all away, in just a blink of an eye? I wonder if he still thinks of me. If he questions what happened to me or if he just thinks I ran away because I got scared of "forever"? Does anyone care, or wonder what happened to me? All these questions haunt me every day of my tortured life.

"Will I ever be found?" I think to myself, as tears stream down my face. "Will this pain and misery ever end?"

I don't know what is worst – the pain my captor puts upon me, or the torture of the memories of the life I could have had, both of which are exhausting, and more than one person should have to endure.

My head still a little dizzy and getting dizzier by the moment, I lie back down on my bed and cover my face with my blanket. As I lay cuddled with my pillow tucked in front of me, I imagine that Kamrin is lying there beside me. The warmth and comfort of the thought of him in my arms overcomes me, and I am at peace. Without warning, I fall asleep and dream of that day – that wonderful day, when Kamrin slipped over to my parents' house to see me before the wedding. He took my hand, and the last words I heard him say was that he loved me and always would and that he could not wait to marry me that day.

In an instant, I am in my room waiting the minutes until I am his wife. My mom comes into my bedroom and tells me it is time to go. I look up at the clock and realize that my thoughts must have drifted from my task at hand, because all of a sudden three hours have passed, and I am nowhere close to being ready for the wedding. Panicked of being late to my own wedding, my heart begins to pound with excitement, as I run through the house gathering up all my things I need to get dressed for the wedding.

Suddenly, my mind flashes again, and I am at Kamrin's house. I am dressed in my beautiful white wedding dress, with only my veil left to put on. As I await my dad to come in and tell me it is time to go down to the garden, I look outside and sneak a peek of Kamrin in his perfectly fitted white tux. He is so stunning standing among the flowers with his best man, Jeffery. They both are talking and laughing, enjoying the day, neither of them having a care in the world. The sun, bright that day, shining all around making it look as if there are diamonds placed just so within Kamrin's dark brown hair. His eyes . . . his beautiful bright blue eyes seem to twinkle as they always did when he is determined. His face is strong and young, that of a twenty-six-year-old man; he is perfect. I stand in his bedroom window and watch him, thinking how lucky I am to have found someone as wonderful as he.

My mind flashes again, and I am no longer in his bedroom. I am at my dad's side. We are walking down the floral, sprinkled path toward Kamrin's waiting arms. We keep walking and walking, however, never reaching our destination. I can see Kamrin, but I cannot reach him. I begin to panic and run toward him. Suddenly, distorted faces begin flashing in front of my face – each person laughing harder and harder as the faces appear in front of my face quicker, becoming more distinct. They are all laughing at me. I continue to run, trying to get away from laughter, trying to get to him. My body slams into a force of the unknown, and I am hurled to the ground. I try to get up, but the force keeps me down, holding me to the ground, as if thousands of hands are covering my body, pushing me, keeping me down. I look up. Kamrin is now standing above me, reaching for me. I try to reach for his hand, but I still cannot move. Suddenly, he begins to fade, until he is nothing more than a ghostly figure standing there with a look of desperation upon his face. I beg for him not to leave. I hear his voice as he ensures me that he will not leave me. With his ghostly hand, he reaches again; this time I feel his touch. Suddenly, I am able to free myself, and with the help of his strong hands, I lift myself from the ground and take his hand into mine.

Then, as with every dream, I begin screaming, my heart pounding, lying in a pool of sweat – my daydream turning into a nightmare, as he turns to look at me. It is not him. I scream again, as I see the man dressed in black, waiting for me in the dark corner of bedroom. The man that took me that day. As I awake, my body cringes. I can still feel his hot breath on my neck, as he whispers in my ear, "You will never be his," then placed his hand across my mouth, drugged me, and took me away from everything I knew, everything I loved.

There was no time to scream or even to make a noise, as it all happened so quickly. I had tried to fight back, but the powerful drugs took control, and I became putty in his arms. There was no one around, and the struggle didn't last long, leaving no time for anyone to see what was happening.

"Why was I so stubborn and insisted that I am left alone to get dressed that day?" I start questioning myself. "Why didn't I let my mother be with me like she had requested?"

I wipe my sobbing, tired eyes. I can't let him see me cry; that is one of his most enforced rules. He says that he takes care of me, and there should be no sadness, and when he sees me cry, it makes him become vicious. After receiving a broken arm, I learned quickly that it is best not to say or do anything. Just listen, do as told, and whatever pain or sadness you are experiencing, do not . . . I repeat . . . do not let him see you cry. I know by doing this, I am not weak, that it is my way of surviving until I can get back to the loving arms of my family.

I know I have to get my mind off the past, as when I think of "what might have been" for too long, it always makes me become extremely depressed, and I cannot take the chance of losing focus on what is around me for any length of time. I have to always be aware of my surroundings as much as possible. To get my mind off things, I decide to look around. I do that to pass time. Sometimes, it pays off to look within the shelter he has me in. I have found some pretty interesting things and some things I can use. Some he lets me keep, others he takes away if I misuse them. I think he puts things in here just for me to find. I guess it's his way of being nice to me without wanting me to know it. Or at least that is what I tell myself. Everyone has to have a nice side to them, don't they?

As I turn my head, I get a quick reminder that this is not the case with this man and his sick mind. As in the corner sits my dirty, battered wedding dress I wore on that dreadful day. He makes me keep it there, so I am constantly reminded of how my life could be. He says if it wasn't for him I would have no life at all, that without him my life would be a deep, meaningless, empty hole. I know he is wrong; I would have had a wonderful life with Kamrin and maybe even a child by now.

I stand staring at the dress for a while longer.

"I wonder what it would have been like to dance with Kamrin that day," I think to myself, as I take the dress from its stand and slip it over my gown.

It was big on me now, and it was nowhere as beautiful as it was the last day I had put it on. It is dirty and has holes throughout it where rats had chewed pieces of material off. Closing my eyes, I ignore what it looks like and begin imagining the way it was. I take the stand on which it lay, hold it in my arms, and begin twirling around. I am with Kamrin now, and we are on the dance floor. I am in his strong arms, and we are dancing our first dance. We are both laughing and smiling, enjoying each other. My dad comes in and taps Kamrin's shoulder. It is now his turn to dance with the new bride. We dance for only a few moments, before Kamrin comes back and steals me away. I lay my head on the shoulder of the stand, acting as if it was him. It's not as soft as his shoulder was, but with a little imagination, I am able to convince myself it is.

I dance around my room for more than an hour, before I realize what I am doing. I am never to touch this dress. Panic stricken, I take off the dress and put it back on the rack. I have to ensure it is placed exactly the way it was. After a few moments of moving the dress around, I am satisfied that it is in its exact spot and the dress is lying perfectly. However, paranoid, I step and look once again.

"Perfect," I think to myself.

Saddened by the sight, I quickly look away and begin my search once again.

The room is dim with just a small stream of light to brighten my way. The walls are dark, gloomy, and covered in mold from where the ceiling leaks from outside. The floor, where carpet once lay, is now covered in dirt and rat droppings. I hate that I have to walk on it with my bare feet, but I have no choice, as he no longer allows me shoes. He says I misused my shoes, and I have to earn new ones.

When in actuality, the only thing I had done wrong was place my shoes on the shelf pointing the wrong way. I will admit I had done it on purpose, as it was my only way at getting back at him. Now, I had planned on putting them back before he came in. But I was too late. He had walked in and seen them before I could fix the problem. That is when the punishment began. Now you would have thought taking my shoes away would have been punishment enough. Well, to him it was just the beginning. He took the shoes, made me cut them up. Then, as with every punishment I endure, I had to place my hand on his chest and repeat the words, "I am yours forever . . . You are my savior," over and over again, until he was thoroughly convinced that I meant what I was saying. Although I never meant a word, I did what I knew I had to do to rectify the situation. Then and only then was I be spared the torture of having to continue saying such things, that I no way in hell I meant.

I gave up trying to understand his logic a long time ago and just endure what punishment he has for me. Although sometimes painful, this is the best way to avoid any further confrontations with him, as confrontations ensure more pain. And with all that I have suffered in the past years I have been with him, I know this is my only way of saving myself. I have to keep my emotions from escaping from within me.

Although, looking around it is obvious that I have not learned my lessons too quickly, as my room now is bare with only a few things remaining. Scattered around is my beat-up, old furniture, which he has allowed me too keep so far. He says that this is all that I deserve. Now, at one time I had decent furniture, but every time I got punished, an item would disappear and would be replaced with something old and rotting. He says my surroundings should fit my personality, and with the way I act, I only deserve ugly things. Afraid of him taking everything away, I have learned to act like I like them, and I always make it a point to thank him. I don't know if this angers him, but so far it has worked, and nothing more has been taken away.

I continue walking around, feeling the dirt and rat droppings squish between my toes, as the carpet is still a little wet from the last big rain we had gotten. It feels disgusting, and I wish for shoes once again.

It seems that the room has stayed the same since I was last punished. I am just about to give up, when a sparkle in the corner suddenly catches my eye . . . a sparkle I have never seen before. My eyes are drawn to it, and I walk over. There in the darkened corner sits a mirror.

"I know I walked past here earlier, why didn't I see it then?" I ask myself.

I look around for some indication that he has been there recently, or maybe he is still in here with me. There is no sign of his presence, not even his footprint in the dirt. I walk around retracing my footsteps I had made earlier, ensuring that there were no footprints except for my own. I learned a long time ago to walk a certain path; that way any other footprints that I might see is a sign that he has been here or possibly could still be here. It's the only way I have any indication of what is going on, as I seem to be sleeping more these days as my body continues to weaken. I don't think he knows that I follow my footsteps, and I would hate to see what would happen if he did.

"Wow, could I have been so preoccupied with looking for food, that I missed seeing the mirror?" I ask myself.

Shaking my head in disbelief that I could have been so oblivious to what is around me, I look back at the mirror. It is a big mirror. In fact, it is a full-length mirror, one that I can see my entire body in.

"I must have missed it before," I say to myself, shrugging shoulders. "There is no other explanation."

I am leery to why it is here, but I decide to take the chance and get closer to it. Slowly I walk toward it, taking each step with great care and apprehension. I stop and look around to ensure I am alone. I still see no one, so I continue on my way. After a few minutes, I start feeling silly about the way I am acting; after all it is just a mirror, and here I am acting like a wild animal sneaking up on its prey.

As I come close enough to the mirror to see my reflection, I realize that the mirror is covered in mesh, which makes it difficult to see.

"I guess the mesh is so that I don't break the mirror and attack my captor," I think to myself with a slight giggle.

I step back and run my bruised, cut fingers through my hair. A sharp pain shoots through my head, a quick reminder of what could and probably will happen if I were to break any more rules.

"Hmm, well, my hair is longer. In fact, it is a lot longer," I think to myself.

I stare at my hair some more, looking at it from all different angles. It looks really dirty, to where it no longer has the beautiful, bright blonde shine that I once took such great pride in. I think back to the past and realize I had never had it that long before and decide right then that once I escape I will never cut it again.

Examining the rest of my body, I begin moving my dirty, battered gown around, analyzing every inch of my body. My skin is filthy, and I wonder how long it has been since the last time I had a shower, as I am only allowed a shower once in a while which usually consists of a little soap and a cold hose from outside. I'm used to it now, and I don't even mind. In fact, sometimes I just let the cold water fall on me as the water feels nice against my sore, abused body. Plus, there is nothing like the feeling of being clean. Especially, when you have been forced to live in such filth for so many years.

I inspect my body some more, focusing on every new bruise and scar I have gotten since this whole nightmare began. I am amazed on how many scars I have gotten and begin running my fingers across each one trying to remember what I had done to deserve each new lesson. I crouch down in front of the mirror staring at my face, studying every line, every scar. I begin to cry. Whereas, staring back at me is a repulsive, abused woman, where a once vibrant, angelic, young women used to be.

"Would anyone recognize me? Could anyone love me again?" I think to myself. "I mean, how anyone could love something so detestable?"

I am utterly disgusted by what I am seeing; however, I cannot look away. I inspect myself some more. Due to the lack of sunshine, my skin is pale white, and my eyes have dark circles around them, both of which cause me to look like I am suffering from malnutrition. I lift up my gown and inspect my midsection. It is obvious that I have lost at least thirty pounds, as all my ribs seem to protrude from under my skin. Taking my fingers I outline each bone, feeling them as if they are some type of foreign object in my body.

I sit and look in the mirror for hours studying my entire body, astonished of how much I have changed and how many wounds I have endured. I touch each scar over and over again until they are embedded in my mind.

"How could someone do this to another human being?" I ask myself as I continue outlining every disfigurement of my body.

I wonder once again, just how long I have been in this gloomy place. I used to count the days, but my captor says that there is no need for that, as we will be together for eternity, and eternity has no measurement. However, without him knowing, I would still try to count the days in my head. That was until my punishments became more frequent and more violent, causing me to lose days on end.

I am lost in my thoughts and am not aware of the goings-on around me. Suddenly, I feel a hand on my shoulder. I jump away from the mirror and sigh quietly to myself. I know he is there, and he has been watching me the entire time. I am afraid to turn around, but I know I have too. With great caution, I turn slowly. Standing in front of me is exactly what I fear. It is *him*. He is in his usual black mask. He says true love has no beauty; therefore, there is no need for him to show me his face. Often I wonder what he may look like. But I know the day he finally let his face will be the day I will be killed.

Unconscious to what I am doing, I find myself staring into the emptiness of his shadowed body. Panic stricken by my actions, I hurry over to my designated spot in the middle of the floor and take my position.

"I'm sorry, I'm sorry, I did not hear you come in," I cry, as I cower down into my crouched position.

I peek through my sorrowful eyes and see his dark shadow. He is standing right in front of me. I look up slowly, hoping that he will see the remorseful look upon my face. I know I am taking a chance by doing so. But I want him to know how truly sorry I am that I had not met him in a proper way.

Never looking into his eyes again, I scan his entire body. He is wearing a pair of old jeans and a button-up shirt, both of which I have never seen him wear before. It is almost like looking at a real human being and not the evil man that has kept me captured for so long. It is a nice change as I am used to him wearing a black shroud that covers his entire body. A slight grin appears on my face as I look up his perfectly toned body and see that underneath is a merely a man.

"What a beautiful smile!" he says in a sinister, almost inhuman tone.

I look up. I am quickly reminded that he is nothing more than that of true evil, as his mask shows his true identity, that of a dark and heinous person.

His eyes dark and soulless, sends a chill up my spine, causing me to look away quickly.

I see that his hand is on his hip now, as if he is agitated with me. In his other hand, he is holding a big plate of food and a big white box tied with a beautiful, shiny, black bow. Both of which I had not seen seconds before.

"I was going to give you these, but I see that maybe you are a little into yourself to deserve them," he says with a growl.

"No, no, I was just looking at . . . ummmm . . . my hair and how much I have changed. I'm sorry," I say in desperation, afraid he will take the food away.

"*Liar!*" he screams.

"No, sir, I am not lying," I say in a pleading voice.

"You don't like how I have changed you? Do you?" he screams as he throws my food and box on the floor. "I might just have to rethink your reward."

My head begins to scream in fear as he grabs my hair and drags me over to my newfound mirror.

"Look at yourself! I have made you beautiful!" he screams as he slams my face into the mesh. "You would be nothing without me, you understand!"

"Yes, sir, I understand. I did not mean to disrespect you. I, I, I . . ." I stutter in fear.

"Never mind! You sit and think of what you have done. I am going upstairs. I need to be away from you right now, before I do something that I might regret!" he screams as he slams my face into the mesh once again.

Storming out of the room and up the stairs, he begins to mumble words I cannot understand. Abruptly, he turns and runs back down the stairs toward me. My heart begins to beat faster as I run back to my spot and take my position. I start clenching my teeth and close my eyes, hoping that I do not get punished again. However, I know it is inevitable and I await my punishment.

Within a fraction of a second, he is standing in front of me bent over with his lips placed against my ear.

Without warning, he screams as loud as he can, "I should kill you now!"

His words pierce not only my ears, but also my soul. I am scared out of my mind, as he has never in all the years I have been with him said that to me. Instantly, my entire body begins to shake uncontrollably, and I cannot stop it. I try to cease the shaking, but the rising fear inside me will not let my body relax. This is it, my time here is over. I am petrified, not because of death, but the thought of the pain he will put upon until my body finally fades. It is more than I can take. I want to scream, "Just do it!" but my mind refuses to let the words escape my mouth.

Without warning, my captor leaps toward me, and with his hands he grabs my neck. Slowly by slowly, he begins applying a small amount of pressure, tightening his grip until I find it hard to catch my breath. However, before he assures me certain death, he stops. I look up at him, thankful that I can breathe. To my amazement, he lets go completely and begins talking within the room, as if he is arguing with some unseen person. I move my eyes around scanning the room for someone, for anyone, that he could be talking to. I see no one. After a moment or two of arguing within himself, he stands back, grabs my hair, and slams my face onto the floor, then turns and walks back toward the stairs, screaming the entire way.

I am relieved that he has left, and I have not endured very much pain, besides a sore neck and a cut or two. I wipe my bloody nose I had just got from the mesh on the mirror and from the hit on the floor. I look down at my gown and see there is very little blood. Relieved, I take a quick look in the mirror and see that the new wounds are minimal, and there are only a few finger marks on my neck . . .

"Just a small scratch," I think to myself. "One of his easiest fits I have seen him go through. Well, except for him choking me. That scared the hell out of me."

I try and shake the whole thing off, as I am used to his fits by now and know there will be more to come. I am just glad it is over, and I am still alive. I know it sounds strange that after all that I have been through, I do not want to die. But I know in my heart that some day I will escape and that I will be back in the arms of my true love.

I look over to where the argument began and see that the food is still on its plate, that in fact it has landed upright and is all intact. To my surprise, he has also left the package, and it also awaits me. I am happy to see both, so I run over to where they lay.

Curious about the present I have received, I grab it up off the ground first and start to open it. I have not received a gift like this in a long time. In fact, I have never received a gift. Well, at least not from this man. I cannot help myself as I rip through the paper like a child on Christmas day. I am so excited to see what it is that my enthusiasm will not allow me to open it slowly. Therefore, only taking seconds before the floor is sprinkled with torn-up wrapping paper. My hand begins to shake in excitement.

Stopping abruptly, I decide that I want to savor the moment, as enjoyment is something I have not been allowed to have for a long time. Taking the lid off slowly, I anticipate what is waiting for me inside. I close my eyes and feel the paper inside. Immediately, my imagination takes over, and I begin imagining many different things that can be in there. Maybe it is a new pair of shoes, or maybe a new blanket. All things that I need and have been wanting for some time now. To my surprise, a smile appears on my face, something that has not happened in what seems like forever and a day. I can't take it anymore; I have to know what it is, and I have to know now!

In a flash, I open my eyes and tear open the paper. To my delight, wrapped inside white tissue paper are a beautiful gown and a new pair of shoes. I am shocked. What had I done to warrant such a lavish gift? Instantly, I jump up and begin walking around. I am afraid to touch them, afraid that maybe it is some sort of trick or another one of his twisted jokes. Reaching my foot forward, I touch the box lightly with the tip of my toes, as if it is a snake ready to bite me. Nothing happens more than the box moving slightly. However, not thoroughly convinced, I begin to walk around again. I know I am being silly. I just can't stop myself. After all these years, I have became paranoid and for good reasons. I begin walking slower and slower around the box, all the while talking to myself.

"Pick them up," I say to myself. "It is a present."

"No, it has to be a trick," another voice in my head says. "He would never be nice to you, he couldn't."

I continue to walk around the box, staring at the dress and shoes, until I come to the conclusion that he has for some unforeseen reason, honestly, just gave me a gift.

Still a little uncertain to his motives, I look around the room, ensuring that I stay aware of all that is around me at all times. After all, I do not want to put my guard down and be hit with a hammer again. After a few glances around, I am convinced that I am still alone. I reach down and pull out the dress and shoes to admire them. The dress is long and baby blue, with little rhinestones around the neck. I am excited to see how beautiful it is and lay it against my body to admire its beauty. It is perfect, something I would have picked out for myself. Maybe for a formal dinner or a night on the town.

Without thinking, I run over to the mirror and start admiring my new dress. I cannot believe what is happening. I have finally received a new dress and a new pair of shoes, and they are amazing. Looking into the mirror, I begin dancing around. I feel like a little girl again trying on her mother's clothes.

My mind is taking me back to past years when I was a child. I remember how I would sneak into my mother's closet and try on her clothes. My mother would always catch me, but she would never get mad. She would help me pick out clothes, and we would play dress up together. I have to laugh when I think of the times I had put makeup on her, and no matter how awful it would look, my mother would always tell me she loved it. I remember how my mom and I would get dressed up for my father and wait for him to come home from work, then we would all dance around to old '50s music in the living room. It was a time of innocents. A time I wish I could go back to.

After playing with the dress for a while, I begin to question his motives again to myself. I carefully lay the dress back in its box, assuring that I do not let it touch the floor. I then turn my attention to the food that has been lying next to the box. It is no longer there! I turn and see that he is once again standing in front of me. I jump back in complete fear and cover my face, afraid I am going to get hit again. After standing there for a few moments with my face covered, I realize I am safe. So I uncover my face and look his way. To my surprise, he has a new plate of food in his hands.

I don't hesitate; I take the food from his hands and begin to eat it as if I have not eaten in weeks. The food tastes rotten, like it had been sitting out for days. I ignore the taste and keep shoving fistfuls of food into my mouth . . . He touches my shoulder. I slow down my eating, as I know that means I am eating too fast, and if I don't slow down, he will take my food away.

I think to myself, "Wait, I haven't eaten in days," and begin to eat faster, so fast that I almost choke.

He begins to chuckle as if he thinks it's funny that he almost starved me to death; in fact, he seems to be enjoying what he has done to me. I hate that he gets such enjoyment from my suffering.

He continues to laugh.

I am starved; therefore, I ignore his laughter and continue to eat. When I am finished, I hand my plate back over to him and begin licking the extra food off my fingers. My stomach begins to turn as I realize that my hands are covered in maggots. I blink my eyes, as I cannot comprehend what I am seeing. Did he intentionally feed me rotten, larva-infested food? Why? I stare at my hands in disbelief, as maggots continue to crawl around my fingers. I am disgusted. I want to get the maggots off me. But I am afraid to move.

I look up at my captor with eyes filled with confusion, in hopes that he will give me permission to wipe my hands off. He never moves, not in the slightest. Right then, I know I better do nothing more than take my new lesson and learn from it. Suddenly, I feel something move against my lip. I know what it is. It is a maggot! My stomach is no longer able to keep the food in, and I begin to vomit onto the floor. I try to stop the vomiting, but un-processed maggots coming up from my stomach begin to move in my mouth, causing me to become violently ill. My head begins to sweat, and vomit spews out of my mouth as I continue throwing up everything I just ate. I am now covered in vomit, as he has not let me move the entire time I am getting sick.

Furious that I have thrown up the food he gave me, he reaches down, grabs most of it off the floor, and puts it back on the plate.

"Eat it!" he screams violently.

My stomach begins to turn again, and sweat begins pouring down my face. I want to beg him not to make me eat it, but I know not to confront him on his decision. I take the plate from his hands, look at him with saddened eyes, hold my nose, and begin eating it as fast as I can. He becomes angrier and rips my hand off my nose, insisting I smell everything I eat. The food, smelling of rotten flesh and vomit, turns my stomach even more. Instantly, my stomach tries reversing the food back up to my throat. I know I have to keep it down or he will make me eat it again, and that is something I do not want to do. It is bad enough that I am being forced to eat it this time; I do not want to throw it up again and have to eat that also. It is obvious that this could become a pattern and that I may never get away from this disgusting ordeal unless I force myself to deal with the task at hand. I have to stop and take a deep breath before I continue, as this is the most digesting thing he has ever made me do. I try not to cry, but tears begin forming in my eyes.

"You can do this," I tell myself. "Just think of something else."

After I manage to eat everything he has put on the plate, he walks over to the new dress he has brought me and rubs the remaining vomit from the floor onto it.

Handing me the dress, he says that he is sorry he has to punish me in such a way, but until I become like him, the lessons will have to continue. He also says that I am to take a shower and get dressed and that we were going to go visit some people.

He then kisses my forehead and walks up the stairs.

His lips feel like dried snakeskin against my forehead, and I try not to show it, but my body cringes at his touch. I am appalled that after all he has done to me in past and what I know he will do to me in the future, he has the audacity to show such a kind gesture.

"How dare he touch me so!" I think to myself.

I don't know if I am more bewildered because he has shown me a kind gesture, that he is taking me to see some people or because I heard him speak in a normal tone. I hadn't heard him speak in such a tone since the first day he took me, and all he said then was, "You will never be his." I will never forget those words; they haunt me every day. My stomach is still upset, however, I know I have to forget what has just happened and what I just ate. I have to keep my mind focused on what is happening now. Where are we going and why are we going there?

CHAPTER 3

The Game

I STAND IN the area he has designated for me to take a shower. The memory of his disgusting lips on my forehead shoots a shiver through my body, and my stomach begins to turn again. I know I can't throw up again, as that will only prolong my agony. I swallow the vomit that has gathered in my throat and continue on with my shower. I take my time letting the cold water run over my head, easing the pain from my last punishment and the pain from my sore, worn-out body. The water feels nice, and it is refreshing to have my skin and hair clean again. After my shower, I stand in front of my dress, happy to see something new for me to wear. I carefully remove the dress out of the box, taking extra care not to let the vomit spread any further. I then clean the spot as best I can, with the water from the hose and the gown I have just taken off. I am happy to see that with only minimal cleansing the vomit is gone.

With my new dress in hand, I walk over to the mirror to get dressed. To my surprise, sitting now next to the mirror is a brush and a few bits of makeup. All things I have not seen in a very long time, as I am only allowed a toothbrush and a comb. Both of which have broke some time ago. All these new things excite me, but I know I have to be careful. This kindness he is showing me has to come with a consequence. This I am sure of.

Taking in consideration the sick mind of the man that has me captured, I examine the brush for any type of torture devices. I know that may seem strange for someone to do. But with this man, I know anything is possible. I know this for a fact, because one time he took my toothbrush without me knowing it and replaced it with a brush that was hard like a razor, which caused me to cut my gums tremendously the first time I used it.

I take the brush, and with great caution, I feel each bristle, ensuring that each one is soft, and then I run my finger gently around every edge to make sure that they are not razor sharp. Everything is perfect, leaving me with the confidence to use them. I begin to brush my hair, trying to brush out the tangles and knots that I have acquired from the improper brushing and cleansing. It takes a while, but with persistence, I finally get it done.

As I prepare for the night, I wonder to myself, "How does he plan on keeping me quiet? What makes him think that I won't yell and scream? That I won't tell the person that he has kept me captured for all this time?"

All of this making no sense to me, I try to be optimistic and start thinking of any positive scenario possible. I start to smile. Maybe he is going to let me go. I know, I will tell him I won't say anything to anyone if he will just let me go. He can trust me. I will never break my promise. Besides, who would believe me and the horror stories I would have to tell? Not to mention, I have never seen his face, so it will be impossible for me to ever describe him to anyone. As far as I know, he could be someone I know in the past, maybe even a past friend.

Instantly, I come to the conclusion that I will not beg. He hates begging. In fact, the last time I begged, I had my lips super-glued shut for a week and was fed through a straw. It wasn't that bad though. At least I didn't have to eat his disgusting food, as I was only fed such things as nutritional shakes and pudding.

"That's it. I won't beg. I will just let him know I won't say a thing, and maybe he will let me go," I think to myself as I continue brushing my hair. "Wait! He won't let me go. If we are going to go see people, he will have to take his mask off. He will never let me go after seeing his face."

With that last thought haunting my mind, I start to get worried.

"What is he going to do to me to keep me quiet? Or maybe these friends of his have been part of the plan all along," I whisper softly.

Without warning, my mind becomes flooded with horrendous thoughts.

"Oh my god, they could be as sick as him, and they are going to take turns torturing me!" I think in a panic. "No, they can't! I don't know how much more my frail body or mind can take. They just can't!"

My entire body begins to shake all at once, as tears fill my eyes.

"I can't cry. I won't cry," I say to myself. "Just keep it together. You have to be strong to make it through this night."

I continue brushing my hair and applying makeup to my scarred face, taking my time studying every new punishment I have encountered. As I take the makeup and try to hide my hideous scars, I realize that the once-beautiful woman I was will never be seen again. Unable to look anymore at what he has made me, I close my eyes, turn away from the mirror, and continue to brush my hair – as it is the only thing left on my body that did not disgust me. After what seems like a few minutes more, I am dressed and ready to go.

"Wow!" I hear from behind me. "You look so beautiful. More exquisite than the first day we met."

"The first day we met?" I question myself. "Had I known him from before or is he talking about the day he drugged me, and took me away from my family and my one true love?"

"Well, none of that matters. I have to concentrate on what is happening now and how I can convince him or his friends to let me go," I think to myself.

He takes my hand and puts it in his. The feeling of warmth overcomes me. It feels nice to once again have human contact.

"Wait, this is the man I despise. The man who has taken my life away from me. The man who tortures me daily! Then how can this feel so right?" I wonder to myself.

I look up with a diminutive smile on my face. My smile fades quickly, as I see him once again standing there emotionless, wearing his same black mask. I am with no one special, no one that cares for me. I am with him, and I am sure that he doesn't care if I were to die right now. How could I have let myself ever think anything more than that? My mind yells at me to rip his mask off and show his true identity. But I don't, as I know that would probably be the worst thing I could do. My heart drops, and the smile disappears. I try to hide the fact, but I am too late. He has seen.

"What happened to that beautiful smile you just had?" he asks, as he releases his grip on my hand.

"Oh, sorry," I explain in a soft, quivering voice. "I was just hoping that I was going to see you."

"You can see me," he says sarcastically.

"No," I exclaim.

"The real you. You without the mask," I lie. "I just want to see your beautiful face."

He shakes his head and says, "Now, we can't have that, now can we?"

He then lets out a little chuckle as he walks around me, looking over my body like an animal ready to pounce its prey.

Without warning, he stops and grabs my hand into his. This time he takes hold of the hand that has the stitches. His grip gets tighter and tighter as we walk through the room toward the stairs leading out. I don't want to ask him to hold the hand without stitches, but the pain becomes intense, and I am afraid that my stitches might burst and start bleeding again. Besides, I do not want anything more to disrupt my concentration, and the pain that he is putting upon me is doing just that.

"How can I change hands without him knowing what I am doing?" I ask myself. "It has to be something so obvious that he will never question what I am doing."

Thinking quickly, I begin limping, acting as if something is wrong. I stop and act like I have to fix something. I slowly take my hand from his and reach down and begin messing with my shoes. Taking my time, I take each shoe off and shake it out, acting as if something has gotten into them. Surprisingly enough, he stands there and waits for me, never making a sound. Whereas, I think for sure he will tire of my nonsense and punish me for stopping.

"Sorry, there was something in my shoes," I explain. "I didn't want to meet your friends limping the way I was."

"That's OK. I understand, first impression is the most powerful of all impressions," he says, as he laughs the most horrifying laugh I have ever heard come from within him.

All my efforts to keep him from holding my sore hand were useless, as suddenly he grabs my damaged hand again and starts walking. I have no more tricks. There is no other way to handle this situation except to either deal with the pain or ask him to switch hands. I am uncertain as to where we are going and how far it is, so I deem it necessary to take the chance and ask him.

"Excuse me," I say beneath my breath. "The hand you are holding is very sore. Is there a way we can switch, so that you are holding my other hand?"

Suddenly, he stops and swings my body to where it is facing his.

"Are you talking about this hand?" he screams, as he holds it in front of my face and begins to squeeze it tighter and tighter, causing me to cringe in pain.

"Yes, sir," I answer, trying not to show him my distress.

"Hum, well, let's see. Maybe I would have, that is if you hadn't tried to trick me before," he screams as he tightens his grip once again.

"No, sir, honestly I was not trying to trick you before," I beg. "I really had something in my shoe."

"Oh, really now? Because I did not see anything fall out of either shoe," he says in a condescending voice.

"Please, sir. I am sorry. Can you please release my hand? I am begging you." I plead. "I don't want to meet your friends with tears in my eyes."

"You know what?" he screams as he throws my hand away from his face. "You're right. I don't want these people to meet you and see how much of a crybaby you are."

He then grabs my shoulders, and with one swift movement, swings me around to where I am now standing on the other side of him. He grabs my hand in his and starts to walk, never saying another word about it. I am appeased that he has seen my point of view for once and has relieved me of any more pain. I look at him and smile softly, showing him my gratitude for the kindness he has just shown me. He smiles back, and for a brief second, his eyes change from the dark, uncaring black eyes that he usually possess to a beautiful bright blue. In that instant, I see a speck of kindness and caring in his eyes. I have to blink and look into his eyes again to ensure what I had seen was real. His eyes are black, leaving me no indication that they were ever anything but the uncaring black they have always been. I am confused.

"It's OK, Lue." He chuckles. "Trust me."

Walking hand in hand with my captor, I can't help but think I have also heard that same chuckle before. It is so calming and makes me feel like I am at home again. I want to hear it one more time so that I can ensure the feeling. But he is now silent.

"I know his eyes changed," I convince myself, "and I know those eyes, and I know that laugh."

The room silent, I continue to think.

"Where have I seen those eyes and heard that laugh before?" I ask myself. "I have to figure this out."

This is the first time in over three years that I have any clue at all to who this man is. I just have to concentrate.

My mind begins scrambling, but I cannot figure out from whom I would have heard such a laugh and seen such beautiful eyes. I continue to let my mind wonder as I search through every memory of every person I have ever known, trying to figure out who laughs in such a manner, whose eyes make me feel at home. But the memories seem to have faded, leaving me with only distorted faces and nothing more than emptiness within my search.

I don't realize that during my exploration through my memories that we have stopped walking and are in fact now standing in front of the staircase. I snap out of my trance and study the stairs. They are empty and unwelcoming, and sense of regret overcomes me. I do not want to walk any further. I am afraid to see what awaits me through the door at the top of the stairs. But I have no choice, as he is now pulling me up the stairs, leaving me with no other option but to do as he wants. As we head up the old, rickety stairs that leads away from my room, I try to calm myself by thinking of my family and how some day I hope to be with them once again. The stairs creaking beneath our feet, sounding like an old horror movie, erases my hopes and reminds me of the true horror I am in. I am headed into the unknown, and the unknown is not a place I want to be.

"Can we stay here on the steps for a while longer and talk?" I ask in a soft whisper.

"Why?" he asks.

"I just thought we could talk a little, and honestly I am nervous about meeting your friends. I haven't seen anyone in so long," I say nervously.

"Well, you don't have anything to worry about. They are all really nice girls, and they are shy also. In fact, they don't talk much," he says with a devilish laugh beneath his breath.

"Girls? Does he have other girls locked up like me?" I begin to wonder. "Is this another one of his sick tricks?"

"Are they just like me? I mean, friends like you and I?" I ask politely, trying to get more information of who these girls could be.

"If you mean, are they close like us and are going to be together for the rest of our lives? No, Hun," he says. "They can never be like us. You are my special girl, and you always will be. You see, some day you will love me for who I am, and then we will have a life you could never imagine."

I take a shallow breath and say nothing, as he has just affirmed that he never has had the intention of letting me go, letting me live a normal life again. I am now truly disgusted.

We continue up the stairs. They seem to go forever, but I don't mind. I am terrified. I know that he had said that I would be his some day, so I feel more confident that he does not have my death in mind. But he also loves to torture me, so I am uncertain too if that is what awaits me beyond the doors. All I know for certain is that no matter what he has planned for me, I still have hope that one day, when he least expects it, I will get away.

Unexpectedly, we stop in the middle of the staircase. He releases his tight grip on my hand and tells me to turn and face the wall. Afraid to question his demands, I instantly do as I am told. Suddenly, a loud sound comes from behind me, sounding as if a large brick wall is sliding across the wooden floor. I try to peek back, but I am afraid to move my head, afraid that he might see me do so.

"OK," he says. "You can turn around."

I turn quickly, and there to my surprise is a pathway, one that had not been there seconds before. Forcefully, he takes my hand back into his and begins walking into the dark path that led to the unknown. The stairs are narrow, making it impossible for us to walk side-by-side. Still holding my hand, he walks in front of me, pulling me behind him. The staircase is dark and gloomy and has a smell about it that turns my stomach. Worst of all, the stairs are cracked and missing pieces of wood on them, causing it to be almost impossible to walk down. I know this because my foot falls into a few different holes, causing me to suffer new cuts on my heels. I try to keep my balance by holding onto one of the walls, but the wall is slimy, ensuring that I have no grip at all. I reach for the other wall in hopes that it will not be as slimy as the other and I will be able to have some sort of stability. I feel nothing. I move over closer to where the wall should be and reach again. Still there is nothing; in fact, it is like reaching into an empty hole. I move my foot toward the side of the stairs; it also is empty. I'm confused.

"How could there be no wall or stairs beyond where I am walking. How is this possible?" I ask myself.

I reach again, determined that there must be a wall somewhere; I reach as far as I can. Without warning, my shoes become caught on a large sliver of wood that is sticking up, and I lose my balance. Suddenly, I find myself falling into the emptiness of the unseen wall. I reach around to grab something, anything, but there is nothing except the hand of my captor.

"Help!" I scream, as I feel myself begin to slip from within his grasp.

Suddenly, I am being pulled back by the masked man, and he is laughing.

"You don't want to go there," my captor laughs, as he pulls me back to safety. "Well, not yet."

Although I have no idea what he meant by his last remark, I am thankful that he has saved me from a fall that I am certain would have broken my arm or leg, or possibly both. I look up with the intention of smiling at him to show him my gratitude; however, when I do, I see that we have reached our destination, as there behind him is an old, wooden door. Any smile that I intended to show quickly fades, and complete and utter panic sets in.

"I am going to let you go in first so that you can get to know the others," he says abruptly. "I will be back in a few minutes to check on all of you. Maybe I will even bring you all some tea and sandwiches."

My heart drops, as I had hoped that the staircase was going to lead to the outside. Now I know why he isn't worried about me saying anything and why he didn't take off his mask – we are still inside the house. It is now obvious that he never had the intention of taking me to the outside world and that these women that I am going to meet are just like me.

"These women are captives also," I say in a low, saddened voice underneath my breath. "I wonder how long they have been here."

"What?" he demands.

I look at him with a stunned look.

"Did he hear me?" I wonder.

"Oh, nothing," I say. "I am looking forward to meeting them."

I give him a big smile, not too big though; I don't want him to know that I am faking. He has already caught me in one lie today. I don't want to take the chance of him catching me again, as I know I had been lucky before and only suffered minimal pain compared to the wrath he could have put upon me.

"It will be OK. You will get along just fine with the others," he whispers in my ear, as he tightens his grip on my hand. "Don't worry, they can't hurt you."

He reaches over and opens the door. The room is dark as an empty field on a moonless night.

I think to myself, "I have at least a little light in my room."

I am afraid of what may be waiting beyond the dark doorway, so I peek my head in just a bit. Instantly, my eyes tear up as I am overcome by a horrific smell.

"What is that smell?" I wonder to myself.

It is a smell I have never experienced before, and I wish it would go away. I plug my nose, trying to escape the stench that is escaping from the room. It doesn't help; the smell is so strong that it instantly is embedded in my nose and in my mind, leaving me with no escape from the stench. My stomach starts to hurt, and I feel sick. Within seconds, some of the rotten food I ate earlier begins to come back up and is now burning my throat like a hot poker against sunburned skin. I swallow, in hopes that my saliva will relieve the pain a smidgen. It doesn't work, and my throat begins to burn more causing the tears from my eyes to run down my face. Without hesitation, I wipe the tears away as best as I can, as I know I have to keep my vision clear.

I know whatever it is that smells up the room cannot be good, and I don't want to go in. I'm afraid to go any further, and I don't want to meet these people! I want to be back in my room! I panic and try to step back, but he blocks me with his foot causing me to fall to the ground. He is angry that I have tried to leave. Instantly, he grabs my hair and violently pulls me off the floor, all the while ripping a large amount of my hair out. Then, with a sudden brutal thrust, he pushes me through the door, causing me to plummet to the floor inside the room.

"I will be back in a few minutes. You girls play it nice now," he says as he lets out a laugh of pure and utter evil and slams the door behind me.

I rub my head trying to relieve the pain from the fistful of hair he has just pulled out. The pain begins to subside, so I stand up. I try to look around, but the room is too dark, and I can't even see my fingers that are now five inches from my face. I begin to wonder how I am to get around this room in such darkness, or is locking me in this dark, smelly room his plan all along? I shake my head, as all of this is making no sense to me at all. Why would he bring me here? There has to be a reason. If he wants me in complete darkness, he could have just blocked the small window I have presently. It has to be another one of his lessons, as he calls everything he does to me a lesson.

Tiring of all that he does to me, I decide that it be best to just get it over with. I start by feeling the web-infested walls desperate to find a light switch. However, I end my search abruptly, when I feel a spider crawl up my arm. Or at least that is what it feels like. I blink my eyes hoping that they will adjust to the darkness so that I can see my arm. But it is too dark, and my eyes have nothing to adjust too. The blackness becomes paralyzing, causing panic to engulf my body. I do not like this game!

I start to yell as loud as I can, "Is anyone in here?"

I hear a voice, then another. I try talking to them. But the voices are soft and quiet, making it hard to understand what they are saying. I look around trying once again to see in the darkness. But it is no use, and I know I have no other choice but to feel my way around and take the chance of a spider biting me. I just hope if one does bite me, it will not be poisonous. I reach again for the wall nearest me and run my hands up and down it. For a brief second, I think I feel a person standing next to me. I jump back, and then quickly feel again. The person is gone.

"It must have been my imagination," I think to myself. "There is no way someone could have moved away that quickly. Besides, I am sure I will have heard them as they walked by me."

I continue on with my search, feeling the walls with great caution.

"Sit in the chair next to you and relax. He will turn on the lights soon, and we will be able to see each other," an unknown voice demands.

I feel around, but there is no chair. I walk a little further into the room, reaching my arms out as far as they will go, feeling my way through the room. I feel no chair.

"I can't feel a chair," I yell.

"Come a little closer," someone says. "You are almost there."

Knowing the consequences if I were to ignore the person's demands, I decide it be best to continue with my search for the chair.

"What are your names and how long have you been here?" I ask, while I continue feeling my way around.

I hear nothing.

"Hello," I say again.

"We can hear you," a voice says from the corner. "Just sit down."

Without warning, a chair appears next to me as if it is placed there at that moment. It seems a little strange to me, but I decide to sit down anyway.

"My name is Samantha, over there is Christina, and to your right is Lynn. What is your name?" Samantha asks.

"My friends call me Lue," I explain.

"Nice to meet you, Lue," a new voice says.

"Who's that?" I ask.

No one answers.

"Hello? I can't see in this darkness," I say as I look around once again.

Dead silence overcomes the room.

"How long have you been here?" I ask, hoping to hear someone's voice.

Still no answer.

"Are you still here?" I ask again in a panic.

Still no response. I start to feel sick again, not only from the smell, but because it's dark and no one is talking anymore. I feel alone and helpless. I do not know who these women are or what I am doing there. But I do know this game is scaring me, and I wish we could play another that did not involve darkness or this horrifying room.

"I mean, this lesson," I say under my breath. "He would never call it a game, although that is exactly what it is."

Questions begin rushing my head: Are these women captive, or are they part of his sick scheme? What do they want, or do they want anything? Why after so long of being captive did he bring me here? All things I want to scream aloud but dare not to, as I am unsure if he could hear from wherever he has gone, ultimately angering him.

"Maybe, that is what he is waiting for. He wants me to break. He wants me to give into him," I think to myself. "After all, he knows how frightened I am of the dark."

I know I can get through this; all I have to do is keep aware of my surroundings and be strong. I close my eyes, breathe in deeply, and slow my heart rate. This is allowing me to hear only the sounds of the room around me. Listening closely, I can hear shallow breathing. However, I cannot tell which direction the breathing is coming from. I tilt my head and try to listen more intently, but the sounds seem to bounce off the walls and echo through the room, leaving me with no indication at all of where the sound is coming from.

"Please talk to me, I am very afraid," I say in a shaky voice. "I have been locked up for a very long time, and I just need someone to talk to."

No response again.

I decide that I will get up and feel my way around again, as there is no point in me sitting in this chair. I have to know where the voices are coming from. I have to find the women that were talking to me before!

"Stay right there!" I hear a loud growling voice scream.

Startled by the tone of the voice, I begin to sit back down. I reach for the chair, but it is no longer there. I turn in every direction feeling for it, but it is nowhere to be found. I move a few inches in every direction feeling my way the entire time. The chair is gone. This is getting ridiculous, and I am tired of the game that is being played. I am becoming angrier by the moment.

"The stupid games this man plays!" I yell in my head.

The anger grows inside, and I can no longer hold it in. I begin rubbing my hands together, as this is the only way I have to release my feelings. They begin to bleed as the fresh stitches reopen. Now I am mad as hell. This man has made me hurt myself. Unable to hold in my anger any longer, I begin to scream.

"No!" I yell. "I want to see you! This is scaring me!"

No one answers.

I begin to feel around; the walls are cold, wet, and slimy, and I can feel drippings of water as it cascades down the walls. I feel around some more, working my hands up and down every inch of the walls. There are metal objects hanging about. Using my fingers, I concentrate and outline each individual object. Some, I am able to recognize. One feels like a saw, another like a chain. I continue feeling; however, I am not able to figure out most, as they feel foreign to me. They do, however, all have one thing in common; they feel sharp and feel as if they could inflict a lot of pain on someone. My heart skips a beat. I do not like what I am feeling.

"I do not want to be in this room anymore!" I scream, in desperation. "Do you hear me? I don't want to be in here anymore!"

Silence.

Instantly, I begin to wonder if I am here for that reason, that I would be receiving a new form of punishment and these are the tools he will be using.

"Where am I?" I ask myself. "Is this the room I am to die in?"

All of a sudden, I feel a strong force slamming me down. I find myself on the floor, startled and confused as to why one of these women would push me down. I lift myself off the floor, bracing myself for another possible blow. Disoriented, I swing my arms around hoping to hit whoever is around me. My frantic arms never touch anything but the open air around me.

"Who is that?" I demand to know.

Once again, no answer.

"This is not funny," I yell. "What the hell is going on here? Why are you doing this to me? Don't you think I have been through enough already? I am not the enemy here. That person is upstairs!"

The room is filled with silence once again, except for a few faint giggles that seem to surround me. I continue to feel my way around the room, looking for any indication of another person. All of a sudden, I feel a sharp stabbing pain across my face. A gush of blood runs down my cheek onto my new dress. Applying pressure to my cheek, I try to stop the bleeding. I look around; I cannot tell where the person came from. I hold my cheek in pain. Another breeze of wind goes by, and I am cut again. My face is now cut on both cheeks. The slashing comes to an abrupt end, and I fall to the ground. Holding my face with the bottom of my dress to stop the bleeding, I hold back my tears the best I can.

"Why are you doing this? Why do this to me now? Am I being punished for something? Please . . . please leave me alone. I am sorry for whatever I did," I scream in pain.

I instantly know that it is my captor doing this to me, as I cannot understand why anyone else would want to hurt me.

I know begging is not allowed, but I don't see a reason to care anymore. I am in pain and do not know what is going to happen to me next. Something about being in this room is horrifying, as it possesses a certain evil about it. I am more frightened than I have ever been before. Is he going to keep slashing my face until there is no more skin to cut? Or is this just the beginning of much more horrible things to come?

I look at the floor where I had just been standing and see a small shiny object. I reach for it slowly, ensuring that any of the lurking eyes do not see me do so. I feel it with my fingers; it's sharp and pointy. I pull it toward me and carefully feel it with my fingers. It is a knife. He has dropped his knife! I look around and quickly scoot it under my dress and into my underwear, hopeful that no one has seen me do so.

"Now I have protection, and if he touches me one more time, I will be prepared," I think to myself.

Afraid to move, I sit in the middle of the floor holding my face. I feel comfortable here, and I am confident that with the knife under my dress, I will be able to reach it quickly, as I have my dress raised slightly with the knife ready to be grabbed. Hours pass, and to my relief, no one has hurt me again. However, not only has my captor disappeared, but the voices have stopped also, leaving me wondering what happened to the women I heard before.

"Maybe it isn't my captor that is slashing me after all," I say to myself, as I hold my cheeks. "Maybe it has been the women all along, and they are waiting for me to be unprepared before they start torturing me again."

Whoever it is, I am ready.

Hours seem to pass, and I find myself wondering how long I have been in here and how much longer it will be before I am either hurt again or released from this horrific room. I know it has been a long time, because I can no longer smell the stomach-turning aroma I had experienced when I first came in. Confirming that I have been in here long enough that my sense of smell has became immune to the stench. I am confident that I can take my dress from my wounds, and they will no longer be bleeding. Slowly I take a side off at a time and feel the wounds. I am right. The wounds have coagulated and are no longer bleeding. However, as soon as I take the pressure from my hands away, blood rushes back to the wounds, causing the wounds to throb. I am in more pain than ever.

"Why?" I cry. "Why?"

"Because you won't see the truth," I hear a soft voice growl from behind me.

Stunned, I turn around. I see nothing but the darkness that continues to engulf the room.

Suddenly a strange smell fills the air, overtaking my senses.

"What is that?" I question myself.

My lungs begin to burn, and I feel as if someone is taking the breath from within me. I cover my face with my blood-soaked gown, trying to escape the smell. The smell is too powerful, and the dress is too thin. The smell is all around me, leaving me with no escape.

I can't catch my breath!

I can't breathe!

CHAPTER 4

The Others

"WAKE UP! WAKE up!" I hear someone screaming in my ear. I now find myself lying on a cold metal table. My face is throbbing from the wounds I now possess, and my left eye is burning. I try to open my eye, but it wouldn't budge. I know something is wrong, but I am too stubborn to admit it.

"OK, there has to be a reason for this," I think to myself, as I try to ease the fear that is growing inside of me.

Taking great care in what I am doing, I begin concentrating on that eye and that eye alone, keeping my mind focused on opening my eye and on nothing else. But no matter how hard I try, the eye will not open. Without warning, someone grabs my arms and holds them down. I try to look up and see what is happening, but the room is still dark, and I cannot see who is around me. Suddenly, something is put into my right eye, and it too is now burning.

Both my eyes are now cemented shut, and no matter what I try, they will not budge. Petrified of what might happen next, I frantically move my eyes around hoping to loosen the grip on whatever has a grasp on my eyelids. I know I must get them open, as I am defenseless in my new state of blindness. I try to free my hands, but the person holding me down is too powerful and refuses to let me free. I am powerless against all that is happening, and I know that if something doesn't change soon, I will never escape the torture that I am sure will be soon to come. I begin to cry, but no tears can escape. My eye sockets, filling like two damned river of flowing water, feel as if they are going to bust from the pressure of the pooled water.

"What is going on?" I cry out loud.

I hear nothing, but a door slam from within the room. I try to move, but my hands are now tied, keeping me bound to the table. I begin moving my wrists around, hoping that the ropes are tied loosely, as I had learned a long time ago that my captor could not tie a very strong knot.

The skin from my wrists begins to feel as if it is being peeled from my bones. The pain is agonizing, but I know this is my only way of freeing myself. Ignoring the pain by focusing my mind elsewhere, I keep moving my wrists in large circular motions until I feel the knots start to budge. Within minutes, my efforts work, and I manage to get one of my hands free, then seconds later, the other.

Panic stricken, I rip the remaining ropes from my arms and legs and jump off the table.

"I have to get my eyes open, and now!" I think to myself in frenzy.

Without thinking of the pain I am about to put upon myself, I begin pulling at my eyelids. Harder and harder I pull, but my efforts seem to get me nowhere, as every lash seems to be glued individually.

"Superglue," I think to myself as I shake my head.

I want to scream aloud, "Can't you think of anything original!" But I don't, as I know that will definitely be the wrong thing to do. I know there are many other things in this room he could have used on me that would have caused a lot more pain and agony, or worse yet, could have caused my death. This is actually minimal, and for once, I am happy with his choice of torture.

The thought of me dying now throws my body into a frenzy. I do not want to die in this room. If I am to die, I want to die in my room, a room I have learned to call home, and not this way, not blinded. I want to look into the eyes of my killer as I die, ensuring that the image of my dying soul never leaves his memory.

"Not here! Not now!" I scream in my head.

As fast as I can, I begin pulling each individual eyelash from my eyes. The skin housing my eyelashes becomes tender quickly and begins to bleed. Although I hate the thought that I will have no more lashes, I know it is the only way I will be able to get to the eyelids themselves, and that is where the main gist of the superglue is. The pain is overcoming; however, I endure my suffering and continue with my mission until there is not a lash left on either one of my eyes.

Knowing time is of the essence, I stop for only a brief second to debate on what is the easiest, but yet, fastest way to do this. Coming to only one conclusion, I take my fingers, and as slow as I can, I begin at the corners of my eyes and start pulling my eyelids apart. But no matter how gentle I try to be, I cannot escape the deep agonizing pain. The sensitive skin of my eyelids continues to rip apart, exposing raw, torn skin. Instantly, blood mixes with the escaping pooled-up water, causing tears full of blood to stream down my face. I try to open my eyes. However, stopping abruptly, as the dirty, dungeon air comes into contact with my fresh wounds, causing my mind to scream in agony. My reflexes instantly take over, causing me to clamp my eyes shut again, refusing to take the pain anymore.

I know I have no other choice. I will have to fight myself to keep my eyes open; I have to be able to see. My body will just have to endure the pain.

The blood, now inside my eyes, has made my vision blurry. However, I can see that there is a dim light on in the corner opposite of me. Taking my dress, I lift it up and try to find the cleanest spot I can. After just a few seconds of searching, I am convinced that there is not a clean spot left on the dress, as it now is covered in dirt and blood. I decide it be best to use my hand to wipe my eyes, thinking that they are cleaner than the dress I am wearing. I wipe my eyes as best I can, trying not to injure them anymore than they already are. They are raw and cut and hurt when the skin from my hand touches them, but I continue to wipe them until I can see better. Managing to get most of the blood out of my eyes, I take a look around and can now see the things that I had felt on the walls earlier. They seem to be exactly what I had feared. I have never seen such objects, as they all look like they are used for nothing more than to torture someone in the worst ways possible. In fact, they are the most horrific torture devices I have ever seen, and the majority of them are stained with dried blood. A chill runs up my spine, and I have to look away, as I think about the fact that while I was passed out anyone of those horrible devices could have been used on me.

"The best thing to do is to stay calm and look around for a place to get out," I think to myself with confidence. "This is an entirely different room than mine, and there might be a route of escape."

With my afflicted eyes, I begin scanning the room for any possible indication of a different door than I had came in, or passageway out. All of a sudden, I see a figure in the corner opposite of me. I blink my eyes ensuring my vision. My eyes had not deceived me; there is truly a figure in the corner. But who or what is it? My heart begins to rapidly pound. Is it *him*? Has he come back for more? I peer again into the corner, staring at the figure, hoping for some type of movement. The body never moves.

"What is that?" I ask myself as curiosity overtakes me. "Is it a person or a piece of clothing?"

Now, you would think that by now I would have learned to keep my distance from the unknown, but I haven't. I know no matter how much I try to talk myself out of it, I am eventually going to walk over to see what it is. I have to know if there is going to be a need to defend myself from whatever is leering in the corner. So without any further delays, I reluctantly walk toward the darkened shape.

As I walk closer to the figure, the corner becomes brighter and my eyes become more focused, until I can see the definite shape of a human. It is as I thought. It is a person, and it is not moving. As I put my hand onto my knife, I cautiously continue to walk toward the waiting figure.

"I'm ready for you," I whisper beneath my breath as I continue walking.

I am now directly in front of the figure.

In that one and only instant, I wish it was "him."

"Oh my god!" I yell in revulsion.

Whereas, standing in front of me is a lifeless, deteriorated, naked body. The body of what looks to be a woman. It is hard to tell, but she looks like she is a younger woman – a woman that I am sure someone is looking for. I say this because next to her is a damaged picture of a young woman. A picture I am certain is of her or of what once was her. Sadness overtakes my heart and soul, as I cannot believe what I am seeing. I look down and immediately notice her feet and begin to cry. She is shoeless like I had been for so long, and her feet are so filthy that it looks as if it has been at least a year since she has showered. I don't know why that bothers me so badly. But it does. So without truly thinking about what I am about to do, I take my dress and tear a piece off it and begin trying to clean her feet. I cannot stand the thought of her being filthy in death also. I know that sounds like a funny thing to do, but I want her to have some kind of love and kindness, something that is apparent she has not had in a very long time.

"What the hell!" I scream as I jump back.

Suddenly, her two big toes fall off, and the remaining eight stand straight up toward the ceiling. It is as if the dirt was the only thing that had been holding them in place, and now I have ruined that for her also.

"I am so sorry," I cry as I shake my head in complete sorrow. "I didn't know."

I close my eyes and reach up toward her leg. I want to say a prayer for her, and I want to be touching her so that she might feel the sincerity coming from my words. When my hand touches her leg, it is instantly stabbed by something that feels like a razor blade, causing me to quickly pull my hand away. I look down and see that I now have a deep puncture in my hand.

"What in the world could have caused that!" I wonder to myself.

Something overpowers me, and I have to know what it is that has cut me. I begin scanning her legs. I am appalled by what I am seeing, but I cannot look away. It is like someone has overtaken my mind and is making me look and want to see more. I don't know if it is because I can't believe that this is all real, or if it is because I am happy to still be alive, and I want to see what could still happen to me at any moment. All I know for sure is that I am scared to death, and what I am seeing is the most disgusting and loathsome thing I have ever experienced, but I have to see more.

For those reasons alone, I begin to study her body.

I can't believe what I am seeing; her legs are bound in barbwire that is wrapped so tightly that the razor-sharp edges has encased her skin, making it look as if the barbwire is part of her shriveled body. I look down at my hand and feel ignorant that I was worried about the minimal scratch that I had endured compared to what she must have suffered.

"You poor thing," I whisper to her as I continue scanning the rest of her body.

Her midsection is worse than her legs, whereas her stomach is sliced so deeply that I can see her spine where her stomach once housed her intestines. I look over at her sides and see that her skin is pulled back and is being held there by large hooks, making it look as if someone had pulled her apart and left her stripped for everyone to see. Instantly, I know I cannot leave her exposed like this, as I am unsure if there are others like me, others that he will bring in here also. I have to close her up. I do not want them to see the atrocity that this woman had experienced, nor the terror that I have seen. Without further thought about what has to be done, I reach over and try to unlatch her skin from the hooks so that I could ensure that her stomach is closed back up. However, to my dismay, the skin is dry and is permanently attached to the hooks that holds it captive and will not separate from its powerful hold. Totally disgusted by the sight of her hollow stomach, I start to look away. I cannot take the pain I am feeling in my heart for her anymore.

Without warning, her arm falls and hits me on the shoulder. I look up and see that her hand has detached from her arm and is now dangling on the rope that had once bound her. I begin to cry. I want to fix her. I want to make her better. But I know it is too late for her. I look over at her other arm, in hopes that it is still attached to her hand. It is, however, completely covered in cuts and gashes, the same kind of gashes that I have gotten since I have been in this hell.

It is so horrific that I cannot comprehend how one human could have done this to another. Suddenly, a horrifying thought rushes through my mind. If he did this to her and has tortured me for so long, how many others will there be or has there been? Depression overtakes me, and I start to walk away, but I can't. I have come this far and figure I may as well look at her face, as I now know my destiny and I need to see how bad it is going to be for me. Deep in my heart, I have known all along that my captivity is going to end badly, as I already have endured so much. The worst fear I have had since I have been here is that if God forbid I am unable to escape; he will mangle my face to the extent that when he finally disposes of my dead body, I will be unrecognizable to my loved ones, never leaving them with the peace of seeing me one last time.

I take in a deep breath and then continue to look at my destiny.

The rest of her body is mangled so badly that there is no way her face can be much worse. I close my eyes, take a deep breath, let it out slowly, and then quickly look up.

Her face! My god! Her face is so mutilated that I wish I would have walked away and never looked at it. It is more horrifying than anything I could have ever imagined and made the rest of her body look as if it is flawless. In fact, if it isn't for me knowing that I am looking at a human's face, I may not have recognized it at all as such that.

Whereas, where her eyes once were, there are now empty, dark sockets, leaving only her eyelids to occupy the empty space. To my dismay, that is not the worst of it. Her mouth had been sliced from ear to ear, and the skin had been folded back and stapled around her face, keeping her mouth from closing. I think back to a time when he had stapled my lips shut and think how lucky I am that he had not cut my face as he did hers.

I shake my head in disbelief and continue searching for a possible piece of her body that he had not disfigured. I look past her eyes and look at her hair; shockingly enough, it has not been touched. In fact, it looks as if it has been recently brushed and maybe even washed. The thought of someone brushing her hair after her death is so disturbing that a chill runs through my body, causing large goose bumps to take over every inch of my skin.

"What a sick and demented man!" I say softly. "I wish there is something I can do. I hate to leave her standing here like this, naked and vulnerable to everything in this horrible room."

I start searching the area around her for anything I can cover her with. Within seconds of my search, I find a blue tarp that I am sure he is going to use to bury her. I grab what looks like some shriveled-up organs attached to a cord and remove it from on top of the tarp. I then take the tarp from the table, and with great ease, I wrap it around her fragile body ensuring that I do not disturb her anymore than necessary.

I take a bottle of superglue that I have found next to the tarp and open it. I want to use it to glue her eyes shut so that she can be at peace. I know in my heart that although this is one of his ways of torture, by me doing so I'm not torturing her; I am keeping others like me from seeing into her soulless eyes. I am positive this is something she would have wanted. Taking the opened bottle, I reach as high as I can and grab her lower eyelid and place a small amount of superglue on it. Then, as fast as I can, I reach for the upper eyelid and put glue on it also. With both of my hands, I grab both her eyelids and begin closing them.

Instantaneously, an enormous amount of bugs gush out of her eye sockets and down her cheeks. Within seconds, her face is overtaken by the rushing insects. I jump back and scream in horror as the insects enter her mouth, overcoming her dry, shriveled tongue. Immediately, the insects become too heavy for her bottom jaw, causing the bones of her mouth to crumble. Without warning, the bugs spew down her body and onto mine.

I am in hysterics. I run in circles screaming and smacking my clothing, as I scurry to get the bugs off my clothing. Within moments they are gone, leaving only the sound of their bodies hitting one another as they continue to crawl down her throat and into her hollowed body, like millions of tiny metal pieces slamming together.

I have to turn my head; I am going to throw up. I run to the corner next to her deteriorated body and crouch into a ball, as any remaining food I might have had in my stomach begins to expel from within me. Tears begin falling down my face causing my eyes to hurt more and the fresh cuts on my face to burn. I do not care about the pain and continue to let myself cry, until my crying becomes so intense that I am no longer in control of my emotions.

"How could you do this?" I scream as loud as my weakened lungs will allow, all the while looking around the room in hopes to see him standing there.

I want to face him; I want him to admit that what he is doing is wrong.

I see no one.

"What pain and anguish this poor girl must have endured before she finally passed!" I cry to myself.

"What a sick man! I always knew he was a sick man. Now I see just what he is capable of," I yell inside my head.

I have to calm myself down. I have to keep a straight head. I do not want this to happen to me. I sit for a moment more and try to forget what I have just seen. However, the vision of her body and all that had been done to her is embedded in my head and will not release from my memory. Suddenly, images of her and all the torture devices on the wall begin flashing in my mind, one picture at a time. The picture of her face eventually turning into mine, becoming mangled even more with every image that flashes before me, until they become so disturbing that I have to slap myself in the face to escape the trance I am putting upon myself.

I think back to when I had first came here and how my punishments have became more severe throughout the years. I know I have to get away before I suffer the same fate. I decide to look around some more in hope of finding the hidden passageway that I yearn for so badly. I wipe my mouth and stand up quickly. I have to act fast, as I know I already have been in here for some time, and I am uncertain how much longer it will be before he comes back in.

When I stand up, I feel a sharp pain in my leg. Frightened to what it could be that causes such a pain, I look down and feel inside my dress where the pain had originated. I feel the knife I had hid before; it has shifted and now is cutting my leg. Happy to still have the knife, I forget the pain quickly.

A faint smile now on my face, as I know that although he is way more powerful than me and obviously a twisted man, I still possess a small dim of hope. I close my eyes and grasp the knife beneath my dress and begin imaging all the things I will do to him to ensure that he suffers as much as this other woman and I have. I begin to giggle at some of the thoughts and almost begin to laugh as I think of the most horrific things possible.

"I could never do those things," I think to myself. "That would make me no different than him, if I did."

I take in a deep breath and exhale it slowly, as I know no matter how much I think I would love to torture him, I would never be able to do such things.

"I still need this for protection," I say under my breath. "So I better think of a better hiding place than against my leg."

I walk carefully over to a far, dark corner. I have to move the knife so that I do not cut my leg anymore and so that he will not see it sticking out from within my dress. I slowly take the knife out, all the while searching the room to ensure that I will not be seen by anyone that may be around.

"I'll put it in my new shoes," I think to myself. "I don't think he will look there. Besides, if I am careful in my step, I will be able to avoid any further cut."

I bend slowly, careful not to make any sudden moves that will make me look suspicious. I lift my dress and slowly remove the knife from beneath my underwear, acting as if I am adjusting my slip. I then slowly put my dress back down and reach for my shoes. I know I had used this trick before, but at that moment, it is the only thing I can think of doing. Talking one shoe off, I shake it out, acting as if I have dirt in it. Casually, I insert the knife into my shoe, making sure that the knife is positioned in such a way that it will not cut my foot or cause me to suffer a limp. I know any strange behavior on my part will cause him to become curious, and he might search me; so I must be careful in everything I do.

The thought of what he will do to me if he suspects I want to harm him causes my heart to instantly beat out from my chest. I take a deep breath and try to shake off the feeling of despair, as I continue on my way without any further disruption.

First, I scan each individual area, trying to find a possible light coming from within the darkness, indicating that there is a window or door, anything that will allow my escape. But my mind is finding it hard to concentrate, as what I had just seen keeps replaying in my head over and over, until my mind is clouded with nothing more than the vision of her standing there covered in insects as they ate their way throughout her body.

Shaking my head with disgust, I continue to search. Suddenly, I see a ray of sunshine coming from within an area that is completely dark. I know there has to be a window or maybe a door that is allowing the sunshine to sneak through. I just don't know if it is covered with shards of glass like my window. Without further hesitation, I begin to walk as fast as I can to the darkened area of the unknown I am about to encounter. I have to find from where the light is coming.

The lights go out!

I am stunned by the sudden darkness. I instantly freeze. Fearful that I might trip on something I may not have seen before, I stand still, feeling my immediate area with only my feet.

In the silence of the room, I can hear of only my own heartbeat as it beats louder than ever before. He is back, and he is here to finish the job he started earlier! I will not let him do the things that I know he has planned for me. Not without a fight! Right then, I know I have to get back into a corner and hide the best I can so that it will be hard for him to find me. I needed that time to get my knife, without the possibility of him sneaking up behind me before I can do so. As quickly as I can, I begin maneuvering through the darkness, taking extra care that I do not bump into something that could cause a loud sound and possibly give away my position. Or worse yet, bump into him. Continuing, I walk around the room until I finally reach another corner. The area is the blackest black, and I can see no more than an inch in front of me. Something leaps out at me, causing me to jump back. Immediately, I become paralyzed from the fear that has taken over me. I am scared out of my wits. I cannot move! I cannot breathe! I have walked right to him!

"Get the knife!" a voice screams from within me.

As fast as I can, I bend over and start to reach for the knife, however, stopping abruptly, when I hear faint breathing coming from behind me. I stand back up, freezing instantly.

"I hope he has not figured out what I am doing," I say to myself as I stand there motionless.

Suddenly, I can feel the warmth of his breath on my neck! He is directly behind me!

"Oh my god!" I say in a low, quivering voice. "He has been here the entire time. He had seen me hide the knife, and he knows what I am up to."

I turn my head slowly. If I am to be punished, I don't want it to happen from behind me. I want to see it coming so that I will be prepared. I reach my hand out, feeling my way toward where I think he is standing. I can feel the outlining of a body. He is ten inches away from me. My heart is beating so fast that I expect that at any moment it will stop instantly from the accelerated pounding.

I now know for certain that he had seen me when I put the knife in my shoe, as I am standing only about fifteen feet away. I jump back, preparing myself to run. The body moves.

I scream in terror!

"Don't scream. He will hear you," a soft voice says within the darkness.

"Who is there?" I ask as I try and focus my eyes again.

"It's me, Samantha. I spoke to you earlier. I'm sorry, I stopped speaking to you before, but I passed out again," the woman explains. "There is a small lantern over on the table. Get it, light it, and come closer to me. Then you will see why I am hoping that maybe you can help me."

Although I am frightened that it is a trick, I decide to do what the voice has asked. After all, if it is him and I do not do as I am told, the punishment will be more severe; this I am sure of. Without questioning her or "its" motives, I turn and feel my way over to the table against the east wall and begin feeling around it. It is as bad as the walls I had seen earlier, as it too contains many things that could cause someone unnerving pain. I know this because as I search I can feel the sharp edges of the things that lie there, lie there waiting to hurt someone.

Luckily, I am able to locate the lantern within a few moments and do not have to search for too long, as each time I touch one of the objects, tears fill my eyes, knowing some of these objects were probably used on the girl in the corner.

Holding the lantern in one hand, I run my fingers up and down the sides, hoping it is the type of lantern that does not require a match to light it. Within seconds of feeling around the edges, I find what feels like a switch. Quickly, I flip it in the opposite position than it is in. To my surprise, the lantern works, and the area around me lights up. It is not very bright, but I am happy to have the little amount of light that the lantern is putting out.

I look down at the table where I had found the lantern in hope that maybe there is another. There on the table is exactly what I had thought. It is covered with torture devices, some of which seem to have fresh blood on them, others dried blood.

I look at my hands and realize that some of the blood has gotten on my hand during my search for the lantern. Sickened by the thought of the blood of a murdered woman on my hands, I frantically begin rubbing my hands onto my dress. I have to get her blood off me!

Satisfied that my hands no longer possess someone else's blood, I look at the table once more. I want to take one of these horrible things with me back to the corner. However, I am certain he will see me, so I leave everything where it lays and turn my attention back to the person in the darkness.

Reluctantly, I begin walking back to the corner, back to the unknown person that awaits me. I walk slowly as I hold the lantern as far out from me as possible, lighting the area directly in front of me. I feel this way I can at least try to run if I have to, although I am uncertain to where I will run, unless it is back to the "table of death."

"You should have grabbed the knife from your shoe before you lit up the lantern," I tell myself.

I can't believe how foolish I had been, that I did not think about the knife while I was there, alone in the dark. I shake my head in total disbelief that I had been so careless.

"It's too late now," I say to myself and continue walking.

"Wait," I stop and think, "what if I acted like I am dropping the lantern, flip the switch off, and when I bend over to pick it up in the darkness, quickly take off my shoe and grab my knife?"

"That might have worked. But now that you stopped, he will know what you are doing," a different voice in my head says. "So just continue on. You already blew your chance. Now you have to live with what you have done and whatever he has waiting for you."

I know the voice is right and that there is nothing more for me to do but to continue on with my journey to the corner and endure whatever pain awaits me. The closer I get, the brighter the corner becomes from the light of the lantern. To my relief, I can now see that the figure is actually a figure of a very slim woman. She is as the other woman I had seen; she seems to be shackled to the wall. I look over to her hands expecting to see that she is being held there by chains. But there is nothing binding her; it's as if she is being held there by some unforeseen power. I look down at her feet; they are the same and seem to be stuck where they lay, but there is no sign that they are being held there besides the stagnant air that surrounds us.

"This is impossible," I say softly. "How could this be?"

I blink my eyes and look again. All of a sudden, chains appear and begin encasing her wrists and ankles as if some invisible force in front of me is taking her hostage at that very moment, leaving me in total disbelief and helplessness. Only there is no one there. The chains bind her tighter and tighter, until the skin around her wrists explode, exposing muscle and bare bone. Suddenly, the open wounds begin oozing with green pus, as if they had been festering there for weeks.

"I must be losing my mind," I say to myself as I rub my eyes with my hands in disgust. "There is no way this can be real."

I look at her wrist again. The chains are now in fact holding her, and her wrists are infected. I look down; her ankles are the same, leaving no indication that they had ever been any other way.

"This is getting really strange," I say to myself as I reach over and feel the chains, ensuring myself that they are indeed real.

The room becomes muggy, so muggy in fact, that instantly my hands begin to sweat. My fingers lose grip on the lantern, and the lantern falls to the ground. As I quickly reach down to pick it up, I get a whiff of scent that overtakes my senses. My nose begins to burn, and my eyes begin to water. I look up and see that her legs are covered in what looks as if to be her own feces and there are cockroaches crawling on her feet and up her legs. Quickly I grab the bottom of my dress and try to scare the insects away, as I know there is no way she could do it herself; she is powerless in her state of restriction.

"Thank you," I hear a soft voice whisper.

"You're welcome," I say in a sorrowful voice as I stand up slowly, all the while scanning her body for any possible way I may be able to ease her pain.

Although she is not completely naked like the other woman I found, most of her body is uncovered, showing her exposed wounds like a sick and twisted trophy. As I try to move her ragged clothing around her body to better cover her, I see that she has deep gashes throughout her body, some of which look as if she has suffered recently. A sense of sorrow overcomes me, and I begin frantically to try to free her from her chains. I have to save her! I just have to!

The chains are too tight and do not budge. I pull harder. Still, they refuse to release her. I take the lantern and frantically begin slamming it into the chains hoping that the constant pounding will cause the chains to weaken.

Nothing!

"There is no need to try an' release me," she says in a soft voice. "I'm already dead."

Her words are piercing my heart, as what she said replays over and over in my head, like a broken record. I stand and face her with the intention of trying to console her. I want to let her know that she is not alone and that I am here for her and will do anything I can to help ease her suffering.

I look into her eyes and instantly understand. She looks tired, and it is obvious that she has given up on survival some time ago.

My heart breaks as I listen to her words of defeat. Although at times it is difficult to understand her, to look into her saddened eyes finishes any story she is telling.

She continues to talk, telling her nightmare of how she too was taken from her family and brought to this dungeon. I listen as best I can, trying to get as many details of her horrific story, but her words are reserved.

I try to lean forward, hoping that I can get close even to hear her softened voice, but her head is inside some kind of strange contraption. It is metal, with razor-sharp points protruding around the inside edges, and around the middle of the contraption is a chain that is hooked to a device behind her. There is no possible way she can move her head without enduring pain, as every time she does, she will endure a cut. However, it does not look like the cuts that she sustains are deep enough to cause instant death; it's just a tremendous amount of pain. I look at her neck closer and see that it is obvious that she has been wearing the contraption for some time, as there is scarring from where she has been cut numerous times. I start to look away, however, stopping abruptly when I see that she has no hair on her head. I look closer only to see that not only has it been shaven off, parts of it have been skinned off, as her skull is partially showing and is still bleeding. It is obvious that her hair has been removed within the past few days.

"This poor woman," I say within myself.

Something catches my eye, and I look over to the stand that sit in a distance. There is a winter cap lying on the table. I want to put the cap on her head so that her skull will not suffer the same fate as her wrists and become infested with insects.

The table is farther than I thought, so I have to abandon her for a moment while I walk over and get the cap.

"I'm going to help you," I say as I walk toward the darkened table. "I'll be right back."

"Please leave the light," she cries. "I have been in the dark for so long."

I know I need the light to see where I am going, but her words of desperation shot through my heart, leaving me with no other option. I leave the lantern at her feet and continue to the table.

Within a second, I am at the table and begin feeling around it. Luckily, there are only a few things on the table, which makes it easy to find the cap quickly. When I go to lift the cap from the table, the cap gets caught up on something and does not budge. I pull as hard as I can, but it only budges slightly. I take my free hand and feel around the outer edges of the cap in hopes to find what is attached to it. It doesn't take long to figure out that the hair that was once on her head is attached to it by the dried skin of her skull. Once again, I find myself delighted to be in the dark, as I do not want to see what I am feeling.

As fast as I can, I grab the strands of hair and begin ripping pieces away from the cap until the cap is free of any remaining hair. Disgusted by what I have done, I wipe my hands as best as I can and scurry back.

Without saying a word, I reach up and start to put the cap on top of her head, ensuring I do not cause her any more pain. However, as soon as the cap touches her skull, her wounds rip open and green pus begins oozing from her skull and onto her face. I don't know what makes me do it, but without thinking, I reach up and grab the cap back off as fast as I can, ultimately making things worse. As when I lift it from her head, the remaining skin attaches to it and starts to peel from her skull. My jaw drops, and tears fill the corner of my eyes. Right then, I know that I have not helped her, that in fact I have made things more detrimental for her. My stomach begins to burn as the thought of the extra pain I have just inflicted on her rips my heart in two.

I do not want her to know how bad she looks, so I quickly turn my head until I can compose myself once again, ensuring that she does not see the tears that now are streaming down my face.

"There is no reason to cry," Samantha says with a smile. "It's almost over, and then I will finally be at peace."

"I'm sorry," I say. "I did not mean to hurt you."

"That's OK. I am sure I would have reacted the same," Samantha says with a sigh. "You are only trying to help me, and I appreciate the kindness you are trying to show me."

"But I hurt you," I cry again.

"No, you didn't. I have been in pain for so long that my body has become immune to much of the torture and pain he puts upon me," Samantha says in a fading voice. "Not to mention that I have not been able to move in such a long time that I can no longer feel my legs or arms."

"Are they still attached to me?" Samantha asks in a certain desperate chuckle.

"Yes, and they look fine," I lie.

"I am sure they do," she says as a small smile appears on her face.

I know she does not believe me and that she is trying to make me feel more at ease, but I have to try and convince her anyway; I want her to have some kind of peace.

"There is another girl in here. She is in the opposite corner from me. I have not heard from her in a very long time. Did you see her?" Samantha inquires.

"Yes, I did," I reluctantly reply.

"Is she OK?" asks Samantha.

"I am sorry, she has passed," I say in a low voice.

A small cry escapes from Samantha's lips as she begins to sob. I hate to see her cry, but I understand how she feels, and I am sure that she needs to let her emotions out. I know that the best thing I can do for her is to comfort her in any way possible. I rip a piece of cloth from my dress and try to comfort her by wiping the tears from her face, but she flinches, and I know that the rough cloth against her exposed skin is hurting her. Afraid to hurt her anymore, I stop abruptly and let her tears fall down her cheeks.

"I guess she is in a better place. The last time I heard from her, she was in a lot of pain and was awaiting the day that they would take the . . ."

Samantha passes out!

"Samantha!" I scream.

Nothing.

"Samantha!" I scream in desperation.

Nothing!

"Don't die!" I scream. "Please don't die!"

Panicked, I begin pushing her chest trying to revive her.

Silence has overtaken the room once again.

I lower my head in grief and lie my head on her chest.

"I hope you are at peace," I whisper to her.

Suddenly, I realize that I can hear her heartbeat.

"Samantha," I cry.

She moves.

"Am I in heaven?" I hear Samantha say in a whisper.

"No, honey, you are not," I say in a remorseful voice.

"Oh," Samantha sighs. "I guess I passed out again."

The desperation and sorrow in her voice is heart wrenching, and I wish that she is in heaven and that she would never have to suffer any second of pain again.

"Did you see anyone else?" she asks. "There are other girls in here."

At first, I am a little confused. We started this same conversation just moments before she passed out, and now she is repeating herself.

"Yes, sweetie, we were just talking about one of them. I told you that she has passed away," I say softly. "You said she was waiting for them to take something from her, then you passed out."

"I said that?" she asks.

"Yes. What was she waiting for them to take?" I inquire again.

"I don't know," she says. "I can't remember."

There is no reason to push the issue; it is obvious that she is in a lot of pain and is having difficulty comprehending everything that is going on.

"Earlier, I heard a couple of voices. Are there more than you two?" I ask abruptly.

"There were three of us at one point, but I have not heard from either of them in a while. Now that I know that Lynn has passed, I am sure that Christina has too. She has been here the longest," Samantha says, heartbroken.

"But I know I heard more voices. Where did they come from?" I ask.

"He likes to play tricks like that. There are speakers set in different spots throughout the room. He watches through the cameras and speaks through a microphone from somewhere in the house. That is why I was not sure if you were "real" before," Samantha explains.

"I can understand that," I say. "I thought that might have been what was happening when I heard people speaking when I first came in."

"Yeah. He has a sick mind and thinks it is funny," Samantha whispers. "He is too stupid to realize we figured out that trick a long time ago."

I start to laugh along with her, however, keeping the laughter to a low chuckle in case he is listening.

"How long have you been here?" I ask.

"I lost count over two years ago," Samantha answers.

"Can I ask you something?" I ask abruptly.

"Sure, ask me anything," she says.

"Have you always been like this? I mean, have you always been tied up like this?" I ask in a sorrowful voice.

"No, I once was free to roam. But after I refused to allow my body to house his child, I was put up here and tortured," she answers. "You see I did not want to give him a child, afraid that the child will be evil like him. Or worse yet, what he might do to the child. So I decided a long time ago that I would suffer whatever pain he puts upon me to ensure that an innocent child did not suffer because of my weakness."

"Why didn't he force you to have one?" I ask. "I mean, he has us captured. He can pretty much do anything to us that he wants, and we will be defenseless."

"I don't know," she says in a low voice. "All I know is that when I refused, he got angry, and the longer I refused, the worst my punishments got, until I found myself here."

This seems all so strange to me, as my captor has never tried to push himself on me and has certainly never mentioned anything about a baby. I am glad that he has not put that demand upon me, as I hate the thought of someone taking my innocence in such a way.

"Do me a favor," she continues. "He will be here soon, and the last time I heard him talking with someone, they said that I was ready and that I could now be seeded. I am unsure to what that means, and I surely do not want to find out."

"There's more than one person keeping us here?" I ask her, interrupting her abruptly.

"Yes, I believe that there are many of them," she answers quickly.

"That would explain a lot," I think to myself, as I think back to the time when I had heard my captor speaking to someone else within my room.

"I wonder what they had meant by seeding you," I say, continuing my conversation with Samantha. "I have never heard of such a thing."

"I don't know, but whatever it is, I am sure it is not good," Samantha says as she closes her eyes. "All I know is I cannot take this torture anymore. I think you were sent here from heaven to help me."

"What do you mean?" I ask.

"I had a dream about you last night," she explains. "You were in a beautiful blue gown like the one you are wearing now. You took all the pain away. You saved me."

"How did I save you?" I ask.

"There is a switch on the wall next to my right hand. If you push it up, it will tighten this contraption around my neck, and I will finally be at peace," she says as she signals toward the right. "He put it there and then told me that I could end all this on my own if I wanted to. Then he broke my wrists so that I could no longer move them."

I take the lantern and point it in the direction that she has indicated. There, to my surprise, is what she has explained; there is a switch.

"I can't!" I cry. "I don't have it in me to take someone's life."

"Please! Please! You have to! You won't be taking my life," she whispers in desperation. "You will be giving it back to me."

I know what she is saying is probably right. I just don't think I can do as she has requested. After all, what she is asking me to do is murder. Or is it? Standing next to her for a few minutes, I debate what will be the right thing to do. I know I do not have it in my soul to kill someone, but I also don't have it in my heart to leave this girl suffering the way she is. I look toward the area of the other woman I encountered earlier, and pictures of her midsection and face start flashing in my mind. When I think of how she has suffered so badly and endured such horrific torture, I know she would have wanted to end it sooner and probably prayed every night for it all to end.

Thinking about what still could happen to Samantha, I look into her eyes. Her eyes show nothing but complete horror and sadness.

Silent, I continue to stare into her brown eyes.

Here is a woman that although is alive, she is suffering dearly, and there is nothing I can do to help her, except to take the very life from her. Right then, I decide I have no other choice. I will do as she asks and relieve her of any more suffering.

Before flipping the switch, I walk to Samantha and kiss her forehead gently. Whispering, "Go in peace," in her ear, I reach over and put my hand on the switch.

I look into her eyes and smile; she is smiling back.

With one last gesture of gratitude, she winks at me and whispers, "Thank you."

I close my eyes and flip the switch. Within seconds, the sound of chains slamming together echoes throughout the room as the contraption tightens around her neck, until it has crushed every bone. A heartbreaking gurgle comes from her mouth as she lets out one last breath, leaving the echoing sound of death in my mind.

She's gone.

CHAPTER 5

The Escape

IT HAS BEEN months since the day I was taken into his room of death. I pray every night that how thankful I am to have not met the horror and torture that the others endured and that I may forget what I have seen.

The visions of the other girls still linger in my head, and depression has overcome my emotions, making it difficult for me to function anymore. At one time, I would get out of bed and look around the room in hopes to find something that would occupy me for the day. Now I find myself sleeping until he comes in. I take my daily beatings, and when he is done, I lie on the bed again, never moving unless I must.

The days go by slowly, and I feel my day is coming soon, as I now know that I too will suffer the same fate as the others, as my punishments have become more severe. My spirit has been broken, and unless I can escape soon, I am afraid that I will become like the other girls and look forward to nothing more than the day I will diminish in his torturing hands.

There is a small part of me that has remained strong and wants revenge for me and for the others. But I know I am weak, and I am only one person. So I am uncertain if I can do it alone. But I know, when the time comes, I will not give in easily. I will fight to my death!

I look down at my empty plate of food and realize that I have not seen my captor today, and I wonder why.

"Usually, he has already been in here to hurt me at least once by now," I think to myself.

"Maybe it is better for him that he does stay away," I say in a hushed voice. "With the way I am feeling today, I could kill him."

"Kill, kill," a voice keeps repeating in my head.

I killed an innocent woman. Although I know that if I hadn't she would have died eventually, I still am having a hard time dealing with the fact that I have taken the life of another.

"No, I helped her!" I scream within myself.

"She would have suffered more pain and more anguish if I wouldn't have killed her," I try to convince myself.

My emotions are no longer in control as the anger grows inside me with every thought of Samantha and Lynn. I put my face into my hands and begin to cry uncontrollably. His punishments are inevitable. Therefore, I allow myself to cry whenever I want to and no longer care what he says about it.

The thought of those poor girls and what they went through haunts my memories every moment of every day.

"Punishment? This is the ultimate punishment. Pain goes away, but the memories will haunt me forever," I think to myself.

I gather my thoughts into something more pleasurable, like my plan of escape.

"I must get my thoughts trained on just that and nothing else," I think to myself. "Or I will give into my depression, and I will never get my chance for freedom."

"Snap out of it," a voice within me suddenly screams. "You did what you had to. Now get over it and get out of here!"

Quickly, I turn over on my bed and check within my mattress. The knife is still there. I smile as that means he has not found it yet. Ensuring that I am not seen by any possible hidden cameras, I reach under my bed and into the springs, checking to see if the few escape tools I have hidden are still there. This includes a small rope that I found while in the other girl's room and a small piece of material I ripped from Samantha's dress. I can't help but smile when I look at it, as I have planned to use it to gag him. Just a little souvenir so that he never forgets what he has done.

"I hope he chokes on it," I say out loud.

I quickly look around to make sure he has not sneaked in the room. I wipe my forehead as I am relieved to find the room is still empty. I double-check the area. Then as quickly as I can, I put my treasures back into my secret hiding place.

Without warning, I hear the door open. I turn my head in a panic. I am nowhere near the area I am to be when he comes in, and I do not have enough time to get my knife before he reaches the area himself. I am left with no other choice except to run as fast as I can to the middle of the floor and abandon the knife for now. I know if I am not there by the time he reaches the bottom of the stairs, I will be punished dearly, and with the way my punishments have been getting worse, I am afraid to take the chance. Although I know that I will still suffer some sort of punishment, I do not want to add to his fire of rage.

As fast as I can, I run to the middle of the floor, take my position, and wait. I am sitting there for about five minutes before I realize that he is not coming. Slowly, I look up toward the area of the stairs. There sitting on the top stair is my morning meal, but he is nowhere to be found. I am a little confused as to why he has set it on the stairs and left. But I am hungry, so I decide it be best to just go get it from where it lies. Slowly, I get up and walk toward the staircase, all the while ignoring the sense of apprehension that is growing deep inside of me.

"It will be OK," a voice inside me demands. "Just be careful."

I want to believe the voice, but something is telling me that all is not right. I stop at the end of the staircase and look around. I see no one, ensuring me that I am completely alone. However, I am not thoroughly convinced that this is not a trick. So I listen closely, trying to hear any possible movement outside the door. Everything is silent.

"I'm just being paranoid," I say to myself. "If he is going to do something, he will just do it. He has no reason to hide."

I continue up the stairs, all the while shaking my head in disgust that I have to live in such a constant state of panic.

Without warning, the door springs open. Startled by the sound of the door hitting the wall, I look up. There standing at the top of the staircase is my captor, and he is outraged. I try to turn and run back down the stairs, but I am not fast enough; he is already leaping toward me. I try to keep my balance, but the force from his body hitting mine is too powerful, and I go tumbling down the stairs.

When my body finally reaches the bottom of the staircase, my head slams into the hard ground, causing my ears to ring and my eyes to blur. Instantly, I know he is here to either take me back to the other room to torture me like the others, or to kill me.

"I can't pass out," I say to myself in a panic. "I have to get to my knife. I will not end up like the others. Not without a fight."

I look up and see that he too has fallen down the stairs and seems to be dazed, as he lay motionless next to me on the floor. Afraid that he will snap out of it soon, I jump up with the intentions of running to my bed. But before I can take more than one step, he grabs my leg. I trip, but I do not fall this time and continue toward my bed.

Despite the fact that he is still on the floor when I start running, he manages to reach the bed at the same time as me and tackles me down, slamming my body into the hard mattress, face-first.

I know that being in this position I am defenseless, so I try as quickly as I can to flip myself around. However, before I can move an inch, he is on top of me, holding me in my present position. Now, sitting on my back, he holds my arms out in front of me. I try to move, but as soon as I do, he ensures his grip on me, leaving the upper half of my body powerless.

I have to get free any way I can. I begin kicking his back with the heel of my foot, hoping that the blows to his back will make him move. It works; he changes his position to relieve his back from the bashing it is receiving, enabling me to squirm my arms loose. Franticly, I begin feeling around my mattress. I have to find my knife, and I have to get it before he takes control of me again. Within seconds, I am able to locate it within my mattress. It is only inches away. I reach as far as I can, but only my fingertips are able to touch it. I have to move closer. I will have to continue kicking him, until he moves.

I kick as hard as my captured legs will allow. But no matter how hard I kick him, he does not budge, as he is totally preoccupied and has all his attention on the rope he is wrapping around my neck.

"If I don't reach this knife, I am going to die, right here and right now," I think to myself as I feel the rope tighten.

In desperation, I kick him again, this time hitting him directly in the ribs. He changes his position once again, all the while keeping a death grip on the rope. The rope is so tight around my neck that I can now barely breathe, and I can feel myself fading into unconsciousness. I know this will be my last chance to reach the knife before I die. I take a shallow breath and stretch as far as I can. It's right there! I can reach it!

Without hesitation, I grab the knife from within the mattress and plunge it into his arm. As the knife rips through his skin, he jumps off my back, holds his fresh wound, and begins screaming in some foreign language that I have never heard him use before.

"How does it feel to be on the other end of the pain?" I scream.

He says nothing as he stands there holding his bloody arm.

"Well! How does it feel!" I scream again, all the while lunging toward his direction with the knife.

It is obvious that he is not scared in the least, as the entire time I am lunging for him, he stands there staring at me with a grin upon his face. After a few minutes, I start becoming intimidated, because no matter what I say or how many times I thrust the knife toward him, he stands his ground in the middle of the floor.

As I look into his evil eyes, I know I will have to reach deep inside myself and gather every piece of courage I possess. I will need that strength to take him over. With blood dripping from my hands, I hold the knife in confidence and stare back at him, suggesting that I am not going to back down.

"I guess you're not as stupid as I thought you were," he says with a sinister look.

"I guess not," I snap back.

"But what are you going to do now!" he screams as he let out an evil chuckle. "I am strong, and you are weak. I will get that from you, and when I do, the things you saw that the other girls had went through will be nothing compared to what I will do to you. You will beg me to let you die!"

"Beg you? I will never beg you! You don't deserve the satisfaction of hearing me beg, you crazy asshole! You tortured me and who knows how many others. I will die tonight before I let you do anymore to me," I yell as I swing my knife in front of my face like a crazed woman on the edge of insanity.

"Is that right?" he asks as he let out a menacing laugh that echoes throughout the room.

His laugh is not that of the other man's, and I begin to wonder if this is an entirely different person.

"Well, I am waiting." He laughs again. "Give me all you got."

That is it! I can no longer take anymore sarcasm from him! It is time! I am going to follow through with my plan, and I am going to do it now! I lunge forward in a rage of fury, as my captor stands his ground in the middle of the floor and awaits my first blow. My knife strikes him. I am uncertain to as of where, and I don't care. I keep frantically plunging the knife, but his clothes seem to be that of armor, never allowing the knife to come any closer to his skin. Desperate, I continue plunging the knife until my arms begin to burn and my body tire from the frenzy I am in.

He stands there laughing, never moving an inch. I ignore his ignorance and continue with my mission. I have to kill him or be killed myself.

Suddenly, I feel the knife rip into his skin. He yells, grabs his midsection, steps back, and looks at his stomach. His eyes, that of disbelief, staring right through me, as if he is looking for someone else, someone to help him. Blood overtakes his clothing, and within seconds, it is drenched with fresh blood coming from within him. He falls to the ground and screams my name as he reaches up toward my uncaring figure. I have finally hurt him, and he now knows what it feels like to suffer in pain and no one around to care.

I find myself staring at him. I want to see him suffer. I have to. I have finally gotten revenge for me and the others, and I don't want to miss a bit of his pain.

"Here, use this to stop the bleeding," I say sarcastically.

I rip the dirtiest piece of cloth from my dress and throw it at him.

"Why did you do this to me? You have been treated like a queen here," he says in a low voice.

He takes the cloth and tries to stop the bleeding, but blood continues to ooze out from between his fingers.

"Like a queen? Like a queen?" I yell.

I begin pacing back and forth next to his still body.

"Does a queen get treated like this?" I ask, kicking dirt onto his face. "Well, does she?"

"Or how about this?" I scream.

I take my urine bottle and try to force him to drink it.

"How many times did you make 'this queen' drink her own urine because I had run out of water?" I ask. "Is that the way a queen is treated?"

"Well, is it?" I demand to know.

As I kick him in the area to where the knife had cut him, I scream, "And what about the others? How were they treated? Were they queens also?"

"Oh, I'm sorry. I guess they were," I yell. "I guess that contraption around Samantha's neck was a crown."

I throw my arms up in a rage of fury.

"By the way, did you know they had names?" I scream.

My emotions were in complete control of me. I continue kicking him harder and harder in the stomach.

"They all did. Just to let you know, one was named Samantha, the others were Lynn and Christina. They had families like mine and all wanted to live, just like me," I continue.

"I'm sorry," he cries.

"Sorry?" I yell. "Well, I guess that makes it all better then, doesn't it?"

He curls into a ball, trying to escape my foot as I continue to kick him. "You don't understand. I didn't mean to harm the others. I loved all of them. I had to make them like me so that they could . . ."

"Loved? Don't you ever say that word again, you sick bastard!" I say as I bend down and scream in his ear, ultimately interrupting him before he can say another word. "You don't know what love is."

"I loved Samantha," he cries. "And you took her from me."

"How dare you say that you loved her, when you showed her nothing but hate and pain?" I scream. "You don't deserve to use that word!"

Every word coming out of his mouth enrages me more. I kick him harder.

"Please stop," he cries. "Help me."

He lifts his arms, indicating that he wants me to help him from the floor.

"Sure, I will help you," I say, grabbing the hardest thing I can find. "I will give you the choice. I can leave you here to die slowly. You never know someone might come around and help you. Or I can kill you now! Which will it be?"

"Too late," I scream instantly. "I choose for you to die now!"

With a smile on my face, I hit him as hard as I can across the head. A loud crack and blood begins oozing from his skull.

"How is that, my king!" I say as a giggle escapes my lips.

I turn to run up the stairs but stop. I want to see who this man is. I have to see the face of the man that has tortured me for so many years. Quickly, I turn back around so that I am facing his lifeless body. I start to reach for his mask but decide I better ensure that he is either passed out or dead. I kick him lightly in a few different places on his body to make sure he does not move.

After only a few moments, I decide it is safe. I quickly bend down and reach for his mask. As soon as my hand touches it, a moan escapes from within him, and he reaches up for me, taking hold of the bottom of my dress. Scared out of my wits that he is completely coming to, I take the knife and stab his hand, knowing that by doing so he will let go. I then take the freshly, blood-covered weapon from the ground and hit him over and over again across the head, ensuring that he will never move again. Satisfied that I have killed him, I run up the stairs.

To my surprise, the door is still open, as he forgot to close it before he attacked me. Forgetting about the possibility that someone else might be there, I run through the door and into the main part of the house and keep running until I find the front door. I stop and look at the front door knob as tears fill my eyes. I am finally going to be free, and there is nothing stopping me except for turning the doorknob. I close my eyes, turn the knob, and stand completely still. A breeze of fresh, untouched air enters through the open door and onto my face.

As I take my first step out of the door, I start to look back but quickly decide not too. Instantly, a feeling of freedom overcomes me, and I start to run. I keep running and running and running, never looking back.

I am weak and had only been running for about thirty minutes, before I have to stop and catch my breath. The fresh air smells good and is refreshing. I take in deep, long breaths, taking in as much air as my lungs will allow. I had been locked up in that dingy dungeon for so long that I have forgotten the wonderful feeling of fresh air in my lungs. I sit silent for just a moment and take in all the smells that are around me, trying to identify each and every one. One scent is that of fresh grass. The other, that of oak trees. Most importantly the smell of freedom.

I am free! Free from my captor! But I know I have to concentrate. I am not out of the woods yet. I will have to find help. *But which way will I find it?* I look around. I can either go through the empty field that seems to lead to nowhere, try hiking up toward the mountains in hopes of finding a trail, or I can walk through the forest and hope that I find someone there. I look over my options again as I debate which way is the best way to go.

"If I go through the field, I will be seen easily," I think to myself. "But is that something I want? Are there wild animals around here? If so, the field will not give me any protection."

"If I go toward the mountains, I may find myself in a terrain I am not used to being in and might find myself needing more help than

I do now. So that is definitely not the way I want to go," I convince myself.

"I guess the best way is through the forest," I say out loud. "I will have a little protection, I think. Plus, it will be easy to find firewood if I don't find help by nightfall."

Wasting no more time, I get up and begin running again. I run deep into the forest and keep running until I can no longer see where I began.

It isn't more than an hour, before I tire again. I do not have the stamina I once had. I tire easy. I need to rest. I look around for a place that I can rest my tired, beaten body for a while longer. Within seconds, I notice a small meadow in the distance. I slowly walk the rest of the way there.

The meadow is so beautiful and so inviting that all my worries seem to instantly fade into the distance. I lie down in the meadow, letting the sun rest on my pale white body. It feels good to have the warmth of the sun on my skin. I look around. The meadow is still plush green. Sunshine peeks through the hundreds of trees that outline the meadow, making the grass look like it is sparkling with every color of the rainbow. I look up at the trees. There are thousands of them that encircle the meadow where I now lie. A sudden breeze passes by causing the trees to move in sync, looking as if they are all dancing to the same song. I listen closely; I can hear the song also, so I start dancing along with them, swaying my body back and forth as I lie in the soft grass. It is all so beautiful; I never want to leave. Forgetting at that moment everything except for what is in front of me, I lie here enjoying the moment.

I am not worried about him coming after me. I had killed him with the last blow to his head. No one could have survived what I had done to him. The blood left on my hands and dress is proof of how hard I hit him. As I lie here, I study my hands and dress and realize that I am more of a mess than I originally thought. My hands are covered in blood and so is my dress. I guess I could have taken my time and looked for something to wear before I left the house. But I was scared that someone would catch me, so I did not dare. After all, Samantha thoroughly convinced that there are more than one of them. And although it seems that she might have been wrong, I have my suspicions also.

Relieved that I had not come in contact with any of them during my escape, I take in a sigh of relief. Instantaneously realizing what I am doing – I am wiping his disgusting, dirty blood onto my face. The thought of any part of him on me appalls me to no end. I have to get his blood off me. Frantically, I begin spitting on my hands, trying to wet the dried blood. But it is of no use; my mouth is too dry and only a few drops of saliva come out. Determined to get the blood off my hands, I try to wipe off what blood I can onto the grass. However, only a small amount comes off, as most of it has already crusted into the wrinkles of my dry skin.

"I hope he rots in that room and the rats eat him," I say out loud as I leer at my hands.

I am so excited to be free that I begin yelling it as loud as I can, over and over again, until my throat becomes dry and sore and a sound no longer escapes from within my mouth.

A wave of exhaustion overcomes me. I am tired from the lack of food and all the fighting and running I have done this day. I yawn, then smile. I will never have to look into his soulless eyes again, nor see his horrifying black mask.

"I will close my eyes only for a moment," I say to myself. "Then I will get up and search for help some more."

I must have been lying for hours, as the next thing I know I am opening my eyes to a near-dusk sky. I jump up in fear, and for a moment, my heart begins to pound faster, as I think of the dungeon and all that waits for me if I were ever to be caught. I look around, ensuring that I am truly in the meadow and still alone. The meadow is silent, and there is no indication that anyone is around. It is getting dark, and I don't know where I am, and I do not care. I will no longer endure the pain that another human could put upon me, and I will no longer have to feel his wrath. I am as free as the bird that is flying above me. A smile appears on my face as I twirl in a dance, knowing that he cannot, and he will not ever touch me with his disgusting hands again.

After dancing for a while, I decide I should seek some type of shelter for the night, as now the sun is setting behind the trees, causing the field to become dark and uninviting. I know it will be only a short time before I am no longer able to see, and I am afraid I will walk back toward where I just left.

Agreeing with myself that it will be best to leave my celebration for another time, I start to walk.

As I begin my journey again, I walk slowly, taking in everything that the forest has to offer. It isn't long before I start noticing different types of animals. First, I see a squirrel, and I stop and watch him as he gathers nuts from the ground and packs his cheeks full. I know he is bringing food home to his family, and that makes my heart melt. After watching him for a while longer, I decide to let him gather his food in peace, as he seems a little nervous about me being there watching him.

Continuing on my way, I stop only one more time and that is to watch a baby deer playing with his mother. I have never seen something so beautiful, so close to me. They seem to dance around with complete grace and serenity, neither caring nor noticing that I am there.

"I'll let you be, so you can play with your mama," I say softly, then continue on my way.

I am looking for only a while longer, when all of a sudden I come across a small abandoned shack. It is pitch-dark outside by now, and I am not able to see to go any further. I will have to stop here, no matter what is inside. That is unless I am wrong and someone is living there, someone who will not welcome me or that I will not feel comfortable with.

I knock on the door, lightly. No one answers. I try again. Still no answer. I slowly open the door and yell inside, hoping that if someone is in there, they will let me know before I enter. There seems to be no one, as my calls are left unanswered.

I try to see inside, but it is too dark, and I cannot see a thing. That scares me, as instantly memories of the room with the women come to mind, and I think back to how dark it was in there and what had awaited me inside. With great hesitation, I enter the room and begin to feel the walls closest to me in hopes that I will find a light switch, but there is not one on the wall by the door. Instantly, I know it must be an old cabin, and it probably does not have electricity. Continuing on my search, I feel every inch of every wall hoping not to find such objects as I had in the "room of torture." To my relief, the walls and all that is in the room seem to be that of what you would find in just about in a cabin. I can relax.

A sudden cold breeze hits my bare skin, and I realize that the cabin has a broken window. I will need to find a blanket, as all I have on is my torn-up gown that I have been wearing for days, and it is very thin. Taking my time, I feel everything around the room, until I find what feels like a small crotchet blanket. I pick it up and instantly think of my mom and how every year for Christmas she would make me a new crotchet blanket. How I loved each and everyone she ever made!

I am not real tired, but I am cold, so I decide to cuddle on a small couch that I have come across in my search throughout the house. Lying there, now warmer and more comfortable than I have been in a very long time, I listen to the sounds of nature outside.

My mind begins to wonder as I hear the sounds of a nightingale singing outside my window. It reminds me of the times that my fiancé and I spent the weekend at a cabin. It was a cabin that he had owned that was deep in the woods away from any other person. Therefore, we were completely alone the entire weekend. I remember we would walk for hour's everyday, taking in the clean, fresh air and all the beauty surrounding us. During the last trip, we had found a small pond and played there for hours in the water. It was hot that weekend, so the cold water was refreshing on our overheated bodies. It was so perfect that he had to carry me out of the water to get me to leave.

If he would have just told me then that he had wanted to take me to a waterfall that he had found on one of his solo hikes, I would have left without an argument. Boy, did I feel stupid that I had put up such a fight, when all he wanted to do was take me to that magical place – the place that he proposed marriage to me and I happily accepted.

I hold my left hand out and feel the area to where my engagement ring once was and begin to cry, as the mark from wearing it is gone, leaving no trace that it ever existed. My eyes become heavy, and I fall fast sleep.

I dream of the day we were to be married, the same dream I have every night since the day I was taken away from my life. But this dream is a little different. I do not dream of the man in the dark corner. Instead, I dream of Kamrin and me in front of the podium saying our vows.

I awake this morning with a smile on my face, something I have not done in a very long time. As I lie here with my eyes shut, I realize that this is the first day in, I don't know how long, that I do not wake up in fear to what kind of pain I will have to endure for this day. Instantly, I begin to cry hysterically from the joy and happiness that is growing inside me.

"You have made it this far, but you can't stay here. So get it together and get moving in case there are others and they are looking for you," I think to myself.

A little panicked by the thought, I quickly wipe my tears, open my eyes, and look around the room. The sun is shining through the window, brightening the cabin. It is wonderful to see the sun again. However, it has been so long since I have seen the sunshine that I have to blink my eyes a few times to get them used to the brightness.

Without warning, my stomach lets out a growl that I am sure could be heard throughout the forest. I am hungry, as in the past three months I was allowed only minimal food, and I have not eaten the day before. I decide that before I leave the cabin, I will take the time and search for something to eat.

As I look around, I notice that I am in a much larger cabin than I originally thought. The cabin is clean, but it looks like it has been months since someone has been here, as there is a thick layer of dust on everything.

Taking my time, I look in every cabinet hoping that whoever has been in here before has left some type of food behind. However, with each door I open, my hopes begin to fade as all the cabinets are empty. My quest is unfound, and I know I will have to leave here hungry and pray that I find someone or some type of food soon.

"I'm sure I will find someone today," I say, giving myself encouragement.

Tired and undernourished, I decide to sit for a few minutes before heading out for my long journey home. I start to head back over to the couch I slept on earlier, when I notice a rocking chair in the corner. It is an old rocking chair and reminds me of the one that my grandmother would hold me in and tell me stories, when I was a small child.

"This is perfect," I say to myself as I rub my hands up and down the sides of the chair.

I sit down carefully, making sure that the chair is not old and rotten and is strong enough to hold me. It is a perfect fit and seems to mold around my body. Instantly, the chair begins to rock back and forth as the weight from my body moves with it. As I take in the "at home" feeling, I close my eyes and lie my head back and allow the rocker to continue to move me.

It is quiet and peaceful with only the sounds of the trees swaying outside, and I am enjoying it immensely. I sit and rock in the old chair for at least an hour.

Suddenly, someone screams in my ear, "*Get up!*"

Startled by the sound, I immediately open my eyes and look up.

"What in the hell!" I scream aloud as I jump from the chair.

I cannot believe what I am seeing. Whereas, on the ceiling is picture after picture of women. I look closer. Every woman has been tortured and seems to be photographed right after the death. However, after closer examination, I realize that is not actually the case. There are two pictures for each woman. One before she had been tortured and one after. The strangest thing is that the pictures that were taken after death – each woman is wearing a veil and has a different last name written on them than the "before" pictures. I cannot tell if they have been married before he killed them or after. Either way, the thought is horrible.

"This has to be the same man or people that had me," I think to myself as fear rushes through my body. "I have to get out of here and now!"

As fast as I can, I take down each picture carefully to ensure that I do not rip them. I know I have to take the pictures with me to show them to the police.

"Maybe they will be able to identify some of these poor ladies and give their families a little peace of mind," I say to myself, uncertain whether the names on the pictures are correct.

It takes at least an hour to gather all the pictures, as they are plastered among the entire ceiling. There has to be hundreds of them. Although I try not look at them, I keep finding myself staring at each one as I take them down. Some women had been tortured so badly that they were unrecognizable as women; others looked as if they had been barely touched at all. However, all were suffering the same fate; their eyes were missing, and the mouths were either stapled shut or their lips were missing completely. I cannot comprehend what I am seeing. *Why were some hurt so badly and others not and why are their eyes gone and their mouths the way they were?*

"Were some luckier than others and died before they could be tortured in such a way that even God would have a hard time recognizing them?" I ask myself.

I begin to cry as I see what happened to each one. They had all been tortured in different ways. One had both her legs and arms broken so badly that they were all facing opposite directions than they should have been. Another is missing her feet and hands, eyes sockets stapled shut, and lips missing. It is like each one had learned a lesson and with each lesson came a different punishment. I say this because I remember, once when I had talked back, he stapled my mouth shut for doing so and I had to take the staples out myself. Now I understand, depending on what they did wrong that area of their body would be punished. This is how they learned. Well, at least according to him.

"God, I hope they do not let the families see these pictures," I cry to myself. "I hope that I can help them find this guy! Now I know I have to get away. I have to find help! He can't do this to any more women!"

I gather the rest of the pictures without looking at them, as my heart and stomach can no longer take the pain. I look around some more, until I find an old nap sack to put the pictures in for safekeeping.

"That's it," I scream aloud. "He takes their eyes so they cannot see him, and he takes their mouths so they cannot talk. It all makes sense now. He is afraid that even in death they will tell."

"What a sick and twisted soul this man, this monster must have!" I scream as loud as I can.

With that last outburst, I know I have to leave, as I am sure I have screamed loud enough that anyone near to the cabin will have heard it. Ensuring that if there were others, they now know where to find me.

I run around the room as quickly as I can, looking at every wall. I have to make sure I do not leave a single picture behind. I want to show the police everything. After a few seconds of searching, I am convinced that I have gotten them all, and I am ready to leave.

"You're going to need food," I hear a woman's voice say.

"OK," I think to myself as I frantically look around. "Where did that voice come from?"

I quickly look around the inside and outside of the cabin. There is no one in sight.

"Maybe I am hearing things," I think to myself. "Or maybe it is my self-consciousness I hear, warning me."

Wherever it comes from, I know the voice is right. I will eventually need food as I am unsure of how far the nearest town is or even which direction to go. All I know is that I am in a forest; however, I am uncertain which one, as I was drugged the day he took me and have no idea how far we traveled, or which way we traveled.

I look around some more to make sure that I have looked everywhere for food. All of a sudden, I spot a large freezer, one I did not see earlier. I blink my eyes and look again, ensuring myself that it really exists.

"I was sitting there just a little bit ago," I think to myself. "I don't remember seeing that."

With great caution, I walk back toward the rocking chair, where now sits a freezer next to it. I plug my nose and close my eyes as I slowly lift the lid, afraid of what might be in there. After having lifted the lid, I unplug my nose, thinking that if there are dead, rotting bodies in there, I would rather smell them than look at them. To my delight, I smell nothing more than the smell of a cold winter's day when you walk outside right after a fresh snowfall, the same smell as a freshly opened freezer. I open my eyes, however, still anticipating seeing a dead body or two in there. My heart starts pounding with excitement when I realize that the freezer is full and there is not a body to be found. I start looking through the white packages of meat trying to find one that is not too big to carry with me. That is, until I can get a little further away to start a campfire, so I can cook it and eat part of it.

"They sure do like big pieces of meat," I think to myself as I look throughout the freezer, only finding pieces of meat that look as if they would feed about twenty people. "That's right. He probably was. With all the pictures of the women I found, he must have fed a lot of people."

A sudden sense of urgency overcomes me, and I know if I do not get out of here now, I may never get out. The thought of being in his cabin, knowing that there is a possibility that there could be others like him, helping him, petrified me. I know I need to travel as far away as I can, as fast as I can.

"A man that could do such horrible things to innocent people is capable of anything, I am sure," I say to myself, unconvincing myself that he is truly dead.

I take the package and put it in a separate bag, then the pictures. *I have to make sure they do not get wet.*

"I have to keep these pictures safe," I think to myself.

"Get out now!" a woman's voice echoes through the room.

Right then, I know it is definitely time to go. I do not bother looking around the cabin for any possible explanation of who could have said that. Without any further hesitation, I grab up the pile of things I have found while searching for food. I am ready to continue with my journey home.

"Home . . . Home sounds good to me!" I say as I head toward the door.

I reach for the doorknob. Without warning, an evil, almost sinister, feeling overcomes the room.

"It's too late. He is here!" a woman's voice cries.

The air becomes cold and unsettling, causing the hair on my body to stand on end.

"The hell it is!" I scream back as I open the door and run away from the cabin.

I run as fast as I can, all the while looking back toward the cabin, ensuring that I am not being followed. After five or six miles of running, I decide that I am safe and that no one is following me.

As I slow my running to a brisk pace, I start to laugh.

"What am I running from?" I ask myself. "Ghosts?"

I know that I have probably suffered some type of physiological issues from being locked up for so long. Therefore, the voices were probably not real. I am just being paranoid because of the pictures I found in the cabin. Besides, if there are any others like Samantha had suggested, I think they would have found me by now.

But with my newfound freedom being uninterrupted, I am more confident than ever that she was wrong.

I shake my head and decide to try and forget what happened in the cabin and the voices I heard and enjoy the nature around me. I take in a deep, relaxing breath and look around. The sun is out in all its glory, making it bright and radiant outside. There is a slight breeze, and when it brushes against my body, it is cool and refreshing on my sweaty skin.

I continue to walk, however, uncertain if the way I am headed is the way out of the forest.

"All that matters is that I am headed away from the cabin and the house," I think to myself as I start to hum a song.

It is so amazing being free to walk anywhere I want, sing anything I want, and say anything I want. It's like being in heaven to me, as I cannot see heaven being any better than this complete peace I am feeling at this point.

"I wonder if I can still skip," I ask myself.

I remember as a child, how I always would skip around when I was happy, and I have not been this happy in a long time.

Suddenly, I find myself skipping throughout the forest like a princess in a fairy-tale cartoon. At that moment, I forget about everything that happened in the cabin and begin singing, all the while stopping to smell every flower I come in contact with, taking in their different fragrances. I do not care if it is a nice smell or a bad one; I always stop and smell it, ensuring that I will never forget the scent again.

"What is that sound?" I ask myself as I lift my head up from smelling a rose.

I lift my head.

"I think it might be water!" I say aloud.

A drink of water sounds really good to me. I had tried to get water from the cabin, but I never came across a sink or anything that contained water, so I have not had a speck of water in days, and I am extremely thirsty.

I stop and listen until I can figure out which way the sound of running water is coming from. As my ears finally focus on the sound, I sprint as fast as my tired, weakened legs will carry me to where I know the water is waiting.

"There it is!" I scream in excitement as I run to the spring, almost falling in face-first.

The water is a little cold, but it feels nice on my sore, dry skin. I begin scrubbing my hands, trying to get all the dry blood off that I could not get off yesterday in the field. At first, the blood is stubborn and does not lift from my hands. However, as I continue to move my hands around the water, the blood begins to loosen and melt from my skin. There is much of it, that the sight of the massive amount of blood rushing down the stream sickens my stomach. I turn my head as the rest of the blood is washed away, only looking back when I am certain that all the blood has moved down stream.

I look down and study every inch of my hands until I am convinced that my hands are clean. I then reach into the moving stream and gather water into my hands and splash it onto my face. It is so refreshing to feel the cold water on my face that I continue to splash it until my hair is soaked from the water I am playing with.

"Well, I might as well get my feet wet and try to get them clean also," I say to myself as I look at the filth crusted on my legs.

I take my shoes off, put my feet into the water and splash around for a bit until my feet and legs are clean. I smile and lean back onto my elbows, as I let my feet continue to dangle in the stream, kicking my legs, causing the water to splash all around me. I do not care that it is a little chilly and I am getting wet; I am enjoying the fact that I am cleaning myself because I want and not because I was ordered to.

I look down at my dress; it still has blood drippings on it. Instantly, my stomach turns, and I begin dry heaving. I don't know if it is the thought of his blood still on me or the memory of how his head was drenched and dripped with blood from the beating I had given him. All I know is that, at that moment, the sight of his blood on my dress reminds me of a horror movie, and I feel like the villain. I had now killed two people, and that is something that I will have to learn to live with for the rest of my life. I understand that one of them was the one I was trying to help, and the other was an evil, sadistic man and deserved to die – or should I say needed to die? But no matter how I look at it, I still had taken their lives in my hands and killed them.

"I have to get this blood off me," I think to myself. "If I don't, the sight of his blood is going to drive me crazy. Besides, who is going to want to help someone who comes running up looking as I do, especially when their dress is covered in blood? They will know I killed someone and probably run themselves, thinking they are next."

Without any further debate, I jump all the way into the water, hoping to clean as much off the blood as I can. The water is really cold and causes a chill to instantly rush throughout my body. Now most people would have jumped out right away. But not me; I did not mind the frigid water. In fact, I am used to the cold water, as every time I was allowed a shower, it was from a hose, and the water was usually cold, except for during the summer. The water that had been sitting in the hose for some time in the heat would be the first to seep through the hose, and I would get the feeling of warm water for just a few seconds. I used to love those days. Although they were few and far between, I would crave them often.

As I stand in the water scrubbing my dress, my mind begins to wonder, and I think of how wonderful it will be to take a hot bath again. I would make the water as hot as I possibly could without burning my skin and maybe get some bath beads and put them in there also. That way I could smell pretty, like I did at one time. I would sit there, totally emerged in the bathtub and let the warm water cover my body like a winter's blanket, until my body begins to shrivel and the water cool. I would then get out and find the plushest towel I could and wrap it around me, ensuring that I do not let the feeling of warmth escape from my body.

"God, a hot bath sounds good," I say as I lean back and let my body float on top of the water.

I stay in the water for hours, imagining that I am in the largest bathtub that was ever made and it was made just for me. Looking up into the crystal blue sky, watching the birds as they fly by, I cannot imagine my world being any better.

"Food would be nice though," I say to myself, rubbing my food-starved stomach.

My stomach, no longer upset, is now growling immensely, reminding me that in fact it has been a couple of days since I have last eaten, causing me to instantly jump up from my relaxed position. Suddenly, I begin to shake, and right away, I know it is time to get out of the water, or I will take the chance of fainting and possibly drowning where I stand. I need food now, or my shaking will continue to get worse. I say this not because of the feeling that is stirring inside of me, but because I had experienced this many times during my captivity, when he would starve me for days on end.

Quickly, I get out of the water, ring out my hair and my dress as best I can, and put back on my shoes. My fun time is over, and I need to get moving again. I have to get some food. Taking the blanket that I brought with me from the cabin, I wrap it around my chilly body, gather up my things and head down the stream.

"I will keep walking until I find a decent place to camp for the night," I think to myself. "I have to find something that is a little secluded with just a few trees. That way I can start a fire without the fear of burning down the forest, and I will have something I can climb in case I need to get away from a wild animal."

I knew that by all means I would not be able to climb a tree, but for some reason knowing that I would have the option if need be made me feel more confident about being alone in the forest.

I continue to walk for what seems to be an hour, before I find the perfect spot. It is an open area, however, secluded by trees that seem to encircle the immediate area, making it an ideal place to start a fire and rest for the night.

"This will do," I think to myself as I look around.

Within seconds, I find a large pile of leaves that look as if they had recently fallen from the large tree above and right away know it will make the perfect bed for the night. I am pretty sure I don't have to worry about snakes, as it is early in the fall, and I don't think snakes are out in the cold.

"Now for a fire," I say as I scan the area around me.

I set my gear down next to my bed for the evening and venture off to find firewood. I had heard somewhere that a fire will keep wild animals away, so I know I have to find enough to keep my fire going all night while I slept. I gather firewood for a while, and then I notice that the sun has gone down, and it is getting dark. I know I am out of time, and if I do not stop soon, I might get lost in the dark forest and not be able to find my way back to my home for the night. Afraid that I have not gathered enough wood to burn all night, I look over at my pile of wood. It is then that I realize that not only do I have enough for tonight, but that I have enough firewood to last me a couple of nights.

"I guess I have enough." I chuckle to myself as I clear an area for the fire.

Strategically, I place some of the dried-out leaves from my designated bed down and place a few of the logs on top. After a few strikes of the matches I found at the cabin, I am able to catch the leaves on fire. I am certain that they will burn quickly, but I am uncertain if the wood will catch fire before they burn out completely. I quickly add more leaves to the fire just to ensure that the logs will catch also. I have used most of the leaves from my bed, but that is OK. I am quivering from the wet clothes I am still wearing and need warmth more than I need a comfortable bed. After all, I am used to sleeping on a hard surface.

After making certain that the logs are on fire, I head over to the tree where I had dropped my belongings before and pick up the sack with the package of meat in it, then head back to the fire. As I take out the meat from within the bag, I notice that it has defrosted and, the blood from the meat has gotten all over everything else that is in there. It is disgusting as everything is now covered in blood, reminding me of what I looked like earlier that day.

"Wait a minute," I say to myself in a panic. "I watched a movie once about bears and how they are attracted to blood. I am going to have to burn everything that has blood on it."

Quickly, I look down and see that my hands are now covered in blood again. Panicked, I take the bag and look for the cleanest area and scrub my hands as best as I could. I then take the bag and all it contents and throw it into the fire, hoping that I have not left anything out that has blood still on it.

After looking around the area to where the bag had been lying and searching my entire body, I am convinced that I have gotten everything, and I will be safe for the night.

"I think I will be OK," I say in a soft, relieved voice.

I sit down on a log next to the fire and start to open the package of meat. All of a sudden, I hear something moving about in the wood behind me. Frightened, I jump back away from the sound.

"What if it's a bear or a wild cat and they had smelled the blood before I could destroy it?" I say between my clattering teeth.

My eyes now wide open, I stand paralyzed in one spot and look around for any possible movement around me. I do not see a thing. My body begins to shake so tremendously hard that the clattering of me teeth makes it impossible for me to hear anything around me except the sound of my teeth as they slam together. I have to keep calm. I have to be ready to defend myself from whatever is out there.

"More fire," I think to myself.

As fast as I can, I run over to the pile of wood and begin throwing log after log onto the fire, until it is now raging more than ten feet tall.

"This will keep any animal away, I am sure," I try to convince myself.

However, there is a part of me that is still uncertain, so I grab the largest log that is left in the pile of wood and lie it next to me. I then stop and listen again. To my relief, I hear nothing more than a few birds singing in the distance. I breathe in a deep sigh of relief and sit back down, club in hand.

"The fire must have scared them away," I think to myself as I look over at the large wrapper of meat that awaits me.

I grab my package that contains my dinner for the night once again, hoping that the smell of cooking meat will not arouse anymore animals. I know that there is a good chance that it will, but it is a chance I will have to take. I am starving, and I know that if I do not eat soon, my body will begin to shake again, or worse, I will suffer another episode of my blood sugar being to low and possibly pass out, leaving me in state of unconsciousness that will ensure my vulnerability to any passing animal. Not to mention, I need the energy for tomorrow's journey, as I do not know how much further it will be before I am able to find someone to help me.

I open the white package I had found earlier and study it to see what kind of meat it is. Not that I care too much. I am just curious to what I will be eating.

"What a strange piece of meat this is! I have never seen something so big. Maybe it's a roast. Although if it is a roast, it's the biggest one I have ever seen," I think to myself as I lie it onto a log within the fire and sit back and relax while I wait for it to cook a bit.

Still a little curious of what kind of meat it is, I decide to look at the wrapper, thinking that the type of meat should be written somewhere on the paper.

"I know he probably didn't care what he was feeding us," I say out loud as I think back, remembering that I had gotten the piece of meat from the cabin, I am certain is owned by my captor. "But I am sure he ate it too, so he should have written on the wrapper what it was so he knew what he was eating."

I reach over to the empty wrapper lying on the ground next to me. The dirt from the ground has mixed with the blood on the paper, causing the wrapper to become filthy. As best I can, I shake off the dirt that has gotten on it and study the wrapper looking for any clue to what kind of meat I am about to devour or how old it is. After all, if it is too old, I am uncertain if I should eat it, as this is not a good time to be eating rotten, old meat and getting food poisoning. If that is the case and the meat is really old, I will just eat the worms I saw under the pile of leaves. I know it will be disgusting, but somewhere I had heard that they are a good source of protein, and I am certain that I can force myself to eat them if I have no other choice. Either way, I have to eat something tonight.

I begin to laugh.

"I don't know what day it is, never mind what year. How will I know if it is old?" I say aloud. "I guess I will say . . . if it's from 2009, then it should be OK. I believe that is what the year is presently."

I turn the paper over and see some writing on it. Hopeful that the writing will give me a clue to either the date or kind of meat, I hold the paper closer to the fire so I can better see it, as it is now pitch dark outside. I can barely make out the markings. I think "10/2009" is written on it.

"Great!" I say out loud. "I can eat it!"

Taking extra care with my meal, I sit and watch it closely, turning the meat several times, ensuring that it will cook completely through without burning. I can smell the meat cooking, and at first, it smells wonderful and makes me think of times when my father would barbeque for my mother and me.

"I wonder what my dad would say if he saw me now." I laugh. "I bet he would never believe it."

As I continue to daydream, a sudden horrific smell fills the air causing me to instantly plug my nose in disgust.

"Maybe the meat is old," I think to myself. "That might explain the smell."

Quickly, I grab the paper up again so that I can ensure myself of the date. It is as I thought; it has 2009 written on it.

"Maybe it is because it's on top of a log, instead of an open fire," I try and convince myself. "Or maybe it's the type of meat it is. After all, I have no idea what this is."

Determined to find out what it is, I continue to search the crinkled white paper for some kind of clue to what type of meat I will be eating. Although I try to convince myself that I am overreacting, I have a strange gut feeling inside me, nagging at me to find out what I am cooking, and I know that unless I find out, it will keep haunting me. Finally, after searching the entire wrapper, I see some more writing other than the date I had seen earlier. However, like the date, it is faded, smudged, and hard to see. I hold it closer to the fire, in hopes that the light will brighten it enough so that I will be able to make the writing out. Despite the fact that I am trying to be careful, I come too close to the fire, and an ember lands on the wrapper causing the paper to catch fire.

"Oh shit!" I scream while I am stomping it out.

"Well, I guess I will never know what it is now," I say as I lay it on the ground next to me.

Realizing that I have been so obsessed searching for an answer, I had forgotten about the meat. I quickly look into the fire and see that not only does the meat seem to be done, but it also seems to be burnt.

"Crap, now I will have to eat burnt meat," I say to myself, disgusted that I have let myself become so obsessed that I had forgotten to turn it over, ultimately ruining the only meal I have. "That's what I get, I guess."

I look around and spot a thick, skewer-like stick and pick it up. Holding it in both my hands, I push the skewer as deep as I can into the freshly cooked meat and lift from the fire. I then lay the piece of meat onto the log I presently am sitting on, hoping that it will cool quickly.

"I am so hungry," I say as I blow on the meat over and over again, hoping that it will cool enough that I can at least take a small piece off and eat it while I wait for the rest to cool.

The meat smells better now; in fact, to my starved body, it smells like the most delicious food I have ever smelled.

I continue blowing on the meat, touching it over and over again, as I anticipate the first bite.

"Finally," I say as I tear a small piece of meat off and hold it to my mouth, blowing it off one last time.

Ha-ha, ha-ha, ha-ha.

"What the hell!" I scream as the sound of someone laughing echoes through night air.

I jump to my feet almost knocking my soon-to-be meal onto the ground. I quickly look around, but the forest is dark, and I cannot see any further than the light that is being emitted from the fire.

"This darkness must be getting to me," I think to myself. "Too many bad memories."

Shaking the sound of laughter out of my head, I sit back down to enjoy my meal. I pick the meat up, bring it to my mouth, and take a big bite. Suddenly, a sparkle near the fire catches my eyes. I look closer. It is the burned-out meat wrapper I had thrown down earlier, and it once again is partially on fire. After stomping the rest of the embers out, I pick up the wrapper and hold it in my hand.

I can now see more of the letters on it. I sound it out in my head as I continue to chew. The first word starts with a "C." However, the rest of the second word is hard to read. I continue on with the second word, hoping that it will be clear. The second, in fact, is much clearer, and I have no problem reading it. It reads: Thigh.

"C, thigh?" I question myself. "What does that mean?"

"It can't be a chicken thigh. It is way too large." I laugh, as I take the last bite of the meat that I had cooled earlier. "And it surely does not taste like chicken."

Still holding the piece of meat in my hand, I bring the paper closer to my face and study each letter until I finally make out the words.

"Oh my god! Oh my god! It says Christina's thigh," I yell.

I throw the meat onto the ground and let out a scream that surrounds the forest, traveling for miles. My surroundings start spinning, and my stomach begins to hurt. I turn my head and vomit into the fire and keep vomiting until there is nothing left to empty out of my stomach. I begin to dry heave.

"What have I done!" I cry.

I sit back onto the log I occupied before, put my face in my hands, and begin to cry hysterically. I must have cried for an hour; I cannot believe that I had just eaten another human being.

"I didn't know," I cry to myself. "How could I have known that he had cut her up and put her in that freezer!"

I cannot understand how someone can be so evil. How one human could do such horrible, disgusting things to another? My mind begins to wander back to all the times I ate while I was captured and how many times I might have been eating . . . I begin dry heaving again. The thought that I have just eaten the flesh of a tortured woman and might have eaten more people than that is more than my stomach can take, more than my beaten soul can take.

Tears stream down my face.

"It's OK, Lue," I hear a voice from behind me.

I jump to me feet.

There, in the darkness behind me, is a figure. A figure of a man. I should have been more aware of my surroundings, but I had let my emotions take control. My heart skips a beat as a rush of adrenaline surges throughout my body. How long has he been there?

"No! No! How? When?" I scream at the dark figure. "Leave me alone . . . you son of a bitch! Just leave me alone!"

Quickly, I look around for anything I can use to defend myself. I know that without some sort of weapon I will be defenseless against this man, as it is obvious that he is no normal man. He is inhuman.

"I will not go down without a fight!" I think to myself as I spot the large stick I placed next to my seat earlier and grab it firmly.

"Come on, you sick bastard, I took you down once, and I can do it again!" I yell into the open field.

With my newfound weapon, I firmly stand my ground and look around. The figure has disappeared into the blackness of my surroundings. I study the dark forest as intently as my obstructed eyes will allow, but the glow from the fire seems to make the forest darker, leaving me in complete blindness.

"Am I imaging things? Am I going insane? I mean, I know I heard a voice, and I know I saw a figure. But where did it go?" I repeat over and over again to myself.

I continue to search, but there is nothing to be seen except that of complete blackness and the only sound I can hear is the same two birds that I have been listening to for a while. I shake my head and lower the stick to my side.

"I have to be imagining this," I say to myself. "I am sure it is because I am out here in the dark alone, and I hate being in the dark, especially in an unfamiliar place."

Taking my chances that in fact it is only my imagination, I sit down next to the fire. However, being cautious, I sit facing the area I think I heard the voice. That way if someone is really there, I will be prepared if they attack me.

"See, it was your imagination, silly girl," a voice inside me says.

I finally relax after an hour or so of peering into the emptiness of the forest.

I take a deep breath and lay my head back, as I know I am in fact alone, and I can now totally relax without the fear of being attacked.

"What a beautiful night!" I think out loud as I stare at the stars above. "I don't think anyone could ask for a more perfect sky."

"Or a more beautiful woman," someone says from behind the tree.

I know that voice, as well as I know every wound he inflicted on me. There could not be another person in this world that could have such a sinister voice as he.

This time, it is not my imagination playing tricks on me. It is him!

I jump up and grab my club. He will not fool me again. I know he is here and has been watching me for a while. I just do not know for how long.

"Where are you?" I scream into the emptiness of the night. "Show your face, asshole. Or are you too scared?"

"I'm not scared of you." He laughs from the other side of the area I am in. "You're my Lue. I know you would never hurt me on purpose."

"What?" I scream back. "I stabbed you. I bashed your skull in. I tried to kill you!"

"I know you didn't mean to. You were just scared," the voice in the darkness says. "Let's go home, and I will forgive you. You will be mine again."

"No!" I scream as loud as I can, as I prepare to run in the opposite way of the voice. "I will never go back, and I will never be yours!"

Suddenly, something hits the side of my head. I look down; it is a rock.

"Is that the best you got?" I yell.

Suddenly, I hear a burst of laughter behind me. I turn quickly around, searching for the voice. I see nothing more than complete darkness that has encircled me, trapping me where I stand.

"What am I going to do?" I ask myself.

My heart begins beating so hard that I can hear each and every beat within my ears. My hands begin to sweat, causing the stick to slip. I am in a full-out panic.

"*No!* I cannot allow myself to be taken back," I scream within my head as I reposition my hands, ensuring I have a stronger grip on my weapon. "I can't let him take me back. I don't care what he promises. He will kill me for sure."

Another rock hits me, this time from the back. I swing around, hoping that I will see him this time. He is not there. His evil laughter fills the air as I am pelted by rock after rock. Soon I am being showered with rocks from all directions. My head begins to twirl as I turn around, looking in all directions, trying to figure out where the next rock will come from, but they seem to be coming from everywhere, from nowhere.

"I have to run. Run as fast as I can. I know he can't catch me. I injured him the day before," a panicked voice screams within me.

A sudden horrifying thought comes to my mind, and I know I cannot run as of yet.

"I have to get those pictures. I don't want to leave without them," I whisper softly.

Slowly, I try sneaking my way over to the tree where I had left the bag full of the gruesome pictures. Careful to keep my guard up at all times, I make sure I never lose sight of my surroundings. As I reach the area that I had left them, a feeling of defeat overcomes me, as there is nothing left there except for a pile of leaves. The pictures are gone!

"No! I will never be able to show what these women had gone through and their bodies may never be found!" I cry within myself. "Their families will never know."

Frantically, I begin kicking leafs around in hopes that somehow the bag of pictures had fallen through when I had taken leafs from that area earlier.

Suddenly, someone grabs my wrist! . . . It's him!

"Looking for something?" he asks.

"No," I say softly. "I am getting my stuff so that I could go home with you."

"*Liar!*" he screams in my ear.

I jump back, turn around, and get ready to run. My foot slips on the dew-dusted grass, and I twist my ankle, causing me to fall to the ground. I try to get up and run, but before I can move an inch, he is on top of me and is now holding me down. Suddenly, I am violently turned around by his strong hands, and to my dismay, I am now staring into the eyes that I had wished I would never have to look in again. I can see the true anger in his eyes through the same black mask he wore in the house of torture. He is livid, and I know he wants me dead.

"Please leave me. Take your pictures and let me go," I beg. "I won't tell anyone."

"Now why would I do that? You cut me, and now you must pay," he whispers in my ear.

"I am truly sorry," I plead.

"I don't think you are. I asked for your help, and you denied me of it," he says while gritting his teeth. "You killed my wife, and now you will be mine!"

The earth begins to shake violently beneath me, and suddenly, he is ripped from on top of me as if some unforeseen force has yanked him into the sky.

As his body is ripped from mine, the earth instantly stops shaking. I jump up and look around.

"Where did he go?" I ask myself.

My surroundings are silent.

The earth shakes violently again, and I find myself being thrown to the ground once again. He is back, but from where?

He grabs my arms and holds me down.

"It's OK, Lue," he says in a softened tone. "It is me. I'm not here to hurt you, unless I have to."

His voice sounds sincere, but his eyes confirm he is lying.

"What do you mean it's you?" I say stunned. "It's been you all along, you freak."

He laughs as if he is hiding something.

"Don't worry about it. In time you will understand," he states.

"You said I am your special girl," I scream. "Then let me go. Let me live my life. If you love me like you say you do, then you will set me free."

"I can't let you go. Then you will never be mine, and you have to be mine and mine alone. If you refuse to come back with me and become my wife, I'll have no other choice but to deny you of your sanity and freedom," he says in the utmost disturbing voice. "I cannot let you be . . ."

I interrupt him.

"You think love is pain and suffering," I say in desperation. "You can take me back, you can hurt me, you can torture me, and you take my sanity. But I will never, I repeat, *never* be your wife!"

"Tsk-tsk," he says shaking his head. "Then you leave me no choice."

His voice instantly changing to a deep menacing growl.

"Stubborn bitch!" He chuckles as he takes out a razor and holds it to my face. "The things you must suffer now!"

I don't want to endure anymore pain, but there is no way I will ever be his wife, and there is no way I am going to go back and be his prisoner. I have to fight. I have to get away. I know if I could distract him just for a second, I could get out from under him and get away. In desperation I try to grab his mask, but it hugs his face like a second skin, allowing no place to take grasp.

"Please, don't do this," I cry, as I continue to squirm under his grasp. "I'm sorry."

"Too late for that now, my dear." He laughs as he holds the razor to my face. "It is time for me to teach you your final lesson."

The determination and anger in his voice ensures me that if I do not get away, my death is inevitable. I am going to have to use my woman's intuition and distract him.

"No!" I cry. "I will go back with you, but first I want a kiss."

"You want what?" he asks in a shocked voice.

"If I am going to go back with you and be yours, I want a kiss," I say in the most sincere voice.

He leans down, and with his mask still attached to his face, he places his lips on mine. His mask and lips feel as one. My skin crawls in disgust.

"You're going to love this," he whispers as he begins to kiss me with such intensity that his lips against mine feels like two hard rocks slamming together.

It is time to get away, as he is preoccupied trying to satisfy my desire of a caring kiss.

I bite his lip as hard as I can, ripping a chunk of skin and mask from his bottom lip.

Instantly, he jumps away. As he rubs his wounded lip, I start to squirm from beneath his body. He is too heavy and too strong, leaving me helpless and unable to move.

"So you like it rough?" He laughs. "Me too."

He takes the razor that he still possesses and begins slicing my face. I move around trying to miss the slashing, but his movements are lightning quick, and no matter which way I move I cannot get away from the sharp blade. I scream in pain as the razor cuts deep into my face, my ears, and my head, leaving me no route of escape. Blood starts to gush onto the ground as the sharp razor edges cuts me over and over again. I try to cover my face with my hands, hoping to relieve it of anymore punishment. But it is no use; he holds them above my head and continues lashing at me, never missing a strike.

"I'll be good," I cry. "Just please stop."

"No, I don't think you have learned your lesson yet," he screams, continuing to slice my hands and face with such intensity that I do not think I will be able to escape the wrath that is put upon me.

"Someone, please help me!" I scream in excruciating pain.

"Who do you think is going to help you?" He laughs as he takes his finger and wipes the blood off my face.

"No one will help a crybaby like you." He chuckles, and then with his blood-covered fingers, he wipes my blood onto his face, making warrior stripes across his cheeks.

"A crybaby?" I scream. "I can remember 'someone else' crying when I cut them."

Without warning, he sits straight up on top of me and stops lashing at me with his razor. Rolling his eyes at me, he chuckles.

"Baby, it wasn't me that was crying." He laughs. "I was enjoying it myself. I wanted you like me, and that moment you were everything like me. While you were slashing him, I could feel you in my soul."

I am confused as to why he refers to himself as another person, but then I look into his eyes and remember just how insane this man truly is. I do not press the issue, as it is obvious this man is completely out of touch with the real world and anything further I might say could anger him to the point that he will take the razor he is holding and slash my throat.

"I am a warrior, and you are my prey," he suddenly screams, as he licks the blood from his fingers. "And no one would dare mess with this warrior!"

"I am not prey, I am a woman. A woman who deserves life," I scream.

"The only way you deserve life is if you are mine, and just to let you know, you will be mine no matter what pain I must make you suffer before you realize that!" he says with an evil smirk. "And if you continue to refuse, I will make sure you regret that decision forever. When I get done with you, no one will ever recognize you, not even your mother."

"No!" I cry. "Please, don't."

"In fact, I think I will start right now," he says as he grabs my hands and starts rubbing the razor against the skin of my fingers. "First, I am going to cut your fingers off one by one, then your toes. Your arms and legs will be next, and I will make sure you live through every horrible thing I do to you."

"No! I won't let you!" I yell. "And I will *never* be yours!"

"Baby, you have no idea," he whispers in my ear. "I am a prince, and with you by my side, I will be king and together we will own the world."

"Don't call me *baby*!" I scream.

The adrenaline in my body surges and a sudden burst of strength overcomes me. I am able to push him off. He falls to the ground besides me. Stunned and confused, he lies there laughing an inhuman, sinister laugh.

I jump up, and forgetting about the pain, I catch my balance and turn to run away.

"Where are you going?" he says as he grabs my leg and continues to laugh.

"I'm going home," I say as I pull my foot back and kick him with all the rage and hatred that has built up inside me.

My footprint now embedded on the side of his cheek, he looks up at me, and with a soft smiled he says, "You were always home," then turns his cheek and lets out a laugh that makes a chill run up my spine.

I turn to run, when all of a sudden I spot the bag that possesses the pictures lying beside him. I know that if I am quick enough, I can grab them, as he now lies there silent; I am sure that he has passed out.

"I have to get those pictures," I say to myself as I stand there staring at the bag.

I carefully reach over his lifeless body and grab the bag.

I will never understand the things I do, but in that instant I have to also have his mask. There is something about his mask that every time I see it, I want to rip it off his face. I am sure it is because I know deep inside that this evil man has to look like evil himself. I reach down and . . .

His hand reaches for me.

I jump back and once again kick him in the head with all my might, turn, and run as fast as I can into the dark forest.

Scared, I run for what must have been a mile or two before I realize that I have been running through trees and shrubbery and have been receiving new cuts and bruises on my legs and arms. My face, now sweaty and covered in dirt and blood, causes the mixture of both to drip into my eyes. At first, it is not a big deal, but as I continue to run, the situation gets worse until my eyes burn with such intensity that they feel like at any moment they will close and refuse to open again. I can no longer see, and I know I will have to stop or take the chance of running into a tree. Stopping only for a moment, I carefully wipe my eyes, ensuring that I do not disturb the new wounds on my face.

"That's better," I say as I finish wiping my eyes on my dress and look around.

I do not know what direction I am headed, nor if he is behind me. I just keep running and running deeper into the unfamiliar forest, hoping that I will find someone that will help me. Suddenly, my sides constrict in such pain that I find it hard to take a breath.

"I can't stop. I can't let him catch up to me again," I think to myself. "I will suffer more."

Frightened by the thought of how crazed he is, I know that it'll be best to ignore the pain and keep running. However, my body does not agree with my mind, and I fall to the ground, as my lungs are no longer able to handle the lack of oxygen. As I sit and try to relieve the pain of my burning lungs, I can't help but touch my face, as I have to see how many new wounds I endured from the lashing I just received. I touch my face, searching it in its entirety as softly as I can with my rough, dry hands. Instantly, I know that he has slashed my face more than I originally thought, as every area I touch burns intensely. I take the bottom of my dress and try to wipe some of the dirt away from the wounds in hopes that the pain will subdue. However, that is not the case; the loose dirt from my dress becomes embedded in my new gashes, causing me more pain.

I want to bury my hands in my face and cry, but I know that by doing so, I will not be helping my situation; in fact, I will be making things worse.

"You have to stay focused," a voice in my head says. "Just do what I have taught you to do and think of something else. It will help the pain go away."

I know exactly what the voice is talking about. I have to think of something else besides the excruciating pain I am enduring. I learned a long time ago that if I focus on something else, I can ignore what is happening to me at that moment. It was the only way I could keep my sanity for all those years.

I wipe my tears, close my eyes, and begin focusing my mind onto something more pleasurable, like sitting at home on my front porch on a cool summer's night. It seems to work and only take a few moments before the pain is bearable.

After resting for about an hour, my lungs finally quit burning, however, my legs still ache from all the running and fighting I have done in the last couple of days. I know I will have to walk the rest of the way; running is no longer an option.

"Time to go," I think to myself as I start to stand up.

I am still uncertain if the direction I am walking is the right way, so I stand for a moment longer, looking in every direction. It is then that

I realize that I am uncertain which way I came from. Every direction looks the same.

"Shit," I think to myself, "now I really don't know which way to go. If I go the wrong way, I will head right back to *him*"

I am so angry with myself that I did not pay more attention to where I came from.

"How could I have been so ignorant?" I yell in my head.

I look around some more, hoping to find some indication to the direction I had come from. There has to be something. Maybe a broken limb or some footprints, anything that will show me the way. But it is still too dark to see any further than a few inches in front of me, leaving me disoriented.

"Please, give me a sign," I scream as I look up to the heavens above. "I cannot do this alone."

I don't know if I am expecting someone to actually answer me, but I find myself blankly staring into the night sky.

"What are you doing?" I ask myself. "Do you really think someone is going to show you the way? That someone actually cares what happens to you?"

I lay my head down and stare at the ground, as I know deep inside that I am right. No one cares. No one is looking for me, and I will probably never find my way out of this damn forest.

"Maybe I am better off in that dungeon," I think to myself.

Suddenly, I hear what sounds like water. I listen closer as I turn in every possible direction, until I know the exact area to where it is coming from.

"This way!" I yell as I start walking as fast as I can toward the sound.

I don't know why the sound of the water excites me so, but it does. I know I had been there before, but this time, it is as if something inside me is telling me to go there and to go there now! Almost as if someone is waiting there for me. Someone that will take me home to my family.

I start walking as fast as my worn-out legs will carry me, as I anticipate what could be waiting there for me, getting more anxious with every step I take.

As I continue to walk, the sound of running water gets closer and the excitement of the unknown overtakes me. I have to know what is there waiting for me, as I know it is something that will change my life forever. I begin to walk faster and faster until the next thing I know, I am running.

"There it is!" I yell in excitement, as I run as fast as I can toward the reflection of the moon on the water.

Without warning, my feet begin to slip on the wet bank. I try to catch my balance, but the bank is too slippery, and I fall down, slamming onto the rocky bank that outlines the stream.

"Oh shit!" I scream as I hear a loud snap.

Pain overtakes my leg.

I look down and see that my leg has landed on a large boulder. I try to move it, but it does not budge, and I know right away it is broke! Resting all my weight on my good leg I try to get up, hoping to move away from the bankside. As I lift myself up, my hands slip on the wet sand, causing my body to shift onto my broken leg. Instantly, my leg buckles from beneath me, and I fall back to the ground screaming in pain.

"Is this why I was to come here!" I scream as I look into the sky above. "To endure more pain!"

Within seconds, my head begins to spin and the surroundings around me begin to fade. I try to keep consciousness, but it's no use; the pain is overwhelming.

"You can't pass out!" I scream within myself. "You have to fight this! Think of something else!"

It's no use; no matter how much I try to fight the feeling, I know it is coming, and my eyes begin to close.

"Lue, are you OK?" I suddenly hear a man say.

I look up, and there standing above me is a figure of a man. A man I am sure is there to finish me off. With every bit of energy I can gather from within me, I try to get up and run, but my head is too dizzy and my body too weak, making it impossible to lift my body more than an inch off the ground.

"Help me, please," I say out loud as I reach for him.

My arms are too weak and fall lifeless to my side. My eyes close, and I pass out.

CHAPTER 6

My Angel

I FEEL THE warmth of a fire next to me, and I am uncertain to where I am.

"Hello," I scream as I scan the area.

Suddenly, I see a man lurking in the darkness of the forest. I try to get my eyes to focus, but the fire is too bright, and I can see no further than the shadow of the man that is now walking toward me.

"Just do it and get it over with! I cannot take this anymore," I scream over and over again, as I curl up in a ball and bury my head within myself. "Please, just kill me now!"

Within seconds, I feel him place his hand on my shoulder.

"It's OK," the man says.

I hear his voice, but I cannot understand him as all I can hear is the weeping that is coming from within me.

"Calm down. I'm not going to hurt you," says the man as he pats my shoulder in reassurance.

His voice, now clearer, is not familiar to me.

"He could be disguising his voice," I say to myself, as I slowly lift my head from its tucked position, in order that I can hear him better.

"Miss, are you OK?" the man asks as he continues to reassure me of his kindness.

"You have to look up," I think myself. "If this is your captor, sitting here crying isn't going to do you any good anyway. It's best to say your final good-byes and prepare yourself for death."

As I stay in my partially curled position, I begin to pray, ensuring that I have said my good-byes to everyone I have ever loved.

"Why don't you just kill me?" I scream as I quickly raise my head so that I can face the one that will now be taking my life away.

"I don't want to kill you," the man says in a low chuckle.

Instantly, I have to blink my eyes to ensure that I am truly seeing what I hope is not a dream. Whereas, there standing in front of me is a young man that looks to be about my age. I am not sure, but from where I am lying, he looks as if he is about six foot tall and is slim built. He has bright blond hair which sparkles like gold against the warm fire, and when he smiles at me, it is like an angel smiling down from the heavens above.

"Oh my god!" I scream in pain, as I sit up from my curled position so that I can get a better look at him.

"Be still. Your leg is broke pretty bad, not to mention you have cuts throughout your body," he says with warmth and sincerity in his voice. "I cleaned you up the best I could, while you slept."

"You were the one I saw at the riverbank?" I ask.

"Yes," he answers. "I heard someone screaming earlier. I have been looking in the woods for a while trying to figure out where the voice came from and that is when I saw you fall and break your leg."

"I am so glad it was you," I cry. "I thought it was him!"

"Him?" he asks softly.

"It's a long story," I explain to him. "When you found me, did you see a bag by me?"

"Yes, it was wrapped in your arms when I found you. It must be pretty important to you, because you would not let it go," he says with a concerned look.

"More important than you could ever imagine," I say as I look around the immediate area for the bag.

"Don't worry, the bag is safe," he says as he points toward the bag containing the pictures. "Can I ask you something?"

"Sure," I answer.

"What happened to you?" he asks.

"Where do you want me to start?" I say in a soft laugh.

"Wherever you want, sweetie," he say as he smiles.

"It all started on September 7," I explain as tears instantly fill my eyes. "That is the day I was taken from my home. I mean, from my life."

He never makes a sound, as he sits and listens to my horror story in amazement, or maybe it is disbelief. In fact, the only time he does move is when he looks away for a brief moments at a time. I know that by him doing that, he is trying to hide the tears that have been gathering in the corner of his eyes.

About an hour into my story, he gets up, walks over to me, sits by my side, and put his arms around me. The warmth and comfort overcomes me, and I melt in his arms like putty and begin to cry hard.

"Let it out, let it out," he says as he holds me tighter. "It will be OK now. I won't let anything happen to you."

"Thank you . . . Thank you for saving me." I smile.

We sit together for hours talking about everything, about nothing. I laugh at his jokes, and he cries at my stories.

"What is today?" I ask abruptly.

"It is Monday, October 29."

"What year?" I ask.

"2009," he answers.

"Three years . . . Three years of pain and torture," I whisper to myself. "Three years I have lost from my life."

My mind begins to wander, as I start thinking of what I went through and what will happen next.

"I wonder what my parents will do when they find out," I think to myself.

My body shakes from the pain of my leg, snapping me out of my beautiful trance.

"What are you doing out here all alone?" I ask as I look around my new surroundings.

I have been in my own little world and have not seen that my savior has gotten up and is no longer sitting next to me. In fact, the man that has saved me is now at the other end of the fire, and he looks as if he is preoccupied doing something.

"Look at him," I think to myself. "He is beautiful."

His face seems to sparkle in the firelight like fresh snow on a sunny winter's day, and when the glow from the fire hits his golden hair a certain way, the illumination looks as if he has an angel's halo around his head. When he moves, it is like watching a living piece of art, as he moves with such grace and beauty. He is the most stunning man I have ever seen, and I find myself staring at him, mesmerized by his beauty.

"You must be starved," he says as he holds a plate of food out to me.

I jump back and almost fall from my seat as I have been so caught up in my fantasy that I did not notice that he has walked back over to my side.

"What?" I ask.

"It's OK. I won't hurt you," he says in a soft voice. "I guess I will have to be more easy with you."

"I'm sorry. I didn't see you there," I explain as I shake my head trying to bring myself back to reality.

"Are you hungry? I made you some food," he asks again.

I have forgotten all about not eating in days. That is until I smell the food that is now in front of me.

"Thank you," I say.

I grab the food from his hands and begin eating it as fast as I can. I really don't think to use the silverware that is lying on the plate, as I had not used any in over three years. My captor always said that using silverware was a luxury and I would have to earn it.

"I guess I had never graduated to that level," I say in a low chuckle.

"Excuse me?" the man asks.

"Oh, nothing," I answer in a soft voice and continue to eat. "I am just thinking out loud."

I am starving, and with every bite I take, my stomach growls, as if it is screaming for more food. At first, I am a little embarrassed by the way I am acting, that is until I look up at him and see that he has a look of concern on his face rather than a look of disgust, like my captor always had.

"This is delicious," I say, ensuring him that I am enjoying everything I am eating.

While stuffing my face, my mind wanders back to the recent event when I had eaten . . . I shake my head in abomination. I have to stop thinking of such things from the recent past and concentrate on now. Besides, what will he think of me if I tell him I had eaten another person? I am sure he would run away as fast as he could, or think I am insane.

Looking up at the man standing in front of the fire, I look into his eyes. He does not look like he is capable of doing such things as my captor, so I decide to end my story of Christina unheard, as I am still a little uncertain how he will react to such a horrifying, disgusting detail of my life. By looking at me, it is obvious that something has happened to me, but the story I have shared with him so far is outrageous; I don't know if I would have believed it myself.

"I'm sure he believes you. What else could have happened to you to make you this way?" I think to myself. "Just relax. Everything is going to be OK."

Putting my attention back to my food, I begin eating as fast I can, as I believe if I do not eat it all within a specific allotted time, it will be taken away from me, and I do not want that to happen. I am starving, and the food I am devouring is not rotten; in fact, it is the most delicious food I have ever tasted.

After eating everything on my plate, I look up to find that he is standing next to me with another full plate of food. Right then, I realize how ridiculous I must look and start laughing so hard that I almost choke on the food that I am presently chewing. I decide it will be OK to slow my eating, as it does not look like he will be taking my food away, like I half expected him to. Besides, I am afraid that I might choke to death, if I continue in the eating frenzy I am in.

"I don't want to die from choking on this food, not after all I have been through." I giggle to myself.

The thought now embedded in my mind, I become self-conscious about my eating and slow it down to a turtle-like pace.

"Don't be embarrassed," he says. "Go ahead and eat. I have more for you if you like."

"I'm sorry. I have not eaten for days and have not had a decent meal in years," I explain. "This is the best food I have had in a very long time."

"Well, then you eat up. You need your strength until I can get you to a hospital tomorrow," he says.

"Tomorrow?" I ask.

"Yes, it's too dangerous to go out in the dark. We will have to wait until daybreak," he explains. "It is only a few more hours."

"But he is still out there," I say in a panic. "He will find us."

"I will stay up, don't worry about it. I will never let him touch you again. Besides, I have a gun. He wouldn't dare come around here," he says as he taps his side.

"You don't know him though. He is evil, and he won't care about a gun. You don't understand. I don't even think he is human. I stabbed him. I knocked him out, and he always came back for more," I explain as my voice cracks. "Besides that I saw him disappear into the sky and return, unharmed."

My savior sat quiet for a moment.

"What?" he asks.

I knew he didn't believe me, as I did not believe myself.

"Nothing," I say quickly. "Just know that I think he is immortal."

I expect at any moment that he will fall to the ground laughing at accusations, but he doesn't. Instead, he begins pacing back and forth.

"Bring him on!" he yells. "I hope he does come, and I would like to kill him myself. That sick bastard! Do you hear me? I'm waiting for you!"

"Please, please," I beg. "Not so loud, please for me."

"OK, OK, I will be quiet," he says as he sits beside me again.

"Thank you," I sigh.

I finish my dinner, both plates, in fact, then lean back, resting against his side.

"You should sleep," he says. "I will stay up and watch the camp."

"I'm OK. I can stay up with you. I just need to lie down for a second." I laugh. "I think I ate too much."

"You can lie here and use my lap as a pillow," he offers.

He stretches his legs forward, places his jacket on his legs for a pillow, and taps on his legs as if inviting me to do so.

I am tired, and I know deep inside, it would be best if I lie down and rest. So I take him up on his offer and lay my head on his lap.

"Is that comfortable?" he asks as he looks down at me.

I look up into his baby blue eyes and a feeling of warmth overcomes me. Suddenly, I am tongue-tied, and I can barely say a word.

"Yes," I say quickly as a feeling rush through my body like never before. "It is perfect."

I am a little shocked at myself that I can have such a strong feeling about a man I have just met. But being here with him is like being with my missing half. I force myself to look away, as I know that the feeling is unreal and in fact is nothing more than the gratitude I feel toward him for saving my life. I have heard of people falling for someone who saved their lives or taken care of them when they were sick. And I do not want to fall in love with someone for those reasons alone.

"What time is it?" I ask abruptly.

"It is 3:00 a.m.," he answers, never looking at his watch.

"Why?" he asks.

"I am trying to figure out how much longer before daybreak," I answer him with a smile.

"Just about two or three hours and we will be on our way," he says as he answers my unasked question.

"OK, I can do this," I think to myself. "It's only a few more hours you have to stay up."

I lie there for a while staring at the stars through the trees, trying to talk about anything I can think of. I need to stay awake, and I know that if I do not keep talking, I will fall asleep instantly.

"What's in the bag?" he asks.

"It is a bag of horror. A bag that shows how evil one person can really be," I explain.

"A bag of horror? That's a strange way to describe a bag." He laughs.

I begin to explain what I had seen in the cabin that day and how the ceiling was wallpapered with the many pictures of the tortured women I now have in my possession.

"This can't be true. There is no way that there is someone out there capable of doing what you are explaining," he says as he lays his gun next to his lap.

"Well, no human anyway," he mumbles beneath his breath.

I look at him with a strange look. Did he say what I think he said? He sits silent, and I am sure that he has said nothing of the sort. I take a deep breath and continue talking.

"I wish it wasn't true. But it is, and I hope that the pictures inside that bag can help capture him," I explain in desperation.

He begins to rub his hands through my hair. A sigh escapes from within me, as his kindness is something that I have been missing for so many years. Instantly, my heart and soul is relaxed, and I begin to fall asleep. However, before I fall completely asleep, the sound of despair fills my ears. I peek through the corner of my half-closed eyes as I hear his soft weeping. He is crying.

"Thank you," I say softly as I lift my hand slowly and wipe his fresh tears.

"For what?" he asks in a soft voice.

"For caring," I say as I smile at him.

"That is what I am here for," he says as he smiles back at me.

Now I know I should have questioned his last remark, but I don't. I have never met someone with such compassion, and truthfully I am taken in by his genuine concern.

"Go to sleep, little one," he whispers to me. "Everything is going to be fine."

Within seconds, I can hear the soft hum of a song coming from through the forest. The sound, that of complete serenity, sounds like thousand angels humming the most beautiful song I have ever heard. I cannot tell where it is coming from, as it seems to be coming from everywhere. It is magnetic, relaxing, and fills my soul with peace. I know he is right. Everything is going to be OK.

"That is the most amazing song I have ever heard," I say as I lift my head. "But maybe you should turn the radio down so that he does not find us."

He chuckles, then says, "I will be sure to do that."

I lie my head back down on his lap and continue to listen to the beautiful music. Within seconds, the music begins to hypnotize me, and I find that I can no longer keep my eyes open. I look up at my savior, smile, and then fall sound asleep.

"Good night, my sweet Lue," I hear him whisper, and my mind enters dreamland.

When I awake the next morning, I find myself lying on a bed of plush blankets. My leg is now wrapped in a fresh white cloth and the pain has subsided. The fire that was raging the night before is now a pile of burnt, smothering embers.

I quickly scan the camp for a sign of the man who saved me the night before. I see no one. I sit up to get a better look. Still no one. Suddenly, something catches my eyes. It's a black piece of material scrunched up next to the fire. I begin to panic, as a flash enters my head of my captor in his black mask. I try to stand, however, my broken leg stops me from doing so, and I fall to the ground.

"I have to see what that is," I think to myself.

I slowly scoot my body across the dirt and leaves working my way over to where the black object lies. I pick it up, and to my dismay, it's the mask!

"*No!*" I scream in terror. "It can't be!"

The sound of my screaming echoes throughout the forest, my voice bouncing from tree to tree until the forest is filled with the sound of my terror. Suddenly, silence overcomes my surroundings as if the sound of my voice has scared everything around me away.

"Why?" I cry to myself, as I hold the mask in my hands.

Without warning, the mask begins to move in my hand, overtaking my skin as if it is liquid.

"What in the world?" I scream as I try to rip the mask from my skin.

The unwelcomed mask is now embedded into my skin, taking over my hand. I can feel evil growing inside me and the need for my captor growing intensely.

"What is happening?" I cry to myself as I continue to fight the feeling that is taking over my mind and body.

Suddenly, I hear a noise behind me, and I scream again.

"Hey, it's OK. It's me," I hear from behind me.

Without warning, the material releases from my hand and the mask falls to the ground.

"You're him! You're him!" I scream again. "Get away!"

"No, no, I'm not. I found that mask this morning in the woods. I brought it back to show you and for possible evidence. I swear I am not him," he tries to convince me.

"Where did you find it exactly? Is he close?" I ask not fully convinced that he is telling the truth.

"I went back to the stream where I found you, and it was lying in the area where you fell," he explains.

"How do I know you're telling the truth? This might just be another sick joke," I cry as I try and scoot my body further away from him.

"Don't you think I would have killed you last night?" he snaps. "And from what you told me about the man that kept you, he would never have given you the pleasure of eating before he killed you."

"I don't know. You never know. It might be your last way of torture," I say as I grab a large stick. "I mean, what better way to torture me than to show me some kindness just to take it all away?"

"Calm down and put the stick down. I am not here to hurt you. You have to trust me," he says with a calming smile. "Just look into my eyes, and you will know the truth. I have to learn to trust someone."

This is not fair. I have no idea if he is telling the truth or not. But what could I do? I can't run. I lower the stick in defeat. I wouldn't be able to fight him off anyway . . . Not with a broken leg.

He slowly walks to my side, hands me a plate of food, and says," Eat this, and we will be on our way. If I found the mask out there, then he is still around, and I need to get you to safety."

He turns and walks away with his head down. I could tell by his actions that I hurt his feelings, and I know that my captor would have never reacted in such a way. In fact, he would have laughed at me and then would have hurt me in anyway he deemed appropriate for the lesson I would be learning. Or worse yet, he would have taken the very breath from within me.

"What are you doing?" a voice in my head says. "This man is here to help you. You know that in your heart. Just look into his eyes."

"Sorry for my actions." I turn in his direction and smile, ensuring him that I believe in him and that I am truly sorry for how I reacted. Accepting my apology, he nods his head, smiles back, and winks at me.

I feel better that he has accepted my apology; however, I am still a little embarrassed by the way I acted. I put my head down and begin eating the eggs and bacon that he has served me, never looking up to see what is going on around me. When I finally finish my food, I slowly raise my head and look around. To my surprise, he has the camp completely packed up and is ready to head out.

"How are we going to get out of here?" I ask softly.

"I will carry you. It's not that far to my truck from here. Maybe an hour or two walk," he says with confidence as he flexes his muscles at me, causing me to laugh.

"Just give me a stick, and I will hobble out with you," I say with a smile.

"No, I can't take the chance of you hurting your leg any more than it is already hurt. Besides, if he is still out there and watching us, I want you as close to me as possible," he demands.

"Wait, you can't carry me and all your gear," I exclaim.

"I will come back for it after you're safe. Besides, it's not that important, just a few things, all of which can be replaced if it is taken," he explains.

Before I know it, he swoops me onto his back and we are headed down the path, leading to his truck. We walk for a while, and then I insist that we stop so that he can rest from the extra weight that my body is putting on his back. At first, he argues with me and says that he is fine and does not need the break. However, after my constant nagging for him to rest, he finally gives in and stops for a moment.

He gently takes me off his back and sits me down on a log. I cannot help myself but to watch him as he moves his perfectly toned body around, stretching his muscles in all different directions. It is obvious by the way his shirt clings to his body that he is a man of great strength.

"He is my guardian angel," I think to myself as a ray of light peeks between the trees, shining on only him.

"What are you smiling about?" he asks with chuckle.

"Oh, nothing, I am just thinking that you must be an angel," I answer.

A loud laugh comes from within him as he smiles at me.

"We better get going. We are almost there, and that leg of yours needs attention." He laughs.

In one swift movement, he lifts me from the log and puts me on his back again.

As we start to walk, I lay my head on his shoulder and take in the smell of sweet candy.

"Thank you and I'm sorry for before," I say in a soft voice.

"I don't blame you. I would have been scared also," he explains. "And I want to apologize myself for snapping at you the way I did."

"Let's just say, we both overreacted and let it go," I say.

"I think that would be best," he says as he reaches back and touches my hair.

For some reason, whenever he touches me, even with the slightest touch, it is calming and makes me feel warm inside.

"I was thinking. I never asked your name. What is it?" I ask.

"My name is Angel," he says with a chuckle. "That is why I laughed before, when you said I must be an angel."

"See, you are my angel," I whisper in his ear. "I knew you were."

We both begin to laugh as he continues walking, still carrying me on his back.

"I have something I need to tell you," Angel says, breaking the laughter that filled the air moments before.

"What?" I ask a little concerned about what it could be.

He admits to me that he had looked inside my bag and was horrified on what he had seen. Also, that he had heard noises in the woods the night before. But worst of all, he admits that the mask he had said he found by the river was actually found about one hundred yards from our camp.

"You see, that is why I have to get you out of here as fast as I can," he says in a concerned voice. "I can't take the chance of you ending up like those other women, and truthfully, I am not thoroughly convinced that there is only one person that is responsible for all this."

"He is right," I think to myself. "That would explain how no matter how bad I hurt him, he kept coming back for more. It wasn't always him, at times it was someone else."

I cringe at the thought of my captor or captors being so close to us and instantly begin looking around in fear that they are right behind us.

"Did you see that the women in the pictures that were wearing veils had different names on them than their originals?" I ask.

"Yes, sweetie, that is why I think there is more than one or two. I think there is a whole gang of them," he says in a concerned voice.

"More than one or two?" I think to myself as my grip becomes tighter around Angel's neck.

Instantly, I find myself becoming more and more paranoid at the thought of how many of them there could be and that they could be watching us right now, waiting for the perfect time to attack.

"You might want to loosen your grip there. I have to breathe you know." He laughs.

"*Oops*, sorry about that," I whisper as I loosen my grip around his neck and reassure my grip on the bag of pictures. "The thought of how many of them . . ."

"I know," Angel says as he interrupts me. "Don't worry about it. Look ahead."

As I look into the distance, a sigh of relief seeps through my lips, as a few yards in front of us is his truck.

"See we are only a few yards away from my truck. Besides, they would have never of taken you without a fight from me," he says as he lies his hands on my arms. "And believe me, that is not a fight they want to be in."

I can tell by the tone of his voice that he is serious and would have fought to his death to save me. I just don't know why, and truthfully, I don't want to ask him why. I am just happy that it is a man like he that has found me.

"Here we go," he says as he gently places me into the front seat.

Before I can turn to put my seat belt on, he is sitting in the driver's seat of the truck and has the truck started. I am relieved as I know I am on my way home and no one could stop me now.

"Are you ready?" he asks.

"Boy, am I ever," I say as I take a look around the forest I hope to never see again.

I lay my head against the back of the seat and relax, something that I have not been able to do in years.

"Do you feel that?" I turn and ask Angel as he put the truck into gear.

"What?" he asks.

"Freedom," I say as I smile at him.

Angel never says a word. He just turns his head and smiles at me.

Suddenly, a chill overcomes my body, the same way it always did when my captor would walk into my room. I lift my head and peek through the rearview mirror. Standing there in the shadows of the trees in which we just left is not only one dark figure, but the entire forest seems to be lined with them. I scream!

CHAPTER 7

Homecoming

I T IS EITHER the rumble of the engine or the complete relaxation that puts me asleep. I am not sure how far we have traveled. I do know though that I have been asleep for a while because it is now dark.

As I look down the empty highway, I see in front of me a sight I thought I would never see again – the lights of a big city. It is amazing how the lights from the buildings sparkle around like stars in the sky. I am truly going home! I look over at Angel and take in a deep breath.

"Hello, sleepy head," he says with a smile as he patted my head.

"I'm sorry. I didn't mean to fall asleep. How long have we been traveling?" I ask.

"About eight hours. We are almost there," Angel says. "First stop, the hospital."

"What city is that?" I ask in curiosity. I want to know how far I am from home. From my family.

"That is Jackson Hole. It's about forty-five minutes from your hometown of Swan Valley."

"Can't we just drive the extra few minutes and go to my hometown?" I ask.

"I would rather take you to the hospital in Jackson Hole. I have a friend there who is a doctor, and I know he will take great care of you," Angel explains. "You can give me the names of your family and anyone you want me to come in touch with, and once you are settled in your hospital bed, I will contact them. Don't even try to argue with me on this one. Your health comes first."

"OK, you win," I say. "I am feeling a little woozy from the pain. Maybe this way is best."

The rest of the ride is quiet, and I can tell that Angel is tired, as he is not talking as much as he did the day before. That is fine with me, because my mind is elsewhere, thinking about my family and dreaming of my fiancé.

We arrive at the emergency entrance soon after. Before Angel can get me out of the truck, a funny man with a wheelchair comes running toward us.

He is a tall, skinny man with a bald head. He wore his pants above his waist, his shirt is tucked into the high-waist pants, and he moves in quick, jerky movements. I can't help but laugh as the sight of him is so comical, like an old black-and-white comedy.

"Was it a car accident?" the funny man asks.

"No, she fell and broke her leg," Angel answered the man. "She has other wounds that need attention also."

"I see that," the little old man says in a nervous tone.

"Dr. Johnson is waiting for us," Angel further explained.

After that, everything moved fast, and before I know it, I am out of the truck and being wheeled into the hospital emergency room.

"Let's take you into this room," the old man says, as he wheels me into the first room we come to.

Suddenly, nurses begin coming out from everywhere, and within seconds, my room is engulfed by them, blocking my view of Angel.

"Angel!" I scream frightened by all that is going on.

"I'm still here," I hear from behind the crowd of people. "I will be right back. I just have to tell the doctor what has happened. Don't worry. If you get scared, just yell my name, and I will be right there."

I feel like I am being poked and stuck everywhere. Whereas, as one nurse is putting an IV in my right arm, another is taking my blood pressure on my left arm. I must look a mess as they all seem like they are panicking. Within seconds, I begin to feel claustrophobic as it all becomes too much at one time, and I am uncertain how much more I can take. I yell for Angel once again.

Within a blink of an eye, he is standing by my side holding my hand.

"Are you OK?" Angel asks.

"I am starting to feel a little intimidated," I admit.

"I know this is probably a little scary and maybe a bit too much all at once. But these people are here to help you," Angel says with a smile. "No one here is going to hurt you."

He then puts his lips on my forehead and kisses me gently which makes everyone else seem to fade, until I can no longer hear or see anyone else but him. I know I have only known him for a day or so, but every time he looks into my eyes, my heart goes pity-pat and all my worries instantly disappear.

"I need to finish talking to Dr. Johnson, Lue. I will be right back," Angel says as he gently kisses my forehead one more time before leaving the room.

I really don't want him to leave again, but I understand that he has to talk to the doctor, so I do not protest him leaving. I merely sigh and close my eyes in hopes that the nurses will be done soon, and I can rest here in peace.

"There you go, sweetie," a nurse says. "I could see that you were nervous with all the people around you, so I had them all go away for now."

I open my eyes and see that everyone has left the room, leaving her and me alone.

"Thank you," I say as I smiled at her.

"You're welcome," she says as she lightly touches my hand, then walks out the door.

The room is finally silent with only the sounds of machines beeping in the background, and I can finally recollect my thoughts of something more pleasurable than all the machines I am hooked up to.

"Where did Angel go?" I think myself.

Suddenly, I see Angel waving at me from a distance.

I look closer and can see that Angel is not far away and that he is still talking with the doctor.

He is a quirky little doctor, and from where I am lying, he looks as if he is all of five foot tall, making him even look short against Angel's tall physique. He is an older man, maybe in his early seventies, and I know he is wearing a toupee, as every time he turns, the piece of hair on his head shifts, causing his hair to lie in different directions. I have to laugh as it is the funniest thing I have seen in a very long time.

Suddenly, Angel looks at me and with a wink, indicates that I should not be laughing. It is like he knows exactly what I am laughing at.

I quickly look back into his eyes showing him my innocence. In return, he shakes his head and smiles, then turns and continues to talk with the doctor.

They would talk for a while, then the doctor would look my way and shake his head. I could see the sadness and pain in his face growing with every word that is being said. At one time, I see the doctor lower his head as he talks to Angel. This scares me as I think that maybe there is something extremely wrong, such as them having to amputate my leg.

"I hope that is not what they are talking about," I think to myself as I continue to watch every move that they make.

"Is there anything you would like?" a nurse asks as she suddenly peeks her head in my room.

I am shocked by the sudden break in silence and jump back in my bed.

"Can I get a soda?" I ask, startled.

"No problem," she says with a smile, then heads back out of the door.

I have not had a soda or anything close to that in over three years, and an ice-cold soda sounds really good. I close my eyes and think back to the last time I had a cold drink, and I can't remember when that would have been.

"Hi, Lue! Are you feeling better?" Dr. Johnson asks.

"Yes, thank you," I reply as I quickly open my eyes.

"We have to do some x-rays on your leg to see how bad the break is. But I am sure it will be fine," the doctor says further.

I breathe a deep sigh, as I am relieved to hear the good news.

"Don't worry, we will take great care of you here, and I promise no one will harm you while we are around," Dr. Richardson says as he holds my hand tight.

"Thank you," I say as I give him a big smile.

Tears fill his eyes. Suddenly, he jumps up, kisses my forehead, and whispers, "I am so sorry this happened to you." Then he turns and leaves the room.

I know Angel has told him everything, and soon the whole hospital will know, if they didn't already. I am a little embarrassed of the things they must be thinking, but I am not mad. I know he had to tell.

Well, at least I won't have to talk to anyone. Well, not yet and that I am happy for, as all I want to do is forget the past three years of my life.

They don't want to move my leg anymore than necessary, so the nurse comes in, and they do the x-rays right there in my room.

It isn't long after the nurse leaves that I see Angel walking back my way. He looks tired, however, he is still beautiful. I watch as he walks toward my room; it is like he is floating on air. Every move he makes, he makes with such grace and poise. I am in a trance watching him and cannot stop staring. In fact, I don't think anyone can, as every nurse has now stopped what they are doing and are watching him as he walks by.

"They have to do surgery on your leg right away, sweetie. It has gotten an infection and they need to stop it before it gets worse," Angel says with the look of solicitude on his face.

"What?" I want to cry.

"Don't worry, I will be here when you wake up. Tell me the names of the people you want me to reach, and when you get out of surgery, they will all be here waiting for you," Angel says in reassurance.

I begin giving him the names and numbers of all the people that I want him to contact. The list isn't long, as I am an only child, and I do not to give him the information on my fiancé as I surely do not want him to see me. Not now, not in this condition.

My eyes become heavy and my mind cloudy, and I am not sure if I am talking coherently. The nurse has put something in my IV that is causing the way I am feeling. I do not want to go to sleep. I am afraid that I will wake up and realize it has been all a dream.

Angel tightens his hold on my hand and whispers in my ear, "It's not a dream. When you wake up, your leg will be better and your family will be by your side. Now go to sleep."

"I am supposed to get a soda . . ." I slur.

"I will get you one when you wake up." Angel laughs.

"OK," I slur again. "I love you."

I continue to talk, uncertain what words are coming out of my mouth. I know I must have not made sense, as I hear Angel chuckle often. Angel kisses my head gently, and I fall fast asleep.

"Go to sleep, little one," Angel says softly.

It is daylight when I open my eyes. I am still a little groggy, but I can see that I am in a bright white room with gadgets everywhere. I still have an IV in my right arm, and my leg is raised in some kind of strange contraption. I look around, and to my delight, I see Angel in the chair next to me. He is fast asleep and looks to be at total peace. I rub his hand gently and smile. I can't believe that he has waited for me. He is truly my angel.

A nurse comes in a few seconds later and asks if I need anything. In a hushed voice, I politely tell her no, trying not to wake up Angel. However, it doesn't work; he begins to squirm as soon as he hears my voice. He raises his arms to stretch, then rubs his sleepy eyes. After another big yawn, he is coherent.

"Good morning," he says, "how are you feeling?"

"I feel much better now," I admit.

"They did a wonderful job on your leg, and they say it should heal up just fine. They also stitched up some of your wounds you had on your face," Angel says with a wink. "You're going to be as good as new before you know it."

I start to feel my face, and instantly, I can feel new stitches. It isn't hard finding them as there are so many. In fact, they seem to cover my entire face. I sigh as I know how horrible I must look. Reality starts to set in, and I begin to cry. I know I must look like a monster from an old Frankenstein movie. I try to look away from Angel. I do not want him to see me cry. Angel takes my hand and holds it firmly against his heart. I can feel his heart beating beneath my hand, and it calms me enough that I can turn and look back at him.

"What's wrong, sweetie?" Angel asks as he wipes the tears from my cheek.

"I know I look like a monster," I say with a broken heart.

"Who said you look like a monster?" Angel asks as he wipes the tears from my eyes.

"I know I do, just look at me," I cry. "Look what he has made me."

"Sweetie, you are beautiful," Angel smiles. "And don't let anyone tell you different, including yourself."

"Look," I cry as I look around. "My parents didn't even come. They didn't want to see the monster I have become."

"That's not true," Angel explains. "I called the numbers you gave me, but they have all changed. You have to remember, it's been a long time since you have been home. Swan Valley is a small town, so I am waiting to make sure you are OK, then I am going to go down there and see if I can find anyone that you have named. I did call the police though. They came, and I told them all that you had told me and gave them the pictures. I hope you don't mind."

"No, not at all. What did they say?" I ask with concern.

"We agreed that it is important that you got some rest so that you could heal, and then I will take you to the police station to give your statement," says Angel.

"But they need to go now so that they can catch him!" I scream.

"Don't worry. I told them where I had found you. They are headed up there now to look around," Angel assures me as he touches my hand.

"The cabin, did you tell them about the cabin with all the pictures and the frozen body parts in the freezer, and, and, and . . ."

Angel interrupts me.

"Frozen body parts?" Angel asks.

Instantly, I realize that I had kept that part of the story from him; now I find myself speechless.

"Yes, body parts," I cry. "There were so many of them, Angel. There were many of them."

"You need to relax. I told them everything except about that. I did not know the details of the freezer. If you want, I will call them and let them know right now," Angel says, consoling me. "But you need to calm down, or they will kick me out of here and allow no one in."

"No! Don't leave me," I cry. "I'm sorry for yelling. You can call the police later."

I lower my head, awaiting to be hit for raising my voice.

Angel sits on the bed beside me.

I jump in fear.

"I'm not going to hurt you," Angel says in a softened tone.

He then leans back and lays his head on my shoulder. The warmth from his body is welcomed by mine. It has been such a long time since I felt compassion from anyone. I close my eyes and engulf the feeling.

"I'm not going anywhere," he says with a big smile. "I'm your guardian angel, remember?"

"Yes, you are," I say as I touch his hand.

"And just remember this, guardian angel will never lay his hands on you in such a manner to hurt you," Angel says as he lifts my hand and kisses it.

We lie next to each other in the bed for over an hour, before a nurse comes and interrupts us, insisting that she needs to talk to Angel for a few minutes outside the room. At first, it scares me, and I think something has happened. But then as I lie there, I start thinking that if there is something wrong, I am sure they will talk to me also. Anticipating Angel's return, I lie here and wait for his warm body to be next to mine again.

"I brought you something," Angel says as he walks back into the room and hands me a small box.

"What is it?" I ask as I take the package from his hands.

"Open it," Angel says with a smile. "It's something I think you might like."

I have no idea what it can be. But whatever it is, it is kind of heavy and rattles if you shake it. So I know there is more than one object in the box.

"Are you going to open it?" Angel says sarcastically as he laughs. "Or are you going to just sit there and shake it?"

I look at Angel and begin to laugh, then open the box as fast as I can.

"What in the world!" I laugh as I stare at the contents of the box.

"I thought after all the time you have been gone, you might want something like that," Angel says as he starts pulling objects out of the box. "Besides, I promised you one of the things in the box."

"I guess you did," I say smiling as I open an ice-cold can of soda.

I take a sip. It is the best soda I have ever tasted, and I find myself guzzling it down as fast as I can.

"You might want to drink that a little slower." Angel chuckles. "Your body isn't used to stuff like that."

"I'm sorry." I snort as the bubbles from the soda I am drinking tickle my nose. "You have no idea how good this tastes."

Angel sits and laughs with me as I continue to drink the first can of soda until it is gone and then open another.

"What else is in this box?" I ask, taking a sip of the second soda.

To my surprise, it is full of all of my favorite junk food. There are candy bars, chips, suckers, even a cheeseburger. All things that I had craved so badly while I was captured and all things that I had been denied!

"How did you know that I had been craving these things?" I say as tears begin forming in my eyes.

"Let's just say a little bird told me," Angel says as he winks at me.

I don't know how he is in such tune with everything about me. But I am happy that he is here and that he is thoughtful enough to do such a kind thing for me.

"Let's not disappoint that little birdie," I say as I pick up the cheeseburger and one of the candy bars and begin eating them, simultaneously.

"Let me take the box, and I will set it over here on the table. That way you can reach it whenever your sweet little heart desires," he says as he takes the box from my lap and sets it on the table next to my bed.

"Please don't take it away," I cry.

"Don't worry, it will be right there for you. No one is going to take it away from you," Angel assures me. "In fact, if you want more, I will go get you more."

"I'm sorry," I explain. "I guess old habits die hard."

Angel reaches over and kisses me gently on the cheek. "No one will ever take food from you again." He smiles. "I won't allow it."

His voice is that of certainty, and I believe everything he is saying.

"Thank you, but don't you want any of it?" I ask as I continue to stuff my face with the cheeseburger.

"No, thank you. I am fine. That is all for you." Angel smiles as he taps the box. "Just don't let the doctor see it."

I begin laughing until I find myself crying in hysterics. I don't know if I am crying because I hoped to see my parents or if it is because I know I am truly free and here in a hospital getting better. I have made it. I am alive!

"I should go and find your family," he says softly. "I won't be more than a day."

"You said you wouldn't leave!" I yell.

"But I can see by the way you're acting that you need your parents here." Angel smiles, walks over to my side, and rests his hand on my shoulder.

"That's not why I am crying," I say as I calm my crying down to a soft whimper. "I was just thinking about how I am free and that no one can ever take that from me again."

"Are you sure you don't want me to go get your mom and dad?" Angel asks, concerned.

"I am sure," I answer, giving him the biggest smile I can conjure up.

"I guess it will have to wait then. Your happiness comes first," says Angel. "Maybe the police can find them. I'll call them later and give them the information."

"Actually, Angel, I have been thinking it might be better if they aren't contacted. It might bring the media into it, and I am not ready for that," I say with a deep sigh. "Besides, my captor will know where

I am, and he might come here after me, or worse yet, go after my family!"

"You may be right. That might be for the best," Angel agrees as he kisses my head gently. "At this point, I am sure he has no idea where you are. Best to keep it that way."

Angel insists that he stay with me, and I am happy he does. He makes me feel safe, and I need that feeling right now, as I am still a little worried about the man who took me before, showing up here and taking me again. Although, I do feel bad that he stays here without leaving; I can't see myself being here without him. I need him.

The first couple of nights, he tries to sleep in the chair next to the bed. After a couple of days of waking up and seeing him crouched in the chair asleep, I convince the nurses to bring in a small cot for him. He is a trifle embarrassed that I have made such a fuss, but I think he is also grateful, as it is obvious that the chair is starting to make his back stiff.

The days and nights go by slowly, as I am limited on what I am allowed to do. They have kept my leg elevated. They say it will help it heal. I understand that they have to do what is best for me, but after a few days, my legs begin to cramp, and I have to ask if they could please lower my leg so that I can let it rest a little more comfortably. I am lucky as they listen to my plea and finally take it down.

Angel tries to keep me occupied by bringing in some games and playing them with me. At first, it is a lot of fun, and we laugh so loudly that the nurses come in and hush us. Making us laugh even harder. However, after a few days, the games become boring, and the anticipation of going home and seeing my parents and fiancé continues to grow inside me.

Angel, persistent to keep me happy, comes in dressed as different things and hops around the room, causing me to laugh so hard that my sides begin to ache. The funniest of times is when he comes in dressed like a funny old doctor and begins acting like he is operating on me, although he is doing nothing more than tickling me. The funniest part about that is that my doctor has walked in right when he is making fun of him. When the doctor first walks in, I think for sure he will be mad that Angel is making fun of him, but he isn't; in fact, he starts laughing along with us. In turn, the nurses see what is going on, and one by one they come in until the room is full, and before I know it, the entire room is laughing and joking around.

Angel seems to have that effect on people. He is so charming and an all-around great person. I love that he is here with me and now find that I cannot imagine my life without him, and I know I am beginning to fall for him, and that confuses me.

Sometimes, I watch him sleep at night, studying the perfection that he is. Never moving or making a sound while he sleeps, I can see that he seems to be at complete peace at all times. It is as if he has everything that he wants in his life and has no worries to haunt him in his sleep, which I am jealous of. I want that peace in my life.

My sleep is still interrupted every night by the haunting memories of the man that had me captured for so long. It is as if he is here, haunting me every night, never allowing me a peaceful sleep and never wanting me to forget him. I do not want to bother Angel with what is haunting my mind, so I don't tell him about the nightmares I am having. I think he knows though, as every morning I wake to him wiping sweat off my forehead and holding my hand.

The worst incident is the morning when I woke up to find my arm lying in a pool of blood. Angel was standing over me holding my arm down as the nurse cleaned up the mess and bandaged my arm. I remember when I first woke up that day and saw that someone was holding me down, I panicked, and for an instant, I was back in the dungeon. It wasn't until I saw Angel's kind eyes looking at me that I snapped out of my trance and was brought back to reality. When I asked what happened, Angel informed me that in the middle of the night I had started tossing and turning in my sleep and ripped my IV out of my arm.

After this incident, the nurses talk to the doctor about keeping the IV out of my arm, afraid that I might do it again. I am happy that he has agreed, because I hate that thing as it reminds of the times that my captor would stick needles deep into my arms as a type of torture. The pain would be so overwhelming that I would usually pass out.

I hate when the bad memories come back. But they seem to be carved into my mind, never allowing any others to escape. Angel knows the agony I am in, so he has come up with a way to try to help me forget. He says that with every bad memory that begins to haunt me, he wants me to think of two good ones and not to stop until I am able to think nothing more than them. It seems to be working, as I am not crying as much as I used to.

The nurses are great also. They make it a point to stop in everyday to visit me. Some coming in on their days off, bringing their babies for me to see. Others bringing in food for both Angel and me. So much so that Angel and I now share the food with others on the same floor; there is so much of it. The patients love it; they say the food here is bad and they look forward in eating what Angel brings them. I don't see the problem with the food from the hospital, as it is better than anything I was ever feed in the dungeon. Although, I will admit that sometimes the food does look like something from out of this world.

I have not been treated with such love and care for so long that I enjoy all the attention I am getting. However, sometimes I get extremely depressed as I watch families go in and out of other rooms, visiting their loved ones. I want my parents here with me so bad, but I know it is better that they stay away. I have to keep them out of the clutches of that evil . . . evil . . . man, as I am still uncertain if he knows who my parents are, and I can't bring it upon myself to the chance of him seeing them come in and out of my room and following them home and possibly hurting them.

The police have not found him yet. Leading me to believe he is still out there somewhere looking for me. I know that Angel is here by my side and that he will never let that man come near me again. But I still worry about my family and the ones I love.

"Lue, you need to stop worrying yourself," Angel says as he takes my hand into his. "You're going to make yourself sick."

"I can't help it," I cry. "I'm so afraid that he will find my family and hurt them as a way of punishing me for running away."

"Don't worry. I will do everything in my power to keep your parents safe," Angel says as he kisses the back of my hand.

"I know you will . . . But who is going to keep you safe?" I ask.

"Me? Don't worry about me. No one can touch this," Angel says as he stands up and flexes his muscles at me.

I begin to laugh as he proceeds to flex his muscles in many different positions. He is very comical when he wants to be and is always able to make my sadness disappear into laughter. After flexing his muscles at me for a while, he sits back down.

"Now that's better. I only want to see smiles and laughter. No more sad faces," Angel says as he crosses his eyes and gives me a silly smile.

CHAPTER 8

Evil Returns

I HAVE IN the hospital for over a week, every day talking to the police on the phone about what had happened and giving them any information I can about where I was kept and the man that had held me hostage. I know I am not much help, as all I am capable of doing is telling them my memories of the dungeon I was kept in, what I had been through, and the pictures that I had found.

Every day I talk to them, I am told that they are still looking for the cabin or the house I was kept in, but they have not been able to find either as of yet. However, they will continue to look, and I am to call the office if I can think of any new information that may be of help to them. This I do not understand, because I know Angel has told them where he had found me, and I know that the house or cabin could not be that far from there. This all makes no sense to me, as there is no reason why they wouldn't be able to find one or the other. But no matter how many times I try to tell them that, they keep insisting that there is no house or cabin and as far as they can tell there never were.

In fact that within a thirty mile radius of where Angel found me, there is nothing more than trees, fields, and mountains.

They also have insisted that I go home and rest, and when I am healthier, they want me to come down and talk to them. They say that although it is of great importance that they talk to me, I have to heal my mind and body before I come in. That way I may be of better help to them. As of right now, they feel that I am still too distressed to think coherently enough to give exact details.

The phone call I am on now is the worst of them all, as the man on the other end is acting like he isn't convinced that what I am telling him is the truth, insinuating that maybe Angel is the one that has done this to me and that I am too afraid to tell the truth. After screaming at the man for sometime, I finally am able to convince him that there is no way that the man sitting next to me has ever harmed me in any way, that if it wasn't for him, I wouldn't be on my way to recovery and finally going home.

"Home. What a wonderful word!" I think to myself.

Excited to be going home, I didn't want to talk about it anymore. I hang up on the man without saying another word.

I cannot say that phrase enough: "Going home."

I am free, I am healing, and I have an angel to thank for that. He has saved me and has been there every minute of every day since he found me on the riverbank.

With that thought in mind, I suddenly reach over and give Angel a kiss on the cheek.

"What is that for?" Angel asks as he smiles at me. "I mean, don't get me wrong. You can do it again if you want."

"I am thanking you for everything you have done for me," I say as I kiss his cheek again.

"You're acting like you will never see me again," Angel says in a soft, saddened voice. "I will always be here for you when you need me."

"I know," I say in a smile.

I am happy to be going home today. But on the other hand, I am sad at the thought of never seeing Angel again. I know we both agree that we will see each other again, but I know that once we leave the hospital and I am home again, things will go back to normal and he will fade into the distance once I am back with my fiancé.

My heart drops as the nurse comes in and tells us that the doctor has said that I am able to go. She gives me some instructions on care for my cuts and broken leg and walks back out the door. I know this is it; it will be the last day I will see my "Angel."

"Wait, I have a surprise for you," Angel says as he hands me a big, white box.

"What's this?" I ask.

"Something beautiful, for a beautiful girl." Angel smiles.

"You have done so much for me already. You shouldn't have." I smile back.

"Now, I can't let you go see your family wearing a nasty old hospital gown, can I?" Angel chuckles.

"When did you have a chance to go get anything? You never left my side," I ask.

"One of the nurses went and got it for me," Angel replies. "I snuck out while you were sleeping and told her what to get. I hope you like it."

I unwrap the beautiful pink bow that is wrapped around it. Quickly becoming very emotional, I begin to shake and cry, as I remember the terrifying day that my captor gave me a box just like this one. The day, I was brought into the room with the other girls. The day I killed Samantha.

I stare blankly at the opened box.

"What's wrong? You don't like it?" asks Angel.

"I love it," I say as I lift the contents of the box to my body. "Just a bad memory."

"I'm sorry, I was hoping it would be something that would make you happy," Angel says as a frown emerges on his face.

"It is. It is. Thank you!" I say as I give him a big hug.

"Now leave the room so I can try it on." I giggle trying to lighten the mood.

The dress is a beautiful baby blue, just like the one that I had been wearing when Angel found me, except this one is sleeveless and flows down past my knees. It fits perfectly, as if he has had it tailored just for me. I stand wobbling in front of the full-length mirror admiring my new dress. Although I had seen myself in the mirror in the dungeon, I never quite got a good look at myself, as it was hard to see through the dirt and mesh that had covered it. Now that I can really see myself, I am amazed on how thin I have gotten.

"I must weigh no more than a hundred pounds," I say to myself as I brush my freshly washed, long, blonde hair.

It shines for the first time in many years and feels soft to the touch.

I reach to my tray to get some of the makeup I borrowed from the nurses and begin applying it to my face, maneuvering around my fresh stitches. At first, I am a little shocked, as I expected to see more stitches than I do.

"He must have not slashed my face as bad as I thought," I think to myself as I study my face.

I look different, as the makeup helps hide my other scars that I am ecstatic about.

"OK, you can come in. I am ready to go," I yell out the door.

Angel opens the door, stands in the doorway, and stares. I pose for him, hoping to impress him I guess, when deep inside I know no one could fall in love with someone who looks like me, someone whose face has been abused to the point of hideousness.

"You were beautiful before, but now you are *B E A U T I F U L!*" Angel exclaims as he holds out his arm for me to grab, "my lady."

I smile as I take his hand, and he leads me to my awaiting wheelchair.

"Wait," a nurse yells.

Startled, I leap into my chair and almost knock Angel onto the floor.

"I have to bandage those stitches up. We don't want any dirt getting in them, now do we?" the nurse exclaims.

Happy that it isn't anything more serious, I calm myself, allowing my heart to beat at a normal pace once again.

The nurse comes over and begins placing large white gauze on my face, until my face feels like it is now encased by nothing more.

I am relieved and ready to go once again. However, a little disappointed that my face is now engulfed by bandages, covering any makeup that I had put on. Now, I am certain that my family will never recognize me.

As we head for the waiting truck outside, I am greeted by the nurses and the doctors I have met since I have been here. Every one of them hand me different gifts. I am overjoyed by the attention I am receiving and the genuine concern that these people have for me. I feel like a movie star or someone famous that is being bombarded by the paparazzi. I am enjoying every bit of it.

After hugs that seem to last for hours, I am headed outside. I welcome the sun on my face as we walk to the edge of the curb. Watching me, Angel must have realize that I am enjoying the sun, so he pauses and lets me sit for a few moments as I let the warmth soak into my skin, soaking in as much of the sun as I can.

"It seems a little extra sunny today, doesn't it?" I say with a smile.

I close my eyes and lay my head back.

"Yes, it does," Angel replies. "Yes, it does."

"I know what will make it brighter," Angel continues.

"What?" I ask, in the utmost happy tone.

"Let's go see those parents of yours." He smiles.

"Yes," I reply. "Let's do that."

I smile larger than life upon my face; I begin to whistle a tune.

A curb and a short walk down the parking lot, and we are at Angel's truck.

He places me gently into the front seat, sets all my gifts from the nurses and the doctors into the backseat of the truck, and then walks over to the driver's seat. He pauses, reaches back behind him, grabs something, and hands it to me. I open the bag, and inside is a stuffed toy of a little boy angel hugging a little girl angel, and when you touch the little boy angel, it hums the same song I heard in the forest. It is adorable.

"This way I will always be with you. As you are my angel also." Angel smiles.

"Thank you," I say as I fight back a tear. "I will keep them with me always."

Reaching over, I give him a soft kiss on the cheek and thank him once again.

Angel smiles and starts truck. The sound is inviting, as I know I am on my way home and will finally be in my loved ones' arms once again.

"You ready to go find your family now?" asks Angel.

"Yes!" I yell in excitement as I hold the angels tight in my arms.

During our ride to my hometown, I decide to find out more about the man that saved me. After asking hundreds of questions, I find out that he is thirty-two and single and that he has just moved to the outskirts of Swan Valley and come from a very wealthy family. He owns quite a few restaurants, homes, and travels a lot. I am impressed that not only is he gorgeous, he is also very successful.

"I must be keeping you from your work," I say.

"No, not at all. The restaurants pretty much run themselves," he says with a smile. "Besides, I have to make sure you get home to your family."

I am so excited to see my family, but at the same time I am nervous. It has been years since I have seen them, and I am sure that they have went on with their lives by now. Not to mention that I am a little worried about the reaction they may have, as I am sure by now they have come to believe that they would never see me again.

"I wonder if my fiancé has married by now. Or if he will want to see me," I think to myself.

I am sure he thinks that I had gotten scared and ran away the day we were to have been married, as there was no sign that I had been taken. Even the local police station has no record of an ongoing investigation for my disappearance.

As we come closer to my parents' house, my stomach begins to burn, and I commence to shaking so hard that I can feel every piece of my body vibrating from my nerves.

Angel holds my hand in his.

"It will be fine," he says, reassuring me.

"I'm just nervous. It's been such a long time since I have seen anyone, and I am sure that they all think I'm either dead or hiding. Either way, I am sure they gave up on ever seeing me again," I reply. "Besides, I look horrible. I have scars all over my face, and I have lost a lot of weight. They won't believe it's me."

"You're being silly. They will be so ecstatic to see you. Nothing else will matter," Angel says with a smile. "And if it does bother them, then they don't deserve you."

We pull up to my parents' house. The house looks different. Something has changed. But what is it? I stare out my window and study every part of the house and its surroundings until I finally figure it out. The flowers that once lined the driveway are dead. The big willow tree in front that I played on as a child is dead. I take in a deep breath and release a loud sigh. It's all dead, like I am sure their hearts were when I disappeared. Dead!

"Are you OK?" Angel asks.

"Yes," I reply. "I was just hoping that everything would have been the same as I had remembered."

"Material objects change, dear, but how someone feels never will." Angel smiles.

I know he is right. After all, we were such a happy and close family before. What is stopping us from being like that again? Apprehensive, I walk up to the door. I reach for the doorknob, then release it and step back. I take Angel's hand and squeeze it tight, then take in another deep breath.

"It will be perfect," Angel says as he winks at me and nudges me back toward the door.

As I reach for the doorknob, I suddenly hear my mom's and dad's voice inside. It is the most beautiful sound I have ever heard. Excitement overcomes me, and I grab the door handle and swing open the door with such extreme force that I knock over the vase that is sitting against the wall. Ignoring the fact that I have just made a mess, I hobble into the house as fast as my crutches will allow. The TV is on, but I don't see anyone.

"Mom, Dad? It's me, Lue. I'm home!" I yell.

There is no response. I stop and listen, as I can still hear them talking. I release Angel's hand and begin hobbling through the house looking for them. I go into every room of the house but cannot find them anywhere. The voices seem to be coming from every direction, leaving me helplessly searching. I am confused as to why they don't come to the sound of my voice. I continue searching, all the while screaming as loud as I can. After searching in every room twice, I hurriedly hobble back into the living room where I had left Angel.

"Can you hear that?" I ask with a confused look on my face. "It's like their voice is coming from everywhere. But I can't find them."

Angel is sitting leaned over in my dad's favorite chair. He has his face in his hands, and I can hear a soft weeping.

"Angel? What's wrong?" I ask.

Angel does not reply.

"Angel! What is it!" I demand.

He slowly lifts his head. Tears stream down his face as he hands me a piece of paper. My heart skips a beat, then another, as a sense of despair overcomes my entire being. I grab the paper from his hand and begin to read in disbelief.

"No!" I scream.

Instantly, the room begins to shrink around me, closing in on me. Trapping me. I am in hell again! I become light-headed. I cannot catch my breath, and my knees become weak. I can no longer stand. I try to catch myself before I hit the floor, but my hands miss the chair, and I begin to fall fast to the ground. Luckily, Angel is right beside me and catches me before my body plunges to the ground below and gently sets me on the floor. I stare at the piece of paper he gave me, reading it over and over again in disbelief. The letter read:

> I see you made it this far. You will not make it any further. You are mine and always will be. I don't know the man you are with. But I will find out everything about him. Do not get too attached to him, as he will not be around for long. When he least expects it, I will capture you and him. You will watch as I'll slowly kill him in front of you! As for your parents, this is your punishment for what you did to me. I told you I would get you back! Now suffer in the hell I am going to put upon you!

My mind begins to race.

"Has he killed them? Is he torturing them?" I scream. "What is he doing to them?"

"I don't know, sweetie, but I'm sorry. I was blinded. I didn't see it coming," he says as he holds me tight. "But let me tell you this. I will find him, and I will bring your parents back to you!"

Angel sits on the floor with me in his arms.

I know he will never find them. That he is merely trying to calm me down.

"I should have let them come and see me!" I cry. "At least I would have been able to see them one more time and warn them that this might happen. Or I should have had the police watching them, ensuring that no one would harm them."

"Now stop it, Lue. You can't blame yourself for what this sick, demented man has done," Angel says as he pulls my body from his and looks into my teary, bloodshot eyes. "I will not have you blaming yourself for something that is out of your control."

"But it wasn't out of my control," I cry. "I could have warned them."

Without warning, the door flies open, causing me and Angel to jump back in fear.

"Stay right there. Don't move!" a man screams from the front door.

Startled, I look up expecting to see my captor standing there, ready to take Angel and me away. To my surprise, it isn't him; it is a police officer.

"It's OK. I used to live here with my parents," I explain. "I am Lue Walters."

"Lue? Lue Walters?" the man in blue asks.

"Yes. You can call the station. They know I am coming here today," I continue.

"You can't be Lue. She disappeared over three years ago. Besides, I think I would know my brother's ex-fiancé," the police officer snaps.

I lift my head higher from Angel's shoulder, so I could get a better look at the man standing in front of me. It is Jeffery. He is a little older and a little bigger. But I know it is him just by looking at his eyes. He has eyes that look like that of his brother's – deep blue, calming, and relaxing. Eyes that you can melt into.

A smile comes across my face as I look into his deep blue eyes. Finally, a familiar face. Someone who had known me before this whole horror story began!

"Jeffery!" I scream in excitement. "It's you!"

Jeffery stands there staring at me in disbelief. Suddenly, a smile takes over his face, and he runs in my direction.

"Oh my god! Lue, it is you!" he says as he leaps toward me.

Jeffery grabs me up, swings me around, and then holds me as tight as he can. So tight, in fact, that after a few seconds I find it hard to breathe. I am happy to see him, so embrace the feeling. I squeeze him back, holding him as tight as my thin arms will allow.

"Be careful with her," I hear from the other side of the room.

It is Angel. He is watching us with a concerned look.

"Who the hell are you?" Jeffery snaps at Angel.

"I am her guardian angel," Angel replies.

Angel and I begin to laugh.

"I am a little confused. Is this the man you left Kamrin for?" asks Jeffery.

"No! I didn't leave Kamrin for anyone!" I yell as Jeffery sets me down. "Just look at me. Isn't it obvious that something has happened?"

"How do I know? He could have done that to you," Jeffery snaps at me, then points toward Angel.

"Excuse me!" Angel screams as he jumps out of his chair and leaps toward Jeffery.

I don't know how I do it, but I manage to get between Angel and Jeffery lightning fast and stop them before they start fighting.

"How dare you accuse this man of doing this to me?" I scream in Jeffery's face, pointing my finger at him. "You neither know him nor know what he has done for me, so until you do, I think you should shut your mouth."

"Sorry, man," Jeffery says in an apologetic voice as he backs away from Angel. "From what I heard, Lue had left Kamrin for another man. I guess I shouldn't have jumped to conclusions."

"I guess not," I say in an angered voice.

I am mad, and now I know that everyone had thought that I had run away. It isn't fair. I have gone through so much, and the first person

I see insinuates that I had run away with another man. This confirms my suspicions and makes it obvious that the entire time I was missing, no one had looked for me. I am heartbroken.

Angel sees that I am upset by what is being said, so he does not press the issue any further. Before I know it, he is holding my hand and is helping me to a seat on the couch facing the fireplace.

"What happened to you, Lue?" Jeffery asks suddenly. "Where have you been?"

"Sit down, Jeffery," I insist. "And I will tell you everything."

I begin to tell him of my captor and the things I had endured. I start off with how I was taken from Kamrin's house and end my story to where I had come in today and found the note.

Jeffery sits with his mouth open through the whole gruesome story never saying a word.

When I finish, we are all crying, and there is not a dry eye in the house. Jeffery stands up, walks over to Angel, and shakes his hand.

"Thank you." Jeffery smiles. "Thank you for saving her."

"And as for you, little lady," Jeffery says as he winks at me, "I guess we are going to have to keep a closer eye on you."

Now normally he saying that would have not fazed me, but his tone is that of uncertainty, and I find myself not believing a word that he is saying.

"Maybe," I say in a condescending voice.

The rest of the day is a big blur as policeman after policeman comes in, takes evidence, and asks Angel and me thousands of questions. I feel like the questions will never end. However, as the day becomes night, people start to leave, and the house becomes quiet. I am tired and want to get some rest. I look at Jeffery and Angel; they both look tired too. I know I will not be able to get any kind of peace until the last person is gone, and that includes Jeffery and Angel.

"Everyone's gone," Jeffery announces as he closes the door and walks over to me.

"What about the voices I heard? Were they able to find where they were coming from?" I ask.

"They found tiny speakers throughout every room. They are all linked to one tape player. So what you were hearing was a recording of your parents," Jeffery replies. "Too bad it is not a live feed coming from some unknown place. We might have been able to trace it."

"So do they know where he is or where he has my parents?" I ask in hopes that they had found some type of evidence that will help them find this man.

"At this point, hun, they don't know anything. The house is clean. No foreign fingerprints, nothing. Whatever they did think would help them, they packaged up, and they are taking all the evidence and information you gave us to be evaluated. Don't worry, we will find them," Jeffery says in confidence. "But for now, they want to take you in to protective custody, just to ensure your safety."

A strange feeling takes over my body, and I do not feel comfortable going anywhere with Jeffery. You know that gnawing feeling you get in your gut and right away you know you better follow that feeling. Well, I had that tenfold.

"Jeffery," I say with heavy eyes, "I really would like to just stay here. I don't think he will come back here, and I need to be around familiar surroundings right now."

"I'm sorry. They won't let you do that. It's still a crime scene," Jeffery insists.

"I'll take her to my house," Angel says abruptly. "I have guards there, and I will put them on high alert."

"Well, the only way I can let you do that is if you allow me to have an around-the-clock policeman stay there also," Jeffery says as he winks at me. "We can't let anything happen to her again."

"That's fine. She will be completely safe with me," Angel snaps. "Don't worry about it."

Jeffery realizes that Angel is not going back down, and the conversation ends abruptly. I am glad to see it end, as all I want to do is crawl into a soft comfortable bed and cry myself asleep.

"Are you ready?" Angel asks as he helps me off the couch.

"Yes," I answer quickly.

I have been in my parents' house long enough and want to get out of there before I become even more depressed. Flashes of their innocent faces being with "Evil" itself is embedded in my mind, and pictures of what they must be going through runs wild in my thoughts over and over again until I can see nothing more.

"Jeffery?" I ask.

"Yes," he answers.

"How is Kamrin?" I ask.

Jeffery, with his head down, explains to me how two years after I disappeared Kamrin had gave up on me ever being found and began dating my best friend, "Cheyenne," how they dated for a few months, then Cheyenne had gotten pregnant. He continues in telling how, although, Kamrin was not ready for marriage; he had decided to do the right thing and marry her. They have been married now for just about a year and have a new baby girl of three months. Her name is Scarlett.

A lump gathers in my throat, and I want to cry.

"He will still want to see you, Lue," Angel insists, although it is apparent in his eyes that he wishes I would have never brought up Kamrin's name at all.

"Yes, Lue, I think it would be a good idea," Jeffery agrees.

"I will have to think about it," I say in a soft, saddened voice. "I think I need a little more time."

"OK, but I have already called him to let him know that you have been found. I told him a little of what has happened, but not everything. The rest I thought you might want to explain yourself," Jeffery says as he puts his hand on my shoulder in reassurance. "Angel gave me his home number. He will contact you there."

"He didn't show up here to see me. It must have not been that important to him," I snap.

"Now, Lue, he is very upset. I told him not to come here. It would be better to see you when all this is not going on," Jeffery explains with a smug look. "You should meet alone."

"I agree," Angel says. "I think your meeting should be when you two can be alone. I gave Jeffery my address so that Kamrin can come over anytime."

I look at Angel in shock. I don't know if it is because a part of me is hoping that he would be jealous and not want Kamrin around me, or because he took it upon himself to think I would want to see Kamrin.

Now that he is married and has a child, I do not know how I feel. I turn in disgust and head for Angel's truck.

"I don't know who I am more pissed off at, Kamrin or Cheyenne," I think to myself. "I bet they had something going on the entire time Kamrin and me were dating, probably even while we were engaged."

I want to scream, yell, and cry. I want to hit something, and I feel if I do not get out of here right now, I will go insane. I am just about to yell for Angel to hurry, when I turn around and see Angel and Jeffery shake hands and go their separate ways.

"Thank God!" I think to myself as I get into the truck. "I need to be away from all of this and think."

We drive down a dark winding road toward Angel's house. It is a quiet ride as neither of us is talking.

"Why did he have to take my parents?" I whisper to myself.

Instantly, tears begin to fill my eyes once again.

I have lost my parents and my fiancé all over again. I know that the police insist they will find my parents. But I know this sick man like no one else, so I find myself trying to come to terms that they are already dead. Or at least I hope they are, as I hate to think of them being tortured in the ways I had been, or worse yet, like the other women I had found.

"They were such good people!" I scream out loud.

I'm not worried about anyone hearing me. I am mad as hell, and my heart is broken. I want the whole world to know how I am feeling.

"Why Angel?" I cry. "Why did he have to take my parents?"

"I don't know, sweetie," Angel says as he turns and looks at me with sadness in his eyes. "I wish I could take it all away."

My tears turn into sobs. My sobs turn into fierce crying, and suddenly my emotions run wild causing me to become hysterical. Angel reaches over and takes my hand. I look over. He is crying also.

"I know, Lue. It will be OK," Angel says to me between sobs. "I will make sure of that."

His voice is so calming and reassuring that I cannot help but smile.

We drive for about thirty more minutes; all the while, I am looking out the truck window trying to get my mind elsewhere. I can see that we are far from town, as there seems to be no other houses, and the streets are empty. I am just about to ask Angel where we are going, when suddenly we pull up to a large iron and brick gate.

Angel stops and puts a card into a contraption like I have never seen before. As the gate begin to open, Angel waves to the policeman that has been following us, directing him to go into the gate first. After the policeman is through the gate, we follow him through a long winding driveway up to the house. It is dark outside, but from what I can see, the driveway is lined with perfectly manicured purple and yellow roses, my favorite.

"Is this is your house?" I ask a little intimidated by the size.

"Yes, this is home." Angel laughs.

"Home? This is a mansion!" I laugh.

I look around trying to see the end or beginning of this . . . mansion. It is the biggest house I have ever seen, and I am certain that the only way you would ever be able to see the entire estate is if you were in a helicopter, as there is no way you would be able to stand at the front door and see it all.

"This is amazing!" I say as I look around at all the statues and greenery.

"Thank you," Angel says with a proud smile, as we pull up to the stairway leading to the front door.

Amazed by what I am seeing, I continue to stare out the window, looking at the beauty that is in front of me. It is an old brick colonial home, which looks like it is from the early 1900s. It has a large stone porch attached to it with enormous pillars which seem to wrap around the entire home. But that isn't the thing that catches my eyes; it is the vines of beautiful flowers that is growing up the outside walls, extending all the way to the roof.

"This looks like a mansion you would see in Scotland," I suggest.

"Actually, I had it made to resemble one of my favorites I had seen one time while I was visiting there," replies Angel.

"Who lives here?" I ask. "I mean, besides you?"

"Just me and a few people that work here," Angel explains. "Don't worry, you will never see most of them."

"I don't want this to sound the wrong way," I say in a hushed voice. "Why so extravagant?"

"Why not?" Angel chuckles.

I will admit at first I think the house is a bit much. However, after looking at it a little closer, I realize that everyone has their own dream house, and this is obviously Angel's. Not to mention mine.

"I will be right back," Angel says as he steps out of the truck and walks over to where the policeman is waiting in his car.

After only a few moments, Angel finishes talking with the policeman and heads back to the truck to help me out. Taking me in his arms, Angel carries me up the countless number of stairs that lead to the front door. He says it is better that way, as he doesn't want me to trip and fall.

The front door is an eight-feet tall double wooden door. It is embellished in wood inlays of roses and vines that surround beautifully stained glass windows. It is so miraculous that I cannot imagine what the rest of the house must look like.

"My lady," Angel says as he opens the large front door.

As soon as the door opens, the sweet smell of candy fills the night air, reminding me of when I was a child and I would visit my grandmother's house at Christmas time. Taking in a deep breath, I inhale the sweet smell, embracing the memory.

We enter the front door to a foray that is as big as my parents' entire home. It is breathtaking. The walls are covered in cherrywood and the floors in the largest Italian tile I have ever seen. Placed perfectly around the room are antique furniture, expensive paintings, and fresh flowers. It is like being in a museum with a touch of home to it.

As I look around, I cannot believe the beauty that is in front of me, until I look up at the chandelier above me. The chandelier looks out of place. It is an old black iron chandelier that resembles something you would see in an old horror movie or a old castle from the medieval era. I must have given off a strange look when I looked up and saw it, because Angel laughed.

"I know the chandelier doesn't quite match the rest of the room. But it is a family heirloom that was given to me years ago," Angel says with a smile.

"Oh no, it's beautiful. I just expected something more . . . glitzy," I say with a confused look.

We stand in the foray for a while as he explains to me how the chandelier had come from an old mansion in Scotland that his great-grandparents had owned and how when they had passed away it went to his mother. He further explains how when his mother had it, she believed that it had the power to keep them safe, so he has always kept it with him.

I study the chandelier some more hoping to understand his story and what power such an object could possess. It is at that moment that I see that the figurines that make up the chandelier are actually that of Angel's. I let out a shallow sigh as the true beauty of it becomes apparent. In fact, the more I look at it, the more I feel at peace, and I can understand why his mother felt it to be that of a safe haven.

"Hum, interesting how a simple object can make you feel so at ease," I whisper beneath my breath.

We continue through the house, as Angel takes me to each room. The first thing I notice is that in every room the ceilings are painted like the Sistine Chapel. It is the most amazing thing I have ever seen, as the angels seem to move around the ceiling, following our every move. So much, in fact, that I have to keep stopping, assuring myself that it is all my imagination. Each room is more breathtaking than the last.

The house is enormous, and it has taken hours to walk through it, as there is so much that Angel wants me to see. He says that he wants to make sure I feel at home, so I have to know where everything is. Although, I do not think I will remember all that he has showed me. I still appreciate his effort and do not want to tell him that I have so much on my mind that more than likely I will forget by morning where everything is that he has shown me.

"What do you think about the house so far?" Angel asks as we leave the last room, downstairs.

"It is more than I could have ever imagined a house could be," I say, smiling.

"Well, there is one more room I want to show you," Angel says as he picks me up in his arms and carries me to the second floor.

When we finally reach upstairs, Angel puts me down so that I can walk. He hands me my walking cane, holds my other hand, and walks with me toward a large door at the end of the hallway.

As he opens the door, I gasp. It is not covered in cherrywood like the rest of the house. Instead, it is decorated in pink, rose-covered wallpaper. The room is so light and inviting that I do not hesitate and go right in. There in the middle of the room is a cherrywood canopy bed, big enough for six people. It is draped in a white sheer material that sparkles in light from the candles that rest on the table next to the bed. Stunned by the beauty of all that is in front of me, I stand in the middle of the room and study every inch of the room. Every wall has an angelic painting on it like the rooms downstairs, and at the far end of the bedroom is a fireplace roaring with a warm and inviting fire, adding to the ambiance of the room.

"Will this room be OK?" Angel asks as he stands next to the bed.

"If I could ever pick out a room, it would look just like this one," I answer in excitement as I leap onto the bed.

The mattress is soft. So soft, in fact, that as I lay on it, I feel like I am lying on a cloud of air that encircles my tired muscles. Quickly I sit up, as I become a little embarrassed of my reaction.

"I'm sorry. It has just been so long since I have slept in a decent bed, and truthfully, I have never slept in a bed like this one." I laugh.

"Don't be silly. Enjoy your bed. That's what it is for." Angel laughs.

We both lie down on the bed laughing so hard that my stomach begins to hurt, causing me to sit up holding it in pain.

"We forgot to eat," Angel says with concern. "I bet you're famished."

"I guess I am a little hungry," I admit. "Actually, I am starved."

Angel jumps up, picks up the phone next to the bed, and begins talking to someone on the other end.

"Is there anything that you are craving?" Angel asks as he put his hand over the mouthpiece of the phone.

"No, whatever you want is fine. Well, except for liver." I laugh. "I can't stand to even look at liver."

"OK, so that will be two large orders of liver and onions, and for me, I will have a . . ." Angel starts to laugh so hard that he can no longer talk on the phone.

"Very funny." I laugh as I smack him lightly on the arm.

After ordering enough food for a family of eight, he instructs the person on the other end to bring the food up to my room.

"Oh and hurry, she is getting abusive in here." Angel chuckles and then hangs up the phone.

"I hope whoever you were talking to didn't think you were serious," I say.

"Don't worry, he knows I am serious," Angel says as he jumps from the bed quickly, dodging me from smacking him again.

"See," he says as he lets out a laugh that I am sure can be heard from downstairs.

"You're so ornery tonight," I smile.

"What can I say? I like the company I am with," Angel says with a wink and a smile.

My heart melts with the words that he has said, as I too feel the same way. However, I do not say a word, and the room becomes silent, to the point where it is one of those awkward silences that is hard to break. You know, the ones where you want to say something, but you do not dare, as you are afraid that it will be inappropriate.

"The food should be here shortly," Angel says as he brakes the silence that has taken over the room. "While we wait, if you go into the closet over, there you will find some clothes for you. You can take a bath and change if you like before we eat."

I look his way with a confused expression upon my face.

"Where did the clothes come from? An old girlfriend?" I tease.

"No." Angel chuckles as a hint of embarrassment appears on his face. "While you were talking with the police today, I called over to my house and had the maid go buy you some clothes, shoes, and all the necessities you will need. I knew they weren't going to let you stay at your parents' house after what had happened, and I knew you would have nothing. And honestly, I was hoping you would come here."

I walk over to the closet that is at the farthest part of the room and open it. The closet is the size of an average bedroom and inside are more clothes than I have ever seen. There are so many dresses that two walls of the closet are filled with nothing more than dresses alone. I am amazed as I stare at the sea of dresses that is in front of me, as there is one in every length and every color imaginable. On the wall following the dresses is an area that is designated just for jeans and slacks. I take in a deep breath, let it out slowly, and look over at Angel.

"There's more," Angel says. "If you walk around the area of the dresses, you will see that the room opens up to another closet."

"What?" I think to myself as I do as he says. "There is more?"

There around the corner is just as he has said; there is another closet. This closet contains shirts and nightwear. There weren't just a few shirts or a few pair of pajamas. The closet is lined with every color, every style of shirt and blouse that you could ever imagine, not to mention the '50s or so different style and patterns of pajamas that line the closet, making the closet look like a perfectly colored rainbow. However, this rainbow is made with clothing.

I inspect the closet some more and notice that the closet floor is lined with shoes. It is like a shoe store came in and emptied their entire stock of women shoes into my closet. There have to be hundreds of them.

Astonished, I turn, walk out of the closet, and look at Angel.

"You didn't have to do this," I say.

"I know. I wanted to. After all you have been through, I figure you deserve something nice for a change. I hope you like what they got. If not, we can go buy more tomorrow," Angel replies.

I turn and look back in the closet.

"Are you serious? Everything is perfect!" I say in excitement. "Besides I don't think there is a store left in town with any clothing or shoes left in it."

"You might be right." Angel laughs.

I look at everything in the closet once again, as I cannot believe everything that he has bought. When he told me he had bought a few things, I expected maybe a dress or two. Not my own personal mall.

After searching for a while, I come across a beautiful white gown. It is long and embellished in lace, and I know it will cover my scars well. I take it out and lay it across my body. It is stunning. Looking in the mirror, I admire the way it flows down my body, as if it is made just for me.

"That's perfect," I hear from across the room.

"It is, isn't it?" I say with confidence.

"Yes, it is. No need to get dressed up for dinner when it is so late." Angel smiles.

"No need at all." I smile.

Angel points at the intercom on the wall and explains how to use it.

"Just push this button here if you need me, and I will be here faster than you can blink those beautiful eyes of yours." Angel smiles as he walks out of the room.

"I won't be but a few minutes," I say as I blush and head for the bathtub.

I fill the tub with bubbles and the hottest water my skin will endure. Both things I haven't had in years and always promised myself I would do once I was free. There is that word again – *free.*

I take in a deep breath and sigh, "I am free but my parents are not."

I shake my head in disgust. I want to cry, but I have no more tears to cry.

"I love you, Mom and Dad," I whisper softly.

I'm not trying to be cold or heartless, but I know my heart and soul needs a rest from all the pain, suffering, and sadness I have been through, so I decide that I will try and forget about all my worries for the night and enjoy the evening worry free.

Taking my time, I sit in the bathtub gently, ensuring that my newly cast leg does not emerge fully into the water. At first, the water is so hot that I am uncertain if I will be able to get in, but with a little cold water added to it and a little splashing of the water around, it is still hot, yet cool enough to get in.

"That works out perfectly," I think to myself. "Now I have bubbles I can enjoy also."

I lie there for a long time enjoying the warmth from the hot water as it surrounds my body. It is better than I had imagined it would be; it is like being covered in blankets fresh out of a hot drier on a cold winter's eve.

"This is exactly what I have been wanting," I whisper, as I lower my body further into the water, leaving only my face and leg sticking out of the welcoming water.

I am lying here completely still for about twenty minutes, before I notice the water is beginning to cool, so I decide to completely submerge my face so that it too can feel the warmth before the water cools any more.

I slowly lower my head into the water, and instantly, I can feel the warm water rush over my face. It feels so relaxing that I want to close my eyes and lie here until I can no longer hold my breath, but I am still a little scared to close my eyes completely, as I am afraid I will open them and *he* will be here. Waiting for me. Wanting to drown me. Suddenly, my heart skips a beat, then begins to beat so fast that I can see the water moving in rhythm to my heart.

Scaring myself into doing so, I jump up suddenly, almost causing my cast leg to fall into the water.

"I guess I am done for the evening," I think to myself. "Besides, I have been in here long enough, and I am sure that Angel is waiting for me to eat dinner."

I get dressed quickly, brush my hair, and head out to the bedroom. As I walk, the cool, silky gown feels wonderful against my skin, as the flowing gown captures the still air around me. I feel like a princess. That is, until my cast gets caught on the underneath of my gown, causing me to trip and knock over a vase, then tumble to the ground.

I sit and laugh as Angel comes running into the room to my rescue.

"I heard a loud crash, and then something hit the floor. Are you OK?" Angel asks.

"Yes," I say as I laugh in hysterics. "My gown caught my cast, and I fell."

"I guess I have to watch you a little closer, don't I?" Angel says as he laughs with me.

"I guess so, my angel," I blush as I look into his concerned eyes.

Angel helps me off the floor, and we head over to a wonderfully decorated table full of food.

"You didn't specify what you wanted, so I had a little of everything made," Angel says.

I can't believe my eyes. There is anything anyone could ever desire spread among the table. We sit, eat, and talk for hours. I am full but can't help but eat the dessert that is placed in front of me. It all looks so delicious.

"Did you have enough?" Angel asks as he tries to hand me a plate with a large piece of chocolate cake on it.

"I had plenty. Thank you," I answer graciously.

Interrupting our conversation, Angel jumps up suddenly and runs over to the bay window on the far end of the room. He stands there silent for a second, then turns and looks at me. With a look of despair, he runs out of the room and down the hallway. Stunned and confused about what has just happened, I start for the window to see what might have made him react in such a manner. However, before I can get there, Angel grabs my shoulder and turns me around.

"I'm sorry. I am sure I scared you," Angel says as he looks at my troubled face.

"What is out there?" I ask.

"Nothing to worry your pretty head about. I just see that there is a storm coming, and I think it would be best that you get some sleep," Angel says as he looks out the window again.

Trying to see what he could be looking at, I glance out the window. It is calm outside, and I cannot see a cloud anywhere in the sky. In fact, the sky is filled with so many stars that it is impossible to count them. I am sure he is wrong. But I am too tired to argue.

A tall man comes in and begins to clear off the table and its leftover contents. He is a younger man, so young that he does not look like he would be working as a butler. Maybe in his mid-twenties. His hair is a bright blond like Angel's and sparkles in the candlelight. His eyes are the clearest gray I have ever seen, and when the candlelight hits them, they seem to glow. It is like looking into the clearest of blue skies.

I watch him work as he moves with complete grace. He is like watching a stallion in all its beauty and elegance. I find myself staring at him. It must have been obvious because he turns quickly and looks at Angel, as if he is asking him a question. Angel answers him with a quick nod. The young man leaves.

We sit and talk for a while, and then I begin to yawn. I am tired physically and mentally and want to lie down. Angel must have felt the same way because he too starts to yawn.

After stretching his perfectly toned muscles, he gets up from his chair and helps me out of mine. Angel says a quick good night, reminds me of the intercom, and heads for the door.

"Wait," I yell quickly, "will you stay with me until I fall asleep?"

"Sure. It will be my pleasure," Angel says and walks back to the side of my bed.

He sits next to me holding my hand and caresses it lightly, telling me funny stories that I am uncertain are true. Suddenly, his eyes begin to droop, and I can tell he is getting extremely tired.

"Come, lie next to me," I say as I point at the empty spot on the bed.

Angel looks at me as if he is in shock that I have suggested him to do so.

Truthfully, I am a little shocked that I have offered him to sleep with me. But I am a little frightened and feel that I need someone here with me. Someone I feel like I can trust.

"Maybe for just tonight. That is how I can get used to the house and new surroundings," I say quickly.

Angel smiles softly and lies down beside me. Instantly, the strangest feeling comes over me, and my heart begins to flutter with excitement. It has been so long since I have had someone lie next to me. I find it to be exhilarating.

Inch by inch, I slowly move closer to his side, as I am trying not to make it obvious that I want to be closer to him. I need to feel the warmth of another person against me. However, I am hoping that he will not think that I am being too promiscuous. I just need the feeling of comfort and safety right now, and I need it from him. It must have felt nice to him also, because he cuddles behind me, placing his arm gently around my side.

My mind begins to race.

"How could I have met this man only days before, and every time I am around him, I feel the way I do?" I say to myself. "I almost feel like I have been here before, like I belong here with him."

Now most people would question how I can trust a man that I have not known for very long. All I can say is that every time I see him or touch him, a sense of being home overtakes my soul, making me want to never lose how he makes me feel. It's almost like he is my own addictive drug.

I become sleepy as I think about how lucky I am that such a special man had found me that day in the woods. It could have been anyone that found me, but no, it was a true angel. The angel lying next to me.

My eyes become heavy, and before I know it, I am fast asleep. I start dreaming that I am in my dungeon once again, running to take my place in the middle of the floor like I have done so many times before. As I sit waiting for my next punishment, I feel a gentle hand touch my shoulder. I look up. It is Angel. He stands in front of me, his hair illuminating in the light, emitting a halo around his head, like I had seen in the forest. He never says a word. He is holding his hands out, as if he is there to take me away from all the horror. I smile as I know all will be OK. I reach for him, but before I can feel the touch of his warm hands on mine, a dark figure appears from behind him. My eyes open wide, and my heart begins to pound in frenzy, until I can feel the throbbing of my heart throughout my body. It is the man in the black mask! I start to scream, but not a sound comes out of my mouth. I have to warn Angel! I try again; still not a word escapes from within my panicking soul. I begin to cry, but my eyes do not release a tear. I am paralyzed and powerless, and no matter what I try, I am unable to warn him against the man in the mask. Suddenly, a knife is plunged into Angel's heart. He begins to fall to the ground, his face emotionless. I try to grab him, but the blood that has now soaked his arms causes me to loose my grip, and he falls to the ground. I want to go to him and help him, but I can't. I am now tied to the chair, leaving me with no other option but to sit and watch Angel as his life escapes from his very soul. His heart beating for the last time, he dies.

I awake with my heart pounding and sweat dripping from my forehead. I quickly open my eyes and see that I am still in my new bedroom. A feeling of relief overcomes me, as I know it was only a nightmare.

I need to get back the feeling of "home" again, so slowly I reach for Angel's arm and hold it tight against my body, until the feeling comes back.

"That's better," I think to myself, as I take in a deep breath.

I turn over softly and look at him. He is sleeping as he always does, in complete peace. Slowly, I move my fingers across every line of his face. He is the most magnificent, most amazing man I have ever seen, and he is lying there beside me.

I am afraid to close my eyes, afraid that when I fall back asleep, I will have the same nightmare.

"I will never let him hurt you," I whisper softly as I lightly rub his soft blond hair.

I feel like a child again with a huge "puppy dog" crush on someone. But the feeling doesn't bother me. He is like no man I have ever known, and I know I will do everything in my power to keep him safe as he did for me.

I lay staring at his perfection for a while longer, until my heart returns to a normal beat and I am no longer afraid of what dreams awaits me.

"I will never tell him of the dream I had," I say to myself.

Leaning forward, I gently reach for his forehead and kiss him gently.

"Thank you," I whisper.

Once again, I fall asleep.

CHAPTER 9

The Storm

THE NEXT MORNING as I open my rested eyes, I reach for Angel. He is no longer here. My heart sinks, as I hoped to wake up feeling his strong arms around me. Lying here for a few minutes longer, I look around the large room, taking in the feeling . . . a feeling that is hard to describe. Here I am in the most extravagant room I have ever seen, and there is a man that I am sure only existed in my dreams, somewhere in the house. I am happy. In fact, I feel blessed. But I have a gut instinct that there is something terribly wrong, and I know it has nothing to do with my parents. I pull the blankets over my head to escape the chill that has taken over my entire body, hoping to free myself from the feeling.

"I'm sure it is nothing," I try to convince myself. "You woke up in a new place. You're probably a little disoriented."

I know that isn't the reason, but I try to listen to the voice so that I can relax once again.

"If Angel had been here when I woke up, I am sure I would not be feeling this way," I say out loud.

Suddenly there is a knock on the door, startling me to an upright position.

"Lue?"

"Yes!" I reply.

"Angel would like for you to get dressed and meet him in the yard for breakfast," the voice behind the door says.

I can tell it is the same man that had brought the food to Angel and me the previous evening. My face instantly became flushed with embarrassment. I don't know if I am embarrassed because I had been staring at him the night before or if it is because I am sure that he knows that Angel had spent the night in my room. I could only imagine the things he must be thinking about me. Whatever it is, I know I cannot face him right now. Not with the uneasiness that I am feeling.

"I will be right there," I say to the man outside my door.

"OK, I will wait for you while you get dressed," he says.

"No, no. I can make it down myself," I say quickly.

I know that if I see him right now, I will probably break down in tears from awkwardness and begin to ramble to him about the innocence of last night and how I did not mean to stare at him.

"You know how to get to the backyard, right?" he asks as he lets out a soft chuckle.

It is like he knows what I had been thinking, and he has gotten a kick out of it.

"I think I remember," I say as I pull the covers off me, preparing to get out of bed.

"OK, if you get lost, just yell, and I will come get you," he says.

"Thanks," I respond, "I will remember that."

Forgetting about my broken leg, I jump out of bed and run over to the bay window that is on the other side of the room. It is sunny and beautiful outside with no sign of a storm like Angel had predicted the night before. In fact, it is a perfect day.

I remember the closet and the hundreds of clothing options in it and became excited. I have not had anything nice to wear in many years and certainly nothing clean.

"I still can't believe this," I think to myself as I shake my head. "I don't even know what to choose as everything in here is so pretty."

I want to wear everything right now, or at least try it all on. But I know Angel is waiting for me downstairs, so it will have to wait. I had taken a shower the night before, so I know there is no need for a shower this morning, as I feel if I were to take another so close to the last, I will be taking advantage of his hospitality, and that is something I do not want to do. Besides, I learned a long time ago that a shower is a luxury and is something you get when you are awarded for being good. And in no way should be taken as anything but that.

"You have to stop thinking that way," a voice in my head tells me. "You are not a prisoner anymore."

The voice is right. Before I was taken from my home, I had never before thought twice about taking a shower in the morning, after taking one the proceeding night. Why shouldn't I? I think I deserve one. I have been good.

"There you go again," I scream at myself. "Now stop it!"

I walk over to the bathroom and look over at the bathtub. I want to take a bath, but I want to see Angel's angelic face more, so I decide I will wait until later to indulge myself.

Looking inside my closet of new clothes, I find a beautiful summer dress. It is a prominently pink dress with a rose print. I slip off my gown and put on the new dress. It fits me perfectly.

"Perfect for an outside breakfast," I think to myself as I run my fingers through my hair, trying to get out any knots that I have gotten from the tossing and turning I have done all night.

After finding a matching sweater to wear over it, I hurry toward the bathroom to do something with my hair.

"I think a nice updo will look perfect with what I am wearing," I think to myself.

I pick out the prettiest barrette that lies on the counter, and after brushing my hair, I wrap my hair into a bun on top of my head, leaving a few straggling strands down to frame my face. To my surprise, it looks healthier than it did last night and shines in the light.

"It is amazing how this light makes my hair look healthier than it ever has been," I say softly, admiring the sheen of my blonde hair.

I look around some more and find some makeup, all of which is in new packages. After picking out colors that will go perfect with my pink dress, I start applying it to my face. When I come to the bandages that still overtake my face, I get a quick reminder of reality.

I am hideous, and no matter how I fix my hair or how much makeup I put on, I am still a monster and will be a monster for the rest of my life.

I move my fingers up and down the bandages studying how big they are and how bad the wounds must look. While doing so, one of the bandages becomes loose. I pull it off. I have to see how bad the wounds are, how many more scars will be on my already mangled face. There is nothing there, not a wound, not a scar, nothing but young, vibrant, white skin. I pull off the other. Same! My heart drops. How can this be? I am bewildered on how they could have healed so well.

I search my entire face, taking my time, ensuring I do not leave an area unsearched. Every scar on my face is gone, leaving not a blemish on my face! I am young again.

I begin looking over my entire upper body; it is the same everywhere I look. There are no more scars, just perfectly white, milky skin. It is soft and youthful like it had been before I was kept in the dungeon. I know I have to be dreaming, so I slap myself in the face. It hurts. I look again into the mirror; it is all still the same. No scars. At that moment, the only explanation I can come up with is that maybe this is a magical mirror and somehow when I look in it, my scars disappear. I run to every mirror in the room, staring into them as if I am looking at someone I do not know. They are all the same, all showing me the same person in the mirror.

Right then it dawns on me, not only am I perfect within the mirrors, my skin is perfect without them.

Scared out of my mind, I throw down everything that I am holding in my hands and run out of my bedroom door and down the hall. I begin running down the stairs, when I realize . . . I am running.

How could I be running? I stop in the middle of the stairs and look down. The cast is gone.

"How did I not notice that before? Was it there when I woke up this morning?" I stop and ask myself.

I start thinking back to everything that I had done after I woke up.

"I got up, walked to the closet, walked around the inside of the closet for a while, picked out a dress, and then walked over to the bathroom," I think to myself. "No, it wasn't there."

I look down at my newly healed leg again; there is not a mark on it.

"How could I have missed that?" I question myself as I continue to go over the events of the morning.

I move my leg in small circular movements; there is no pain.

I am frightened and excited at the same time. This cannot happen. A person cannot heal overnight, and scars like I had cannot disappear. In fact, the doctor at the hospital told me that I would have them for the rest of my life. How did this happen? How could this happen!

"I need answers," I say, panic stricken.

At first, I am a little confused on which way to go once I get downstairs. I know it is because of the anxiety that I am feeling that I cannot remember a thing that Angel showed me the night before.

"Which way do I go?" I stop and ask myself as I continue to panic.

"Lue? Is that you?" I hear someone yell. "We are over here."

The sound has come from the right of me, so I know that would be the best way to go. Or at least I hope that is where the sound is coming from, as I am a little confused by the echoing caused by the enormous, desolate home.

"You're correct, go toward your right, and you will soon pass me in the kitchen, and Angel is outside the first set of garden doors you will come to," I hear the voice yell again.

I don't question how he knows what I am thinking. I am just happy that he does, and I will not have to search any further than necessary. As the anxiety continues to grow inside me, I need answers, and I need them now.

Passing the kitchen, I can see the man who served us the night before; he is busy preparing what looks to be our dinner for the night.

Never looking up at me, he says, "Good morning" and then continues working.

At first, I feel as if I should stop and talk to him for a second and thank him for the wonderful dinner that he served last evening. But after watching him for a brief second, I know I will find myself staring again, as he is remarkably unreal.

I finally make my way to the door that faces the garden out back. I look outside, and I can see Angel sitting at a table full of food. His body is turned toward the garden, and his head is faced down toward the table.

"Angel?" I ask.

"Come, sit down, Lue. We need to talk," Angel says in a shaky voice.

I am a little concerned about the tone of his voice, as he does not sound like the cheerful, strong man that I have gotten to know. I walk over to the other side of the table, pull the chair out, and sit down. I instantly know something is wrong, as Angel has never allowed me to pull my own chair out. He insists no true man would ever allow a lady to do so.

"Angel, what is going on? I woke up this morning and all my stitches are gone. My leg is healed, and my scars have disappeared!" I say in a frantic, mumbling voice.

Angel never lifts his head. But I can tell something about him is different. He does not seem the same, and he no longer has the glow he once had.

"Lue, you have to listen to me. I have to leave for the day. You must stay here. Please do not leave the grounds," Angel says in a soft voice.

"Why? Where are you going?" I ask.

"Where I am going, I will explain to you at another time. You have to promise me you won't leave," Angel begs.

"OK, I won't leave. I promise. But you have to tell me what is going on! How did my scars disappear and my leg heal?" I demand to know.

"All in good time. There are things going on that you are not to know at this time. Trust me," Angel says in a stern voice.

"I do trust you. But I am very confused, and this is all a bit much," I admit.

"Look!" Angel snaps. "I don't have time to explain right now. A storm is coming, and I must prepare myself for it. I will be back before nightfall. I want you to wear this necklace and never take it off. It will keep you safe."

Angel looks up at me. His face looks tired and wrinkled, and he looks as if he has aged thirty years. His eyes, the once bright, brilliant blue, are now a dingy dark gray, and dark rings now encircle his outer skin surrounding his eyes. I jump back in my seat as the shock of how he looks startles me.

Angel attempts to hand me the necklace, but he is too weak and drops it on the table. When I reach for it, my fingers rub across his hands. They are dry and weak and no longer soft and strong as they once were. I pick up the necklace, all the while never losing eye contact with him. He looks as if he is in pain, and I want to make him better. But I don't know how to, as I have no idea what is wrong with him.

"What happened to him?" I wonder to myself.

I want to reach across the table and hold him until he is once again the man that found me. But I don't. I am too scared to touch his fragile body anymore than I have already touched him, afraid that at any moment he could fade away and leave me forever.

Without saying a word, I look over the necklace. It is gold with a beautiful crystal at the end of it that illuminates rainbow on the table when the sunlight shines on it. I put the necklace on and ask no more questions. Although I have many to ask, I decide that after everything he has done for me, there will be a better time to get my answers. Besides, he does not look like he is strong enough to say anything further.

I am saddened by the look of pain and despair in his eyes and have to turn away, as I know if I don't, I will soon cry.

After sitting in silence for a few minutes, Angel stands up, kisses my forehead, and whispers, "You stay on the grounds today. Please do not leave with anyone."

He then turns and walks inside.

I sit and stare at the necklace that Angel has given me for quite a bit longer, amazed by the beautiful colors that come from within it. As I continue to look deeper into the necklace, I become hypnotized, as inside of the crystal becomes clearer, and the brilliant colors of the rainbow fade into a blue and white haze that seems to float within the crystal. After closer evaluation, I determine that the inside now looks like clouds floating in the air.

So intrigued by the necklace, I do not notice that the weather has begun to change and the birds that had been singing are no longer there.

There is a bright flash of lightning, then a loud crackling of thunder. The loud sound startles me so bad that when I jump back in my seat, I almost tumble out of my chair. Quickly, I turn and look up to the sky; it is now dark and gloomy, leaving not an inch of blue sky left to be seen.

The rain begins covering the garden with a fresh layer of fall rain. Slow at first, it is nice to experience the smell of the fresh rain on the grass and flowers. I love the smell of the first rain of the season. I close my eyes and lean my head back as I breathe in the fresh, dewy air.

"What a wonderful smell!" I think to myself as I continue to breathe in deeply.

Suddenly, there is another crack of thunder, and the sky seems to open up. It is now raining so hard that I can no longer see the garden I have been admiring earlier.

Crack!

Another strike of lightning, and another crackling of thunder.

"I better get in the house before I get wet," I think to myself. "Or worse, get hit by the lightning."

As fast as I can, I jump out of my seat and run into the house looking for Angel. I do not think he should be going out in this storm, and I am going to insist that he stays here so that I can look after him.

It takes a while, but I search through every room. He is nowhere to be found.

"He must have departed right after he left me outside," I think to myself as I softly sigh.

"He will be back soon," I hear someone say from behind me.

I turn quickly; it is the young man I had seen last night and in the kitchen.

"OK, I am just checking to see if he has already left," I reply.

"Yes, ma'am, he did," the man says in a husky voice.

"May I ask your name?" I ask.

"Sure, I'm John. It's nice to meet you," the man says as he shakes my hand.

I hold out my hand to shake his. His hands are soft and strong like Angel's. However, his touch does not offer the same "home" feeling that Angel's does. I am a little surprised as they are so similar in every aspect that I thought his touch would have the same affect on me.

"It is nice to meet you," I say as I look into his clear gray eyes.

"You too," John says with a wink.

I don't know what about him intrigues me so, but I cannot look away, and once again, I find myself staring into his welcoming eyes. It is like looking into the past, a past that I know nothing about.

He begins to say something to me, when all of a sudden the phone rings, interrupting our conversation.

"Excuse me, ma'am. I need to answer that," John says as he hurries into the study.

I start to walk away, when I hear my name being called. I look around and see that it is John, and he is calling for me from within the study.

"Lue, it is for you," John yells from the other room.

"For me?" I think to myself. "It's probably the police with information about my parents!"

I dash into the study with great hopes that they have found them, *alive*. I take the phone from John and take in a deep breath of hope.

"I will leave you to your phone call. If there is anything you might need, please yell for me," John says with a smile. "I will be right down the hall from here."

"Hello?" I say as I talk into the receiver of the phone, forgetting to thank John for his kindness.

"Hi, Lue?" a man says.

"Yes, this is Lue," I answer.

"Hi, it's me, Jeffery."

"Hi, Jeffery, any news on my parents?" I ask.

"No, sorry. Not yet, Lue. But we are following some new clues. It will be soon, I am sure," Jeffery says in a strange tone.

"How about the cabin or the house I was kept in? Have you had any luck with those?" I ask, hoping that they have been able to find something.

"Lue, that is what I want to talk to you and Angel about. We have searched the forest in the area you described again, and we still cannot find anything. Can you come in today so that we can talk some more?" says Jeffery.

"Angel is gone for the day," I explain.

"Then you can come alone. We really need to go over some things with you," Jeffery states in an elated tone.

I sit quietly for a moment.

"I know Angel asked me not to leave, but I am sure it will be OK with the police," I think to myself. "Besides, he has already met Jeffery, and he seemed to be OK with him."

"Lue, you there?" Jeffery asks on the other end of the phone.

"Oh yea, sorry, Jeff. Yes, I can come. Do you want me to come in with the policeman that is here?" I inquire.

"No, No! I will send a car for you. I want him to stay there and watch the house," Jeffery explains.

"OK, when will you be here?" I ask.

"Actually, I have someone here that would like to pick you up for me," Jeffery says in softened tone.

"Who?" I ask.

"Who?" I ask again.

Jeffery is no longer speaking.

"Hello? Jeffery? Are you there?" I ask.

"Hello, Lue," I hear a different voice say.

It is a new voice on the other end of the phone. A voice that is familiar to me, one that I have yearned to hear for three long years. A moment of excitement jump-starts my heart, accelerating my heartbeat. I begin to shake so hard that I now find myself having a difficult time holding the phone in my hand. I have so much I want to say, so many questions I want to ask that my mind begins to scramble, and I become tongue-tied. Within seconds, my mind shuts down, leaving me empty and speechless.

"Take a deep breath," I think to myself. "This is the moment you have been waiting for. Don't mess it up."

After calming myself, I am able to talk once again.

"Kamrin, is that you?" I ask.

"Hi, Lue. Yes, it's me," Kamrin replies.

I become speechless once again, as tears instantly fill my eyes. I finally, after three years of waiting, hoping, and praying, am hearing his sweet voice. My dreams have come true! It is truly him!

"I will be there shortly. We can talk then," Kamrin continues.

"I can't wait. I have so much to tell you," I say in a soft tone.

"Yea, me too," Kamrin says.

"I look forward to it," I say under my breath as I wipe the tears from my eyes.

I know he is married and has a child; this I am sure is what he wants to talk to me about. That, in fact, he wants to make sure I do not try to contact him or interrupt his new life. My heart plunges to my stomach, and I feel like I have been taken from his loving arms for the third time.

Tears uncontrollably continue to stream down my face. I have waited for so many years to hear his voice again, to see his face again, and now I know it is going to be our final good-bye. This is all wrong. It is not supposed to be like this! It is not fair!

"Lue?"

I have forgotten that I am still on the phone.

"Yes?"

"I love you!" Kamrin says in a soft voice.

My heart starts beating faster and slower at the same time. I cannot believe what I have just heard. Did he mean what he has said, or is he trying to make me feel more at ease? I want to jump through the phone and hug him. Finding myself wishing he was here now so that I can do just that, a smile overtakes my face, and I forget all my worries. He still loves me, and I still love him, and that is something Kamrin, Cheyenne, and I will have to deal with.

"I love you too," I whisper as I look around the room, ensuring that neither John nor Angel hears me.

Angel knows I have a fiancé and that I love Kamrin dearly. However, I feel uncomfortable saying those words in front of him, as he has done so much for me. I am still uncertain as to his true intentions, that is if he has any intention at all. Either way, I am happy that he is nowhere to be seen. I would hate to hurt him in anyway.

Still in disbelief, I blankly hold the phone in my hand.

"Kamrin is on his way!" a voice within me screams in excitement.

I hang up the phone and run upstairs to my room. I want to look my best, so I search through everything in my closet, ransacking it until I am able to find the perfect outfit. I get dressed quickly and then hurry my way into the bathroom to fix my hair and makeup.

When I look into the mirror, I start to laugh, realizing that my makeup is still half finished.

"What an idiot! I must have looked like a fool." I laugh. "No wonder Angel left in a hurry. He was afraid that he will start laughing at me."

"Angel," I think to myself, as I imagine his exquisite features. "Snap out of it, he is not interested in you that way. Think about Kamrin. He loves you, and you love him, and he is on his way here now."

Taking in a breath of confusion, I shake my head, and then continue getting ready for our reunion.

Once again standing in front of the mirror, I cannot help but wonder how my scars could have disappeared. Brushing off the fact that I had not gotten any answers from Angel, I finish fixing my makeup and let my hair down.

"Kamrin always liked my hair down," I think to myself. "In fast, he always would beg me to let it grow long. Boy, will he be surprised when he sees how long it is now."

Running downstairs in anticipation of finally seeing the man that I was taken from years ago, I begin to sing a song that my mom would sing to me when I was a child. Memories of the past overcomes me and tears begin to fill my eyes as the thought of never seeing my parents again is becoming more of a reality with every moment that passes, every moment that they do not find them.

"Have a little patience," I think to myself. "It has only been one or two days since the day they were taken. Or at least that is what the police believe."

I stop and try to convince myself that there is still hope. That it is possible that they will find them alive, as I have heard of many stories in the past about people that are abducted, and they found them alive.

"Look at yourself. You were gone over three years and suffered more pain than any one person could take, and you are here, alive, and without a scratch on you," I think to myself as I admire my scarless skin.

Wiping my sorrowful eyes, I maneuver my way from one room to another, until I find my way into the front living room. I sit on the couch facing the front driveway, in hopes that I will get a glimpse of Kamrin as he pulls into the driveway, like I used to do when he would come over to pick me up from my parents' home. I know that by doing so I am acting like a young girl waiting for her first date. But I need that sense of my past youth in my life again, as since I have been back, nothing has been the same.

I start getting nervous and begin feeling around my neck for my necklace. It is not there. I have forgotten to put it back on. I jump up to run upstairs to get it, when I realize it is sitting on the arm of the couch next to me. I look around to see who might have put it there. There is no one, nor a sign that anyone has been there.

"I know I left this on the sink in my bathroom," I think to myself.

I shrug my shoulders as I put it around my neck.

"The strangest things happen in this house, I swear," I think to myself as I sit back down and look out the window.

I have other things to think about than where the necklace has come from, as that little incident seems minimal at this moment, compared to everything else that is going on.

I sit for more than an hour thinking of what I want to say when I see Kamrin and how I will react when I came face-to-face with him. Then I start thinking of how he will react, hoping that he will grab me in his arms and never let go. I have so much going through my head at one time that I become dizzy.

"Maybe I am hungry. I did forget to eat breakfast," I think to myself as I grab an apple from the table and begin to eat it.

The sky lights up as a loud thunder rips across the sky. Overwhelmed by the sound of the loudness, I jump off the couch, ultimately falling against the coffee table and then onto the floor. Embarrassed about how I must look, I scan the room quickly for anyone that might have seen me fall. Once I am certain that I am alone, I start laughing so hard that I barely hear the knock on the front door. My heart skips a beat and then begins to race. He is here! The moment I have waited for . . . has finally come!

I jump up, run to the door, and grab the doorknob. Suddenly, I find myself paralyzed, afraid of what may happen.

"Just breathe," I say to myself. "Just breathe."

Grasping the knob in a firm hold, I take in a deep breath of hope and swing open the door. Standing there in the doorway is Kamrin. He is as handsome as I remembered him being, with his dark brown hair that flows to just above his shoulder and his bright blue eyes. Looking closer into his eyes, I realize that he still has the power to pull me into his heart, just by looking deep in his hypnotic eyes. As he stands in the doorway with a smile on his face, I am brought back to earlier years, when I would meet him at the front door. He would always pick up, hug me as tight as he could, then swing me around in his arms until we were both dizzy and almost falling on the floor. He was always happy to see me.

A little disappointed that he has not done just that, I stand frozen, staring at him, anticipating the moment when he will.

He has not changed in the last three years, as I am afraid I have. His smile is so warm and inviting that I cannot take the silence and anticipation any longer; leaping forward, I land in his waiting arms. However, hitting him so hard that I almost knock us both to the ground. Laughing at my reaction, Kamrin tightly holds me in his arms, releasing the feeling of desperation between us. We stand outside the doorway holding each other for a while, neither of us saying a word. The moment has finally come!

Kamrin, breaking the silence, takes my hand and asks me if I would like to sit on the porch swing and talk awhile before we go to the police station. I agree, and we do just that.

The storm is still stirring outside, but we ignore it as we continue talking about the past and what has happened. Kamrin holds my hand and listens to every story I tell.

"I'm a little confused," confesses Kamrin. "Jeffery said that when he saw you at your parents' house, you looked bad. He said you had a cast on one of your legs and a lot of scars on your face and body. He said that you looked so bad that he didn't even think that your family would recognize you. But here I sit looking at you now, and I don't see any of what he was telling me."

I don't know what to say to him because I have no clue what has happened either. I sit in silence thinking to myself, trying to think of what to say to him. *How will I explain the unexplainable?*

I remain silent.

"Well, Lue," Kamrin snaps. "How do you explain what Jeffery has told me and what I am seeing here now? I'm starting to think that something is wrong here, like some of the stories you are telling me are not true."

I become aggravated and do not appreciate the tone of his voice. He sounds like he does not believe what I have told him about being taken and held captured for so many years.

"I don't know how to explain," I snap. "Just know I am telling the truth."

We sit in awkward silence for a while, neither of us looking at each other. Kamrin must have realized I am angry at his accusations, because he puts his arm around me and apologizes. I lay my head on his shoulder, and we sit in silence for a while longer, swinging in the stormy afternoon air.

"I'm sorry, Lue. You don't understand what I have been through. We were to get married. I waited for you at the podium. You never showed. We searched months for you, no word, and no clues of where you had gone. After three years, you suddenly show up. Jeffery tells me that you have been abused and have a broken leg. I show up to this house. You are living with a strange man that no one knows, and you look as beautiful as ever. How do you expect me to act?" Kamrin implies.

"You searched for me?" I ask.

"Yes, we did," Kamrin replies.

"Just who is 'we'?" I ask. "According to the police, there was never a report of me missing."

"I don't know who you spoke to," Kamrin grumbles. "There was a report. All you have to do is ask Jeffery. He will show it to you."

I have no reason not believe him, so I let the subject rest with his last statement.

"Now answer my question," Kamrin says in a growl. "What is going on here?"

"I don't know," I say softly. "I just don't know."

Silence overtakes the area we are sitting, leaving only the sounds of the rain as it falls to the ground.

I look up at Kamrin; he looks angry and uncaring. His look becoming more disturbing as the silence continues. Becoming agitated with the whole situation, I lower my head into my hands and begin to cry.

"What you went through?" I cry. "What about me? I was tortured for three years, and I almost died I don't know how many times! Have you ever had someone hit you over the head with a hammer or slice your face with a razor over and over again, until your skin peels from your bones? In the last three years, have you had to wonder when you will eat next and if the food will be rotten and covered in maggots? *No!* You went on with your life. You got married to Cheyenne and had a baby! You forgot about me!" I begin to cry hysterically.

He merely sits there in silence, listening to every word I say, never saying a word. It is obvious that he does not believe a word I am saying, as he no longer has his arm around me and is not comforting me in any way. He looks annoyed and begins picking the paint off the arm of the porch swing where he sits.

I cannot stop crying, and the more I look over at Kamrin's uncaring face, the more intense my crying becomes. I need someone to console me, and I had hoped it would be him. But by the way he is acting I know I will have to continue waiting.

"I just don't understand what happened to your scars and your 'broken leg,'" Kamrin snaps again. "It just seems a little odd to me, how you're so . . . perfect . . . now!"

"Why are you so worried about my damn scars? Aren't you happy that I am here with you now?" I cry. "None of this makes sense, like your marriage to Cheyenne, my 'ex-best friend.'"

"You have no idea about my marriage. You were gone! I was sad and lonely, and I did not know what happened to you. I gave up looking for you, as there was no trace that you had been kidnapped, leaving us to believe that you left on your own. Cheyenne was there for me. Things changed, and we became intimate. She got pregnant. So I had to marry her. I never loved her like I love you! I want you. That is why I am here! Damn it! I want you!" Kamrin screams as he grabs my face and turns it toward him.

"You want me!" I state. "But yet you sit here and accuse me of lying!"

"I'm accusing you?" Kamrin screams. "I'm stating a fact! There is something wrong here! You are perfect, and you should not be!"

"You know what! I am done with this conversation," I yell as I start to get up.

"Sit your ass down," Kamrin screams as he pulls me back to my seat. "I am not done with you yet!"

"You're not done with me yet?" I scream, as I stand up again. "Do you want to know what happened to the last man that said those words to me?"

"As a matter of fact, no, I don't," Kamrin snarls as he pulls me back onto the swing and wraps his arm around me tightly.

In fear that I am going to get hurt, I give into his power and sit arrested in his arms. After a few moments, I realize that his intentions are not that to hurt me, but that to keep me from leaving his side. I lay my head on his shoulder.

Although I feel a little more comfortable, I am still upset that he has bullied me in such a way that he scared me.

"I'm sorry," Kamrin whispers.

Trying to conceive what he must be feeling, I sit silent for a few minutes and think about all that is going on. After a few moments of thought, I understand the confusion he must be feeling. Jeffery has told him one story, and I have told him nothing more than the stories of my abuse from the past three years. But yet here I sit beside him without a scratch, without a scar. I know my stories are hard to believe, and with the lack of evidence to support my accusations, they are nothing more than preposterous stories. In fact, I am uncertain if I believe it myself.

At that one and only moment, I wish that I still had the proof on my body.

"I'm sorry too," I say as I lift my head and look at his face.

"I think you should be," Kamrin says as he brushes my hair with his fingers.

Kamrin begins to chuckle in a sense that makes me very uncomfortable. It is almost sinister.

Nonchalantly, I begin to scoot away from him. Suddenly, he grabs me by my waist and pulls me close to him, once again taking me in his arms.

"I said . . . I want you!" he demands as he forces his unwelcomed lips on mine.

He is getting rough and is beginning to hurt me. I try to push him away, but this just makes him become more persistent. His strength is overpowering, and his actions bring back memories that I have been trying to forget. I try to squirm away, but his grip continues to tighten until I can no longer move. I want to scream for him to stop, but I know it might make things escalate into a worst situation. I am his prisoner.

"It's OK. He is only acting this way because he has wanted you for so long," a voice inside me says. "Just give in to him."

"No!" I scream within myself. "This is not the way it should be!"

"You know you missed me," Kamrin says as he tries to kiss my neck.

I am scared and uncertain how I should react. He is right. I do want him, but I do not want him this way, not forceful and demanding. I want the Kamrin I knew years ago, and this is not him! As he continues to push himself on me, memories of the man in the mask flood my mind. The visions scare me so much that I am afraid to talk, afraid to move, afraid to do anything except sit here and endure what he is doing to me.

The fear of pain overtakes my mind, and I do not want to take the chance that he will hurt me like my captor always did. I know the best thing for me to do is to wait until he comes to his senses and ceases the way he his is invading my mind and body.

Scanning the immediate area, I search for anyone that might be around, someone that will see what is happening and break the tormenting spell that Kamrin is in. I want someone, anyone . . . I want Angel to save me from Kamrin's forceful arms!

"Angel!" I scream within myself.

Suddenly, every speck of hair on my body stands on end.

An earsplitting crash echoes through the front yard, sounding as if a catastrophic bomb has just gone off. We both jump back in our seats, as the sound is so overtaking that it rattles the stone porch that we are sitting on.

"What was that?" I ask, frightened by the sound.

We both look around, and right away, it is obvious that it has been lightning, and it has hit a tree out front, as the tree is still smoldering.

"Thank God," I think to myself, as I am relieved to finally be out of his grasp.

"The storm is getting pretty bad. Maybe we should go inside," I say to Kamrin, trying to ensure that he does not get hold of me again.

"Maybe," replies Kamrin. "That was pretty close."

The wind is now blowing with such tremendous force that the trees begin to fold. Suddenly, the heavens above opens up, spewing out sheets of rain, making it impossible to see any further than the front porch. I know if we stay on the porch any longer, we will be taking the chance of getting wet or possibly getting hit by lightning.

Looking over at Kamrin, I hold my hand out for him to hold. I do not want him to know that I am afraid of him, as I am still having a hard time believing that he would act the way he has been under normal circumstances. I tightly grasp his hand and lead him to the front door.

As we approach the front door, Kamrin yanks his hand from mine and gives me a look like no other I have ever seen.

"What's wrong?" I ask, stunned by his sudden reaction.

"Whose house is this?" he demands to know.

"I told you. It is the guy who saved me when I was out in the woods," I reply.

"No! What is his name?" Kamrin asks in a sharp tone.

"His name is Angel!" I snap back.

"I see that I am going to have to speak slower," he says sarcastically. "What is his full name?"

I look at him and roll my eyes. I am becoming more and more agitated with every word that is coming out of his mouth. He is being rude and mean. Something I have never experienced from him before, and I am not appreciating it now.

"His name is Angel Smith," I say between my teeth.

"Smith, huh? Sounds fishy to me. I would be careful if I was you!" Kamrin says as he squeezes my shoulders.

The pressure from his hands becomes stronger and stronger until I can feel the compression of each individual finger from his hands on my shoulders, and I know if he does not loosen his grip soon, I will suffer new bruises.

"What will Angel think about Kamrin if he leaves bruises on my arms?" I think to myself as I try to release myself from his clutches.

It doesn't work, and his grip becomes tighter until I can feel the bones beneath my shoulders beginning to crack.

"Stop it!" I scream. "You're hurting me!"

I look up at him; he looks angry and out of patience. All the years we have known each other, he has never attempted to hurt me and has never shown me his angry side. I am confused, hurt, and angry all at once and cannot understand why he is so angry at me and at this man that has saved me and is now caring for me.

"Jealousy," I think to myself as I try to ignore the alarming feeling that is stirring inside me.

"Baby," I hear him whisper beneath his breath.

Suddenly, he releases his hands from my shoulders and starts to walk in the front door. However, he stops abruptly as soon as his foot touches the ground just inside the doorway. He looks up at the chandelier that I had once questioned, steps back outside, and snaps at me again.

"I don't feel comfortable being in this 'man's' house! Let's get going to the police station. We can talk more there," Kamrin says as he gestures to the waiting car.

A creeping feeling overtakes my body, and I know that I am no longer comfortable being alone with him. I wish Angel was here so that he could go along, but he has not returned.

I begin arguing within myself.

"What are you scared of?" a voice in my head says. "It's Kamrin . . . your fiancé. You know he is only acting like this because you are at some man's house that he doesn't know. He will change as soon as you leave here."

"But what if he has changed and this is who he truly is now?" I continue arguing with myself.

"Take the chance. You know you have to or you will never know," I think to myself as I finally let my heart take control over my mind, ultimately convincing myself that all will be OK.

"Let me grab a sweater," I say as I head for the living room.

I grab the sweater off the couch where I had left it, turn, and walk back toward Kamrin as he continues to wait outside the door.

Without warning, there is a thunderclap that overtakes the house causing the windows to shake and the lights to flicker. The storm is overhead, and it sounds fiercer than ever.

I run to the door as fast as I can, as the thought of the lights going out completely scares me. I am still scared of the dark, and I do not want to be standing here alone when darkness engulfs the room. Not to mention that I do not know the house well enough, and I know that if I was to get scared, I would try to run in the darkened room and end up knocking something off a table or wall and break it. And everything here looks like it is very expensive and old, and I do not want to have a broken family heirloom on my conscious.

"I'm ready to go," I say as I reach the front door, quick, fast, and in a hurry.

I am excited and scared at the same time. I don't know what the police have to say, but I am hoping that it will be good news. Plus, I know as soon as we are away from this house; Kamrin will treat me with the love and kindness as he did in years past. In my heart, I know that. I just hope my heart is right.

Heading outside, I realize it has suddenly turned chilly, so I pause in the doorway and slip on my sweater. Turning and looking in the house, I feel as if I have broken my promise to Angel. I become confused, and I am uncertain if what I am about to do is the right thing. It's a fight within myself. I want to go with Kamrin, but a voice from deep in my soul keeps telling me I should stay far away.

"Wait a second," Kamrin says as he smiles, takes his jacket off, and shields my head from the rain we are about to encounter. "I don't want you to get sick."

"Thank you," I say as I look up at Kamrin and smile.

At that moment, I feel that I have my Kamrin back, as I no longer see anger in his eyes.

"Lue," Kamrin says as he touches my shoulder.

"Yes," I reply.

"I am truly sorry for before," Kamrin says as tears fill his eyes. "I guess jealousy overcame me. I should have never yelled at you. And I definitely should have never hurt you like I did."

His words seem sincere and heartfelt, and I believe everything he is saying.

A smile overcomes my face as I know right then that my heart is right; Kamrin still loves me, and we will be together again.

Forgetting to tell John where I am going and with whom, I shut the front door behind me and continue on my way.

"I will have to call when we get there and let Angel or John know where I am. I don't want to worry anyone here," I say softly.

"Well, I might let you," Kamrin says sarcastically.

Convincing myself he is kidding around, I brush it off.

We begin walking down the stairs toward the car, when suddenly the sky seems to open up, like never before. Lightning begins hitting all around the car, as if it is trying to keep us away. Determined, Kamrin insists that we continue toward the car, as he grabs my arm and pulls me forward. However, with every step we make, a small bolt of electricity hits in the area we are about to step to. It is as if the lightning knows our next step before we do. I am scared out of my mind and do not want to go any further, afraid that at any moment we will get struck by lightning. Stopping in the middle of the stairs, I pull away from Kamrin's grip once again and freeze in my tracks, refusing to take another step.

I look up into the sky and cannot believe what I am seeing, as there is not a cloud in the sky. The sky is dark, but the stars I had seen the night before engulf the sky once again. I stand there in amazement as I cannot comprehend where the lightning, thunder, and rain are coming from.

"What in the world!" I say out loud.

Within seconds, Kamrin begins looking at the sky also. However, he does not show the same concern as I do about the events that are unfolding in front of us. In fact, he merely stands there and shakes his head as if he is disgusted by the whole thing.

He stares for a while looking at the sky and then begins mumbling to himself. I cannot understand what he is saying, and the tone of his voice is strange.

"So you want to play that way?" I think I hear him say. However, I cannot be certain.

I become nervous and begin fiddling with my necklace Angel has given me.

The necklace becomes very hot, which makes no sense, because it has continued to get colder outside. To the point that I can now see my breath as my breathing continues to escalade.

I look down at the necklace; it is illuminating, and the clouds I thought I saw in the necklace earlier are now fading into hundreds of individual speckles of glowing light. It is hard to believe what I am seeing, but I know I have to hide it from Kamrin, as I will have to explain that to him also, and I am fresh out of explanations.

As fast as I can, I wrap my hand around the glowing necklace and try to hide it. My efforts are useless, as Kamrin has seen what I had done. He quickly grabs my hand and pulls it back out. My hand is still grasped around the necklace; it is now visible for all to see.

The sight of the glowing necklace must have shocked him also, because he leaps away from me as if he has just seen a ghost. His face becomes pale white, and his eyes instantly turn from a bright blue to a dingy gray. I begin staring into his eyes, as they continue to get darker and darker until they are now the darkest gray I have ever seen. In fact, they are almost black. I want to turn away, but I can't; I am hypnotized, as the constant change of color pulls me in.

"What is happening to his eyes?" I ask myself as I continue to stare into his once-beautiful blue eyes.

He becomes very nervous and begins looking around. At first, I think it is because he knows what is happening to his eyes, and he doesn't want me to see. However, as he continues to search the area, it becomes obvious that it isn't me he is afraid of. He is afraid of something else and continues acting like at any moment something or someone is going to jump out at him and take his very life away.

"I have to go!" he says as he stumbles over his words. "We will do this another day. I will have someone come get you."

Kamrin turns quickly and dashes for his car. Instantly, the rain seizes, the lightning subdues and no longer is hitting around his car.

I stand there watching as Kamrin continues to his car. A wave of sadness overcomes my heart, and I don't want him to leave without me, as I am afraid that something will happen, and I will never see him again.

"It's safe now," Kamrin yells as he stands next to the car, holding the door open for me. "Hurry up. You can make it."

"OK," I yell back as I start to run down the final few stairs.

Instantly, lightning starts hitting simultaneously on the ground all around the bottom of the stairs, making a wall of electricity in front of me. Without further hesitation, I run back up the stairs to the porch. There is no way I am going any further, as it is apparent that something is trying to stop me from doing so.

"Never mind," Kamrin screams. "It's not going to happen this time. But don't worry about it . . . it will happen!"

"And tell your boyfriend that," I think I hear him say, but I am unsure, as the wind is blowing so tremendously hard that it is muffling most of what Kamrin is saying. Quickly, I excuse the comment as something merely that of the wind playing tricks with my ears, as it makes no sense to me as to why he would have said that. He knows Angel is nothing more than a friend . . . a savior.

"Did you hear me, Lue?" Kamrin yells. "I will call you later."

"Yes," I yell back. "I look forward to it."

He is undeniably mad, but there is nothing I can do about it, as I am not going to fight the inevitable and get hit by the lightning that has encircled the porch. It will have to be as he said, another time.

"Hey, what about Jeffery? I thought he wanted to see me?" I scream at Kamrin. "Can he come here?"

"I will have him call you and set something up so that you can go see him," Kamrin yells as he scurries to get into his car. "There is no way I will let him come here!"

Suddenly, there is a loud noise coming from behind me. Frightened that one of the lightning bolts has just hit the front door, I jump back and turn to see what has happened. To my relief, it is John, and he is standing in the doorway. Relieved, I turn back around to wave good-bye to Kamrin, but the car is no longer there.

"How could he have left without me hearing him drive away?" I ask myself as I look to where Kamrin was just parked.

There is no sign that a car has ever been here, nor that one has just left. I shake my head and look again.

"There has to be tire marks in the mud or something," I think out loud.

"Is everything OK?" John asks from behind me.

"You saw a car, right?" I ask John.

"A car?" he asks.

"Yeah, when you came out, I was talking to Kamrin. You saw that, right?" I ask as I head toward John.

"Sorry, ma'am, I did not see a car." John chuckles.

At first, I am little confused as to why he is laughing at my question.

"Am I going insane?" I ask.

Pointing toward the direction the car has been, I ask again, "You didn't see a car over there?"

John looks at me and smiles.

"I saw a truck." John chuckles again. "But no car."

The tension is broke, and my mind relaxed.

"Oh, you," I say as I smack him lightly on the arm. "You had me thinking that I am going insane."

John stands there and laughs as if he is proud of himself and his little joke.

"I know. Sorry, I couldn't help myself, "John says between his laughter.

It is then that I know that John and I will be great friends, as he has the same great sense of humor like I once had.

The night goes by slowly, as I am lost within my freedom and do not know what to do. Angel has not returned home yet, and I am beginning to worry about him, as he did not look healthy earlier that day. I continue to look outside the front window hoping to see him pull into his driveway. But there is not a sign of a car near or far, leaving me stranded here with only my thoughts.

Hours continue to go by.

Becoming restless, I begin looking around the house for something to do. By all means I am not trying to be nosy. I am merely bored and need to find something to do before I get too antsy.

After walking around for a while, I find myself in the library. It is the largest room in the house and probably the most elaborate. Shelves filled with novels line the dark, cherrywood paneling making the walls look as if they are made of nothing more than books they house. There have to be thousands of them. I have not read for a while, and reading used to be one of my favorite pastimes, as it always kept my mind occupied when I was bored.

"That's what I need, a good book to lose my thoughts in," I think to myself as I continue to stare at my thousands of options.

I begin searching through the books hoping that something will grasp my attention. I am not sure exactly what I am looking for, but the thought of reading a nice love story sparks my interest.

After searching for a while, I find myself being drawn to a large, leather-bound book that is encircled with gold inlayer. The title of the book is written in a foreign language, and the book is old and tattered making it difficult to read the title. Staring at it for a while, I am able to make out the word, "Archangelous."

"Interesting," I think to myself.

I take the book and sit down on the armchair in the middle of the room. I then open the book and begin flipping through the pages. There are pages after pages of beautiful women and men. The most beautiful people I have ever seen. I cannot stop staring at them, as their beauty is hypnotic to look at. As my mind begins to wander, I start to remember the last pictures of women I have seen, and I begin to cry.

"Those poor women," I whisper as I quiver in disgust.

Trying to shake the images of the mutilated women from my head, I continue looking at the pictures in the leather-bound book.

I am about halfway through the book, when suddenly one particular picture catches my eye. It is that of a man dressed in a silky white robe that flows down his body. His hair is that of bright blond, and his entire body emits off a glow that is hypnotizing to look at. I look closer at the face in the picture. I am astonished! It looks like Angel!

At first, I think it is a painting like the pictures before it, and then I realize that it isn't. In fact, the photograph of the man in the picture is standing in front of a house that resembles this one.

"Why is this one a photograph and the others are paintings?" I question myself as I quickly scan throughout the book.

Quickly I realize that the first half of the book is paintings of men and women, whereas the second half of the book contains photographs. I am a little confused as to why it would be that way; however, I am more interested to know why there is a picture of Angel and why he is in such a book.

Knowing that the cover appears to be old, I look to the back of the book to find the date the book was made. There is no way that Angel could be in a book of such age.

"Maybe I am wrong about the book being old," I think.

To my dismay, the book is dated "1820." Instantly, I know the picture cannot be Angel's. Turning the book back to the page I had seen, I study the picture closer, until my eyes become blurry, and I close them. The picture is stuck in my mind, and I have to look at it again. I wipe my watery eyes and then focus them on the picture once more. The man in the picture has the same eyes, hair, and build as Angel. I am mesmerized by the similarity of Angel to the picture and cannot look away.

"This has to be someone else," I think to myself as I lay the book in my lap and run my fingers around the picture, outlining the man's body. "Maybe a relative from many years past."

The phone begins to ring behind me. I look around. I see no one. The phone rings over and over again. Still no one answers it.

"I wonder where John is," I think to myself as I look around the room expecting someone to walk in at any time to answer it.

It rings again.

"I better answer the phone. It could be Angel or Kamrin," I say in a low whisper.

I set the book down, careful not to lose my page. I want to read what is written under the picture that I have been studying so closely. I walk over to the large wood desk next to the window and answer the phone.

"Hello?" I ask.

"Hi, Lue?" the voice on the phone asks.

"Yes, this is Lue," I answer.

"Oh, hi, Lue, it's me, Jeffery," he replies.

"Hi, Jeff. Did Kamrin get back to you on why I didn't show up today?" I ask.

"Yes, he did. What a strange storm, huh?" Jeffery asks.

"Yes, it was. I'm sorry, I couldn't make it," I say, as I think back to the cloudless sky.

"That's OK. Do you think you can come over tomorrow?" he continues. "We can talk then."

"Sure, do you want to send a car, or should I have Angel bring me?" I inquire.

"Have Angel bring you, if he will. Sorry, but that house gives people the willies," Jeffery replies in a strange voice.

"Oh, OK," I stutter, confused as to why he would have said that, as this house has made me feel as I am at home.

"Just have him drop you off, and we will find someone to take you back to his front gate when we are finished talking with you," Jeffery continues. "There is no need for him to stay. Besides, we are a little uncomfortable around him also."

I squeeze my eyebrows together, roll my eyes, and shake my head, as I am dumbfounded as to why they are acting in such a way. Whatever their reason is I do not appreciate it. In fact, it angers me. I sit quiet for a while before I begin to speak again.

"OK, Jeff, I will be there," I say in an irritated tone.

"See you then, Lue. Just remember, no Angel," Jeffery says and then hangs up the phone quickly before I can say another word.

Sitting at the desk for a while longer, I stare at the phone, going through the conversation in my head.

"Why did they not want me to bring Angel?" I continue to question. "Why are they so uncomfortable around him?"

None of this makes sense to me, as Angel is the nicest person I have ever met. Besides, he gave me my life back. That they should be grateful for or at least I hoped they would be.

"Maybe they are questioning his motives as to why he is taking care of me and why he would take in a complete stranger and do so much for them," I think to myself.

I will say that is something that I have questioned myself, but then I forget when I look into Angel's eyes. I figure he is a kind man, who somehow feels responsible for my well-being. Or possibly, I am the one being blinded.

"Maybe I have craved attention for so many years that I can't see his true intentions," I wonder to myself.

Although I really do not know the real truth, it doesn't bother me as he has been so nice to me, and that is something I need at this present moment. After arguing with myself for sometime, I look over and see the book I have been reading.

I want to look at the picture again and see what is written below the photograph. I walk back over to the chair where I have been sitting and pick the book back up. The pages must have shifted as the picture I once was looking at is no longer there. I begin looking through the pages. I cannot find the picture, and the words have disappeared from beneath the pictures that remain. I am baffled.

"Did I imagine all this? Am I losing my sanity?" I ask myself.

I start over and begin searching through the book one page at a time. I still cannot find the picture that looks like Angel. I become obsessed trying to find it, to the point that I begin looking at the book page numbers, ensuring that they follow suit through the whole book. There is not a page missing. Frantically, I scan through the entire book five times just to ensure that I am not missing something. It is the same each time.

"I should have looked at the page number," I say to myself. "At least I would have known what number I thought the picture was on."

Becoming aggravated, I slam the book onto the table and lean back. I close my eyes and growl a soft, irritated growl. I can still see the picture fresh in my mind, haunting me as if this is all some kind of hide-and-seek game.

"How could that picture disappear?" I ask out loud. "I know I saw it!"

"You should be careful talking to yourself. Someone might think you're going crazy." I hear a voice chuckle in my ear.

Startled, I jump forward, flipping my head around to see who is there. There is no one around me! I turn my head in all directions and ensure that I have looked everywhere in the room. There is no one around. Deciding that it has all been my imagination, I return my attention to the book. When I turn back around, there sitting next to me is Angel.

"When did you get here?" I ask in a shaky voice.

"I just got here," Angel replies.

"How? I did not see you come in," I demand to know.

"I walked right past you, while you were flipping your head around, like a crazy woman." Angel chuckles. "By the way, what were you doing?"

"I heard someone say, 'You better stop talking to yourself, or people are going to think you are crazy,'" I say as I look into his eyes, anticipating him to laugh at any moment.

"And when did you hear this voice?" Angel asks with concern in his voice.

"Seconds before I saw you sitting next to me," I state. "Didn't you say it?"

"No. Sorry, dear, I didn't. Are you sure you heard something?" Angel questions.

"Yes! I know I did. Stop fooling around with me, Angel. I am starting to freak out. I know I heard the voice!" I yell.

"I don't know, Lue. Maybe it has been a long day for you. You're tired, and you thought you heard a voice," Angel says in a voice of concern.

Angel takes my hand and gently places it in his. His hands are soft and strong again. Although still upset about hearing the voice and Angel not confessing to it, I decide to drop the subject, just in case it has been my imagination. Besides, I have other things I want to talk about. Like: Where was he all day? What happened to all my wounds? And why did he look so sick this morning?

Prepared to ask him all these questions, I look into his eyes. They sparkle like they had the first day I met him. His face is young again and glowing in the soft light of the room. I am bewildered.

"What happened to your appearance?" I asked softly.

"What do you mean?" Angel answered with a small grin.

"This morning," I continue, "I don't want to sound rude, but you looked a lot older. Now you're . . ."

I stop talking and start blushing.

"I'm what?" Angel chuckles, teasing me.

He smiles at me, melting my heart . . . making me forget any concerns I once had. It is like his smile makes me forget everything I want to say, and my mind erase any worry or concern I may have. The only thing I can do is smile back at him.

"So what are you doing in here?" Angel asks.

"Looking for something to read, when I came across this book," I say as I look into his mesmerizing words.

"What book?" he questions.

I look down. The book is gone! My heart skips a beat. I know I had the book. I look on the floor to see if it has fallen. There is no book. Glancing around the room, I see that the book is nowhere to be found. My mind is boggled as to where it could have gone. I begin questioning myself, if there was ever a novel. *Am I imaging things, or is someone playing games with my head? What exactly is going on here?*

"I had a book that I was looking at. I had sat it down here when I went to answer the phone," I explain to Angel as I point at the table sitting in front of us.

"That would explain it," Angel says in confidence. "When you answered the phone in the other room, John probably came in and put the book back. He is kind of a neat-freak."

"No, I didn't leave the room," I reply. "I answered the phone over there on the desk."

"Sweetie, you couldn't have. There is no phone in this room," Angel looks at me concerned.

"Angel, stop. I know there is," I state as I walk over to the desk.

There is no phone.

"I know I answered the phone, right here!" I say in a loud tone and tap the desk.

"It's a big house, maybe you got confused," Angel says as he walks over to my side.

"No, Angel. I was in this room. I had gotten a book from over here," I say as I walk over to where I had found the book. "It was a large book bound in leather and looked like it was old. I brought it over to the couch and sat down and started to read it."

I walk over to the couch.

"That could be any book in here," Angel explains. "I am a collector of old books, and I have a lot that fit that description."

"It is called 'Archangelous,'" I say abruptly.

"Sorry, I don't remember a book called like that," Angel says as he continues watching me as I move around the room.

"Anyway, I was sitting here looking at a certain picture, when I heard the phone ring," I explain, becoming more certain that I have imagined the entire thing. "No one answered the phone, so I walked over to the desk and picked it up. I can even explain what the phone looked like. It was an old-fashioned phone. It was ceramic with tiny red and blue flowers painted on it, and the handle was gold."

"There is a phone like that in this house, but it is in your room," Angel replies. "Maybe you remember it from there."

"No! It was here!" I scream, almost crying.

"Lue, sweetie, there is no phone here," Angel says as he points his hands toward the desk. "Maybe you fell asleep while you were in here and dreamed all of this."

"I guess I could have," I say, though I do not believe that I have dreamed this entire ordeal.

I don't know what has happened, but I know I have been reading the book, and I know that I talked to Jeffery on the phone. I sit quietly as I recollect everything I have done, trying to remember what I did with the book and why the phone is not on the desk.

"Wait, that is it!" I think to myself. "I talked with Jeffery on the phone. I can call him, and he can confirm that I had."

"Angel," I say breaking the silence in the room.

"Yes?"

"Never mind," I say as I convince myself that by proving to Angel that I have been talking to Jeffery neither proves that I answered the phone in here, or that I have ever had a book. I have no proof except my memory. Maybe Angel is right. Or maybe I am right; all those years of abuse have caused me to lose part, if not all, of my sanity.

The room is silent as neither of us is speaking anymore. I am busy thinking about everything that has happened today, and I am certain that Angel is thinking that he has invited a crazy woman to live in his house and probably is regretting that decision at this exact moment.

I have to say something, maybe an admittance that it has all been a dream, or maybe ask him what he did all day. All I know is that I have to do something to break the silence in the room, as it is becoming a little unnerving.

"I will be right back," Angel announces as he rises from the chair he is sitting on and leaves the room.

After scanning the room quickly, I jump up and run over to the desk. I have to see if there is any sign of a phone, like a cord or maybe a phone jack. There is nothing. No indication that there ever has been.

"It was a dream," I say to myself as I walk quickly back to where I have been sitting.

I do not want Angel to see that I have gone over to the desk to check. He might think that I am accusing him of lying.

"John has prepared a nice dinner for us out on the patio. Let's go eat. You look like you could use some food," Angel says as he walks back into the room and stands in front of me, reaching for my hand.

I take his hand, instantly taking in the warmth it has to offer.

As we walk toward the door leading to the hallway, I stubbornly take one last look around, hoping that the book or phone has magically reappeared. However, there is still no sign of either, leaving me empty within my search. I take in a shallow breath and sigh lightly within myself.

"Wait, it's storming outside," I say, as I suddenly remember the storm that had stopped me from leaving earlier that day.

"The storm has ended for now," Angel replies.

We walk outside. He is right; it is no longer raining. The ground is dry, and it looks as if it has never rained at all. The stars are shining bright, so bright in fact that they look closer than usual. Almost like I could reach up and grab one out of the sky. I stop and listen to see if I can hear any thunder in the distance. The night air is peaceful now, with only the soft sounds of birds chirping in the background.

Angel pulls out a chair for me and motions for me to sit down.

"Thank you," I say smiling, gracious to be with such a gentleman.

The table is beautiful. It is decorated exquisitely with candles, crystal, and silver, and I find it captivating how the flickering lights of the candles strike the silver and crystal, causing lights of many colors to dance on the fresh white tablecloth. The thing that I am enjoying most, besides Angel's company, is the smell of fresh roses that fill the air from the rose garden that sits a few feet away from us.

Angel and I sit for hours enjoying our food and talking about everything. Talking to him seems to come natural, and when he speaks, it is like hearing angels sing. I could sit and listen to him talk for days, merely to hear his soft, soothing voice. After speaking for a while, Angel asks me if I heard from Jeffery that day. I explain to him how Jeffery called and said that he had something he needed to discuss with me and how he had sent Kamrin over to get me to bring me to the police station. I am just about to tell him about how the storm stopped me, when all of a sudden Angel lifts his head from its downward position, looking at me as if to be in disarray.

"What?" he asks suddenly.

"I was saying Kamrin came over, and I was going to go with him to the police station," I told Angel, surprised by the sudden interruption of my story, "when . . ."

"You were going to leave with Kamrin?" Angel snaps.

"Yes, he was going to take me to the police station to talk with Jeffery," I say in defense.

"I thought . . ." Angel begins to say and then suddenly jumps up out of his seat and runs to the kitchen.

I am confused as to why he has gotten so angry about me leaving with Kamrin. After all, he had been the one that had suggested I see him; in fact, he gave his number to Jeffery just for that reason. Not to mention, Kamrin was my fiancé at one time.

"I wonder what that was all about," I think to myself as I watch Angel scurry into the kitchen.

I can hear Angel and John talking. They seem to be arguing about something of a serious nature. Angel sounds agitated and is raising his voice louder and louder with every word that he speaks. As I sit quietly, I try to hear what is being said, but their voices seem muffled through the walls, and the only words I am able to grasp is John saying, "I took care of it, didn't I?"

The argument seems to quickly settle, with only Angel conveying a few more words. The argument ends, and Angel walks back outside and sits down at the table, acting as if nothing has happened.

"Is everything OK?" I ask.

"Don't worry your pretty little head," Angel says as he caresses the back of my hand. "Everything is fine."

The warmth his hand has to offer mine feels nice. So I grab his hand and hold it close to my face. The kindness and sincerity I feel from him is what I need to feel, as Kamrin had lacked showing me any kind of real affection earlier today. I close my eyes and take in the feeling. Becoming addicted to the feeling, I continue holding his hand, resting it on my face. Patiently, Angel waits.

"So what else happened when Kamrin came over?" Angel asks, as I release his hand from mine.

I told him about the storm, how the lightning was hitting the ground around the car, and how we could not leave.

Angel looks at me with relief on his face, turns back toward the kitchen, and gives John a little wink, and laughs.

"It's better that you did not go. From the way you describe, the storm could have been dangerous to drive in." Angel smiles.

"You're right. I just hope it wasn't something important that Jeffery needed to talk to me about, today," I say as I finish the last bite of my dinner.

"Wait here. I will go get the phone. We can call him, and if they really need to see you, then I will take you now," Angel says as he gets up and walks toward the door.

"It's OK. You don't have to call. If it was important, I am sure he would have insisted that I came after the storm let up. Besides, when I talked to him on the phone, he said that tomorrow would be fine and that you could just bring me," I tell Angel, trying to keep him from wasting his time.

"It's better to make sure," Angel says as he continues to walk into the kitchen to get the phone.

"If you insist," I say, as I have learned a long time ago that it is better not to argue.

Panic rises within me, as Angel does not return right away.

"Maybe it was important, and Jeffery is talking to him about whatever it is that is happening," I think to myself as I scoot my chair closer to the door so that I can hear their conversation.

"Lue, I can't get hold of him," Angel states as he walks out from the kitchen.

I can tell he is lying, as his face shows nothing but deviance.

"What is it?" I ask Angel, knowing that he is hiding something from me.

"Nothing," Angel says as he turns his head away. "I will take you there tomorrow, and we can find out what they needed to see you about."

"It seems like there is something that you are not telling me," I say in a demanding voice.

I look at him in disbelief.

"It's just that, when I called and talked with Jeffery just now . . ." Angel starts to say.

"I thought you said that Jeffery didn't answer," I interrupt.

"I said that because he told me he never talked to you today," Angel states, keeping his head lowered. "I didn't want to tell you, because of how upset you had gotten when you were trying to tell me about the phone call earlier."

He is wrong.

"That's OK. At least I know for sure that it was a dream," I lie.

I do not know why Jeffery has lied to him about talking to me, but in my heart I know it was not a dream!

"I know why he lied," I think to myself. "He is probably afraid that I told Angel that he does not want him to come with me tomorrow, and he did not want to deal with that conversation."

So I let the subject go, with the plan of talking with Jeffery tomorrow when Angel and I are face-to-face with him. As I feel he owes me an explanation and Angel an apology.

"Where did you go today?" I ask, changing the topic at hand.

"There were some things I had to take care of, nothing that you should worry about," Angel replies.

Figuring I must have asked something that is none of my business, I let the subject go and continue eating my dessert.

After dinner, Angel walks to my side, helps me out of my chair, and asks me if I would like to take a walk in the garden. I happily accept his invitation. Hand in hand, we walk along the rose-lined path through the beautiful garden.

The night air is perfect, and the exercise feels good to my rested muscles.

"What a perfect night!" I say within myself as I take in a deep breath of fresh, cool air.

The smell of flowers and freshly cut grass takes me back to times when Kamrin and I would take long walks in the woods. The memories bring me back to a time of love and happiness. I begin to hum a song in my head, the one that was playing in my room the day I was to have been married. It has always been one of my favorite songs, and I know every word to it by heart.

"What is that song you are humming?" Angel asks.

"It's called, 'Lover's lullaby,'" I answer. "It is a song that I had been playing the day . . ."

I do not want to say another word, as I always feel a little strange talking to Angel about Kamrin.

"The day . . . what?" he asks.

"Oh, nothing," I lie, as I think back to that day. "Actually, I forgot where I have heard it."

Suddenly, Angel releases his grip from my hand and begins walking ahead of me, something he has never done before. He becomes quiet as he continues to walk faster and faster toward the house, leaving me far behind him.

"I think we should head back to the house," Angel snaps, abruptly.

It is like he has read my mind and does not like what he is hearing. I begin walking as fast as I can, trying to catch up with him. Finally reaching his side once again, I try to take his hand back into mine, but he slowly moves away from my grasp.

Shocked and a little hurt, I continue to walk beside him, never touching his hand to mine again.

"I am a little tired," I say.

"Me too," Angel says, "and tomorrow is going to be a long day."

We walk into the kitchen where John is still doing dishes. We say our "good nights" and then walk upstairs.

Neither of us talking, the tension seems to grow between us. I do not like the feeling, and I wish he would say something to make it all go away.

Angel walks me to my room, says good night, then turns and walks down the hallway to his bedroom. I am still upset with the way he had become so distant from me in the garden, so I ask him to come in for a bit. He respectively declines and continues on his way.

"Good night," I say loudly in the direction Angel is walking.

My words are left unheard, and Angel keeps walking until he disappears into the darkness of the hallway.

I have a hard time falling asleep this night. I have so much going on in my head. I think about how nice Kamrin looked and how I long for him still. Then I think about the way he had treated me and how forceful he was. Without warning, my mind switched to Angel, and the feel of his touch, and how the mere sound of his voice makes me melt inside.

"How can I have these feelings for a man I just met?" I question myself again. "Why does he make me feel like I do?"

My mind is going in so many different directions at once that I start to confuse my thoughts and do not notice that I have been lying here for hours thinking. That is until I look over at the clock and see that it is now 2:00 a.m.

"I better get some sleep," I think to myself as I fluff my pillow back up. "I don't know what time Angel will want to go to the police station tomorrow, and I want to make sure I am rested."

Without warning, the room becomes cold and uninviting, so I cover my head with the blankets and try to go to sleep. I am just about to fall asleep when I hear the sound of someone walking around my room. I am excited as I believe that Angel has heard me moving restless in my room and knows I am having a hard time sleeping. He is here to tell me he is sorry for the way he acted.

"Angel?" I whisper.

No answer.

"John?" I ask, now a little worried.

No one answers, but I can still hear someone moving about. The sound is getting closer, and I now hear the sound of heavy breathing. I become frightened and start breathing heavy myself. I want to peek out to see who is there, but I am petrified to find out what awaits me beyond the comfort of my shelter. The sound of heavy breathing comes closer and closer with every second that passes. The closer the sound comes, the more my body shakes in fear. Within seconds, I begin shaking so hard that my teeth begin to chatter.

The sound is right next to my bed now. Suddenly, I can feel a hand on top of the blanket as it moves up my leg toward my waist.

"Why is someone touching me like that?" I think to myself as I jump up and pull the covers away from my head.

Standing there next to my bed is a dark shadow. It has no face, as it is wearing a black mask! He is here! He has found me! I curl into a ball and begin to cry as the whole room becomes the darkest dark I have ever witnessed. It is as if someone has taken every speck of light out of the world, leaving me in complete and utter blackness. I can no longer see where the figure is, but I can hear him and feel him touching me and the bed around me. All of a sudden, the feeling of wandering hands engulf my body, encircling it from every direction at once. There is no way one person can move as fast as this person is. Right away, I know there has to be more than one person. Frantically, I begin calling for help as loud as I can.

Suddenly, there is a bright flash that lights up the room, giving me enough time to look around so that I can find the man or men that are now taunting me. He is gone!

"Lue! Lue!" I can hear Angel screaming from outside my door.

"Angel! *Help*!" I scream. "He is in my room!"

The door flies open with such force that it comes off its hinges and belts to the other side of the room, just missing my bed. Angel turns on the lights and looks around.

"Are you OK?" Angel asks as he continues to search the room.

"He is here! He is here!" I cry over and over again as I hold my blanket close to my chest.

Angel runs to my bed and holds me tight within his arms.

"He's gone now," Angel says as he tries to calm me down.

Weeping in his arms uncontrollably, I try to explain to him what I had seen.

"It's OK," Angel assures me, holding me tight within his arms.

Angel almost has me calmed down, when all of a sudden the room becomes cold again, so cold that I can feel the frosty air nipping at my face. I instantly begin to shiver. I panic. He is coming back!

Angel releases his hold on me and looks toward the window. Interested in what he could be looking at, I peer out the window. To my bewilderment, there is a dark figure floating outside the window. Unable to comprehend what I am seeing, I look over at Angel in disbelief. Angel takes my hand and looks me in the eyes.

He looks concerned, and that makes me uneasy. My hands begin to shake, and my heart pounds as the room once again becomes dark and unsettling.

Angel suddenly lifts his arms toward the heavens above, closes his eyes, and sits silent. Instantly the moon illuminates, as if somehow Angel has summoned the power from within it to shine. Although still dark, the now-radiate moon brightens areas of my bedroom. I can now see shadows within the blackness. I do not know what is going to happen, and I am scared for both of us.

"John!" Angel yells.

Angel leaps off the bed and takes the stance of a fighting tiger. His eyes now glowing in the darkness like a wildcat.

Within seconds, John is standing by Angel's side.

Taking the same stance as Angel, he too looks as if he is ready to fight. His eyes are not as bright as Angel's, but they also begin to glow within the darkened room.

A sharp, ear-piercing sound overtakes the room. I look over at Angel and John; they are not moving and do not seem to be affected by the noise. The sound gets louder, until it is so loud that it enters through my ears and into my mind. I have to cover my ears, as I feel if I don't block the screeching noise, my mind will explode at any moment.

Without warning, the moon seems to be covered by some unforeseen cloud, causing the room to be in complete blackness once again. Suddenly, the room begins to violently shake.

I scream!

"It's OK!" Angel screams toward me.

I can hear things falling to the floor, but I cannot tell from where. I crouch into the corner of the bed and cover my head with my arms as I try to protect myself from flying objects. I am more petrified than I have ever been, as the blackness engulfing the room continues to blind me.

"Angel! What is going on?" I scream.

"John!" Angel yells. "Get her out of here!"

"No! You cannot handle his alone!" John yells back.

Angel must have realized that maybe he couldn't, because he does not push the issue any further. Standing their ground, Angel and John prepare for what will come next.

"Lue, stay there! *Do not* leave that bed! I need to know where you are at all times," Angel yells in panic.

The glass from the windows burst, throwing shards of glass throughout the room. I try to cover my body as soon as I hear the flying glass. However, I am too late and receive a few cuts.

I look at the window to see what has caused the windows to burst. To my disbelief, hovering in the window is not only one dark shadow, but now there are two. They seem to have a dark glow about them, almost like a silhouette of an illuminating black haze that outlines their bodies. They are large, and their eyes are glowing bright red beneath their masks. They are unreal; they cannot be human.

As fear grows inside me, I continue to stare at the figures in disbelief.

I need protection, so I feel around the darkness and grab the closest thing to the bed. A large silver candlestick. I sit straight up in my bed. I am ready to protect myself or at least I hope I am.

The two illuminating dark shadows enter the room, causing the room to become more unsettling than before. It is as if . . . evil . . . itself . . . has overtaken the room.

"Go now!" I hear Angel scream sternly.

"Give us what we want, and we will let you be!" the dark shadow demands.

His voice giving me the chills as his evil and immortal tone echoes throughout the room.

"You will have to kill me first!" Angel yells back.

"Then you have to go through me!" John yells.

"Look, our business is not with you," one of the shadows growls.

"If you are here for her," Angel snaps, "then it is my business."

There is a brief moment of silence.

"It would be in your best interest to do as we say," the shadow once again says in a demanding voice.

"No! You have that wrong. It would be in your best interest to leave now!" Angel yells in confidence.

The shadowed men ignore Angel's last remark and start to talk among one another, speaking in a language I have never heard. *Or have I?*

"Good luck!" Angel yells toward the men, as if he understood what they say. "You might want to go get more help. You know you don't have any powers here!" John laughs.

This must have outraged the two men, because all of a sudden a loud, vicious growl escapes their lips. Their eyes become like fire, and the room begins to shake violently. This time more powerful than before. I have to hold onto the headboard of my bed as I feel like I am going to fall off onto the floor at any moment.

Angel, still in his crouching position, stands up and walks over to where I sit still in a cowering position. Whereas, John stands and walks toward the two men hovering at the window.

Although it is hard to see in the dark, Angel and John both look taller and stronger than they had before. One thing is obvious though; they are mad as hell and ready to fight!

"Tell your boss to back off, or there will be *hell* to pay!" Angel laughs, followed by a loud laughter from John.

"You might want to rethink that last threat," the shadow snickers. "I don't think he would mind that at all."

Silence.

Angel takes my hand and whispers in my ear, "Close your eyes, Lue. I don't want you to see this." He then softly kisses my forehead and vaults over the bed like a pouncing tiger attacking its prey.

The two men that were once hovering outside the window are now in the room. John leaps forward attacking one of them, while Angel is at the side of the other one standing his ground. It is still dark with only the illumination of the two men to lighten the room, allowing me to see very little of what is going on.

Suddenly, there are loud crashes coming throughout the room as bodies are being thrown into walls. The sound of glass breaking fills my ears, as fighting men are thrown against tables and dressers. Sometimes coming so close to where I am crouched on the bed that they hit the edge of the bed, causing me to be thrown to the opposite side of where I am hiding. I am horrified. I do not want to be captive of the bed anymore. I want to run and hide.

I sit up quietly as I don't want anyone to hear me move, especially the shadowed men. It is so dark that I can barely see anyone, so I am confident that they will not be able to see me.

"I will slip out of the room and run as fast as I could down the hallway and hide somewhere," I think to myself. "I will be hidden before they know I have even left the bedroom."

That is my plan.

I start to place my feet on the floor so that I can sneak out of the room, when suddenly I hear another loud growl and Angel scream, "Don't move, Lue! Stay on the bed!"

I look down. There is no longer a floor! I can see through the wooden floor to the ground outside; it is as if we are floating in the sky. The emptiness of the floor now lighting the room as the outside sky comes up from underneath. Flabbergasted, I pick up my feet and huddle into a corner on the bed. I cannot believe my eyes.

"I must be seeing things," I say to myself.

Every part of my existence has to know what is going on. I have to know if I am hallucinating, as this is not possible; the floor could not have vanished. I reach down to touch the floor, but my fingers never touch a solid surface as there is nothing but air beyond my bed. Quickly I pull my hand away and sit back against the headboard. I am disconcerted.

"What is going on?" I ask myself as I think back to the walkway that had led to where the tortured women had been and how beyond the stairs was the same as now, an empty hole.

Without warning, something bumps the headboard so hard that I fear that someone has jumped onto the bed. I look up. It is one of the shadowed men. He is now standing next to me. His eyes, glowing like fire, begin to hypnotize me, making me want to go with him. They are so beautiful, as the bright red glow seems to twirl around in his eyes like a fiery hole. I want him. I trust him. I lower the covers from on top of me and move over closer to him; wanting to touch him I begin to reach for his hand, when suddenly I hear a desperate cry come from Angel, causing me to snap out of my trance.

"*No!*" Angel yells as he overtakes the man.

Now furious, Angel picks the man up with one hand and throws him across the room, causing the wall to crash around him. An ear-piercing growl comes from deep inside the man as he stands once again. Angel, without hesitation, pounces on the man again, throwing him into the wall on the opposite side of the room. Showing no mercy on the stranger, Angel moves swiftly to his side, throwing him over and over again, each time reaching his beaten body before the man can get up. I don't know why, but it starts to bother me as I continue hearing the man's limp body crashing into the walls all around me. The sound of bones being broken echoes throughout the room, disturbing my heart and soul.

"Just stop!" I scream inside myself as I hold my hands over my ears, shaking my head back and forth.

I know they have come here to harm us, but the man is tired and weak, and I do not know how much more of a beating he can take, as Angel is not letting up. It is like he is someone entirely different, someone who is capable of viciously killing another and do not think twice about it. I want Angel to stop attacking him, before the man dies. I cannot take it anymore.

Tears stream down my face.

Angel standing over the beaten man screams, "I told you . . . You have no power here!"

The man slowly stands up. Holding onto the wall for support, he leans his head toward Angel's ear and snarls, "Prepare for *hell!*"

A chill engrosses through the room, as the two men simultaneously disappear into a dark haze, leaving only a slight growl fading into the distance.

An eye-blinding light flashes the room, blinding me.

Someone is coming toward me! I am paralyzed from fear, as my eyes are unable to focus on anything in the room. I cannot see who it is.

"Have they come back?" I cry in fear within myself.

Suddenly, someone touches my hand. Instantly, I know it's Angel, as the touch is that of strength and warmth. I feel an overwhelming relief, as I know Angel and John have won the battle, and we are all safe.

"They won't return tonight," Angel says. "You will be safe."

The lights come back, and I can now see that both Angel and John are standing next to me. They both look beaten and seem to be suffering cuts on their arms and faces. I look around. The bedroom is in shambles and looks as if a tornado has hit it. All the beautiful things that Angel had put in the room are now shattered among the floor.

"Is she going to be OK?" I hear John ask Angel.

"She will be fine," Angel assures him.

Unable to comprehend why they are talking about me like I am even there, I find myself staring blankly into Angel's eyes. As I try to ensure them that I am OK, I realize that I must be in shock, as not a word comes out of my mouth. It's like I am there, and I can see and hear everyone around me, but I cannot react to them. Nothing I try to do changes the fear that has taken over my mind and body.

"Lie down now, Lue. It's time for you to sleep," Angel says, as he places his hands on my cheek. I can feel a wave of warmth overtake my body. Instantly, peace overcomes my body, and I fall fast asleep.

The next morning, I wake up with a quick jolt, as the memory of what happened the night before comes to my mind. I sit up in bed and quickly look around. Everything is in its place as if it had all been a dream, as there is not a thing broken.

I continue to search the room for any possible indication of the events of last night.

The windows are no longer busted, and the floor is wood once again. I cannot believe my eyes. It had happened; it was real, and I know it! Last night, the floor was gone, the room was in shambles.

I reach down and touch the wooden floor. It is solid.

Silently, I sit on my bed. I know deep in my heart that it had not been a dream, as I can still see the red fiery eyes of the intruders.

Curious, I get up and look around. Picking up every object in the room piece by piece, I inspect it thoroughly, looking for any indication that they had been glued back together, or in that matter, ever been broken at all. Everything is perfect, with not a scratch on it.

"I have to talk with Angel or John," I think to myself. "I have to know what is going on."

I take a quick shower, get dressed, and head downstairs to find Angel, as I think he is the one I should be talking with.

With the smell of bacon in the air, I know the first place to look is the kitchen, as I know I will find John there, and I am sure he will know the whereabouts of Angel. When I enter the kitchen, I see Angel cooking breakfast as if nothing had happened the night before. The sounds of my footsteps must have startled him, because he flinches and turns quickly around.

"Good morning." He smiles one of his wonderful smiles.

He is wearing a funny apron; it is pink with the words, "Kiss the cook," on it. I begin to laugh at the sight of such a big, strong man wearing a woman's apron.

"What's so funny?" Angel asks.

"Nothing. You just look so cute in that apron," I reply.

"Oh," Angel laughs, "it was my mother's. I wear it whenever I cook."

It seems strange not seeing John in the kitchen, so I look around the adjacent rooms, trying to find him.

"Where's John?" I inquire.

"He had to run an errand for me. He will be back later," Angel answers.

I want to ask Angel about last night, and I know the only way to start the conversation is to just ask and hope that he doesn't think I am crazy, as I am still uncertain if it was a dream or not.

"Angel," I say in a soft voice.

"Yes, sweetie," Angel answers.

"What happened last night?" I ask.

"I'm sorry, I know I acted rudely to you at the end of the night," Angel explains as he places his hand on my shoulder. "I was really tired, and I guess a little grippe."

Now I am really confused. I do not know if he has brought that subject up because he doesn't want to talk about the dark, shadowed men or if he truly doesn't know what I am asking. But I know there is only one way to find out for sure. I have to bluntly ask him.

"That's OK. I understand," I say, "but I am talking about in the room, you know the shadowed men."

"What?" Angel asks. "What do you mean by shadowed men?"

"Last night in my room, there were two shadowed men. You and John were fighting them," I try to explain as fast as I can.

"Sweetie, I never went in to your room last night, and I am certain that no shadowed men were there," Angel says as he gives me the strangest look.

"You have to know what I am talking about," I beg. "It couldn't have been a dream. It was all too real."

"I'm sorry, Lue, I really don't know what you're talking about," Angel says as he rubs his hand lightly on my hair.

"But the floor disappeared in the room. The room was torn to shreds," I continue talking trying to state my case.

"Sweetie, I peeked in your room this morning, and the room was the same as it always has been," Angel says as he starts putting the food he has made onto the table. "I think that maybe you had a nightmare. Just think about it, how could a floor disappear?"

"I don't know, but it did!" I snap.

"Lue, I really think you had a nightmare. There is no way a floor can disappear like that," Angel says as he walks back in the kitchen to get a pitcher of orange juice for our breakfast. "Besides, look at me. Do I look like I was in a fight?"

I look at his body closely to see if I could see any sign that he had been in a fight. His perfect body is without a scratch.

"No, you look perfect," I admit with a smile on my face. "I guess it was a nightmare."

"That's better. I like to see you smile," Angel says as he walks by me, stopping to give me a kiss on the forehead.

"I guess I need to get those nightmares under control." I smile as I help him with the last of the food.

We walk out to the back patio, where he has a beautiful table set up. It has a rose tablecloth that drapes to the floor, with pink napkins to match. The table setting is made up of pearlescent-blue crystal and silver, both of which sparkle in the sun, throwing off rainbows throughout the awning.

"The table looks beautiful." I smile.

"A beautiful table for a beautiful woman," Angel says, helping me to my seat.

The morning air is perfect, no need for a jacket or even a sweater. It is going to be a wonderful day.

I take in a deep breath of fresh morning air.

I love being outside; it is one of the things I missed most of the three years I was kept in that dark dungeon. I could now sit outside staring at the garden all day, taking in the fresh smells around me.

Suddenly, I begin to laugh.

"What is so funny?" Angel asks as he gives me a look of bewilderment.

"I am thinking about how crazy I must have sounded, talking about shadowed men and floors that disappear," I say as I continue to laugh.

"You didn't sound crazy at all," Angel says with a smile. "I have had plenty of dreams that seemed so real that when I woke up, I thought they had really happened."

Suddenly, the phone inside begins to ring, interrupting our meal and our conversation.

"I will be right back," Angel says as he heads in to answer the phone.

"OK," I say as I continue to devour the delicious meal that he has prepared.

Angel returns after only a few minutes. He is no longer smiling; in fact, he looks worried.

"Something wrong?" I ask.

"That was Jeffery on the phone. He needs you to go down to the police station right away," Angel explains.

"Is everything OK?" I ask as I choke down the piece of bacon I have just put into my mouth.

"I'm not sure. He said you should come right away," Angel replies. "I can wrap up your breakfast and take it with us, if you like."

I knew he had wanted to see me today, but when Kamrin was here yesterday, he made it sound like it was not very important. Now Angel is acting like it is urgent. Something must have changed. I don't know if I am more excited at the possibility that they have found my parents alive or more scared that they hadn't found them at all or worse yet, they are dead. All I know is that all of a sudden my heart and mind become flooded with different emotions, leaving me uncertain if I want to laugh or cry.

"No, we better be going," I say as my stomach begins to flutter. "I don't know if I can eat anymore knowing that they called and wanted us right now. It sounds important."

"Are you ready to go?" Angel asks as he reaches for my hand to help me from my chair.

"Sure," I answer, taking his hand into mine.

Angel helps me from my chair, and with his hand in mine, we walk toward the kitchen door.

"Shouldn't we clean up this food first?" I ask, although I am hoping that he will say no, as I want to get to the police station as quickly as I can.

"Don't worry about it. I will have someone clean it up," Angel answers. "I think we should get you to that police station, before your nerves take you over anymore than they already have."

Angel walks over to the area where he keeps his keys hung up, grabs the keys to the truck, and we head to the front door.

Within seconds, we are in the truck and driving down the long winding road toward town.

CHAPTER 10

The Final Good-bye

THE RIDE TO the station seems to take forever. I need to know what Jeffery has to say, and I am becoming impatient.

"Are we almost there?" I ask Angel for the tenth time.

"Just about," Angel answers as he reaches for my shaking hand and holds it tight in his.

I take in a deep breath and sigh out loud. I am nervous, and I do not know what to do with myself. Without realizing what I am doing, I begin fiddling with the radio, turning it from station to station, trying to find a certain song, but I have no idea what song I am looking for.

"I have some CDs if you want to hear something specific," Angel says as he reaches in the backseat and grabs a large black case full of CDs.

"Sorry, I didn't realize I was doing that," I say as I shut the radio off. "I'm a little fidgety."

"I understand," Angel says as he looks over at me and smiles. "But you don't have to be fidgety for too much longer. The police station is right around the corner."

I look up. He is right. I have been so preoccupied playing with the radio that I had not realized that we are already in town.

"Please let it be good news," I think to myself as we pull into the driveway of the police station.

As soon as the truck slows to a crawl, I jump out and begin running to the front entrance of the police station, never saying a word to Angel. I have forgotten to have Angel drop me off like Jeffery had requested on the phone the day before. Before I know it, Angel is by my side. I don't have the heart to tell him what Jeffery had requested, and I don't quite understand it myself . . . so I decide to ignore his request and let him stay.

I tell the lady working the front desk that I am here to see Jeffery. However, before I can tell her why, she is escorting us to a room in the back of the station.

"Jeffery will be right with you," she states as she opens the door to the room.

The room is bright and unwelcoming. The room is empty except for a long metal table in the middle of the floor with just a few metal chairs around it. I have already sat down at the table, when I realize that the table is full of the pictures I had taken from the cabin. My stomach begins to turn, as the thought of looking at them again sickens me. I turn my head and focus on Angel's eyes, as I know by doing so I will be able to stay calm and focused. He is looking back at me with concern, as if he can feel the anxiety growing inside of me. Taking my hand and holding it tight, he tries to reassure me.

"You are strong, Lue . . . Stronger than you think. You can do this," he says with a smile.

The door opens, and there in the doorway stands Jeffery and Kamrin. Instantly, their eyes focus onto Angel. Then simultaneously, they both begin glaring at the table at Angel's and mine hands. Slowly I remove my hands from Angel's, acting like I have to scratch my face, ensuring that I do not hurt his feelings by my reactions. My efforts are useless. Angel seems to know what I am doing and lets out a quiet sigh as he shakes his head.

"Wouldn't you be more comfortable outside?" Kamrin snaps at Angel.

"No! I am fine right here," Angel snarls back.

The tension is thick in the room, and I hope that soon it will be broken, or I fear that Kamrin and Angel will start fighting at any moment. There is a moment of silence in the room and then a loud screech as Jeffery scoots his chair under the table.

"Lue, we went through the bag of pictures Angel gave us," says Jeffery. "In the bag was a message."

"A message?" I ask. "I don't understand."

"Yes, a message," Jeffery bluntly says.

"A message to whom?" I ask.

"Lue . . . it is to you," Jeffery replies.

"I put the pictures in the bag," I state. "There could have not been a message. The bag was empty before I put them in there."

"I don't know what to say," says Jeffery. "There is one now."

"Angel looked in the bag. He never said anything about a note," I state, in disbelief.

"As a matter of fact, I didn't," he states as he turns and gives Jeffery a look of disgust.

"See," I say firmly, "you have to be wrong."

"Maybe you missed it," Jeffery states. "All I can say is there is a note, and it was found in the bag."

"And it's to me?" I ask sarcastically.

"I think I already said that," Jeffery snaps.

I ignore his condescending tone.

"What is the message?" I ask.

Jeffery takes a piece of paper out of a folder and lays it on the table, then scoots it toward my direction for me to read. I hold it in my quivering hands for a minute, never looking at the writing.

"I can't . . ." I sob, as I lay it back on the table. "I just can't do it. Someone read it to me."

You will think I have asked them to kill someone, as all of a sudden no one has a thing to say.

With only the sounds of our breaths, I plead again.

"Please, I have to know what it says," I beg, as I look at everyone in the room. "I just don't have the heart to read it myself."

Jeffery hesitates for a moment more, then picks the note up and begins to read it.

The message read:

> *Death gives me power, and power is what I desire. Every life I have taken has been so that Lue and I could be together forever. I will continue to do this until she gives me what I want.*

That's where the note ends.

The room begins to spin, and my ears ring. I feel as if I am going to pass out. I look around. My eyes become blurred, and I cannot focus on anything or anyone around me. I try to talk, but nothing comes out of my mouth. I have caused all these deaths. In some demented way, I am responsible for these women's pain, and I have no idea why.

Kamrin puts his arms around me. "Lue . . . there is one more thing. We found a picture of your mom and dad on my car today. It had a note attached. They are gone."

"Gone? What do you mean gone? Just say what you mean . . . Dead?" I scream in agony.

"Sorry, Lue. But yes," Kamrin replies as he holds me tight within his arms.

My head starts to pound, and vomit rises to my throat. I try to hold it in, but my emotions refuse. My breakfast is coming back up, and I have no way of stopping it. Angel, being the kind man that he is, hands me a bucket and holds his jacket above my head, shielding me from any onlookers. I become violently ill.

"Thank you," I say as I look up into Angel's caring eyes.

I want to scream, I want to yell, but I know none of that will help those women now, so I sit up, wipe my mouth off, and try to calm myself down. I have so many questions I want to ask and so much information that I want to ensure that they are clear about. Things such as, where the house is and how far away I believe the cabin is from the house. Everything and anything that I can remember, I want them to know. They have to catch this evil, delusional man before he can hurt anybody else.

"You say there is a picture?" I ask as I swallow a lump that is lingering in my throat.

"Yes," replies Jeffery as he hands me a glass of water.

"Were they in a dungeon?" I ask.

"Actually, we cannot be for certain," Jeffery answers. "We have never seen it."

"I want to see it!" I cry. "I have to know if it is the dungeon."

"Are you sure?" Angel asks, holding my hand.

"I don't think that is a good idea," Kamrin snaps as he glares over at Angel.

I sit for a while longer thinking to myself. *I have to know what happened to them and if they were brought to the same place as I!*

"I can handle it!" I cry. "I have to see for myself!"

Jeffery hands me a Polaroid picture. The picture has spots of dry blood on it. The pictures are facing down, and I am happy for that.

I sit and hold the pictures in my hand, all the while rubbing the outside film with my fingers. I want to see, but I am scared to see the horror that I know they had went through. Sitting for a few moments longer, I know what I have to do. Quickly, I turn over the pictures and look at the photos.

"*No!*" I scream as I fall to the ground in a fetal position.

The photos are worse than any I have seen! My parents have been bound in barbwire. Their skin is peeled from their bodies, leaving only raw muscle and bones to remain. They have been gutted, and their intestines are wrapped around their bodies like rope. What they must have went through, all because I wanted to be free! I close my eyes and begin to cry harder than I have ever cried before.

Hyperventilating, I find it hard to catch my breath. I want to run away from everything, from everyone. No . . . I want to turn back time and return to my captor so that my parents could live!

"I will never get away from his clutches!" I scream between my sobs.

I look at the pictures one more time. I want to see their faces. I want to say that I am sorry. I want to say good-bye.

I turn the pictures over one more time, hold them close to my face, open my eyes, and stare. I cannot deal with what I am looking at. They no longer have eyes, and their faces are unrecognizable. They have suffered so much pain.

"Why did he take their eyes?" I kept repeating over and over in my head. "They never saw him. They cannot not 'tell' in death . . . They cannot "tell" in death."

"Are you sure this is them?" I ask in denial.

"Lue, we have not found their bodies, so I cannot say 100 percent that it is them. But so far according to the evidence, it is," Jeffery replies.

"Evidence? There's more?" I cry.

"Each picture came with a little something that we are doing DNA testing on to make sure," Jeffery answers.

"Little something?" I ask.

Jeffery looks around as if he is trying to get an approval from someone to tell me the rest of the story. Kamrin looks back, shrugs his shoulders at Jeffery, and turns away. No one wants to tell me what has happened. I become aggravated and demand to know the rest.

"How much worse can it be?" I scream.

"There were fingers attached to the pictures," Jeffery whispered, "and something else we hoped that you could identify. Well, actually we are hoping that you cannot identify."

"I'm confused. Which is it?" I snap at Jeffery. "Do you want me to or not?"

"We are hoping that you will not be able to, and that maybe they are not theirs," Jeffery explains.

Jeffery takes a little bag from his shirt pocket, opens it, and scoots two wedding rings across the table.

They are parents' wedding rings!

In a rage of fury, I pick the picture back up and rip it to shreds.

"You son of a bitch!" I scream as I throw the pieces of ripped-up pictures across the room, "I will kill you!"

Everyone turns to me as if they are shocked at what I said, or maybe it is because my scream echoes throughout the station, causing people passing by to stop and look into the room.

I begin crying again. I cannot control my emotions. I am madder than hell, and at the same time, I am so sad that I cannot control my crying. I don't know if I want to hit someone or curl in a ball and cry. All I know is that I want all of this to go away.

Did my freedom have to come with so many consequences? It doesn't matter; my captor is killing innocent people and will continue whether I am there or not. That is obvious by the hundreds of pictures that I found at the cabin, some of which was dated over ten years ago. Way before he had taken me. The note makes no sense to me. He is a killer and always will be.

"No matter what I do, people are going to die in the hands of evil!" I scream. "Why me?"

Kamrin is at my side, rubbing my back trying to comfort me.

It feels nice.

"What about the possibilities of other men working with him?" I ask. "Have you been able to figure that out as of yet?"

"No, sorry, Lue," Jeffery says, looking over at Kamrin.

"Well, then it looks like you don't know shit!" I scream.

I am now livid.

"It's OK, Lue," Kamrin says over and over again, still rubbing my back.

I push Kamrin's hand away with extreme force, look up at him, and scream, "It's OK? It's OK? I lost my home . . . I lost my fiancé . . . and now I have lost my parents . . . And it's OK? No, Kamrin, it is not OK! Because not only did I lose all of that, there are a lot of families out there that has lost a daughter, an aunt, a mother, someone they loved – all because of a sick and twisted man! All because of me!"

Kamrin looks aggravated at what I am saying.

"Just go home to your wife . . . Kamrin. She needs you, *not me!*" I scream as I stare into his eyes. "You're too late for me. Where were you three years ago? Just go and leave me!"

Angel gives off a little smirk as if he is enjoying what I am saying. I don't care at that moment. I don't want to be around anyone, and I definitely don't want to be around the man who had given up on me years ago.

Kamrin steps back and looks at me, his expression nothing more than complete pain and hurt. I can see that he had not meant to upset me. That in fact he is only trying to show me compassion, and I have overreacted. I feel bad for what I said, and I want to take it back. But I am too late; Kamrin walks out of the door.

"Angel, take me home, please," I say as I look up at Jeffery.

Jeffery is standing up, his mouth open and tears in his eyes. He looks at me with complete disgust on his face and says, "He is trying to help you. He looked for you for years . . . Lue. Nobody knew where you were!"

I lower my head in shame. My emotions had overcome me, and I had hurt the one that I loved, and now he is gone.

"I know, Jeffery," I say. "Please tell him that I'm sorry. I really didn't mean the things I said."

"I would hope not!" Jeffery snaps. "That was very rude."

I begin to cry again.

"She said she was sorry," Angel yells at Jeffery. "She has been through a lot. Why don't you guys give her a break?"

"Give her a break?" Jeffery snaps. "She has done nothing but lie since she has returned."

"What do you mean?" I scream. "I have not lied to him at all."

"Oh, really? What about the way I found you the other day? You had bandages, scars, and a broken leg. Now look at you. You have not a scratch on you," Jeffery says as he points to the various parts of my body. "As far as we can see, that was all made up. Maybe a little show for everyone so that we don't think that you had been kidnapped, so we don't think that you had left Kamrin for some pretty boy."

"What are you saying, Jeffery?" I yell as I slam my fist onto the table. "You think I made this all up?"

"Well, did you?" Jeffery says in a devious tone.

"You cannot be serious. You have known me for most of my life, what about me would make you think I would ever capable of hurting another person?" I scream as loud as I can.

I ignore the fact that a crowd of onlookers has gathered outside the window. I want Jeffery to know how appalled I am by his accusations.

"Oh, we don't think you hurt these women," Jeffery explained in a sarcastic tone. "We think you found the pictures and made the rest of it up."

"What?" I ask as I glare at him. "What about my parents? Where do you think those pictures came from?"

"That we are still looking into," Jeffery says as he gives me the strangest grin. "So don't leave town until we know for sure."

"You son of a bitch! You think I killed my parents!" I scream as I grab Angel's jacket from the table. "Go to hell!"

I could have solved the whole problem by insisting that Angel explain to John and me how my scars and leg had healed overnight. But with the way Jeffery is acting, I don't think they deserve to know. After all, he knows me and has to know I am not capable of doing what he is accusing me of.

As we head for the door, Jeffery pulls Angel to the side and whispers something in his ear. It must have not been good, as Angel looks back at me with a look of disgust on his face. They talk quietly for a few minutes more and then part abruptly.

The trip home is quiet, as I still don't feel like talking. I stare out the window at the passing trees, thinking about everything that has happened and everything that is happening now. I have lost everyone I have ever loved in my life, and now my fiancé's brother thinks I am lying and that I have killed my parents. How did my life become such turmoil, when all I dreamed about for three years was getting back to my loved ones? Tears begin to fall down my face. I have no control.

I begin crying hysterically. My heart is broken, and I want my mom and dad so bad that it hurts every inch of my body. I never got to see them! I should have let them come and see me at the hospital, and most of all, I should have stayed the scared monster that I was. Then at least I know they would have believed my story, and maybe I would still have a chance of getting Kamrin back into my life. Now all hopes are gone. They are just gone! I start hitting the window with my fist. I am angry!

"I tried to protect them, you know." I sob as I look at Angel. "I kept them from the hospital so . . . so . . . that evil man will not find them."

"I know, Lue. It's not your fault. There is nothing anyone could do. The man is beyond evil," Angel says as he takes my hand into his.

"I didn't kill them," I cry.

"I know, sweetie, and I think they know that too," Angel says as he caresses the top of my hand lightly with his thumb. "There is just so much going on right now that they have to look at every possible angle."

The car becomes quiet again, with merely the sounds of my sorrowful sobs. As we pull up to the front of the house, I wipe the tears from my eyes. The house looks tired and old. It is no longer as beautiful as it once was. The once-amazing flowers are now wilting and dying. The elegant stained glass windows on the front doors no longer glisten in the light, and there is not a bird singing anywhere. It is almost like everything around me, including the house, is feeling my pain. Nothing is beautiful in the world anymore. My depression has come back, and I do not care about anything or anyone, including myself.

Reluctantly, I get out of the truck and walk toward the front door. Before we enter the house, Angel stops and put his arms around me, allowing me to cry within his caring arms.

"Lue, I am always here for you. Remember that," Angel says as he kisses the top of my head.

"Thank you," I say as I lay my head on his shoulder.

As we enter the house, something makes me look up at the chandelier. It looks older than I remember, and the angels that lined the iron around it, no longer look at peace. Suddenly, a drop of water falls onto my cheek, as if the angels that are above me are crying too. I look over at Angel; he merely smiles, takes my hand, and walks me upstairs to my room.

I stay in my room for the rest of the day. I do not want to see or talk to anyone. I just want to be alone.

John comes in a few times trying to get me to eat something, but I am not interested as I can't keep anything down. I am tired, but I can't sleep. My mind is racing so fast that I find it hard to concentrate on any specific thing more than a few seconds.

At times, I walk aimlessly around my room, hoping to clear my mind of all the bad thoughts. It seems to work but only for a moment. Then everything come rushing back worse than before.

"Lue?" I hear at the door.

"Yes," I answer.

"It's me, Angel. Can I come in for a moment?"

"Sure," I reply.

The door opens. Angel is standing in the doorway with a large box. It looks heavy, but he seems to carry it with ease.

"What's that?" I inquire.

"I went and got this for you. I thought it might cheer you up," Angel says as he lays the large box next to me.

I really don't see how anything can make me feel better, but I don't want to hurt his feelings, so I open the box. To my surprise, it is full of pictures – my mom's pictures that she had collected over the years! I smile as I take out each one and look at them. I do not know how or when he did this, but I am grateful he did.

"I will let you be so that you can look at these alone," says Angel, as he walks toward the door.

"No . . . Stay here with me," I insist.

"Are you sure you feel like company?" Angel asks.

"Please," I reply.

Angel sits next to me on the floor as I take out each picture, telling him stories about each one. We sit for hours laughing and crying. It is just what I need. I look at each picture at least three times, as I do not want the memories to fade.

"Thank you," I say, as I smile.

"You're welcome, sweetie." Angel smiles.

"Angel," I ask, "what did Jeffery say to you today?"

"He told me to watch you closely," Angel replies.

"Why?" I ask.

Angel hesitates.

I can tell there is something that he does not want to tell me. His eyes never leaving the ground in front of him, he tries to change the subject many times by asking about different pictures.

"Why, Angel?" I demand to know.

Angel looks up at me slowly, never looking at me straight in the eyes.

"There was another note with the pictures that they found today," Angel says quietly.

"And?" I ask.

"The note named everyone you know and said, 'Be prepared for hell opening up and swallowing them,'" Angel says as he looks at me with sorrow.

"Why would they worry about that the note, when they think I have done nothing but lie?" I ask.

"Jeffery says to watch you just in case," Angel answers.

I still cannot believe that they, even for a second, thought that I would do the things that Jeffery has accused me of. I guess all that counts is that Angel believes me, and I know the truth.

I have nothing to say. I have seen what this man can do, and I know that it is not over. I turn away so that Angel does not have to see me cry again.

The man in the mask has won, and I know it.

I want to go to sleep, so I ask Angel if he would mind leaving as I want to go to bed. Angel stands up, kisses me on the forehead, says good night, and heads out the door.

"Leave it open," I request, as I am still not totally convinced that the night before had been a dream. And I want Angel to hear me if something happens again.

All the emotions I had gone through must have taken a toll on me because I sleep harder than I ever have before. When I wake the next morning, I do the usual. However, without the enthusiasm I once had. I have lost my parents and the man I was going to marry. And I may lose my freedom again, if they prosecute me for killing my parents. That is a reality I have to come in terms with. There is not much for me anymore, except to wait for the conclusion of this nightmare I am in.

I go downstairs to find John once again in the kitchen cooking breakfast.

"He is a sweet man," I think to myself.

"Angel is in the garden waiting for you," John says before I can say a word.

He has a sorrow to his voice, and I know that Angel has told him what has happened.

"Thank you," I say as I walk toward the door.

"Lue, I am sorry for your loss," John says as he walks over and hugs me.

"Now how is it that two men who barely met me knows more about me and trusts me more than people I have known for years?" I think to myself. "I have to find out how I got healed so that I can tell Kamrin and Jeffery, so that they know I am not lying about being taken and kept for so many years."

I have to make this situation better as fast as I can.

I turn around, grab two apples from the table, and walk out the door. I expected to see Angel at the patio table, but he is not there. Suddenly I hear a soft, calming singing coming from somewhere within the garden. I begin walking around the large garden in search of Angel, following the sound as it comes closer and more vivid. The singing is beautiful and the most mesmerizing sound I have ever heard. I want to sit down right where I stand and soak in the feeling of complete peace that the singing is putting upon me. But I know I have to keep looking for Angel. I have to make him tell me the truth.

After searching for a few minutes more, I am finally able to find him in the middle of the garden.

He is busy doing something, but I can't tell what it is. As I get closer, I can see that he has put in a large water fountain. It is beautiful; it has three angels in the middle of it with their wings spread afar.

"I have another surprise for you. I hope you don't mind," Angel says, with a smile upon his face.

I look in front of the fountain, and there lies two new wooden crosses. They are hand-engraved in roses and vines. They are amazing!

"I made these for you. I thought you might want to leave them here in remembrance of your parents." Angel smiles.

Instantly, I forget what I had wanted to talk to him about.

I smile and hug Angel, never wanting to let him go. I cannot believe that I have found such a wonderful man or that such a wonderful man has found me. He always seems to know exactly what I need to take my cares away. Now, I know I have a reason to live. I have my Angel.

"Thank you," I say, as I kiss his cheek.

"I did not put their names on them. I thought that would be something we could do later . . . When you are ready," Angel suggests.

We work in the garden for hours, planting flowers around my parents' makeshift graves. When we are done, each cross lies in a garden of beautiful fresh flowers; they are impeccable. I would not have wanted them anywhere else. They will always be close to me and even if am to leave here. I know that Angel will always be a part of my life, and I can come here anytime I want to visit the crosses.

"Perfect," I say with a smile.

After giving my parents the best and proper burial we can, I talk awhile about my parents, about things they had accomplished in their lives, and how they loved me without limitations. I tell stories of when I was child and how they always were there for me, no matter what mistakes I made while growing up.

I look up to the heavens above and tell my parents how I will miss them with all my heart and how much I will always love them. I am at peace again.

After giving my parents a sincere eulogy, I lie on the grass in front of the crosses and look up to the blue sky. Angel lies next to me, and we both take in the sunshine. I lay one hand on the two crosses next to me and place the other next to Angel's hand. I want to hold his hand so bad, but I do want to take the chance of my touch being unwelcomed by him. That kind of heartache is not what I need right now.

It seems like we have been lying there for hours, when in reality it has only been minutes, maybe even seconds. I can feel the anticipation growing in my body, as I wait and hope that he will take my hand into his so that I can experience the feeling I am longing for.

I close my eyes in disappointment.

Suddenly, I can feel the warm, soft touch of his fingers, as he outlines each and every one of my fingers, before he places his hand into mine. Instantly, my stomach gets butterflies, and I know there is something about him that I want dearly.

We both turn toward each other and smile. I lean forward and kiss Angel softly on the lips. They are warm and inviting, and I do not want it to end. We kiss for a few moments more, as I take in the sweet taste of candy from his lips. As we part lips, I look up to the sky and see two white doves soaring in the sky. Instantly, I know my parents are there with me and always will be.

"Angel? Where are your parents?" I ask.

"They died a long time ago, sweetie," Angel says in a quiet voice.

"Oh," I sigh, "I'm sorry."

CHAPTER II

The Visitors

WE MUST HAVE fallen asleep out on the lawn, as the next thing I know, I wake up to the feeling of water being dripped on my face. I look up; the sky has turned dark, and it is now raining. I am getting wet.

"Oh, crap!" I think to myself as I look over at Angel.

He is still asleep and looks to be at total peace. I lie there staring at him as the rain continues to shower my body. I am getting wetter by the moment, but the rain never seems to touch him. Confused, I look all around us. Everything is wet except him.

"How can this be?" I ask myself.

I look closer and see that he seems to have this magnificent white haze around him that is keeping the water from reaching his body. Astonished, I sit up and lean toward him. I have to know how this is happening. It is the strangest thing. The rain is hitting the haze that is encircling his body, then instantly rolls off, as if he is covered in a thin sheet of glass.

Although I continue to get wet from the rain, I am in complete amazement over what I am seeing. Curiosity overtakes me, and I have to know what this haze is. I reach over, and with the mere tips of my fingers, I touch it. Instantly, the feeling of complete tranquility rushes through my body, then a slight shock. The feeling catches me by surprise. Instantly, I pull my hand out from whatever has overtaken Angel's body.

"What was that?" I ask myself in excitement.

A feeling like no other overtakes my senses, and I have to touch it again. I reach over and put both my hands within the haze. Once again the sense of peace overtakes my mind, as the sensation of a slight shock races through my body. It's exhilarating, as it makes my entire body feel alive and energized. I am not scared in the least, so I continue moving my hands up and down his body, taking in the comfort that the haze is offering me.

Without warning, the haze disappears, and the water falls onto Angel. Instantly, he is as wet as me.

"What the heck?" Angel says in a loud voice as he jumps up from where he is sleeping. "Why did you throw water on me?"

I begin to laugh.

"I didn't throw water on you, it's raining," I say as I continue to laugh.

"See," I say as I point up to the rain clouds above.

"Oh, shoot, we better get out of here," Angel says as he reaches to take my hand.

We both jump up and run for cover. However, by the time we reach the house, there is not a dry area left on our bodies.

"Where did that come from?" Angel chuckles. "It was such a beautiful day."

"It still is beautiful," I say with a smile. "I love everything about the rain, especially the smell outside after a spring shower."

"But this isn't spring," Angel says teasing me. "This is winter."

"True, but it is still nice. A little chilly but still nice," I say as I wrap my arms around myself and start shivering.

"We better get inside and get some dry clothes on," Angel says as he winks at me. "I don't want you to get sick."

"I'm fine," I say as I continue to shake. "I just want to watch the rain a few minutes longer."

"Well, then at least let me get you a jacket," Angel says in a concerned voice.

"OK," I state as Angel walks toward the door to go inside.

I close my eyes and listen to the outside wonder, as the rain hits the roof above me.

"What a beautiful song!" I think to myself.

Before I know it, Angel is back with a jacket for me and one for him. After ensuring that I have my jacket on, he takes my hand and walks me over to an area near the porch that I have not seen before. It isn't like the rest of the porch where it has an awning made of stone; this area looks as if it has been recently built and still has an awning made of plastic where the builders have not finished the roof.

"Let's sit here and watch the rain," Angel says as he leads me to a porch swing, big enough for a party of people. "I always like the way the rain glistens from the light in this area. That is why I am having the porch extended here."

"Looking over the porch, I can see that you are able to see the entire garden from here." He is right; the rain seems to sparkle within the hundreds of lights that fill the garden, making it look like thousands of lightning bugs fluttering in the night air.

"This is beautiful!" I say as I sit next to Angel.

I lean my head on his shoulder and start to think about our kiss. It was a wonderful kiss. In fact, it was magical. I find myself wanting to kiss him again.

"What are you thinking about?" Angel asks softly. "You seem to be at peace."

"I am thinking about our kiss," I say as I look into his eyes.

I'm mortified. I can't believe that I told him what I was thinking about. I wasn't going to, but before I know it, my mouth is spewing the words. Now embarrassed, I lay my head back down on his shoulder and bury my face into his jacket.

"Why are you hiding?" Angel laughs.

"I'm embarrassed that I told you," I say in a muffled voice.

Angel leans back, pulls my head from within his jacket, and with gentle hands lifts my face to his.

"There is no need to be embarrassed," he says as he leans forward, placing his lips on mine.

We engage in a passionate kiss. It is a kiss like I have never experienced before. It is like he has just entered my soul and is stealing every bit of love that I have ever had for any other man and is taking it to be his own.

I don't want it to end. But I am afraid, as I have never felt like this, and I am not sure if I am ready for such a feeling. Kamrin still occupies a piece of my heart.

Without warning, a flash of lightning lights up the sky, causing a clap of thunder to echo throughout the garden. I flinch and instantly stop kissing Angel.

It is now raining so hard that I can no longer see the garden in front of me, as it is now being blocked by a wall of rain.

I look over at Angel; he does not seem to be worried, and in fact, he looks as if he doesn't have a care in the world.

"Should we go in?" I ask.

"If you want to," Angel says as he smiles at me. "But if you're worried about the storm, don't worry, it won't hurt you."

His words are that of certainty. I feel we are safe for the moment.

We sit there for a while longer watching as the rain continues to pour down. The night is beautiful and so is the company I am with, as I am enjoying every moment I am spending with Angel.

"Angel?" I say.

"Yes," he answers.

"Earlier, when we were lying on the grass in the garden, it began to rain," I start to explain. "By the time I woke up, I was wet. When I looked over at you, you didn't have a speck of water. In fact, you had . . ."

Suddenly, the plastic that has been shielding us from the rain rips in half. The pooled-up water instantly descends upon us, soaking every inch of our bodies.

"I guess that is our cue to go inside." Angel laughs as he grabs my drenched hand.

We both run as fast as we can back to shelter. Once again, my question is left unanswered.

"Now we better get you out of those wet clothes." Angel chuckles as he takes my hair into his hands and tries to get some of the water out of it.

"I think you're right." I smile. "I guess our fun is over."

We start to walk toward the kitchen door. I have to stop and take off my shoes. They are drenched with water, and every time I take a step, they slip off my feet, making it difficult to walk.

"I'll race you," I say as I begin to run.

Within seconds, Angel is right beside me and to my surprise gives me a little bump on the side, acting as if he is trying to get me out of the way. I instantly start laughing, however, continue to run as fast as my legs will allow.

We both get to the porch doors at the same time. Angel grabs the knob and swings open the door with such force that it slams against the wall, filling the air with a loud crashing sound. John comes running out of the kitchen, his expression that of complete surprise.

"What in the world happened to you two?" John asks as he starts laughing.

"Long story," Angel says, shutting the door behind him, "I will tell you later. Right now, I think we need to get into some dry clothing."

"I agree." I smile as my body trembles from the cold.

Without another word being said, we both look at each other and begin to run toward the stairs, laughing the entire way. After finally reaching the door to my room, Angel takes my hand, kisses it gently, and opens the door for me.

"I will see you in a few minutes," Angel says, then turns and walks toward his bedroom door.

As soon as I enter my bedroom doors, I close the door and instantly begin peeling off my rain-drenched clothes. After putting on a plush, pink bathrobe that Angel had bought for me, I walk into my closet and pick out something nice and comfortable to put on. A baby blue sweat outfit. Something you would wear if you were to go jogging. I know it isn't the most appealing outfit, but I am freezing, and I want the feeling of the warmth that is has to offer and care less how it looks.

Knowing that if I were to let my hair dry without brushing it, my hair would tangle into a mess that would take hours to untangle, I brush it as best I can and then put it in a ponytail.

"That's better," I think to myself.

Looking in the mirror, I admire the length of my hair, as although it is up in a high ponytail, it still reaches to my lower back.

"Oh my god," I scream, as I get a glimpse of my face in the mirror.

Realizing that the mascara I had put on earlier is now running down my face from the sudden downpour, I soap up a washcloth and begin scrubbing my face.

"I must have looked like a clown," I say laughing at myself.

Suddenly, I feel a rumble in my stomach. Having only eaten an apple the entire day, my stomach is now reminding me of the fact that I am starved and need to get something to eat.

After I am satisfied that I look decent enough to go downstairs, I turn and head out of the bathroom. To my surprise, Angel is sitting at a perfectly decorated table, in the middle of my room. And there on the table is my favorite meal – spaghetti, garlic bread, and a large salad with ranch dressing.

"How do you do that?" I ask.

"Do what?" Angel chuckles.

"Read my mind," I answer. "I was just thinking how some spaghetti, garlic bread, and salad sounds real good!"

Angel laughs and says, "Don't worry about it. Just eat your food."

Although this is the most delicious meal I have had in a long time, I can't help but think that the only thing missing to make this my dream meal is a tall glass of diet soda and a piece of coconut cream pie for dessert.

"Oh, I almost forgot," Angel says as he reaches into a silver bucket full of ice. "I brought this up for you. I know how much you enjoyed it at the hospital, so I thought you might enjoy one."

It is a large glass bottle of diet soda; in fact it is my favorite kind.

"Seriously, you have to tell me how you are doing this." I smile.

"Observation, my dear. That is all it is." Angel smiles, as he pours me a glass of the ice-cold diet soda.

"What do you mean?" I ask. "Observation?"

"Well, one night when you were sleeping at the hospital, you were talking in your sleep about how much you wanted spaghetti," Angel explains. "Then I remembered how much you enjoyed the soda I brought you, so I put the two together and thought I would make you, one of what I thought was your favorite meals. Observation."

"Wow! You remembered all of that?" I ask, flattered.

"I guess so." Angel laughs.

"That's amazing!" I say. "I have a hard time remembering two days ago."

We both start laughing and then continue on with our dinner. It is nice, sitting here, enjoying such a delicious meal with Angel and the sounds of country music playing softly in the background.

"Would you like to dance?" Angel asks as a beautiful love song comes on.

"I'm not very good," I state.

"That's OK, I will teach you," Angel says as he stands and walks to my side.

Taking my hand into his, he helps me from my chair and twirls me in his arms. Fast at first, we twirl around the floor, suddenly slowing to a relaxed pace. I am now cuddled in his arms and can feel his heart beating against mine. He moves to the music with perfect rhythm, moving me along with him. It feels like I am floating in air. We dance until a song comes on that is inappropriate for the way we are dancing.

"Are you ready for dessert?" Angel asks as he takes his hand in mine and walks me back to the table.

"What is it?" I ask.

"I don't know," Angel states. "I guess whatever is in the silver platter."

Angel lifts the lid from a silver platter, and there sitting on the underlying plate is two pieces of chocolate cake, where I half expect to see a coconut cream pie.

"I guess he can't read my mind," I think and laugh to myself.

"I think I will pass. I am kind of full," I politely decline.

"Are you sure? It looks delicious," Angel says as he wipes a piece of chocolate frosting off and walks toward me.

"What are you going to do with that?" I ask, as I back away from his chocolate-covered finger.

"I am going to give you a taste," Angel says with a devious laugh. "Why? Do you not trust me?"

"I'm not sure," I say as I look him directly in his eyes.

"I promise, just a taste." Angel laughs again. "I won't wipe it on you."

"I tell you what," I say, "I will let you give me a taste, only if you hand me one of those pieces of cake so that I will have some type of defense if you're lying."

"Deal," Angel says as he reaches over, takes a piece of cake off the platter, sets it on a clean plate, and then hands it to me.

"Are you ready?" Angel asks as he wipes the chocolate off his finger and takes the other piece of cake into his hand.

"Hey, wait! I didn't agree to you having a full piece of cake," I say as I pick up my cake in my hand, preparing myself.

"Well, I thought if you get a full piece of cake, I should also," Angel says as he walks to my side.

Angel is standing next to me with his cake in his hand, and I know by the look in his eyes that there is going to be a cake battle at any second now. That means I will be taking a shower soon and changing my clothes once again. None of that bothers me, as I will make sure he has to also.

"Now remember, you promised only a bite," I say as I try to give Angel a serious look.

"You worry too much," Angel says as he lets out a sinister laugh. "Now close your eyes."

I know what is coming next, but I do just as he asks and close my eyes. After all, I have my piece of cake ready, and the instant I feel his cake hit my face, I will retaliate with mine.

The next thing I know, I can feel Angel's lips on mine. The kissing becomes pretty intense, and I know I have to make him stop, as I feel that I have been leading him on this entire time. My heart is torn between this man that I want so badly and the man I have been in love with for years. It is obvious that no matter how much I want to hate Kamrin, I am still confused about him, and I am still uncertain as to where our relationship stands.

I know he is married, but a big part of my heart still belongs to him. I can't give into my feelings for Angel, as my heart is not ready for the taking. There is nothing else to do but to softly push him away. Being as nonchalant as I possibly can, I slow the intensity of the kissing to a few soft pecks on the lips and then suddenly pull away.

"I'm sorry, Angel. I'm tired," I lie.

I take a step back and lower my head, hoping to avoid seeing the pain that I have just caused him. I feel horrible, and I want to explain myself, but I am lost for words and can do no more than hide within my self-pity.

The room continues to be silent for a few moments longer, as the tension inside me grows to such intensity that I feel myself wanting to break down into tears. I need to explain myself. I had to make sure that things are going to be OK between us.

Suddenly, Angel reaches over, and with his soft, caring hands, he touches my face. Holding back the tears that have been welling inside me, I reluctantly raise my head to face the one that I have hurt. His eyes, which are of such beauty and innocence, cause the guilt within me to grow. He smiles, indicating that all is well. However, the glow he once had is now fading into the hurt within his heart. I want to turn back time and take away our first kiss, but I can't. I will have to suffer knowing that I have hurt such a great man. I should have never given in to my desires.

I lay my head on his shoulder, hoping that he will understand my feelings.

Angel turns and kisses my head.

"I understand," Angel whispers in my ear.

Without warning, a brilliant bright light overtakes the room, then sudden darkness, the unexpected darkness frightening me so that I hold onto Angel as tight as I can.

"It will be OK," Angel says as he holds me in his arms. "I will go get some candles."

Angel tries pulling my panic-stricken arms from him.

"No!" I scream. "Don't leave me alone in the dark!"

"I am going to walk over to the fireplace and get a candle so that we can see," Angel explains.

"Then I am going with you," I demand, never releasing my grip from his waist.

Still holding me within his arms, Angel begins making our way toward the fireplace. Within moments, Angel locates a candle and lights it. The room now brightened by a single candle relieves my fear.

A loud thunderclap echoes throughout the room, then another bright flash. The lights begin to flicker, and then within seconds, come back on.

Angel releases me from his arms, and we both run to the window to see what is happening.

The outside sky is looking like that of a war zone; it is clear that the storm has become worse. As I stand at the window and look out in amazement; I take Angel's hand into mine and watch as Mother Nature continues to show herself in all her fury. I become worried as the memory of the dream I had days before is still fresh in my mind. The memory overtakes me, and I begin to shake. I want to run and hide.

"Stay right here," Angel insists as he pulls his hand from mine.

Angel suddenly excuses himself and runs down the stairs. His actions shock me, and I don't know how to react to them. Here I am petrified, and he leaves alone.

"He is only downstairs, and he will be right back," I tell to myself, trying to convince my fear that I am going to be fine.

After taking in a deep breath, I stand quietly staring out the window. The lightning becoming that of fantasy, I find myself unable to comprehend the sight. The lightning is like no lightning I have ever seen. I continue to stare in disbelief as I watch small pieces of electricity being thrust from the sky, each bolt looking as if it is being followed by another, until the sky is filled with tiny bolts of lightning, all following the same path. Here!

I am scared, however, hypnotized by the beauty of the rainbow of colors, as each bolt of lightning possess a different brilliant color.

The time goes by slowly, and the flashing from the lightning begins to make me sleepy. I walk over to my bed and lie down, thinking I will watch from here. It probably is safe that way, as the lightning seems to be overhead now.

I never hear Angel come back in the room and figure that he must have finally had enough of the self-indulgent games. I am sure he thinks I am playing. I have hurt his feelings a lot lately, and I don't know why I continue doing it, as I never had hurt anyone like that before. I know in my heart it is from all that has been going on, but that still is no excuse.

Lying in my bed, I continue to think about what is right. *What advice would my mother give me?*

"Choose," I hear a woman whisper in my ear.

The voice of someone in my past; I know it is my mother speaking to me from above, and I know she is right.

I have to figure out my feelings, and the only way to do that is to talk to Kamrin alone. But I feel guilty doing so. I was never a home wrecker, and I don't want to start now.

"That's exactly what you will be doing," I say to myself. "And nobody likes a home wrecker."

I know if I was Cheyenne, I would be worried about me stealing her husband. And that is not right; she should not have to live in that fear. I should have released him from my heart the moment I found out he was married. After all, Cheyenne was at one time my very best friend. I wouldn't have hurt her then, and I am not about to hurt her and her child now. I have to go on with my life without him.

That's it; I need to let him go once and for all, so we all can get on with our lives. I have made my final decision.

"I am going to tell Kamrin that I can no longer see him and that he should forget about me and what we once had. And that he should go on with his life and live happily with his wife and child," I think to myself.

This is the right thing to do.

Although Kamrin does and always will have a piece of my heart, he no longer has all of it. Angel has a great portion of it, and my love for him is growing every day, with every touch, with every kiss.

Remembering our first kiss out in the garden, I get butterflies in my stomach. Instantly, the memory of his sweet lips on mine flashes in my mind, and I know I want him more than any man I had ever known, even Kamrin. I now feel bad for wishing I could turn back time and erase our first kiss, as I now realize that it is a memory I never want to go away.

My heart has made its choice. I am at peace with my decision.

"I love you, Angel," I whisper to myself as I close my eyes and let the fantasy of me and him together take over all my thoughts.

I must have fallen asleep, as the next thing I know I am being thrown out of my bed with great force. I hit the floor with such a hard impact that I can hear the wood beneath me crack. I try to scream, but not a sound comes from within me. I try to get up, but my body feels like it has been nailed to the floor.

It's dark and cold in my room, like it had been in my dream. I can't see anything. I quietly reach around, but can't feel anyone. It is like I had been thrown from my bed by the empty air of the room, as there is no sign of anyone being near me.

Suddenly, the force picks me up again, raising my body up to the ceiling, then dropping me onto the hard floor. The sound of my body hitting the floor echoes throughout my room. I try to run, but once again my body feels as if it is nailed to the floor. Over and over again, someone or something lifts me to the ceiling and throws me to the floor. Each time my body receives a new cut or bruise, I am in tremendous pain, and I want it to stop. But I am powerless, and there is nothing I can do but lie there like a rag doll and let the hidden entity continue to throw me around the room. Closing my eyes I wait for my demise, as I am afraid that my body will soon diminish from the beating I am receiving.

"What were you thinking?" a sinister voice asks me, as he picks me up and holds me close to his mouth, growling in my ear.

I am petrified, as the voice is that of complete evil, allowing my frightened self to say only one word.

"I . . ."

"I warned you, I would be back!" the man growls again, as he throws me against the wall. "Now, are you ready to give me what I want? Or must I take more from you?"

Suddenly, the lights come on. The room becomes silent and begins to warm up. Lifting myself to a sitting position, I begin to cry.

I start to scream for Angel, but I am too late; he is already standing by my side. My body, now trembling with such intensity, I find it hard to stay in my sitting position.

"Who is doing this?" I cry in hysterics. "And what does he want from me?"

"I don't know, Lue. I wish I did," Angel says.

It is obvious by the uncertainty of his voice that he is lying. I become agitated. I want to know what is happening, and I want to know now! After all, I am the one to whom all this is happening, and I am tired of all of the secrets and deception I feel I am receiving. I want to scream out and demand the truth, but my emotions are out of control, and I can no longer speak coherently.

"It will be OK," Angel says as he holds me tight in my arms. "I will never let anyone harm you."

Angel holds me close in his arms. His hold is strong and comforting. I close my eyes and take the comfort in. Continuing to hold him as tight as my shaking arms will allow, I take in deep, long breaths until my shaking subdues. I never want him to let me go.

"I know you love me," Angel says in such a tone that I have never heard.

The feeling of comfort instantly fades, as I hear a sinister laugh coming from the person holding me. Releasing my grip quickly, I step back.

It's not Angel!

It is the type of dark figure of a man I had seen in my dream the other night.

"It wasn't a dream!" I scream within myself. "He's back!"

I try to scream again. I am paralyzed, leaving my voice lost within my mind!

"What's wrong? Were you expecting your 'pretty boy'?" the dark figure asks, laughing the laugh he is capable of.

A laugh that is so sinister, so evil that it instantly makes the hair on my entire body stand on end. Right then, I know that not only is this the man from my dreams, it is also the man that had kept me captured for so many years. He is here to take me back!

"No!" I scream within myself, "I won't go back!"

I want hit to him; no, I want to kill him. He had taken my life, and now he has taken the life of my parents.

The hatred I feel for this man continues to grow with every second that passes.

I close my eyes and gather every bit of strength I can and swing at him with all my might. To my surprise, my fist connects right where I aim – his right cheek.

"Oh yeah, I forgot. You like it rough." He laughs as he grabs me into his arms and begins squeezing me tightly. "Can I dare hope that maybe you like it even more now? Maybe that 'pretty boy' of yours taught you some tricks that you would like to share with me."

Trying to escape his clutches, I begin to squirm, moving my body around in frenzy.

His grip, stronger than ever, begins to restrict my airway.

I can't catch my breath! I breathe again. I keep breathing harder and harder, until I am now breathing so fast and shallow that I know that at any moment I will begin to hyperventilate.

"Concentrate," I think to myself.

I know if I do not calm myself and breathe shallow, I will hyperventilate, and that is something I do not want to do. I have to stay coherent. I have to keep fighting!

I take in the deepest breath I can and exhale it slowly, doing this over and over again, until I am able to catch my breath and keep it at a steady pace.

"Do you want to show me how you kissed him today?" the masked man asks in an evil growl; my face is now directly in front of his.

"He has been watching me!" I think to myself.

"Do you mean the first time in the garden, the time on the swing or just now?" I snap. "Because each time was different. In fact, each time was more passionate than the other!"

I am shocked; I had tried and tried to scream before, but not a noise would escape from within me. Now, words seem to be escaping my mind and out into the open air, leaving me no longer in control of what I am saying, the room air continuing to be filled with my thoughts.

"This is not going to be good," I think to myself as I prepare for the pain I know I am going to experience for saying such things.

Suddenly, he holds my body so close to his that I find myself staring into what I am sure is the black hole of "hell."

I try to turn my face from his, but some unforeseen power has control of me, refusing to let my head move in any direction except for its present position. I can't stand looking into his black, soulless eyes for another moment. I try to squirm out from his arms, but his hands are too strong, and I find myself his prisoner once again.

"I forgot how good you tasted," the dark figure says in an evil laugh. "Now give me that kiss."

His snakelike tongue escapes from the emptiness of his mouth, slithering out like a snake escaping from beneath a rock. I try to move again, but his hold is that of a hundred men, and I am unable to move an inch.

My mind screams in terror!

His tongue continues to grow as it slides out of his mouth like a snake feeling its way to its prey. I close my eyes and await the horror, as I feel the scales from his tongue touch my soft skin. Instantly, my skin is taken over by the feeling of sandpaper as he continues to lick my cheek in long, seductive movements.

My body quivers, and I want to beg him to quit. But once again, I find myself unable to speak, and although I try to get my thoughts to escape like before, my words of hate and fear are left on my own. I have no other option; I will have to stand here and endure everything that he is doing to me.

Suddenly, I can feel his tongue on my lips, slithering around, outlining every inch of them.

Clinching my lips as tight as I can, I try to keep his scaly tongue from invading my mouth. He may have a tight hold on me, but he is not about to make me kiss him.

Determined to get what he wants, he continues moving his morbid tongue around my lips, until he is finally able to pry my lips open and put his tongue into my mouth. My tongue instantly comes in contact with his. His breath, smelling like a dead, rotting carcass, makes my stomach curdle, and I find myself wishing I had a big plate of maggots, as I know that would taste better than his kiss.

His long, slithering tongue continues to explore the inside of my mouth. The thought of a part of his disgusting body in mine repulses me, causing my skin to crawl as if a million bugs are creeping beneath my skin.

I want to bite off his tongue and spit its bloody pieces onto his face. But I am still paralyzed and can't move an inch of my body.

My stomach continues to turn as his tongue never leaves mine, as he continues to force my tongue to move with his.

"I wish I can throw up in his mouth," I think to myself.

But even my vomit is frozen from fear, leaving me in my same state of helplessness.

"That's more like it." He laughs as he licks his lips. "Just like I remember you tasting, like a fresh, untouched piece of meat."

His eyes begin to glow as fire grows within them. My heart is pounding so fast and so hard that I feel like it is going to jump out of my chest.

Suddenly, he releases his powerful hold from my arms and puts his rough, dead hands on my face. They are dark red like the rest of his body and do not look real. Taking his long, pointed nails, he outlines my face, touching every part of it. His fingernails feel like sharp razors, cutting into my face. I want him to stop before he turns me back into the monster he had made me once before, but I am too late. I can feel his wrath against the side of my left cheek as his fingernails pierce my skin. Blood instantly begins dripping from my new wound.

"What happened to the beautiful scars I gave you?" he asks, as he hisses in my ear. "I guess we will have to start from scratch. But don't worry, I don't mind."

Suddenly, I feel a sharp pain as he digs his nails deep into the side of my other cheek.

"Let's start here," he hisses.

"*No!*" I scream within myself, as I think of the dungeon and all that waits for me if I were to be captured again. "Never again will I be the torture toy of anyone!"

A sudden burst of adrenaline surges through my body. Although I once again can move, my body moves in such a manner that I have very little control of my actions, as my mind continues to fight the force that is once again trying to take over my mind . . . take over my ability to function. I am desperate. I cannot let this happen again. Ignoring his laughter, I try to grab his hands from my face, trying to release his power. I am not fast enough, and he catches my hand in midair and holds my wrist tightly within his death grip. It begins to hurt as his grip gets tighter and tighter. Within seconds, I can hear a sound that I had hoped to never hear again – the sound of bones being broken. I look over at my right hand in time to see it instantly turn blue, as every bone crushes beneath his grip.

The pain overcoming every part of my being, I fall to the ground.

"Get up!" he screams as he grabs my arms and jerks me up off the floor. "You have to come back with me now! I wasn't done with you. You are my special girl. You will love me and give me what I want!"

There is no way that I am going to give in that easy. I start kicking and hitting him as hard as I can, until I am able to free myself from his grip. Avoiding his grasping arms, I maneuver away from him and run as fast as I can toward the bedroom door.

I know if I can reach the door, I will be free to run downstairs to find someone to stop this man.

"Leave me alone, you son of a bitch!" I look back and scream as I reach for the doorknob.

He is no longer there!

In fear of not escaping, I reach for the doorknob. My hand instantly being blocked by that of a man, I look up in hopes that it is Angel, and he is here to help me. But my desire for freedom is blocked. He is standing in front me again, ready to capture me in his power.

"Angel, help!" I scream as loud as I can.

"Yell all you want. He can't hear you." The man laughs. "You're not really talking."

"The hell I'm not!" I scream.

He laughs again.

"You are a stubborn one. I like that spunk in a woman," he says as he continues to laugh the most evil laugh. "Keep yelling all you want. I am the only one that can hear you."

For some strange reason, he seems to be right; my screaming seems to be left unheard by anyone. I scream again, screaming as loud as I can over and over, until my lungs begin to burn, leaving me with merely a softened yell that seems to be far in the distance. No one seems to be coming to my rescue.

"Now if you're done with all that noise, I would like to be going," the man snickers.

He may have been ready to go, but I am not willing to give in this easy. I turn and run toward the bathroom with the plan of locking myself inside. Once again, he is waiting for me. As I continue to run around the room for a route of escape, I begin to tire, and my mind weakens. Stopping for a brief second to catch my breath, I turn and look; there is no other place for me to go. He is too fast and seems to know exactly where I am going before I do. I am doomed.

As I am just about to give in to him, I see a sparkle coming from the nightstand by my bed. It is the necklace that Angel had given me and had said that would protect me. I'm not sure of its powers, but I have no other option at this point. I have to do something.

"I am tiring of these games, little one," he snarls. "It was fun at first, but now it's time to go finish this!"

In hopes of fooling him, I act like I am running toward the bedroom door, then quickly bolt for the dresser. It works. He is standing at the bedroom door waiting for me, giving me enough time to reach the dresser and grab my necklace.

An evil laugh escapes his lips. "What do you have there? A present for me? Awe . . . You shouldn't have."

I hold the necklace tightly in my hand, not wanting to show him, holding it so tightly that it begins cutting into my hand. The pain is a bit much. However, the pain from my broken hand is worse. I have to endure the pain, as I am afraid that if I loose my grip I will drop it, ultimately losing the last ray of hope I have. The power that Angel says this necklace has must work. I am frightened, and I know that if the necklace were to fail me, I would be back in his dungeon once again.

"I asked what you have there," he demands. "Now tell me."

In one leap he is by my side, his feet never touching the floor. He grabs my arm and begins squeezing it with such intensity that I have no choice but to lift my arm from my side.

"Your parents didn't put up a fight like this. Actually, they were pretty boring. They put up no fight at all." He laughs in his evil voice.

"You bastard!" I scream as I kick him as hard as I could in the groin.

"Was that supposed to hurt?" he hisses in my ear.

"No, but this is," I scream as I take the candlestick from the nightstand and hit him as hard as I can in the cheek.

"That's more like it," he hisses between his rotten, pointed teeth. "Foreplay."

"You're sick!" I scream.

"Now, no name calling." He laughs. "I want to see what you have there."

"No!" I scream as I hold the necklace tight against my chest.

"Now give it to me!" he demands, as he starts applying more pressure to my wrist.

His power is great, and I know at any moment I will have to give into him. The necklace in my hand becomes as hot as it did that day when I was speaking with Kamrin. I open my hand slowly, keeping a grip on the chain that is attached. The necklace is glowing as it had before.

The dark figure jumps back. His eyes begin to glow like a fierce, untamed fire.

A deep, beastly growl comes from deep within him.

I begin to shake, as I know I have angered him more than I ever have.

"What are you doing with that?" he growls beneath his breath.

"Angel gave it to me," I whisper, as I lower my head. "He says it will protect me from assholes like you."

Once again, I let words slip out of my mouth that I normally would never say. It is like this man brings out every bit of evil and hatred hidden inside me, and I find myself out of control.

The room begins to shake, the walls shaking so violently that the paintings begin to fall to the floor, instantly busting the frames into pieces. I lose my balance and have to hold onto the bed. The floor becomes soft as quicksand, and I know that if I do not get onto my bed, I will take the chance of falling through.

As fast as I can, I leap for the bed.

Something seems different, giving me the confidence that angel will hear me this time.

"Angel!" I scream with every bit of energy left within me.

Before I can scream again, a loud rumble comes from within the hallway. The closer it gets, the louder it is, until the sound becomes deafening. The door begins to rattle more violently than the room, continuing to shake as it turns bright red, until it looks as if it is on fire. Without warning, the door busts into million pieces.

I have to cover my body as the hot embers from the burning door shoots across the room, like an erupting volcano.

There standing in the doorway is Angel, with John standing beside him.

"You need two of you to take me, do you?" the dark figure roars.

"Oh no . . . You are all mine," Angel says with a devious smile.

"John . . . Go stay with Lue. I will take care of this one," Angel demands, as he leaps toward the waiting man.

Instantly, the two men begin to fight. At first, I can't tell who is winning, as they are moving around the room as fast as lightning.

I am still frightened, however, more for Angel this time as I am unsure which of the two is stronger. After a few minutes of watching the two men fight, it is obvious that Angel is dominating the fight, as he continues to pick up the stranger and bash in into different walls throughout the room. The percussion from the man hitting the wall echoing through the room, like loud claps of crashing thunder.

Suddenly, the men stop fighting, leading me to believe that the battle is over. But I am wrong. Angel walks over to the man that is now lying on the ground, picks him up by the throat, and holds him high off the floor.

"Two men?" he says with a smirk. "I think not."

Without further hesitation, Angel takes the man into his arms and starts squeezing him with such intense power that I can hear the man's bones crushing beneath Angel's embrace. The sounds of the bones crumbling within the man sickens me, but at the same time it excites me, as I want him to suffer like he has made me and so many others suffer.

I smile as I continue to listen to his body being destroyed by Angel.

Suddenly, the dark, shadowed man lets out a screech that instantly pierces my ears and enters my mind, causing me to cover my ears in pain.

Before I can blink an eye, there are two other figures at the window. The room begins to shake violently once again, causing John to lose his grip on me. I begin to fall into the emptiness of the floor. Angel grabs me and sets me back on the bed next to John, all the while giving John a harsh look. John shrugs his shoulders, indicating that he is sorry. Angel smiles, indicates to John to keep a better hold on me, and then in a flash, Angel is ready to fight again.

I look around; the man that Angel had been fighting is now gone, leaving only the two dark, shadowed men that hover outside the window.

"I took your leader down!" Angel screams at the black, shadowed men. "He is more powerful than you, what do you think you're going to do?"

With a smirk upon their face, the men look behind them. Within seconds, there are at least ten more of them, all of which possess the same fiery red eyes and skin of lava.

Angel is strong, but I am unconfident if he can take all of these men at once.

"He can't do this alone," I cry within myself. "They will kill him."

"Don't worry, Lue," John whispers in my ear. "It will be OK."

It isn't two seconds after John whispers those words in my ear, that the men enter the room and all at once pounce onto Angel. I can see that he is trying his hardest to fight them off, but they seem to be all over him, hitting him from all directions. I am scared for him, as they continue to pound his body with vicious blows to every inch of his body. I don't want him to die!

"John, go help him!" I scream.

"I can't, they are waiting for me to leave your side. They will take you!" John replies.

"I don't care!" I scream. "Just help him!"

I can hear Angel scream in pain, as one by one the men take turns tearing into him with their sharp nails and their powerful strikes. I can't take the noise anymore. The sound of Angel in pain is tearing my heart and soul into pieces, and I know there is nothing I can do to help him, and it is obvious that John is not going to.

"Leave him alone!" I scream.

I know that my screaming is not going to help Angel in any way, but I can no longer take the sounds of the man I love being in pain.

Suddenly, the sounds of Angel's pain disappear into the room, replaced by that of the other men.

The screaming men sounding like hundreds of wild cats, as Angel gets the upper hand on them and begins throwing them two by two around the room, causing the walls to crash over them. I put my hands over my ears, trying to deafen the sound. But the shrieking is so ear-piercing that the sounds are able to escape through my fingers and into my head.

Without warning, more dark, shadowed men appear within the room, overtaking it in its entirety. John is already moving quickly among the bed, one side, then another, pushing them away.

With more strangers appearing by the moment, I know it will not be very much longer before the fight will end, as it is impossible for Angel and John to continue to fight as they are.

Angel is fighting at least five dark, shadowed men at a time. As it seems that as soon as one will disappear, two will take his place. The fight isn't fair; there are so many of them and only three of us, and out of that three, only one is really fighting, as Angel refuses to let John leave my side. The situation seems like it is getting out of control.

"Get her out of here!" Angel screams at John.

"But . . . Angel!" John yells back. "I will have to . . ."

"I know . . . Just get her out of here. Now!" Angel screams again, all the while fighting off one man then another.

"She will know!" John replies. "There will be consequences."

"I will take my chances!" Angel screams, as he is slammed into the wall next to me.

"Angel!" I scream as I reach for his hand.

He reaches back, barely touching the tips of my fingers. Instantly, I can feel the warmth and strength come through his fingertips and into my hand. I look into his eyes and see that although I know he has to be in pain, he seems to be at complete peace and without a worry in the world.

He winks at me, and then he is gone, fighting the darkness again.

"Hold on . . . Lue. We are taking a ride," John says with a smile.

I am uncertain what he is talking about, but I know I am about to find out.

John takes me in his arms and holds me close.

"I don't know how this is going to feel to you," he whispers to me in a concerned tone, "so take a deep breath."

With me still in his stronghold, he then leaps off the bed. As our bodies begin to tumble through the emptiness of the floor, five shadowed men jump on top of John, all trying to release the grip he has on me. Within seconds, the five men begin to scream in excruciating pain and then vanish in a dust of dark, glittery haze. I want to yell in horror, afraid that John and I will suffer the same fate. As I open my mouth to scream, a sudden feeling of peace rushes through my body, and I instantly know John and I will be fine.

We continue to fall. I can see the ground below us, but it seems to never get closer. It feels like we are never going to stop falling, when all of a sudden a powerful force hits me from the side, instantly knocking me out.

The next morning when I wake, I am in a room that I am not familiar with. Disoriented, I jump out of bed and run to the window, hoping that I am in another room within Angel's mansion and not somewhere completely different.

The garden that I had admired many times before is now a yard full of giant trees. I am no longer in the safety of my home.

Terrified, I scream for Angel. He doesn't answer.

I yell again.

This time, I hear a voice coming from down the hall, but it still is not Angel's.

"He isn't here yet," John yells from the next room.

I feel very drowsy almost like I had been drugged the night before, but this drug is not like the one I had experienced the day I was taken; this one is that of complete peace. I walk into the bathroom and splash some water on my face, in hopes that the cool water will help me completely wake up.

"He's not here yet?" I question to myself as I realize what John had said.

Quickly, I open the door and walk down the unfamiliar hallway. At first, I am not sure which way to go, until I hear the soft sounds of someone singing. It is not the same beautiful singing that I had heard coming from Angel. However, it is still amazing. I follow the sound until I am able to locate the singing. It is coming from John. He is in the kitchen cooking, as he always seems to be.

"Is that all you do?" I laugh.

"Seems that way, doesn't it?" John laughs back.

"John? What happened?" I ask.

"Angel will have to explain it to you, Lue," John replies. "I'm not at liberty to say. I'm sorry."

I shake my head in disgust. Once again secrets, secrets that I may not ever know. This isn't fair. There are so many things happening, all unexplainable and all very strange. And it seems like everyone knows what is going on except me, as I never can get a straight answer from anyone.

"Err," I growl.

John laughs and continues on with his cooking.

I am a little aggravated that he is so amused by my aggravation.

"Are you sure Angel is OK?" I ask, getting impatient.

"He's a strong man. I am sure he is fine. He should be here any minute now," John answers.

I am not totally convinced by John's words, as he too has a look of worry underneath his makeshift smile.

"Where are we?" I abruptly ask John.

"We are in a small town on the east coast called, 'Winter Harbor,'" John answers.

"How did we get here?" I ask, hoping that I will be able to catch him off guard and get a little more information.

"I can't tell you that," John says as he continues to cook.

"John, I remember falling through a floor. A floor that I had walked on many times before but had somehow disappeared," I say as I look him directly in the eyes.

Silence.

"How can that be?" I demand to know.

"I can't . . ."

"Don't tell me. You can't tell me that either," I snap, interrupting him in the middle of his sentence.

"Sorry, Lue," John replies as he looks down at the floor. "Even if I was allowed to tell you, I wouldn't know where to start."

I know it is useless to continue pushing him for information, so once again I let the subject go and ask him if he needs help in the kitchen. I have to find something to occupy myself before I go insane with worry.

"Sure, you can make us toast," John states. "Everything else is pretty much done."

John finishes cooking, while I do the menial task of making toast. When we are done, we both sit down to enjoy our breakfast. I pick at my food for a while and then push the plate aside. I am nervous and worried, so I find it hard to stomach my food without feeling sick inside.

"Don't you like it?" John asks as he stuffs his face.

"I'm too worried to eat," I explain. "I wish Angel would call or something to let us know he is OK."

"He will be here soon, don't worry," John says in a soft tone.

The day goes by slowly. And no matter how I try to entertain myself, I can't stop thinking about what had happened the night before, as everything seems so unreal, so unnatural. But most of all, I can't stop wondering if Angel is OK. I look around the new place we are now in. It is beautiful but not as extravagant as Angel's other house. This house seems to be more personable, as if it is a family home.

"I wonder if this was his parents' house," I think to myself as I continue searching the home for any type of family photo.

Within a few minutes, I come across a set of large doors that seem to be out of place. My curiosity overtakes me, and I have to know what is beyond the big wooden doors. As quietly as I can, I open them. To my surprise, it is a library that in every aspect looks identical to the one at the other house.

I begin searching through the books, hoping to come across the one that had disappeared.

"There it is!" I say out loud as I see it sitting on a table, alone.

I pick it up and scan through the pages. Instantly, I notice all of the same faces I had seen in the book at the other house. It is exactly the same book I had seen before.

"I knew the book existed," I say out loud with excitement.

I continue searching for one certain picture.

"How did it get here?" I wonder.

Flipping through the pages one by one, I carefully inspect each picture. I have to find the picture of the man that looks like Angel.

The grandfather clock against the east wall begins to chime, causing my trance to break.

"What time is it?" I think to myself as I carefully hold the page I am looking at in my hands and look at the clock.

"Four hours," I say beneath my breath. "I have been sitting here for four hours."

I look around the room and let out a soft sigh. Angel is still not home.

Determined to find the picture I am looking for, I wipe my tired eyes and then continue my search.

Within ten minutes into my mission, my search is interrupted when I hear John talking on the phone in the other room. I can barely hear what he is saying, but I believe he is talking about Angel. I lay the book down and walk over toward the door where I am hoping that I will be able to hear John's conversation a little clearer.

He is talking quickly, and his tone is that of panic. Leaning my head slightly out the door, I listen closer. It sounds like he is talking about what had happened the night before and how he had not heard from Angel.

Still uncertain, I look around; I have to get closer to where John is standing. I have to know for sure. Scanning the area around me, I see a phone lying on the table next to the window.

"That will work," I think to myself, as I walk over quietly and pick up the receiver.

I listen quietly on the other end, as their conversation continues uninterrupted. It has worked; my deception has been left unheard.

"They have him, John," the voice on the other end says. "You know they will kill him and then come after her. You must trade her for him, or we will all die."

"More deaths because of me?" I think to myself. "Not Angel! *Not now*! Not ever!"

"All you have to do is take her to the forest where Angel found her, and they will take her from there. The directions that Angel used to find her should be there somewhere on the desk in the library. They will show you the exact location. He had told me he left them there just last week. So they should still be there," the voice on the phone explains frantically. "They will be waiting for you and will give you Angel back. They promise all in one piece."

"I won't do it!" John snaps. "You know how important this is."

"Well, if you're not going to take care of it, we will!" the man on the other end of the phone threatens. "We will not allow this to happen."

As quietly as I can, I hang up the phone and begin searching through the piles of papers on the desk, until I find a paper that has my name on it. I read it quickly. It has directions to the forest where he had found me. Never questioning why Angel possesses such a paper, I quietly fold the paper in half and slip it into my pocket, careful that I do not make any noise.

"If John refuses take me to Angel, I will go by myself," I whisper within my head as I sneak out the front door. "Sorry, John. Please forgive me, but I can't let Angel diminish because of me."

With nothing more than a sweater in my hand, I sneak down the porch. I am not worried about bringing food or clothing as I know once they have me, there will be no need for either. I will be killed or kill myself. I will not live in torture again.

CHAPTER 12

Saving Angel

I AM UNCERTAIN where I am going and how long it will take me to get there. But I know I have to get to the forest quickly. I run as fast as I can down the long dirt road, toward what I am hoping is a road to town. I can't let John catch me, as I know that he will bring me back to the house.

I run for about half an hour, until I find my way to the street and wave down the first car.

"Where are you headed, dear?" the old man in the car asks.

"To the nearest town," I reply.

"Jump on in. I'll get you there," he exclaims.

Although I am little leery to get into a car with a complete stranger, I know I will get to town quicker. Besides, the man driving the car looks to be around eighty years old, so I feel confident that if he were to try anything, I can defend. In my present mood, no one dare mess with me.

The ride is quiet with just the sound of oldies playing on the radio. I enjoy it. I have so much on my mind and need to concentrate on what

I am going to do and how I am going to get there. I have forgotten that I have no money, and I am not sure who I can trust to call for help.

I take the paper out of my pocket and read it over, trying to understand the directions. To my dismay, they seem to be written in a language that I am not familiar with, and I know I am . . . going to need help.

"What do you got there?" the old man asks.

"Directions to where I am headed," I reply.

"And where might that be?" he asks with a chuckle.

I turn and look in the driver's seat. The old man that once possessed the seat is no longer there. It is John!

"You were just an old man!" I exclaim. "How did you do that?"

"No, sweetie, It has always been me. I merely used an old man's voice," John explains in confidence.

"No, you were an old man. I saw you," I demand, as I search around the car for a mask or something that will explain how he changed his appearance.

John remains quiet.

"Well . . . explain," I say in the sternest voice I can conjure up.

I want to see how he is going to get away with this one. I know what I saw; he was a man of eighty years of age, and now he is young and vibrant again.

"Where are we headed?" he asks as he winks at me, changing the topic at hand.

Once again, my questions are unanswered. This will be the last time! After we find Angel, I am going to demand that I am told everything or I will . . .

"You didn't think I will let you go alone, now did you?" John says, interrupting my chain of thought.

"I was so quiet leaving. How did you know?" I ask, agitated.

"I've got my ways," John smirks.

"Err," I growl, "that's what Angel always says to me."

John begins to laugh. "Poor thing, can't get away with anything, can you?"

"Are you mad?" I ask.

"No." He laughs.

Although John deceived me with his looks, somehow, I am happy that it is John who has picked me up, as I really don't know what I am doing. I look into his eyes and give him a quick smile. He smiles back.

"I'm sorry, John. I couldn't let anything happen to him," I explain.

"We will get him back, Lue," John promises, as he lays his hand on my shoulder.

"John." I smile.

"Yes?" John answers.

"I love him," I say as I continue to look over at him.

"I know . . . He loves you too." John smiles.

Before I know it, we are pulling back into the driveway. My heart sinks. John has lied to me. We really weren't going to get Angel. I quickly glance over at John, questioning him with my eyes as to why we are back at home.

"We have to get some things, before we go," John says quickly. "Plus, I need to finish talking with some people about Angel's rescue. They want to help."

The thought of others helping us gives me hope that not only will we get Angel back, but I also might not lose my freedom.

John opens my car door, takes my hand, and leads me into the house. Although we are back for good reason, the house is the last place I want to be. I want to be with Angel. I want to save him from the evil that I know has him!

I sigh.

"Now you sit right here!" John demands, as he taps the seat of the red couch facing the front door. "I will only be a few minutes."

John moves around the house with such speed that I never see his feet hit the ground. Within seconds, he is once again by my side with a larger version of the necklace I am wearing.

"I want you to put this in a place that cannot be found," John says as he hands me the necklace.

Never questioning what I am being told to do, I attach the necklace onto my pant loop and then slip it into my pants. John looks at me and smiles, as if he agrees with my choice of place. I then reach behind my neck and begin to unlatch the other necklace.

"No! Leave that one on. They will be expecting you to be wearing it," John says as he removes my fingers from the latch. "We don't want them to become suspicious and look for another."

"Good idea!" I exclaim.

I am still clueless to the power that these necklaces possess, but whatever it is, it seems to work. As I already feel more confident, merely having them in my possession.

"Let's take a look at those directions you stole." John laughs.

My face turns bright red as I begin to blush. I pull the paper back out of my pant's pocket and hand it to him.

"I'm sorry about that," I say with an innocent grin.

As John reaches for the paper, he winks at me and places his other hand on my shoulder. I know that he has accepted my apology. I wink back.

"Now let's see where we are going," John says as he unfolds the paper.

As John studies the paper, I stand by his side looking at it in complete confusion. All of the writing I am unable to read and the drawing that the paper possesses is that of circle and lines. Nothing that would give anyone any indication as to where the directions would lead. It all looks like scribbling to me.

"What is that writing?" I ask, curious.

"It tells the location that we are going," John explains. "It's difficult to explain how to read this, but trust me. I know exactly where he is."

I continue to stare at the paper, unable to understand the directions.

Suddenly, the phone begins to ring. John, quick as lightning, runs and answers it. I listen from afar, trying to hear what is being said.

"Why can't these people speak louder?" I giggle to myself as I walk closer to the room that John is in.

I can tell by the things that he is saying that he and someone else is making plans to go get Angel. After a few minutes of conversation,

John tells the person on the phone that he will be there in "five" and then hangs up quickly.

I hurry back to the couch, as quietly as I can.

"It's time to go," John says as he hurries back into the room where I am sitting.

"I heard you tell the person on the phone that we will be there in 'five.' How are we going to get there so fast?" I ask.

"Well . . . there is only one way," John says, giving me a strange look.

John takes my hand and leads me down the hall to another room. The door is locked with a large, metal, medieval-looking lock. John takes a skeleton-looking key out of his pocket and unlocks the door.

"Time to break more rules." John chuckles.

John takes my hand tightly into his and opens the door. Instantly I close my eyes, as my senses are taken over by the sugary smell of everything sweet in the world. The same smell I would expect, if I were to open the door to a bakery that had been closed up for a week. It smells so good that my stomach immediately begins to growl.

After taking in another deep breath of the sweet, sweet aroma, I open my eyes.

I am speechless. The room is not really a room. There are no walls, no floor, and no ceiling. Looking into the room is like sitting on a cloud and looking into the star-filled sky above and the blue sky below. There is no end and no beginning, as it is empty but yet overtaken by stars.

"Heaven," I say in a softened tone.

"Close." John smiles.

Squeezing John's hand, I am in complete peace and now know how Angel feels at all times – tranquility.

"Here we go," John says as he holds my hand tighter.

We both leap into the emptiness of the room. Instantly, we begin to fall like we did the night before, when he had taken me from the room filled with the dark, shadowed men. We have only been falling a few seconds, when all of a sudden I am once again hit from the side by a powerful force. Blackness overcomes me, leaving me only with the feeling of peace and the sounds of my heartbeat.

"Lue . . . Lue, wake up!" I hear John yelling.

I open my eyes, only to find that we are now in the forest. It is the same forest where Angel had found me. My heart drops; we are here.

I try to move, but my body feels like it has been drained of all energy.

"Just lie there for a few more minutes," John says as he leans toward me. "You will be fine. It may take a while before you get all of your energy back."

He is right. The longer I lie here, the better I begin to feel. However, I am still a little disoriented.

"Lue, you have to listen to me closely," John says with panic in his voice.

"I'm listening," I reply, still a little groggy.

"You have a necklace in your pants. It is the one I gave you at the house," he whispers in my ear.

"I remember," I say as my mind continues to become clearer.

"They will come and get you. Make sure you take the necklace you have on your neck off, when they ask. Do not show them the other one! This is very important!" John demands.

"Why?" I ask.

"When the time is right, you will take the necklace out and throw it onto the floor as hard as you can," he explains.

"How will I know when to use it?" I ask with a concerned look on my face.

"Trust yourself," he says with a smile, "you will know."

The energy in my body begins to come back, as my adrenaline spikes. Reality sets in, and I am scared out of my wits. I know exactly what is going to happen to me once they get their grim hands on me. I have so many questions I want answered about what is going on. I want to know how we were able to travel the way we had, how Angel had fixed my scars and broken leg, and most of all, I want to know who these people are, including Angel and John.

Not to mention, what did all of this have to do with me being captured and tortured for three years and who was the man that captured me? My mind begins to wander thinking of all the different possibilities, however, only coming to one conclusion. I am certain I will fade into death without ever having a single question answered.

"Lue!" John screams. "Concentrate! They are here. They will take you now!"

I look up at him. He seems calmed on the outside, but eyes tell me different, and I know he can see past the smile on my face and into the fear that dwells inside me also. He touches my shoulder, kisses my cheek, and whispers, "See you in 'five.'" He winks, and in a brilliant flash of a light, he is gone.

I stand alone in front of the stream where I had broken my leg, the same stream that Angel had found me. I am alone, and although I am trying to be strong, I am petrified. My knees begin to shake so hard that I find it difficult to stand. I try to calm myself, but every thought I have is that of terror and pain. Within seconds, my entire body begins to shake uncontrollably, causing my teeth to chatter so loud that I can hear nothing but the sounds of my teeth as they slam together.

"I have to calm down," I think to myself. "I cannot show my fear. They will know I am weak!"

As I stand there trying to calm myself, I am reminded of what Angel had once told me: *For every bad thought you have, think of two good ones. The bad ones will disappear.* I take in a deep breath and do just that. It seems to be working, as my body stops shaking, and my teeth quits chattering. I can now hear the sounds of the birds singing around me.

"That's better," I think to myself as I look around for any indication that someone is walking my way. I feel by doing this I will be better prepared.

Without warning, everything around me becomes dead silent. The birds that were just singing are nowhere to be heard. There is not even a breeze blowing in the trees. I freeze where I stand and glance around, as everything around me begins to wither and die in front of my eyes. Instantly, the sky turns black, and the air around me turns cold, until the once-beautiful forest is nothing more than that of death.

Deep growling now fills the air, as devilish sounds encircle the area around me. They are coming my way!

"Stay calm!" I say within myself.

As the sounds come closer, I can hear the distinct crying of someone. It is Angel. I begin looking around trying to see where the crying is coming from, but it seems to be coming from every direction and all at once. Within seconds, I become dizzy as I continue to spin around, trying to prepare myself for who or what is coming for me.

I take in a deep breath and hold it in my lungs as I hear a deep, immortal voice behind me demand me to take off my necklace. I turn around, and there behind me stands a figure of a man. He is almost seven feet tall and is dressed in completely black clothing. To my surprise, he is not wearing a mask, like all the others had, and I could see his horrific face. It is red like lava and is mangled beyond recognition, as the scars he possess are many . . . taking over his entire face. His eyes, glowing the same fiery red as the others, seem to look right through me.

"Where's Angel?" I demand to know. "You said we would trade. I am here! Where is he?"

"Take the necklace off!" the figure demands again in a loud, growling voice, as his impatience continues to grow.

"*No!*" I scream, "I want to see Angel!"

"This is not up for negotiation, little one. Take the necklace off!" the man demands with such a growl that the skin on my body cringes.

I reach behind my neck, unlatch the necklace and hold it up for the man to see.

"Is this what you want? Then come get it!" I yell as I dangle it in front of me.

The man is angrier than ever.

"Look, we can do this one of two ways," the man yells, tiring of my games. "You can either give it to me, or I will take it from you. But believe me, you're not going to like option two."

The tone of his voice is that of certainty, and I know if I do not give in, I will suffer pain beyond my worst nightmare.

"Fine!" I scream as I throw the necklace on the ground next to him. "Now take me to Angel!"

The man leaps toward me, the percussion from his fast movement almost knocking me to the ground. Standing now in front of me, he lifts his head and his arms up to the heavens and lets out a sinister laugh.

Then with his scaly fingers, he touches me lightly on the forehead, mumbles a few words that I can't quite understand, and then removes his finger. My head begins to spin, and my knees weaken. At first, I try to fight the feeling, but it is too powerful, and I fall into his arms like a worn-out rag doll.

My mind is taken over by blackness once again. However, this time I am not at peace. I am in hell!

"Get up, bitch!" I hear, as someone screams in my ear.

Stunned by the sudden loudness, I open my eyes. Groggy and uncertain as to what has happened, I find myself sitting in a chair in the middle of a dark room. The smell of the room instantly brings horrible memories back. I know I have been returned to my recently escaped dungeon. My heart begins to pound out of my chest. I am going to die, or least that is what I pray will happen, as I cannot live another minute with the thought of being tortured like I had been before.

I have to get the necklace and pray that it helps me in some way. I try to move, but I have been tied down. I begin to cry.

"How am I going to reach this necklace!" I think to myself.

I begin to squirm in hopes that by doing so, I will be able to loosen the ties from within the rope that bounds me. However, this is not the case, and all that happens is that the ties become tighter.

"Come on!" I scream within myself as I continue to move around, "loosen."

I have to get the necklace! Panic sets in.

"Sit still, Lue. You're tightening your knots," I hear from behind me.

I try to turn my head to see who it is, but the muscles in my neck limit my movements. I try again. I still can't see anyone. They have to be directly behind me. I begin hoping my chair around so that I can face the voice. But the room is too dark, and I still can't see anyone.

"Who's there?" I ask as I glare into the darkness.

"It's me, Kamrin."

"Kamrin? What are you doing here?" I cry.

"I am hoping you could tell me that," he says in an almost sarcastic voice.

I begin crying hysterically, as I know it is because of me that he has been kidnapped and brought to this horrible place of pain and torture. And that he will probably be tortured, if he has not been already. I try to get closer to him. I have to touch him. I have to apologize.

"Stop!" he screams in pain. "Every time you move that chair, the rope around my neck gets tighter."

I stop dead in my tracks. I do not want to hurt him anymore than he has already been hurt. Memories begin flashing in my mind of the women I had seen . . . and the woman I had killed. I will not let that happen again! I will get us out of here!

"Are you OK?" I ask.

"Never been better." He laughs sarcastically.

"I'm so sorry, Kamrin. I had no idea that you would be brought into this," I cry.

"Yes, you did!" Kamrin screams. "Jeffery told me that he told Angel about the other note that was found. So you knew this was coming!"

"I'm sorry, Kamrin. I truly am," I cry. "All I ever wanted was to be free again!"

"Do you hear me? That is all I ever wanted! I wanted to be free!" I scream into the darkness of the room. "Why can't you leave me and my family alone!"

"You should have . . . ," Kamrin starts to say.

"I should have what?" I ask as I look toward the direction of Kamrin's voice.

Before Kamrin can say another word, the lights in the room come on. It takes me a few seconds to adjust my eyes from the darkness. After a few seconds, I am able to see. Sitting in front of me is a beaten Kamrin. He is tied up with barbwire that is wrapped around every inch of his body. It has cut his skin so deep that I can see where parts of his skin is protruding through his clothing and is now wrapped around the razor-sharp edges of the wire. He has been bleeding for a while, as on the floor below him is a puddle of blood.

My stomach drops as I see that he has a rope tied around his neck that is wrapped around my chair in such a way that when I move closer to him, the rope will tighten. I want to jump out of my chair and stop the bleeding. I don't want to see him die. But I can't move, as every inch I move, I bring Kamrin closer to his death.

I have no choice. I have to sit here and watch him as he suffers in pain.

I'm as helpless as he, and all I can do is tell him how sorry I am. But I know my words will mean nothing to his wife and his newborn child, as they will lose a husband and a father.

Suddenly, I can hear footsteps coming down the stairs. I know this sounds well, as it is something I had regretted hearing for over three years. My skin begins to crawl, and the anger inside me grows. I know this is the end for both of us, but I am going to make sure that the last thing this evil man hears is my voice as I damn him to *hell!* I look at Kamrin. I want to say good-bye before our time on earth ends. *Surprisingly, he looks calm, or is it that he has lost so much blood that he is fading before me?*

"I'm sorry, Kamrin," I say in a soft voice. "Just remember that I always loved you."

"Then be mine!" Kamrin says in a low voice.

"I always was," I say as I wink at him.

I know in my heart that I had decided days ago to let him go, but this is not the place or time to tell him that. *Besides, what is the harm in showing him compassion and love before he dies?*

Turning my attention away from Kamrin, I can now see the shadow of the man working his way down the darkened hall toward me.

My heart jumps out of my chest as the figure becomes clear as he enters the light! It is Angel! He is coming toward me, and he is alone.

"Asshole!" he screams as he walks past Kamrin. "I wish you would die!"

"I was wrong all along! He is the evil one that had kept me captive!" I scream in my head. "All of what has happened has been another one of his sick games!"

I am mad as hell. *How could I have been fooled by this man?* I want to jump up and kill him, but the ties that bind me refuse to loosen.

"These damn ropes," I scream out loud as I squirm in my chair uncontrollably, trying to untie my bindings.

I start biting at the ropes that has my chest and arms held down, hoping that by some miracle I can bite through them enough to loosen the rest of the ropes. But the ropes are too thick, and the only thing I manage to accomplish is to make my mouth bleed.

"You bastard!" I scream, "How could you do this to me? Why did you even bother taking me home and making me better . . . if *this* was your plan all along! You should have killed me then. You sick excuse for a man!" I scream as loud as I can.

I am in frenzy. I can't stop screaming. I am so pissed off that I can feel the veins on my face popping out. I have never felt so much hatred for one person in my life! I want him dead, and I want John dead for bringing me here. Most of all, I want to be the one to do it!

Angel comes running to my side. He looks tired and beaten. I am confused as to why he looks the way he does.

I stare at him, and for a brief second, I feel sympathy for his pain.

But I know it is him, and I want him nowhere near me. I turn my head so that I no longer have to look at him, as I know if I do, his beautiful eyes will mesmerize me like they always do, and I will believe anything that he says.

"You killed my parents!" I cry "And then you tried to make me feel better by making them a grave. Why would you do that? You sick, demented man!"

I spit in the direction of his face, hitting him on his left cheek.

"Never mind. I know why," I yell. "It is just another sick and twisted lesson of yours, isn't it?"

"Lue, you have it wrong. I'm not the bad guy," Angel says as he wipes the spit off and lays his hand on my shoulder. "This is all a show. They are trying to make you think that I am the evil one. Just look at me, and you will know the truth."

His voice sounds so sincere and desperate, but I am still certain that he is lying. I shrug away, trying to escape his touch, but it is of no use; he continues to rest his hand on my shoulder. I looked up and give him a stern look; I want him to release me. I want every wonderful memory of him to fade. He looks back with sadness in his eyes and smiles.

"You have to believe me . . . Lue. This is all a trick. An evil soul's trick of deception," he says as he touches my cheek.

His touch is warm and calming as usual, and I become disoriented, as his voice becomes hypnotizing. I want to believe him so badly, but everything points in the direction that he is the one deceiving me. I do not know what to believe anymore as everything is so confusing.

"Don't listen to him, Lue," Kamrin begs. "He is the one. He brought me here. He tied me to this chair with this barbwire. Look at me, Lue. I'm dying."

Kamrin takes in a deep breath and then begins to cough. His mouth is now covered in blood from within his beaten body.

"Liar!" Angel screams. "Stop trying to confuse her, you son of a bitch! You are the twisted one! You have been for years. Just let this one go!"

Angel turns my chair around carefully, so I am no longer facing Kamrin. He looks in my eyes and with a wink gives me a soft kiss on the lips. His lips are as warm and inviting as I had remembered, causing the confusion that is brewing inside me to grow to the extent that I am even uncertain as to who I am.

"Don't touch her!" I hear someone growl from behind me. "She loves me!"

"Oh, really?" Angel snaps. "Then why is she kissing me and not you!"

I put my head down and stare at the ground. I don't know what to do or who to believe. All I know is I want these games to end. I begin praying that it will all go away, and what will eventually happen, will happen now. I just want it to be done and over with, and whoever is truly the evil one, I want him to perish into the gates of hell!

As I become deep in my thoughts, I, for an instant, forget what is happening around me. Suddenly, I feel someone messing with the ties that restrain my arms. I look up; it is Angel. He is trying to release me. Instantly, I begin to question why. Is this another evil trick, or is he really trying to help me? My thoughts shoot in every direction, causing my mind to become clouded.

Angel is able to loosen the ties enough that I can move my arms and release them from the ropes. I reach in my pants to check if the necklace is still there. It is! I don't want to pull it out yet, as John said I would know when the time is right, and it doesn't feel like it is time.

Wait, John is Angel's friend. If Angel is the man that is responsible for all of this, then John is his helper. A flash of John winking at me enters my mind, and I find it hard to believe he could have a speck of evil within him, as he has one of the kindest faces I have ever seen and seems to have a heart of gold. There is no way he could hurt anyone, including me.

Angel is now kneeling in front of me trying to untie the ropes that are cutting into my ankles. He looks up and smiles. His eyes are that of the brightest blue, and when I look into them, I know he could never be the evil man I accused him of. I start to smile back. However, my smile quickly fades into a look of fear.

Hovering behind Angel is a man dressed in black.

"What in the hell?" I think to myself.

My eyes open wide, and I want to say something to Angel, but no words comes out of my mouth. It is like someone has taken every bit of air from within me, leaving me unable to speak. I am frozen, or maybe I am in shock. All I know is that no matter how hard I try to signal Angel in anyway, I cannot move. Angel stands up and looks at me with a bewildered expression upon his face. I can do nothing more than look at him with complete fear in my eyes, as I try to warn him. But I am too late. Without warning, the man dressed in black plunges a knife into Angel's heart. A blank expression overcomes Angel's face, and he falls to the floor.

"I guess you now have no other choice," I hear from behind me.

I quickly turn around; it is Kamrin! He is standing behind me, no longer bound by the barbwire. I look up at him as his body begins to float high in the air. He lets out an evil laugh that bounces off the walls, filling the air around me with millions of sinister laughs. His face begins to change. It is no longer the handsome man I once loved. His face is now as red and scaly as the rest of his body and mangled with scars. His voice, immortal.

"That will teach you." He laughs as his eyes light up like fire. "Consider that lesson two! . . . Never trust anyone!"

"Lesson two? What was lesson one?" I scream in complete hatred.

"Lesson one? Well . . . that was never disobey me," Kamrin says with an evil smile.

"It was you!" I scream as I fall to the floor, my ankles still tied to my chair. "It was you all along!"

An array of evil laughs fills the room, taunting me from every direction.

"Now you're mine." Kamrin laughs as he walks over to me and places his disgusting lips on mine.

"Get away from me!" I scream. "I never want you to touch me again!"

"But, sweetie, you're mine. You better get used to it!" Kamrin chuckles.

"I will never be yours again!" I yell as I look up at Kamrin.

"Are you hoping that your 'pretty boy' will save you?" Kamrin snickers as he kicks Angel in the ribs. "I don't think he can get up right now."

"You're just lucky," I snap. "Because if he could get up, he would kick your ass, like he did the other night!"

Kamrin lets out an immortal howl that echoes throughout the room.

"Did you hear that, boys? He's going to kick my ass!" Kamrin says as he tilts his head slightly and looks at me with his evil, soulless eyes.

Sinister-like laughter erupts all around the room, encircling me where I stand.

"Now come here!" Kamrin screams as he sticks his snakelike tongue out and licks my face. "I want another kiss, and I want your boyfriend over there to see it before I finish him off!"

"*No!*" I scream as I run to Angel's side.

He is lying in a pool of blood but is still breathing.

"I'm sorry this has happened to you," I cry.

I look into his eyes; they are changing from the beautiful bright blue that I love so much into a dark dingy gray. He is dying, and I don't know how to help him. Desperately, I rip the shirt from my body and press it tight against his heart, trying to stop the bleeding. It doesn't help. I hold his hand to my heart, then reach down and kiss his lips, for what I believe the last time.

"I love you," I whisper in his ear.

"I love you too." Angel smiles and then closes his eyes.

"You, *bitch*!" I hear Kamrin scream as he leaps toward me.

I grab the necklace from my pant's pocket and throw it as hard as I can onto the floor. Instantly, the necklace explodes into a million different pieces, whizzing around the room like shooting stars. It is so amazing to watch, as each illuminated piece of crystal moves about the room as if it has its own destination.

Kamrin suddenly stops, covers his face, and lets out an ear-piercing hiss that lingers in the room. Within seconds, there is a brilliant white flash, and then the room is in complete blackness. I can hear scuffling all around me, and although I am scared, I know I am the only one there that can protect Angel. I manage to untie myself, lie down beside him, and shield him with my body, trying to shield him from what is happening around us.

I momentarily look up and instantly become captivated by what I am seeing. The ceiling is now replaced with blue sky and fluffy white clouds. While the floor looks as if it is a bottomless pit of fire. I am in total disbelief, but I can't look away. I have to see more, as this is one of the most amazing sights I have ever seen. I have to see everything. As I continue to watch in amazement, the entire room is overtaken by bright sparks of colorful lights, and balls of fire continue to crash into one another, each time one of them diminishing into the darkness.

"What is this?" I ask myself. "My eyes must be deceiving me."

All of a sudden, the room is filled with the sounds of people screaming in agonizing pain. I squint my eyes and search throughout the dark room in hopes to find where the sounds are coming from, but I can't see anyone, leaving the screaming souls unforeseen. I bury my head within Angel's blonde hair and peek out.

The fight continues and so does the screaming, until the balls of red fury finally begin to dissipate, leaving only the mesmerizing illumination of the sparkling crystals.

"Lue?" Angel whispers.

"Yes," I reply, happy to hear his voice once more.

Angel tries to say something, but his voice seems muffled.

The room becomes silent as the fight seems to come to an end. At first, I can't tell who has won, as the room is still engulfed with complete darkness. I blink my eyes a few times as I try to focus on anything around me. But the blackness only allows me to see that the ceiling and floor has now returned to their original forms.

I lay my head on Angel's and kiss his forehead.

"I will get you out of here and get you help," I whisper.

"He doesn't need any help," I hear beside me.

Angel begins to laugh. "Why did you have to say something, John? I was going for a kiss."

I look down to where Angel lies; a dim light is now shining from the roof and onto his body. I touch where the knife had been shoved into his heart. There is no blood. Frantically, I start ripping his shirt open, looking for the wound. There is nothing, not even a scratch. In fact, there isn't a bruise or cut on him; he is perfect. I roll my eyes at him and turn my head, indicating I am angry. Angel grabs my face, pulls me closer, and kisses me. His lips are soft and warm and still taste like sweet candy. I am so happy he is alive that I forget all that has happened around me and continue kissing him.

The kissing continues for quite a few minutes, both of us oblivious that the lights have come back on, and John is still standing beside us.

"Helloooo . . . , people are standing here." John laughs. "I would like to get out of this place."

"Oh yeah, we should get going before . . . Angel stops."

"Before?" I ask.

"Should we?" Angel asks John.

"Why not? We have already broken all the other rules," John snickers.

I take Angel's hand in mine and help him up.

"Wait," I say as I stop, "what about the room that he had brought me into once? There might be others in there by now."

"Sorry, Lue," Angel says as he kisses my hand gently, "there is no one else here alive."

I don't quite know what he meant. *Did he mean that there were no new women, or that there was, but they are now dead?*

"Is anyone coming back?" I abruptly ask.

"Do you mean, Kamrin?" John asks.

"Yes," I answer as I look around the room, "or any of the other men."

"No, sweetie. We are alone," Angel says in confidence.

"Then can I have a minute?" I ask.

"Sure," Angel answers.

I release my hand from within Angel's grip and look around again, ensuring that we three are alone.

"There it is," I think to myself.

"Do either of you have a knife?" I ask with an almost sinister laugh.

Angel and John look at me in total confusion.

"No. Sorry, we usually don't carry around such objects," Angel says with a grin. "Why?"

"It would have made this just a little easier," I state as I walk over to where my old, battered wedding gown still stood.

"What?" Angel asks as he gives me a strange expression.

"This!" I scream as I proceed to rip into the dress with my bare hands, ripping it to shreds.

The anger inside me continues to grow with every piece of cloth I tear. I am in my own world and do not realize that I am screaming and yelling; cussing Kamrin out the entire time I am shredding the dress. I am out of control, as every bit of hatred I have for the man continues to pour out from within me.

"There!" I say calmly as I stand back and admire my newly shredded wedding dress. "That's better."

I turn and walk back to where Angel and John wait, both looking at me in total amazement.

Angel never says a word; he merely takes my hand and leads me out of the dungeon and up into the main part of the house. It is all too familiar. It looks the same as the day I had escaped. I take one last glance around as we leave the house. It is horrifying, as everything about this place screams *evil!*

I want to go out as quickly as I can, so I ensure the grip I have on Angel's hand, grab John's hand, and run out as fast as I my feet will carry me.

"Let's get out of here," I say with a smile, as I pull the two men behind me.

The night air is still and cool and everything seems to be back to normal, as I now can hear birds chirping in the background. I know the evil, dark, shadowed men have left or hopefully have been killed. A feeling of relief swarms my body and mind.

The three of us walk to the middle of the field and sit down on the grass. It is a perfect moonlit night, and I am finally back with the man I love. I can't imagine a better ending.

"This should be a good seat, don't you think?" Angel asks John.

"Perfect," John replies.

"Why aren't we leaving?" I ask Angel.

"I want to show you something," Angel says as he smiles at me.

"But I have seen this field before," I say. "And truthfully, I don't feel very comfortable here."

"You don't want to miss this," John abruptly states.

"John's right. This is the best part. Look over toward the house, Lue," Angel says as he points toward the house we just left.

Angel lifts my hand and kisses it gently.

"See." Angel smiles.

Suddenly, there is a bright light that overtakes the area surrounding the home. Within seconds, the light begins gathering until it forms an illuminating beam of light coming from the accumulating clouds above. Slowly bright, glowing objects in the shape of women and men begin to rise from the house, following the path of the light until they disappear into the clouds. The beauty and intensity of what I am seeing takes my breath away.

We all sit in silence, as hundreds of forms escape the house and fly into the heavens above.

"Angels?" I ask.

"Yes. They are now free. Thanks to you." Angel smiles.

I lay my head on his shoulder and continue to watch. My heart is full of joy, as I know that these women and men are now free . . . Free from the evil clutches of the unknown. I take in a deep breath and then let a deep sigh escape my lips.

"Are any of them my parents?" I ask softly.

"No, sweetie," Angel answers in a whisper, "I'm sorry."

CHAPTER 13

The Prankster

IT HAS BEEN weeks since the day we had saved Angel, and things have remained surprisingly calm and peaceful. We are back in the small town of Winters Harbor as we have not returned back to Swan Valley. Angel says it's better this way because they are almost certain that they had not killed the "man in charge." Although I am certain that he had meant Kamrin, I gave up asking questions long ago. They never seem to get answered anyway.

John is still with us, and I enjoy his company more every day. He has turned out to be quite a jokester and likes to play little tricks on me. Although I try to get back at him, I am not as clever as he. In fact, I am still awaiting a time when I can get back at him for putting a trout in my bathtub. I haven't quite figured out a plan of action yet, but I am working on it.

I never heard from Kamrin again, not that I had expected to. I just cannot come to terms with the fact that he had been the one that had kept me captured for all that time and had tortured me so. He had said he loved me, and I find it hard to understand why he would hurt me or others the way he had. It just goes to show that you may never truly know someone until the end of your relationship. As all the years before Kamrin took me captive, he was the most loyal and loving person I had ever known. "Man, what actor he turned out to be?" I whisper to myself.

Jeffery tried to contact us, but Angel refused to give him any information about where we are living as Angel is not sure what part Jeffery has in this whole situation, and he doesn't want to take the chance of them coming for me again. Although I may never know if they find my parents, I understand his decision, and I do not blame him in the least. In fact, I am happy that he has chosen to keep our whereabouts a secret.

I still don't know what I have to do with all this, but Angel promises me that he will tell me when the time is right. I trust him completely now and await the day he can tell me more about what has happened and why.

I have my suspicions of who or what Angel, John, and Kamrin are. But I do not dare say. Although I have wanted to ask Angel many times about my theory of what is happening, I know it is so far-fetched that I find it hard to believe myself.

"You have too much time to think of crazy scenarios," I tell myself. "You need to find something to do."

I laugh as I know my last statement to myself is true.

It's two o'clock, and Angel is still not home from his errands. I don't know what he had to do today, but he was gone before I woke up this morning. I figure it must be important as he rarely leaves, and when he does, he never leaves without at least kissing me good-bye.

My stomach suddenly reminds me that I have forgotten to eat lunch, so I head into the kitchen to find a snack. I pause abruptly when I hear John speaking on the phone. He seems excited, and by what he is saying, I believe that he is making plans of some sort. I become nosey. I have to know what he possibly can be so excited about, so I stop and listen.

"I can hear you," John laughs.

"John? Oh . . . Hi," I stutter, "I didn't see you in there."

"Uh hu, sure you didn't?" John replies as he laughs even harder.

"Really, I didn't. I am headed in the kitchen to make a snack. Can I get you something?" I giggle.

"You're going into my kitchen?" John says jokingly.

"Just to make a snack, don't worry," I say.

"OK, just remember the refrigerator is the big square thing in the corner." John laughs in hysterics.

"Oh . . . you are just the funny one, aren't you?" I say as I throw a pillow from the couch his way, barely missing his head.

Walking away, I shake my head and start mumbling to myself, "How do they always hear me? It's like they are in my head and know what I am going to do before I do."

"I know . . . What pains in the butt we are," John yells from the other room, "but you still love us."

"That I do," I scream back with a smile, now convinced more than ever that somehow that are tapped into my mind.

Looking throughout the kitchen, I decide to make myself a sandwich. As I take the bread and lunch meat out of the refrigerator, I get an idea. I set my soon-to-be meal on the table and look around. The kitchen is exceptionally clean and everything in its place.

I will move only a little around, I laugh within myself.

I begin by turning the toaster upside down. Then, I move the pictures that hung on the walls to different spots. But I don't stop there. I also hung them upside down and crooked. I step back to admire my work.

"Needs more," I chuckle to myself.

I start to laugh and proceed with my payback. I open the cabinet doors and decide to also move the dishes around. Taking the plates from their designated area, I replace them with the glasses. I continue moving things to different places until the whole kitchen is turned around. I start to laugh out loud, but I know if I do, John will hear me and know I am up to something. So I hold back my laughter as best I can, make my sandwich, then continue on.

After finishing my sandwich, I stepped back to admire my work once again.

"Nope, still needs more," I giggle to myself.

Proceeding on, I move everything on the countertops to new places, most of which I either set upside down or sideways. I am enjoying myself tremendously as I know this is the ultimate payback for all the tricks that John has played on me. I know this because he spends most of his time in the kitchen because he loves to cook and makes sure it is always kept a certain way. So much so that this kitchen is exactly like the one at the other house. Down to the last fork.

Fork? I think to myself. *What can I do to the silverware?*

Suddenly I get a brilliant idea and decide to take the silverware out of the drawer and hide it in the freezer. Taking the entire contents out of the silverware drawer, I quickly, but yet quietly, wrap the silverware in one of the towels from the drawer, afraid that if I were to use the one that hung on the stove, he would become suspicious and probably search the kitchen for it. I then place it in the drawer of the freezer.

"Perfect," I whisper to myself and head out of the kitchen.

Barely able to hold my laughter in anymore, I scurry into the other room, sit on the couch, and burry my head in the couch pillow. I begin laughing so hard that tears instantly fill my eyes and start falling down my cheeks.

"Lue, are you OK?" I hear from behind me.

It is John. He must have heard me from the other room. Unable to lift my head from the pillow in fear that he will see my laughing, I keep my head buried and shake my head indicating a yes answer.

"What happened? Why are you crying?" he asks in concern.

I shake my head trying to indicate to him that nothing is wrong. He places his hand on my back and begins patting it as he continues to try and comfort me.

If you don't calm down and let him know that you are not crying, he's not going to go away. I think to myself as I try and concentrate on something besides the little prank I had just pulled on him. Finally, after a few minutes of deep thought, I am able to peek out from under the pillow just enough so that I can assure him that I am OK.

"If you're sure that you are OK, I'm going to go start dinner," John says as he starts to get up off the couch.

Every bit of my mind begins to scream at once. I have to distract him. I can't let him go in there yet.

The phone rings, John jumps up and runs into the other room.

"Thank God." I laugh relieved that I have at least a few more minutes before he finds out what I have done.

He seems to be talking to the same person as the conversation begins resembling the last.

I listen closely.

"I'm working on it. But . . . someone . . . around here has big ears," I hear John say.

I look back toward the room, and John is looking in my direction.

"Busted again," I say to myself.

He begins to laugh and gives me his usual charming wink, then continues his conversation on the phone. However, speaking softer than before so I can no longer hear him.

I start to feel bad for what I have done to his kitchen. I know that he had tricked me a few and by all means I have been wanting my revenge. But maybe I have gone a little too far. After all I had messed with something that he cherished, and from what I had learned about John, there are very few things that he holds dear to him, one of them being his kitchen and all that is in it. Besides, cooking is his passion, and I have just messed that up for him as I know it will take hours for him to fix the kitchen back to the way he likes it.

"I have to go fix this before he goes in there," I say to myself. "He is too sweet of a man for such a harsh prank."

I lay the pillow back on the couch and stand up, all the while looking for John. I have to ensure that he does not walk past me and head for the kitchen. I glance into the surrounding rooms. No John. Relieved I start my way back to the kitchen. I am hoping that wherever he has gotten off to, that he will be busy for a while so that I can fix everything before he knows what I have done.

He will never know. I think to myself relieved.

Suddenly I am grabbed from behind and pulled back onto the couch. Instantly, I am being smothered in kisses, and I know exactly who the co prêt is that has pulled me down . . .

"Did you miss me?" Angel asks as he continues kissing me.

"Always . . . How could you not miss these kisses?" I say as I kiss him back.

We sit on the couch, kissing and enjoying each other's company and ignoring everything else around us. It is nice to have him in my arms again, as whenever he is away, it is like a piece of my soul leaves with him.

Angel's kisses, like the sweet taste of candy, are addicting and have become my own obsession. I have found myself many times feeling out of control as the kissing becomes too intense. But Angel, like me, is old-fashioned and waits for the day we will marry to consummate our love. Although at times, I know we both find it hard to follow the path we have set out to take.

"What did you do today?" Angel asks as he sits back against the couch.

"Nothing really . . . read a book . . . made a sandwich," I say as I begin to laugh again.

I had forgotten what I had done to the kitchen as soon as Angel had started kissing me, and it isn't until I say "sandwich" that the memory comes back to mind.

"What so funny?" he asks.

Before I can explain myself, John yells.

"Lue!" John screams from the kitchen.

I turn, look at Angel, and shrug my shoulders as I belt out in laughter.

"Sorry . . . I got to go," I say as I kiss Angel on the forehead and run out the room.

"What did you?" Angel laughs as I run away.

John is right behind me. He is holding a spatula in his hand and is laughing in hysterics. I begin running as fast I can, maneuvering my way through different rooms.

Finally, I am able to loose John and hide under the desk in the library. I am laughing so hard that I know it won't be long before he will find me. As quietly as I can, I adjust my body so that I can get up and run one more time. I am too late. I can hear him come into the room.

"I know you're in here, Lue. Come on out and face the music." John laughs.

Placing my hands over my mouth, I try to keep my laughter at bay as best I can. He is coming closer, so I quietly tuck my body in as far as I can and lean forward, ultimately burying my head into my lap. I wait.

It must have worked because soon after I can hear John leaving the room.

I'm safe! I think to myself as I relax.

I jump up ready to run. But before I can take a step, John is standing in front of me holding out the spatula.

"Where did you come from?" I laugh.

"I'm everywhere." John chuckles.

Taking my chances, I look John in the eyes and give him the most innocent look I can come up with. Then, still holding my laugh in, I hold out my arms to give him a hug. Ready to hug me back, John lowers his spatula and holds his arms out for me to hold. I reach into my side pocket and pull out a spoon. Then, taking a step back, I place it in his hand.

"Are you looking for this?" I laugh as I turn and run as fast as I can out of the room.

As I run back toward Angel, I quickly look back. I can see John is right behind me and is catching up quickly. I pick up my pace and start running faster, causing me to slightly slip on the newly waxed floor. Within seconds, I loose my grip completely beneath my feet and slide into a table next to the staircase, causing a vase to tumble over. Catching the vase before it hits the floor, I place it gently back on the table and begin my journey once again.

I look behind me, but John is nowhere to be found.

"I wonder where he is," I question myself, "I know he was here a second ago."

Aware that he could come around a corner at anytime, I continue to run into the living room. Angel is still sitting on the couch, and I know he must have been wondering what is going on.

Hoping that John will give up if he sees me with Angel, I leap for the couch. Landing in Angel's arms with such force, I cause the couch and us to tumble over. John comes running in to see what the ruckus is and finds us on the floor, lying upside down on the couch, laughing.

"What have you two been up to?" Angel laughs.

"Just a little payback," I say as I try to catch my breath.

John holds up his spatula and chuckles. "You just wait little girl." Then he turns and walks away.

Angel helps me off the ground, and then together we put the couch back to its upright position. I am laughing so hard that my side begins to hurt, and I have to sit back down on the couch. I now have tears streaming down my face as I did when I first had pulled the prank. I don't know what it is about someone laughing like that, but it's contagious, and before I know it, Angel and John are laughing just as hard as me. We sit for a while talking and laughing as I explained what I had done.

Angel begins to laugh even harder, gives me a big hug, pats me on the back, and says. "Good one."

"I'm glad you think it was a 'good one,'" John snickers as he turns and walks away, "I'm the one that has to go fix it now."

I am worried that I have angered him when that is never my intension.

"Is he mad?" I ask Angel with an expression of worry.

"No, he just wants you to think he is mad." Angel laughs, "but I would be careful, his retaliations can be pretty bad."

I become worried. Although I know John is not capable of hurting me, I still have the fear of men.

"What's wrong?" Angel asks as he sees that my tears of joy have changed to tears of anguish.

"Nothing," I lie.

"Oh sweetie, I didn't mean he is going to hurt you," Angel says as he hugs me, "he would never hurt you, no one here would."

"Oh," I say softly.

"I'm sorry, I should have been more selective with my words," Angel says as he continues to hold me in his arms, "I meant he will get you back, but in a fun way."

I take in a deep sigh of relief.

"I know. I just always still have that fear," I state.

"Will this help you forget?" Angel asks as he suddenly begins smothering me with his soft, sweet kisses.

"I'm not sure," I say as I begin to giggle, "I think I need more of those."

"I think I can manage that," Angel chuckles as he continues kissing me entire face and head. After about an hour of hugging and kissing, angel suddenly stops.

"Are you feeling better?" Angel asks.

"Yes," I smile.

Angel gets up from the couch and kisses my hand.

"I have to talk to John about something. Why don't you go upstairs and take one of those bubble baths you love so much? I will be up shortly."

"You know what? I think I might just do that," I state as I get up, give Angel a quick peck on the cheek, and head toward the bedroom.

Angel never comes into the room, and at first I wonder what he has been doing as I have been in the bath for an hour. Anxious to be by his side again, I quickly get out of the bath, get dressed, and walk to the kitchen in hopes that he is still talking with John.

"Do you know where Angel is?" I ask, scanning the entire kitchen for Angel's presence.

"He had to go back to town for something. He said to tell you he would not be more than an hour or two," John explains as he continues to put things back in their original place.

I decide to offer my help. However, John has already put most of the things back into their designated spots and is now standing over the stove cooking everyone's dinner. I stand and watch him for a while as he gracefully moves around the kitchen. He is singing the most beautiful song, and I can't get enough of it.

"Smells good," I say in an apologetic tone.

"It does, doesn't it?" John says in a smug laugh.

"Can I help?" I ask.

"Sure," he answers.

I am a little shocked. He never allows anyone in "his" kitchen when he is cooking. Happy that he is not mad at the trick I had pulled on him, I enter the kitchen ready for my first task.

Wait a minute. I think to myself. *This might be his retaliation.*

I become a little paranoid and find myself questioning everything that he is doing or about to do, that is until I finally come to my senses and realize I am overacting.

He wouldn't do anything tonight. He knows I will expect it. I think to myself, *so just enjoy the moment.*

John shows me some of his secrets on cooking as I watch in great enthusiasm. I had never really watched John as he worked in the kitchen. I find myself intrigued on how much he knows. His food always looks a work of art as he is never satisfied unless it is.

Succeeding working with him for a while in the kitchen, he decides to give me the task of setting the table. He shows me where the expensive china is, and then gives me a quick lesson on how to properly set a table. I let all the information he is giving me sink in as he always sets such a beautiful table, and I am excited that he is helping me to do so also.

After finding the most extravagant tablecloth, I place it on the table. I then go over to the armoire and take out the rose-patterned china John had shown me. After placing the plates and bowls exactly how John had explained, I stand back and admire my work. The table is pretty, but it nowhere as beautiful as the ones that John sets. It needs more. I look around the room until I find two silver candlesticks. Placing them exactly the same distance apart from the end of the table, I know they are in the perfect place.

Taking another glance around the room, I spot the vase of fresh roses Angel had picked for me the day before. They are red, fully bloomed, and match perfectly with the rose-patterned china and the white lace tablecloth I had placed on the table earlier. Turing off the lights in all the surround rooms, I then light every candle I can find in the dinning room. Then, I stand back and admire my work once again.

"Perfect," I hear behind me.

I turn to find Angel behind me.

"Well, thank you," I say proudly, "not bad for my first time."

"I didn't mean the table," Angel says as he winks at me.

Blushing, I reach up, wrap my arms around him, and gave him a passionate kiss. Then looking back at the table, I realize that John has already placed the food on the table and is sitting patiently for me and Angel to stop kissing so we can eat.

Angel, taking my hand in his, walks me over to the seat next to where he normally sits and pulls my chair out for me. As I am sitting, John stands and waits until I have sat down and pushed my chair in. Then, he takes his seat once again.

Such gentleman. I think to myself.

John says the most amazing prayer that night . . . a prayer . . . that brought tears to my eyes. Looking over at John when he is finished, I can see that he had been very passionate about what he had said. I smile at him and wipe my tears.

The food smells so wonderful that I don't know what I want to eat, so I take a little bit of everything. Now for any average dinner table that would not be very much food, but with John's table, it is a complete Thanksgiving dinner every night. He always says that he wants to make sure no one leaves the table hungry. I look down at the table.

"Like that will ever happen." I laugh to myself as I look at the enormous amount of food.

Before I know it, I have enough food on my plate for two people. I am little embarrassed at first, until I look over and see that Angel and John are busy filling their plates also, and their plates have more food on them than mine.

"These all look really good," I tell John as I look around for silverware.

"Thank you," John replies.

"Yes, compliments to the chef," Angel says as he raises his glass of wine toward John.

As I start to get up to get the silverware, I am interrupted by John.

"Is everything OK?" John asks.

"I forgot the silverware," I say a little embarrassed.

"Don't worry about it. I'll get it," John says as he walks into the kitchen. "I want to make sure that things don't get magically turned around while you're in there." He laughs.

Angel and I sit silently for about fifteen minutes waiting for John to return. We know he is in the kitchen as we can hear him moving things around. But what can he be doing, that is taking so long?

Angel is just about to go check on him.

"I'll be right back," Angel smiles as he gets and scoots his chair from the table. "I better go see what is taking so long."

Before Angel gets up from his chair, John emerges through the kitchen door holding a napkin full of silverware. He is giving me the funniest smile.

This can't be good. I think to myself as John continues to give me a look of amusement.

As he walks around the table, he places a setting in front of each of us, never saying a word. Angel picks up his fork ready to eat. Suddenly he too gives a strange look.

"I probably will regret asking this, but why is the silverware freezing?" Angel chuckles.

I had forgotten I put the silverware in the freezer. Looking over at John, I smile in hopes that he is not mad. However, when I look at him, I am uncertain as he is sitting at the end of the table with a stern look about him. Right away I am certain he is mad. The room remains silent, and John's face remains stern as he continues to glare into my eyes. Seconds pass like hours, and I feel I should apologize for doing such a dastardly deed. I am just about to tell him how sorry I am when suddenly the room is filled with laughter. John is now laughing so hard that he can barely speak.

"You might want to ask Lue." John continues laughing as he winks at me.

I am so overjoyed that he is not mad at me. I leap out of my chair, run over, and give him a hug.

Angel looks a little confused on what is going on as he sits and watches us laugh. As I walk back over to my chair, I explain that I had also put the silverware in the freezer when I pulled my little prank. However, I had forgotten I had done so.

Angel shakes his head and begins to laugh, making everyone laugh so hard that none of us can hardly eat.

"I guess I am going to have to limit your playtime together," Angel chuckles.

"Aw, man," John and I say instantaneously.

After everyone has finally settled down, we all are able to finish our meals. The food is great, but what I enjoy most is the company. I love to hear the stories that Angel and John tell. Listening with the utmost attention, I always try to figure out some of their past. But they never give away too much information, and if one of them starts to, the other will interrupt him and the conversation will change. It is obvious they have a lot secrets that they are not ready to share with me as of yet.

John excuses himself from the table and then goes into the kitchen to get dessert. I am full, but I might be able to fit a little dessert into my stomach as it had smelled so good earlier. Besides, I know how hard John works on dinner, and I don't want to hurt his feelings by not at least trying some of it.

While John is in the kitchen preparing our dessert, Angel reaches over and kisses my cheek.

"I love you and everything about you," Angel whispers in my ear.

"I love you too," I whisper back.

Angel gives me a soft kiss on the lips, smiles, takes my hand into his, and looks into my eyes. I find it amazing how we can communicate by doing just so. It is like I can hear his thoughts, and he can hear mine. Although I know it is just the way he looks at me with those baby blue eyes, that I can tell how he is feeling, I like to think that we are connected by more than our love.

I can look into his eyes forever, I think to myself, *and get lost in my own little world and never care to come out of it.*

"Wow, that looks delicious," Angel abruptly says.

I look over at the kitchen doorway and see that John had returned with a strawberry pie in his hands. It looked scrumptious, and I know right away that I want a large piece, even though I am full. After John places the pie on the table, he walks back to his seat and patiently waits for the pie to be passed to him. I can see that the pie is already marked in a certain way to be cut. I became suspicious and begin to wonder why as he has never done that before. In fact, he always left it up to us to cut our own piece, so that we got the size we want. John peeks through the corner of his eyes to see what I am doing, making me more suspicious. I know he is up to something, I just don't know what.

"Is something wrong?" John asks as he peers toward the uncut strawberry pie.

"No," I answer, "I am just trying to figure out the smallest piece to cut."

I am afraid to cut into it, thinking that maybe it is not actually a pie, and when I do, it will explode all over me. I had seen that done on a TV show I had once watched. I think it was Funny Videos or something like that. Uncertain to his motives behind cutting the pie ahead of time, I decide to be very cautious.

"Here, I will do it for you," John says impatiently as he walks back toward Angel and me. "If I wait for either of you to do it, it will be breakfast time."

After cutting and serving the pie, John excuses himself for a moment why he goes back into the kitchen for some milk.

To my surprise, Angel gets up quickly snatches my pie from in front of me and exchanges it quickly for the pie that is sitting in front of John's chair. Confused to why he would do something like that, I start to ask him what is going on. But before I can say a word, Angel places his fingers on my lips to hush me, and then gives me a quick wink.

"I can play too . . . you know," Angel whispers, "just eat your pie like nothing happened."

John returns with three glasses of ice-cold milk to go with our pie. He still has a smirk on his face, so I know he is defiantly up to something. I take the glass of milk, raise it to my lips slowly, and smell it, ensuring that he has not put something disgusting in it. It smells good, so I continue to drink it. It is a perfect glass of milk.

John is at the other end of the table watching every move I make. It is obvious that he is holding back laughter. I just can't figure out why as so far everything has been perfection.

"How's your pie?" John asks as a chuckle escapes from within him.

I look over and start laughing hysterically. Angel then follows my lead, both of us unable to control our laughter. John sits at the other end of the table confused as to why we are laughing so hard.

"Ours is great," Angel manages to say between laughter, "how's yours?"

Figuring something is wrong, John gets up from the table and walks over to the mirror on the wall. Looking into the mirror, he too begins laughing so loud that it echoed throughout the room, making the windows rattle.

John turns and smiles at us.

"How did you know?" He smirks showing his newly dyed teeth.

"Just a hunch." Angel laughs. "Oh and by the way . . . blue is defiantly your color."

CHAPTER 14

A Night to Remember

I T'S SATURDAY NIGHT, and Angel has arranged a special dinner for us. He has not told me where as of yet, but he did say that I should dress formal. Therefore, I am taking extra time getting ready for our date as I want to look as beautiful as I can for him.

I go upstairs and fill the bathtub up with the hottest water I can handle and the pink, rose scented bath beads that Angel had bought me, instantly filling the bathroom with the smell of flowers.

I love that smell. I think to myself.

I put my hair into a bun on top of my head, ensuring that I did not get it wet, then cautiously get into the hot tub. Relaxing in the tub of bubbles, I am reminded of the night before my wedding to Kamrin. The night that I thought was going to be . . . A chill runs through my body, and I have to shake off the memory.

"Why can't I let those memories go?" I scream within myself, "Stop it! Think of only good things, and let the past go!"

Enjoying the rest of my bath, I begin thinking of Angel and how much I have grown to love him. The warm water feels nice on my body, and I become extremely relaxed. I must have fallen asleep as the next thing I know, I being woken up by the sound of someone screaming in my ear. I don't understand what that had yelled, but it frightens me to the extent that I want to be out of the tub quickly.

After wiping my tired eyes, I begin working my way out of the tub. Suddenly an unforeseen force pulls me back down and holds me in place. It is like my entire body is glued to the surface of the bathtub. I try to move again, but I am pinned to the bottom, and I am unable to move even a smidgen. I try to yell, but I am pulled under the water as a hand comes up and grabs the back of my hair forcing my head into the water. I begin to fight with every part of my body that is not glued down, leaving me with only my arms as defense. I am not going to die, not this way, not in Angel's house!

As quickly as it all had started, it is over. My head is released, and I am able to breathe once again. I look around and see no one except a dark shadow that escapes through the bathroom door. Frightened, I jump out of the tub, grab my clothes, and run into the bedroom. I rush directly over to the other side of the room, so that I can grab the necklace off the bureau. Quickly I put it on. I know I am safe once again.

"How do they know where we are?" I ask myself as I walk back into the bathroom to clean up the water that had been splashed out during my last fight for life.

I don't want to spoil the night, so I decide not to tell Angel about what has happened. I open my bedroom window and let the night air fill my room. I'm not worried about anyone of the "strangers" coming back and coming into my window as I learned a while ago, that if they want in, a closed window will not stop them. Besides, I can hear birds chirping outside, and that always is a sign that there is nothing evil around. Feeling a sense of relief, I continue getting ready for the night that Angel has planned for us.

I look over at the clock and realize that I am running late and I will need to rush if I am to be ready in time. I put my makeup on in a flash and then dry and curl my hair. I slip on my dress and shoes. I am ready to go.

Angel is at my door again, and I can tell he is getting impatient because he is now knocking on the door every five minutes.

"Lue, we really have to get going, or we will be late," I hear Angel yell from outside my bedroom door.

"I'm coming right now," I yell back.

I look in the mirror one more time and admire my gown. It is one of the most amazing gowns I have ever seen, and I can't believe that Angel had it made especially for me to wear tonight.

Twirling around in front of the mirror, I continue to admire its beauty.

The dress is that of a white, satin gown, with gold stitching. It is sleeveless and form fitting down to a little past my waist, leaving the rest of the dress to flow perfectly out into a beautiful ball gown. I had never thought I was a very pretty girl, but I have to admit that I look really nice tonight. Not only is the dress a perfect match for my body, but I had taken extra time on my hair ensuring that my hair is in a flawless bun on top of my head and that the strangling pieces that line my face are perfectly curled and my makeup is nothing less than perfection.

"Maybe I should wear my hair down?" I ask myself as I continue to look in the mirror, "or leave it up?"

I continue to debate as I look at my hair in from every direction.

Suddenly a vision of my face consumed by scars appears in the mirror. My heart begins to pound so hard that I expect that at any moment, it will explode.

I run out of the room with tears in my eyes.

"I can't even look at myself in the mirror without seeing the ugly monster that I once was," I cry to myself.

I stand in the hallway alone, until I can collect my thoughts and calm myself down. I do not want Angel seeing me cry, not tonight.

After sitting alone for a few moments, I am finally able to control my emotions. I wipe the tears from my eyes and quickly glance in the hallway mirror, ensuring that my mascara has not run down my cheeks. My makeup is untouched.

With my hands, I smooth out my dress, and I grab my shawl from the chair outside my room and then prepare to walk downstairs to meet Angel.

I am hoping it will be nice outside tonight as I don't want to wear a jacket over my new gorgeous dress. When I come to the top of the staircase, I can see that Angel is waiting for me at the bottom of the stairs. He is so handsome in his black tie and jacket, I want to stay home and keep him for myself. I pause for a moment, so I can take in his beauty, smile, and blow him a kiss.

As I grab the staircase railing, I look down and see that Angel has put red rose petals on each of the stairs. I feel like a princess in a fairy tale as I walk slowly down the stairs.

He is being secretive about where we are going, but he promises it will be a night I will never forget. I can't wait to see where he is taking me. I know it has to be somewhere spectacular because the dress he asked me to wear is so extravagant.

After taking Angel's hand in mine, we walk to the front door. The night air is perfect, but Angel insists that I take a jacket in case it cools off. I do not understand why he is so persistent about it. We will more than likely be inside most of the evening. But I know that there is no point in arguing with him as all he has to do is look at me with his hypnotizing eyes, and I always give in. I take the jacket, hold it in my other arm, and then open the door.

The entire porch is lined with white bags filled with candles, the dancing flames throwing off a slight illumination of flickering light.

"This is beautiful," I say to Angel as I look around at the hundreds of candles that are lit.

"There's more," Angel says with a smile.

Angel and I walk down the porch stairs. Pulling Angel by my side, I head for his truck. Angel stops me.

"We are not taking that tonight, Lue. I promised you a night to remember, and that is what you will get," Angel smiles.

Within seconds, I hear the sounds of horses as their feet prance on the stone pavement.

I look toward the end of the house just in time to see John come around the corner. He is driving an exquisite white, gold-trimmed, horse carriage that is being pulled by two white stallions, their manes as pure white as their bodies, however, accented with gold ribbon. I am amazed by the beauty of the carriage as I look at the detailed gold flower pattern that encircles the rounded carriage. It looks as if they had taken it straight out of a fairy-tale book.

"Where are the mice?" I ask, kidding around.

"Haven't you ever watched the show?" Angel laughs.

"I have turned the mice into horses."

"Well, we better get going then. I have to be home by midnight, or we will be walking back when this carriage turns into a pumpkin." I giggle.

John, in a white tuxedo, holds the door open for us as Angel helps me in. The inside of the carriage is as amazing as the outside. It is covered in plush red velvet, with white rose petals lying about. There are candles hanging on the sides of the large window on the opposite side of the carriage. The light from the candles seem to dance as a breeze from outside gently hits the flames, allowing only a small amount of light to remain inside. It is perfect.

As the stallions gallop down the dirt road, I stick my head out the window and look up to the sky. There is a full moon out tonight, and every star is twinkling in the sky like diamonds, lighting our way down the road. The sky is amazing, and no one could have asked for a more beautiful night.

"Keep looking out, Lue. There's more." Angel smiles.

He is right! As we make our way further down the road, every tree on the path is lit up with white sparkling lights. Each bulb placed perfectly next to the other.

This had to take them forever. I think to myself as I continue to look out of the window in complete and utter awe.

We drive through town. It is the same as every tree is lit by the same type of white sparkling lights and white paper bags filled with candles. It is like looking at heaven above, as the freshly dewed streets sparkle within the light.

"How did you do this?" I ask.

"I have my ways." He teases as he smiles his wonderful smile. "Now shush and listen."

I concentrate more to the sounds outside and begin to hear the soft sounds of music. It is numerous instruments all playing at once. But as one, it sounds like angels singing. My heart melts. I can't believe anyone would do so much for one person. I look over at Angel and smile. He is staring at me, watching my every move as if he is uncertain if I am enjoying myself. I sit back in my seat and lay my head on his shoulder, never losing sight of outside.

The ride seems short as I am enjoying the sights and sounds of the drive. I can't think of anything more I wanted to do but sit here in Angel's arms.

At that moment, no one else in the world exists except for Angel and me.

"We are here," John announces.

I hesitate moving from my spot at first as I do not want to leave Angel's side.

Angel looks out his window and smiles.

"So we are," he replies.

John comes around to the side of the carriage and opens the door for us once again. Angel steps out first and then reaches for my hand.

"My lady," he says as he bows toward me.

I begin to blush as I take his hand and make my way out of the door. After I am safely out of the carriage, Angel takes my arm in his, leans over, and softly kisses my cheek.

"Are you having fun so fat?" Angel asks with a sound of uncertainty in his voice.

"Immensely." I smile, then raise his hand to my lips, and kiss it softy. "Thank you."

"The best is still to come," Angel whispers.

John walks in front of us carrying a lantern as he leads us down a small red-carpeted path that is surrounded in roses. I inhale a deep breath, taking in the wonderful smell of the flowers.

We walk for a while until we come to a small garden. It too is surrounded in candles, allowing the flowers to glisten in the light. In the middle of the garden is beautifully set table.

I continue to look around as Angel leads me to the table.

The crystal and silver that is placed perfectly on the table puts off an array of colors that dance in rhythm to the flickering candles.

Angel walks me to the far end of the table, pulls my chair out for me, and whispers in my ear, "You look gorgeous."

"Thank you," I whisper as I am somewhat embarrassed by all the attention I am getting and find myself wondering what I have done to deserve such nice things.

After I am situated, Angel sits at the chair directly across from me. He waves his hand, and instantly, the sound of music surrounds the area as if he queued the music from everywhere around us. I sit quietly and listen. It is the same music I had heard on the ride up here.

I look over at Angel and smile, showing him my approval of the music.

Angel is captivating, and I can't help but stare at him as when the light hits his hair, it sparkles like a million tiny crystals, causing illuminating aura to encircle his body. His eyes, a brilliant, light blue, glow within the luminosity of the candlelight. His untouched beauty is mesmerizing and makes my heart melt.

"I'm going to get a complex if you don't stop staring." Angel chuckles.

"Oops, sorry. I can't help it. You look so . . ." I stop in the middle of my sentence as I am unable to find a word to describe the beauty I see in him.

"So what?" Angel asks.

"So . . . amazing, beautiful, handsome," I continue until Angel interrupts me laughing.

"OK . . . OK. I understand you think I look . . . decent." Angel laughs.

"Something like that," I reply as I wink his way.

We sit and eat the wonderful meal that John has prepared for us, neither one of us talking much. Angel seems nervous and quiet, which worries me as he always has something to talk about. I begin imagining different things that can be bothering him as the memory of earlier today came back to mind. I begin to fiddle with my food, which is always a dead giveaway that something is bothering me.

"Is everything OK, Lue?" Angel asks.

"Everything's wonderful," I reply. "It's all very breathtaking."

Angel smiles as if he is proud of his accomplishment. I smile back, ensuring him once again that I loved everything he has done. The night air becomes silent once again as we return our attention to the food in front of us. I am still a little uneasy and wish I know why Angel is being so quite.

A strange feeling overcomes me, and I find myself becoming paranoid. I have to look around. My eyes catch a glimpse of a figure, lurking in the shadows. I try focusing my eyes toward the darkness, but the area is too dark, and I can't clearly see the figure in question. I look toward Angel, and I can tell that he is unaware of what I am looking at.

I try to get his attention by clearing my throat, but he seems to be in his own world. I turn to look again, but I am too late. The figure is headed our way. My heart drops, and I become unsettled. I start to tell Angel about the figure that is walking our way, but before a word can escape my mouth, the man is standing at the table. I look up . . . It is John. I sit back in my chair, take a deep breath, and sigh in relief.

"Did I scare you?" John asks.

"No . . . I always think shadows in the dark are good. I have had such luck with them lately." I laugh.

"I'm sorry, Lue," he apologizes.

"It's OK," I reply, taking in another deep breath.

"Is everything ready?" Angel asks John as he gives a little nod.

"Yep, everything is ready and perfect if I say so myself," John says confidently.

Angel gets up from the chair he has been sitting at and walks my way. He takes my hand, helps me away from the table, and we begin walking to the other end of the garden. The path at the other end is dark, so John walks in front of us with a lit candle, the light illuminating the walkway just enough for us to see.

"Where are we going?" I ask Angel.

"I have one more surprise for you," he replies.

"You have already done so much. Much more than any one woman could ask for," I say as I look into his eyes.

Angel stops and takes my hand from his. For a second, I think that maybe I said something wrong and have upset him. I am just about to apologize when all of a sudden he wraps his arms around me and picks me up.

"What are you doing?" I ask.

"I don't want you to get that beautiful dress dirty," he answers.

He then begins walking, however, this time almost tripping on a log that is lying on the path. After regaining his balance, he repositions his grip on me and continues walking without any further problems. Except for one, the dress I am wearing is so voluminous that it has taken over both of us, making it difficult for Angel to see. In fact, I have to keep pulling it down from his face, so that he can see the path in front of us.

"You should put me down. I'm too heavy for you to walk all this way," I say, "plus, this dress keeps getting in your face."

"I carried you once further than this if you remember." Angel laughs. "Besides, we are here."

I lift my head from his shoulder and look in front of me. We are now lakeside. The water is completely still, throwing off a mirror-like image of the moon and stars and all that is around it. It is like looking at the sky above, however, on the ground, with the twinkling lights bouncing off the water and the soft reflection of the clouds shimmering through.

Angel put me down, resting my body onto a picnic blanket that John had set up for us earlier that evening. My dress covers most of the blanket, leaving only a very small area for Angel to sit. He tries pushing the dress aside, but it is no use, the dress is winning the battle.

I begin to laugh at the sight of Angel being engulfed by the lace and tulle from my dress.

"You're the one who had the dress made." I laugh while I continue to watch him.

"I guess, I didn't think far enough ahead." Angel laughs as he continues moving the dress around.

Becoming a little aggravated, Angel finally gives up and sits in the grass beside me.

"There . . . that's better." He laughs.

"Are you sure about that?" I start giggling as the dress continues to keep us at a distance between each other.

"I don't know now," Angel says as he tries to get up, ultimately slipping on the material from my dress that lay past the small blanket.

We both laugh.

"If I can get up, I will be better." Angel chuckles as he pushes the dress aside once again.

I sit and listen to the surroundings around us, while Angel fiddles with a picnic basket that John had left behind. It is relaxing hearing the birds chirping in the night air, and the sounds of fish jumping out of the water chasing lightening bugs fascinates me.

"Can I help you look for something?" I ask Angel after realizing that he has been looking in the basket for quite a while now.

The sudden sound of my voice must have scared him because he leaps backward, losing his balance and lands on his butt with his legs in front of him. I feel bad that I have startled him, so I reach my hand out to help him.

"I'm fine." Angel laughs as he lifts himself back up. "Just sit there and relax."

Within seconds, he is back searching within the basket. He seems to be looking for something specific; however, he is having a hard time finding it. I don't want to startle him again as he looks as if he is on a mission, so I lean back on my arms, lay my head back, and take in the sounds of nature.

"There it is," I hear Angel whisper.

"What?" I ask.

"Oh . . . Um . . . the champagne," Angel mumbles.

"Champagne?" I ask, "what are we celebrating?"

"You," he says and kisses my cheek.

Me? It's not my birthday, is it? I think to myself. *No that's still months away.*

Angel becomes quiet again as he pours each of us a glass of champagne. He no longer seems a little nervous to me. He now seems like he is in an all-out panic. His hands are shaking so hard that as he finishes pouring the champagne, the bottle slips from his hands, luckily landing upright on the ground in front of me. Ignoring what he has done, Angel hands me my glass of champagne and toasts to a long happy life. I like the sound of that and toast back.

Fiddling around, he then drops something in front of me and has to retrieve it. At that time, I did not know that he had done it on purpose. It isn't until the following happens that I understand what the whole night is about.

Angel kneels on the ground in front of me and takes my hand in his. In his other hand, he is holding a small velvet box. My heart begins to beat faster as I can't believe what is happening. Instantly, a smile from ear to ear appears upon my face. My smile so large and intense that my cheeks begin to burn. My forehead begins to sweat, and my hands shake. Taking in a deep breath, I listen to what Angel has to say.

"Lue?" Angel asks.

"Yes," I reply as a tear trickles down my cheek.

"From the moment I met you, I knew you were the one for me. I loved your smile, your laugh, everything about you." Angel continues as he opens the box and places the ring on my finger. "Will you do me the honor of being my wife?"

The ring is amazing. It is the most beautiful ring I have ever seen. I look at it closer and see that it has two angels intertwined together with a large diamond placed in the middle that sparkles like fire and ice at the same time. Angel sits quietly, while I admired the ring. After a few moments of silence, he clears his throat. I look up at him, he has beads of sweat appearing on his forehead and looks as if he is panicking that I have not yet given him my answer.

I jump forward, knocking him onto his back.

"Yes!" I scream, "yes, yes, yes! A million times yes!"

Angel pulls my face to his, and we engage in a long, passionate kiss. I want to say sweet back to him, but the happiness that has filled my body has left me lost for words, except three.

"I love you," I whisper to Angel.

Looking deep into his eyes, I find it hard to understand how a man so perfect would want to marry someone as average as me.

We lay there for a while longer kissing, enjoying the moment. Suddenly a loud, booming sound echoes through the peaceful night air, instantly startling me. I jump straight up into a sitting position as at first I believe it to be a gunshot. I look up, and to my surprise, the sky is now filled with fireworks, throwing off the brightest of brilliant colors. The sky above mixing with the water below, allows the fireworks to light up the entire area. It is amazing.

I turn and look at Angel. He has a smile on his face as large as mine.

"Thank you," I say as I kiss Angel's cheek.

"For what?" Angel asks.

"For loving me and giving me the perfect night." I smile.

March

April

May

June

CHAPTER 15

My Surprise

THE WEDDING DAY is approaching quickly, and everyone in the house is busy preparing for the special occasion. I had requested a simple wedding, with merely me, Angel, John, and a preacher. At first that is how it seemed it would be. That is until I gave in and let John and Angel be in charge of it. Now, I didn't lose complete control of it. One thing I insisted is that the wedding be lakeside, in fact in the same place that Angel had proposed. John and Angel agreed without any argument. So there is a lot that has to be done.

This last month, everyone seems to be working day and night on preparing for the wedding, most of which I am clueless about as Angel and John has kept the final details a secret. I don't mind, they seem to be enjoying themselves and that's what is important to me. Besides, it takes a lot of pressure off me and everything I need to do.

John is the biggest help of all. At first, I felt bad that he was working so hard helping us with everything, but he keeps insisting that he doesn't mind. I am happy that he feels that way as I don't have my mother or father to help me with certain things, and I had grown to think of John as family. He helped me picked out my dress, flowers, and cake and ensures that they will be ready in time. That way I will not have to rush later. So besides everything else I still have to do, I am pretty much done.

I know that he has to be overwhelmed with everything that he is doing because if he isn't helping me do something, he is out with Angel, helping him. I am afraid that if he keeps up such a pace, he will wind up sick, so I suggested that maybe we should have the reception catered. Boy! Was that the wrong thing to say? He alleges, "They would just mess it up." So he insists he makes all the food. He says I shouldn't worry about it. He will have plenty of time to make a wonderful dinner for the reception and that he is not stressed in the least. I laugh every time he praises himself as he is humble man.

John and I have become good friends and will go for long walks and talk when Angel is away. I have come to enjoy his company more each day. Sometimes we will sit in front of the fireplace and talk about our childhood and the silly things we had done and laugh for hours.

"You know what next week is, don't you?" John will tease.

I will always smack him gently because he knows I am stressed and that I will run to check the calendar to see what date it is. I am still not good at keeping track of the date since I have been free from my captor. It is something that I never have gotten comfortable doing and will forget often what day it is.

This has been the norm for the past month as he finds fun to tease me often. I love his sense of humor, so it never bothers me.

Today has been a slow day, and once I find myself walking around trying to find something to occupy myself with, I start thinking back to all the times that John had teased me about the wedding coming closer and decide I should go check the calendar, merely to see how many more days it will be before I am Angel's wife.

When I think John is not looking, I go into the kitchen to check the calendar.

"Caught you!" I hear from behind me.

I jump back, roll my eyes at John, and begin laughing.

"You think you're funny, don't you?" I smirk at him. "Guess what is in three days?"

John's face is now that of panic, and he grabs the calendar from me and looks at it in shock. I guess he had been so busy teasing me that he hadn't realized how close it has come. He drops the calendar and begins running around like someone in an old comedy movie. I stand and laugh as he looks so comical.

"Did you get your dress?" John abruptly asks.

"Yes." I laugh. "You were with me when I picked it up."

"Did you or Angel confirm the cake?" he continues.

"Yes, and they say they will deliver it early." I smile.

"Did . . ."

The panic that he is showing is like the panic that a father would show to his daughter before her wedding. I loved his concern, but I hated seeing him worry. I interrupt him, walk over, and put my hand on his shoulder.

"John, you need to relax. Everything is done that needs to be done," I say as I smile. "I want you to go sit down and relax for the rest of the night."

"OK," he says, "as soon as I make dinner."

"I'm making dinner tonight, remember," I say as I walk him over to the couch, insisting that he sit.

John and Angel have been so busy the last month and now with Angel gone away on business, I want to do something special for my guys to thank them for everything they have done for me. I had to beg John to let me make a special dinner for them. But after coercing him with my begging eyes, he finally gave in and agreed.

He acted like he was not happy about it, but he said he would allow me to do it . . . this time and then laughed.

It has been so long since I had cooked anything, I am a little nervous I will mess it up. But at the same time, I am excited to try it once again.

My menu has been planned for a few days now, so John made sure that I had everything I will need. I look at the clock. Five o'clock. The roast I had in the oven would be done in an hour. It is perfectly timed to be done when Angel walks in the door. I still have other things to make, so I decide that I better get busy. I begin pulling out everything I will need. I am making a mess, so John comes in every few minutes and tries to clean up. I just laugh at him then make him leave. That never lasts long as when I am not looking, he sneaks back in and tries to put things away, making it a game of hide-and-seek for me. I don't mind. I am having fun. So much fun in fact that I find myself singing, something I never do as I have the most horrible singing voice. Although some people disagree, I know I can't carry a tune to save my life.

I am busy preparing dinner for all of us and don't hear Angel come in. The next thing I know, I see a shadow being caste from behind me. Instantly, I think it is John again, so I decide to get back at him. I put a little flour in my hand and quickly turn around, throwing it toward where I believe John would be standing. I begin laughing, that is until I realize that it isn't John. It is Angel! He has been standing here watching me for some time.

"Is this the way you are always going to welcome me home?" He chuckles.

"No." I laugh as I smack the flour off him.

"Don't worry about that. Just come over here and give me a kiss." He smiles.

I reach my arms around his strong body and begin kissing him. We had only been kissing for a few seconds when I suddenly feel something warm and wet running down my head. Instantly, I step back and run my fingers through my hair. I can't believe what I am feeling. He has poured gravy on my head. I begin to laugh so hard that I could barely stand.

"Oh. It's that way, is it?" I ask jokingly as I reach back and continue to feel around until I find the coconut cream pie I had made earlier.

I scoop a small piece into my hand and wipe it down Angel's cheek. That is all it took. The food fight is on, and everything I have been working on all day is being thrown all over the kitchen, never paying attention to what food I am throwing. I just keep grabbing whatever is closest to me and throw it. By the time the food fight is over, we are a mess and the kitchen is worst. Both of us, covered in food from head to toe, slip on the wet floor and plummet to the floor, laughing.

"John is going to kill me." I laugh.

"I think he is going to kill both of us." Angel chuckles as he wipes a piece of pie off my face, "Maybe we should clean it up before he comes in here."

"I think that might be best," I laugh, "Or he will never let me in here again."

Angel gets up off the floor and then reaches down to help me up. We had just started cleaning up the mess when John comes in to see what all the noise is about.

"What in the world happened?" John asks as he looks around the kitchen. "Did the stove blow up?"

Angel and I both look at each other, point toward one another, and instantly begin to laugh again. It isn't so much that we are laughing because we had pointed to each other as it is that we both have been watching a piece of pie that has continued to slip on the ceiling above John's head.

I slowly turn and look at Angel, indicating that maybe he should warn John that he is about to have a piece of coconut pie fall onto his head. Angel is just about to warn John when the pie falls onto Johns head, splattering all over his hair and down his face. Angel and I begin laughing harder than ever, causing us both to slip and fall back onto the floor at the same time.

John wipes his face off and looks down at the pie that is now in his hand.

"I know I shouldn't have let you back in my kitchen." John laughs. "I thought it would be bad, but I had no idea it would be this bad."

"Sorry, I'll clean it up," I tell John as I look at him with my best saddened puppy dog impression.

"Don't worry about it. You two go get cleaned up, and I will take care of this . . . mess." John says between his laughter.

"Are you sure?" I ask.

"Yes, now get going before I change my mind." He laughs.

As Angel and I are walking out the kitchen door, Angel turns and yells back toward John, "Hey! Can we get some sandwiches when you're done fooling around there?"

John picks up a piece of the mess that is lying on the table and throws it toward Angel, ultimately missing him and hitting the wall.

"I think we better go." Angel laughs as he takes my food-covered hand in his, both of us scurrying our way upstairs.

Angel goes into one bathroom, while I go into the other. We both needed showers in the worse way.

I don't know if it is because there is so much food on me or because I am laughing so hard in the shower, but I have to wash three times, ultimately taking me thirty minutes to shower. I am finally clean and can't wait to get downstairs and be with Angel. As fast as I can, I put on my new set of clean clothing and brush my hair.

"Good enough," I say to myself as I reach for the bathroom doorknob.

When I open the door, I see that Angel is already sitting at a table.

"Where did the food come from?" I ask curiously.

"John had it already prepared. He said it was in case your dinner was messed up." Angel laughs.

"That brat!" I scream and then laugh, "I'm going to get him."

"Don't worry about him right now. It's all about us," Angel says with a smile. "I missed you so much and counted the days until I would be back home."

"Me too," I smile back.

We sit and talk for hours. It is nice having him back home, and I hope that he won't have to leave like that often. I know he has to work. I just hate the times that he has to leave for days and hope one day that he will feel that it is safe enough for me to go with him.

I know he is tired from the long trip. You can see it in his eyes. I begin yawning. I am tired myself.

"Are you ready for bed, sweetie?" Angel asks.

"Just about," I reply, letting out another big yawn.

"Do you want me to stay in here tonight?" he asks softly.

"Yes," I whisper back.

We had only been lying down for a few moments before Angel falls fast asleep. I lay there staring at his beautiful face, remembering the first night he had laid with me and how the comfort of his arms felt so right.

"I knew you were my Angel from the beginning," I whisper as I kiss his cheek and fall asleep.

The next morning is incredible as I awake to Angel standing over me with a tray of food. Bacon, eggs, and pancakes, my favorite. As I eat my breakfast in bed, Angel tells me that he has planned a special surprise for me. He insists that all this wedding business has been too much for me and that I need to get away. I agree with him but make him promise me that we will be home the day before the wedding as there are still things I need to do.

He promises to have me home in time and then packs a bag for me. While he is busy in his room packing a bag for himself, I get dressed and then wait for him in my room. When he is all finished and ready to go, he grabs both overnight bags, and we go downstairs to have a cup of coffee with John before we go.

John reassures me that he will get everything done and that I should not worry about a thing. I know he will as he is a man of perfection, and everything he does is amazing.

We do not leave right away as I remember there are a few things I have to get done before we leave. After convincing Angel to let me do so, I run upstairs to finish the wedding present I have been working on for him. I know I won't have time when we get back, so I spend as much time as I need ensuring it is finished before we leave. It must have took longer than I thought because when I finish, I look outside and the bright summer day has turned into dusk.

After putting the present in a safe hiding place, I run downstairs in a hurry. Looking throughout the house, I find Angel and John standing in the kitchen packing a basket full of food and wine.

"I thought maybe you got lost." John laughs.

"No, just lost track of time, that's all," I reply with a smile. "I'm sorry,"

"Are you ready to go?" Angel asks.

"Yep, I'm ready," I reply to Angel and smile.

"OK, I have a few things to go over with John. Then I will be right there," Angel says as he turns toward John.

I take Angel's last remark as a hint that I should wait outside. It is obvious that they have something private they need to talk about as I feel I had interrupted a conversation when I had walked in before.

"OK, I will be outside in the garden," I say as I kiss Angel and John on the cheek.

"You behave while we are gone. I don't want to see anymore blue teeth," I laugh as I wink at John.

John picks up the kitchen towel that lay on the table in front of him and throws it at me. The towel landing on top of my head catches me by surprise, and I begin to laugh.

"Now, I have to go take a shower," I tease.

Angel grabs the towel from my head and snaps me on the butt with it.

"I don't think so." He laughs.

"Fine, I will see you outside then," I tease.

As soon as I step outside, I can't help but notice it is a perfect summer evening. The flowers are out in full bloom, and the sky is clear. Stopping to smell the flowers in the garden, I notice two crosses. They are the same crosses that Angel had placed for my parents at the other house, and now, they are here lying against a similar fountain.

The thought of what had happened to them comes rushing back into my mind, and a feeling of sadness and despair takes over my body. I sink to the ground and pick up both crosses.

"How can I allow myself to be so happy? How could I be so selfish?" I say aloud as my eyes fill with tears.

I begin crying hysterically as I remember the last conversation I had with Jeffery . . . the day that he showed me those horrifying pictures of my parents.

Putting my head against the crosses, I look up to the heavens above and tell my parents how much I love and miss them that I am truly sorry that their lives had ended in such a manner and beg them for their forgiveness.

"It will be OK. Don't worry about me and your dad. We are happy," I hear a soft woman's voice behind me.

The voice is the voice of my departed mother.

I drop the two crosses and quickly look back, only to see a white dove behind me eating from the food I had lay out the day before.

Looking back up to the sky, I wipe my tears as I know that my mother had heard me and she and my father are happy. A slight smile comes back to my face as I watch the white dove fly away into the clear blue sky.

"Thank you," I whisper.

I set the crosses gently back against the fountain, all the while staring at them as I run my fingers around the outline of them. How I miss them so and wish I could have protected them more. Kissing my fingers and then placing them on the two crosses, I stand and begin to walk away.

Angel has been standing at the porch watching me. He looks sad, and I can tell he want to help me with the pain I am feeling inside. But no one can help me, they are gone, and I have to come to terms with that on my own time.

Angel walks over and takes my hand in his. Lifting it to his lips, he kisses the back of my hand gently. We stand and look at the crosses for a while as butterflies float around them. Shaking my head in disbelief and complete disgust, I turn and begin to walk away.

"Where we going?" I ask Angel as we walk toward the truck.

"To a secret place of mine," he replies as he loads the bags into the truck.

Angel holds the door open for me as I get into the passenger side of the truck. I sit and stare in a blank daze as we pull out of the driveway. As I try and snap myself out of my depression, I look over at Angel as he changes the radio station. He is absolute perfect in everyway, and I know I am lucky to have him. Powerless from his beauty, I unbuckle my seat belt and scoot to the middle of the seat so I can lay my head on his shoulder.

Listening to the soft music that is playing on the radio, I am able to calm my nerves completely. I began thinking of the day I had met Angel. The day the music was playing in the forest and had seemed to come from nowhere. I look up at Angel and once again begin to wonder about him and about his past.

"What are you thinking about?" Angel asks.

"I'm just thinking that there is so much I don't know about you. So many questions I want to ask," I reply.

Angel stops talking, and the truck becomes quiet once again, with only the sounds of the music playing in the background. I put my hand on his leg indicating to him that it is OK. I know he will tell me more when he is ready to do so. Until that time, I have to learn to be patient.

The ride down the winding road is beautiful . . . so beautiful in fact, I make Angel stop on the side of the road, so I can get out and look at the city lights below. Angel pulls the truck in backward, so we can put the tailgate down and enjoy the view.

It is now dark outside, and all the lights in the city look as if they are on. The twinkle of the lights make the ground sparkle like million of diamonds in the sunlight. It is breathtaking.

A cool breeze begins to blow, causing a chill to come over my body. I try snuggling up to Angel, but he too is cold now. Angel reaches over and pulls out a blanket from one of the bags and wraps it around both of us. It don't take long before the warmth of our two bodies together warms us up.

We sit for hours looking at the lights below and talking about the upcoming wedding. I am shocked to learn that Angel is also excited as I always thought men do not really get excited about such things as weddings.

"I guess I am not like other men." Angel smiles.

"No you're not. I have not ever met a man as compassionate as you," I say as I wrap my arms around him.

"I guess it's the Angel in me." Angel laughs and winks at me.

"It must be," I say as I wink back.

Angel kisses my forehead and asks. "You always talk about me, why can't you see how special you are?"

"I never thought of myself as being special," I reply.

"Well, you better start now because you are very special to me. You are the one I have been waiting for all my life," Angel says in a soft voice.

I have never had someone be as charming and wonderful as Angel is to me every time we are together. I did not know what to say as those are the sweetest words I have ever heard someone say, especially to me. As I lay my head back onto Angel's shoulder, I touch my lips to his and kiss him softly.

The night becomes colder an indication that it is time to get back on the road. I help Angel fold the blanket and put it back into the bag. We then take one last look at the amazing lights below us, get back into the front seat of the truck, and head back down the road.

"Where are we going?" I ask.

"I thought a short camping trip would be nice," Angel replied. "I know how much you enjoy the fresh air."

"That sounds good, just us and the fresh air." I smile.

"I knew you would like the idea, since you have been so busy in the house with all the wedding details," Angel says as he caresses my hand.

"Actually, John has done most of the work." I admit.

"I know he is such a good man. I'm sure it is his pleasure. He loves doing things for people," says Angel.

"I can tell. He is always there to help me, no matter what I am doing," I giggle, "even if it is to clean up a mess that I have made."

"He loves you, Lue. He tells me all the time how he thinks of you as a sister." Angel smiles.

"I love him dearly," I wink, "as a brother."

I nudge Angel with my arm indicating that I am being ornery, Angel nudges me back. We both begin to laugh as we continue on our drive.

Our drive ends at the other end of the lake where Angel had proposed to me. It is dark with only a lantern to light our way. After helping Angel grab our bags and gear out of the car, we walk to the edge of the lake. To my surprise, there are tents, tables, and everything we need already set up.

"You're full of surprises," I say as I wink at Angel.

"I couldn't have you sleeping on the ground now, could I?" Angel winks back. "I knew we would be late getting here, so I set everything up early this morning and then sneak back in bed."

"I'll never understand why you go through so much for me. I don't think I am worth all the trouble you go through," I say.

"I do," Angel says as he kisses me on the cheek.

With nothing to do but build a fire, I sit and relax while I watch Angel prepares to light the logs. He already has a pile of wood that he had stacked earlier ready to go. So it isn't long before the fire is raging, keeping the campground warm.

Although it has been a while since the incident in the bathroom, I am having a hard time forgetting it. I had not wanted to tell Angel about it. However, I am afraid what might happen if I don't. Laying my head on Angel's shoulder, I go into deep thought of what will be best.

After just a few moments of thought, I raise my head and look at Angel. I know he will protect me, and he should know everything about what has happened in case it happens again. Besides, I still am not sure what those figures were. All I know is that they are the epitome of evil and for some reason want me.

I look up at Angel again and smile.

"I will tell him tomorrow," I think to myself.

Knowing it is late and we both have grown tired, I decide that it would be better to tell him in the morning when we both are more awake.

Besides, he seems to be in deep thought himself as he stares out into the emptiness of the dark. It is obvious that he too has something on his mind as he is quiet and unresponsive. I have only seen him that way a few times since I have known him, so I know it must be something important that he is concentrating on.

Suddenly Angel turns to me, his face with the expression of determination and smiles.

"Lue," Angel says.

"Yes?" I respond.

"It's time." Angel smiles.

"Time?" I ask.

Angel shakes his head.

"Time for what?" I continue, all the while looking at him in confusion.

"Time for you to know everything," Angel replies.

"Everything?" I ask.

"Yes. I want you to know everything about me, what has been going on, and who you are to me," Angel says as he holds my hand close to his heart, "Everything."

CHAPTER 16

The Truth

MY HEART BEGINS pounding in excitement. I know I had wanted to know about him and about what had been going on. However, I am not sure if I am ready to hear it, as there have been so many strange things happening, all of which are unexplainable. Taking in a deep breath, I hold Angel's hand tightly in mine and prepare myself for what he is about to tell me.

"I know I have been secretive about who I am and what is going on, but I have good reason. When I am done, I hope you would have a better understanding of why I have kept from you for so long," Angel states.

"OK," I say as I sit and await what he has to say.

"Where to begin," Angel says to himself, "I guess the very beginning will be best."

I sit contently and wait to hear his story.

"Now I want you to sit and listen with an open mind. This might all seem a little strange to you. But I want you to know I am telling the truth," Angel says as he looks at me.

I could tell that he is serious but also worried about what reaction I might have.

"OK, I'm listening," I say trying to assure him that I will be OK with whatever he has to say.

I love this man with all my heart, and I know that no matter how crazy his story might be, it would never change the way I feel about him.

"I will start with where and when I was born." Angel says, then hesitates and walks over to where our bags are kept.

"But first I want you to have something, it will help you understand more of what I am saying," Angel continues.

Reaching in to one of the bags he had brought from home, he pulls out a large book and hands it to me. Looking at it closely, I can see that it is the book I had found in the library – the book that had mysteriously disappeared a few different times.

Taking the book and laying it in my lap, I look up at him in confusion. Angel reaches over and directly opens the book to a certain page. I look down; it is the page that I had seen before – the page that disappeared – the one with Angel's picture in it.

Still confused, I look back up at Angel.

"I'm sorry I had to take the book before, but I couldn't let you see what I am until it was time. It could have changed everything if you would have known too early," Angel apologizes.

Staring back at the book, I try to understand what he is about to tell me. I know this man in the book looks a lot like Angel, but I also know the book is over two hundred years old and so the picture cannot be him. Or at least I can't comprehend how it could be.

"Maybe it is a past relative," I think to myself.

Angel comes over and takes a seat in front of me. He looks down at the book then up at me. It is as if he is trying to read what is on my mind.

Now, facing directly in front of me he begins his story.

"That book, there in your hands, contains a picture," Angel begins.

"Yes," I say as I anticipate his next words.

"The picture looks like me," he continues.

"Yes," I say patiently.

"That is because it is me," he says softly.

"How could it be you? The book is really old," I say as I look down at the picture.

"Just listen and I will explain," Angel continues.

"OK, not another word," I reply.

"I was born in 1810 to a woman in Scotland. She was a young lady that had been raped by a farmer down the road. Her family, unable to deal with what had happened, kicked her out of the house along with me with just the clothes on her back." Angel says as a tear wells up in his eyes.

"1810? How could that be?" I ask in disbelief. "You would be over two hundred years old."

"Just listen," he interrupts.

"With nowhere to go, my mom managed to make ends meet by cleaning for the wealthy people of her town. We lived in a small shack in the outskirts of the town and every day she would walk down a long dirt road to different houses where she worked, sometimes working late into the night.

"One night she was later than usual, and I became worried. I knew where she had been working that day, so I decided to walk down the road to meet her. After reaching about half way to the house, I thought she would be at, I heard a woman screaming. I began running toward the sound and found my mom engulfed by men. Well, I don't want to say men, they were black shadows."

"Like what I have seen?" I ask interrupting his story.

"Yes," he answers as he continues on with his story.

"I couldn't tell what they were doing to her, but it sounded like they were hurting her, and she was in a lot of pain. I tried to get to her, but there were so many of them that I got scared and became paralyzed from fear. Her cries for help became louder, and I knew that if I did not help her, she would die. Confused and desperate, I overcame my fear and jumped into the pile of men. I began hitting them as hard as I could and as fast as I could until I was finally able to reach my mom. She was sitting on the ground crying. Standing my ground, I was able to hold the men back as I helped her up. Within seconds, one of the big men started screaming at her in a strange language, one that I did not understand. I stood there and held on to my mom's dress as tight as I could. I was determined that if they were going to kill her, they would have to kill me also. My mom tried to pull me away from her dress, but I was too stubborn and would not let go. In desperation, she started yelling at me to run home, but I refused. I could not leave her there alone. Standing in front of her protecting her from the men, I was petrified. My mom kept screaming, "You can't have him." I didn't understand what she meant. But I did know she was talking about me. The men became outraged as she tried to hold me back and vaulted toward us, trying to take me from her. At first, she tried to fight them off, in fact we both did. There were just too many of them, and they were the strongest men I had ever seen. It was only a few minutes later that I knew that we were damned and will probably die because of these men. My mom also must have known that, because suddenly she began screaming as loud as she could, "I will never let him be like you!" She then took a knife out of her jacket. Now, I thought that she was going to go after the men with the knife, but that is not what happened. She looked into my eyes and with the most desperate look I had ever seen, she plummeted the knife into my heart. I don't know why, but I knew that she did it out of love. I mean, don't get me wrong, I was in total disbelief that she had killed me. But something told me she had no other choice. But most of all, I remember hearing an immortal growl coming from the crowd of black shadowed men. I looked over, and the largest of them all was standing next to my mom, looking as if he was saddened also. That, to me, was the strangest thing," Angel explained further.

"Who was the man?" I ask.

"Just a minute, and I will explain that," Angel answers.

"OK," I say with a sorrowful heart, as his story so far is very sad.

"Within seconds of being stabbed, I fell into my mom's arms – dying. She sat me on the ground, lay me in her lap, and began to pray. I remember what she said in her prayer as if it was yesterday.

"Please, Lord, forgive me for what I have done. I had no other choice, and I could not let them have him.

"Then she looked down at me and said, 'I love you Angel, please forgive me. I did not want you to become one of them. Now, I know you will be an angel – the angel I always knew you would be.'

"The next thing I knew was that all my fears and pain disappeared, and I was walking toward a bright light . . . I was in heaven," Angel pauses as he takes in a deep breath.

Looking into Angel's eyes, I can feel his pain as he tells his story. I want to jump up from where I am sitting and hold him in my arms until all his pain is gone. But I know he has a lot more to say, so without saying a word, I let him continue with his story.

"You see the man that had raped my mom was a man from the dark side. A man of pure evil and he had raped my mom, knowing that she would get pregnant. He wanted me at his side as he ruled the clan he had created. My mom knew that the only way to keep me from a life of evil was for her to take my very breath from within me. It was a sacrifice she had to make, and I am happy she had done it." Angel pauses.

"In heaven, I wanted to ensure that there would never be another woman that would have no other choice, but to take the life of her child to keep it safe. I was sent back to earth ten years later as a thirty-year-old adult – the person you see standing in front of you. Now there was a stipulation, and that was, that I was to be earthbound for at least two hundred years and that I would continue to hunt the men down and try to help as many women and children as I could. I went on with my life in secret – moving many different times, following the men from the dark side as their group continued to grow, quickly. It wasn't long before I was outnumbered and knew I was going to need help. Slowly, one by one, I received helpers from above," Angel explains.

"John?" I ask.

"John is what is called a guardian angel. He helps individual people like you and helps me keep things in order," Angel replies.

"And you? Are you a guardian angel?" I question more.

"No Hun. You see, there are different types of angels. Take me and John for example, we are both angels, but we have different powers and different duties. I am an archangel, so I have more power than a guardian angel and more responsibilities. I watch over the entire earth, whereas a guardian angel usually only cares for a few people,"

"So is that the only kind of angels there are?" I ask.

"No, there are more." Angel smiles and says, "For instance, do you remember seeing the balls of light during the fight when you came and saved me?"

"Yes," I say as I listen closely.

"They are called 'Thrones.' They come to earth to fight demons and are seen as balls of light and never in human form," Angel explains as he watches my expressions.

I will admit I am a little confused about what he is saying, as I always had believed in angels but never knew that they really did exist.

Angel continues with his story.

"John has been with me for about 150 years. He is one that I tried to save, but was too late. He had also died in his mother's arms, as she tried to keep him away from the demons. He was angry at what had happened and wanted to help me, so he was sent to earth as a guardian angel to the women we were trying to help." Angel smiles.

"Demons?" I ask, "Is that what those dark shadowed men are?"

"Yes," Angel answers, not looking away.

"What do I have to do with all this?" I ask.

Becoming silent, Angel lowers his head and begins staring at the ground. I can tell that he does not want to tell me what I have to do with all of this, and honestly, that scares me.

"Angel," I ask again, "where do I fit into this story?"

Angel raises his head slowly, looks into my eyes, wipes a tear from his cheek, and continues once again.

"I knew that the leader of the demons was here somewhere, and he had a woman he was after. I had been looking for you for sometime, but through the years, they have learned how to hide their main homes. The home like you had been in – the one you were tortured in for many years.

"We were uncertain who they were after, as they had learned to hide their identities from us, making it harder to help the victims before they get to them. By the time I was able to figure out who they were after, they already had taken you to their main home. Hiding it between heaven and earth and making it impossible for me to find you," Angel says as he holds my hand in his.

"What do you mean between heaven and earth? I was kept in the forest – the forest you found me in," I state.

"The forest that you thought you were in didn't really exist. It was only made to make you think it did. You were actually in an unknown dimension, one that they had made without my knowledge. It was well hidden and protected, so I could not find you as long as you were in the house. But once you escaped and were able to get through the "make-believe" forest, it was only seconds before I know where you were. Or at least that is what I thought. I became disoriented and could not find you at first. I had been looking for hours, before I was able to find you at the riverbank," Angel explains further, "Unfortunately, I was too late and you had already fallen and broken your leg."

His story, although interesting, seems far-fetched and hard to understand, as it all sounds like some old folktale that would be passed down from generation to generation. Angel must have realized what I was thinking because he continues without hesitation.

"When I found you, I fell in love with you instantly. I knew that I was to find truelove once in my lifetime. However, I did not realize it would be you . . . The women I was trying to save," Angel says as he winks at me.

"Who is Kamrin?" I ask.

"Kamrin is the leader. The day he had come to get you from the house, John realized what he was. That is why he had to stop you from going with him," Angel continues.

"Lightning?" I ask.

"Yes, that was his only way of defense, as he was not sure how many more of them were around. When I got home, he explained to me what had happened. It wasn't until that day in the police station I realized who Kamrin truly was," Angel says as he rubs my hand gently.

"You mean, besides the leader?" I ask.

"He is the man that had tried to take me that day – the man that had gotten my mother pregnant. Lue . . . He is my father," Angel lowers his head once again.

I could feel my mouth drop open as soon as he said the word, *Father.*

"How could Kamrin be your father?" I ask. "He is the same age as me, and you say you were born in 1810."

"You see, Lue, demons are the same as me. They too live forever. Kamrin has lived many more years than me," Angel explains.

"Why didn't he just marry me then? Why did he take me and torture me for so many years, when he could have gotten what he was after anytime he wanted?" I ask.

"He knew I was coming and that we are soul mates, before I did. You see, it was always your destiny to be with me, and he knew that merely marrying you would not keep us apart. That in fact, I would find you and you would fall in love with me.

"Because of that I am your destiny there was only one way to make you truly his. He had to change you. You see, you always had a heart pure as gold, and for you to be his, he had to take that from you and make you the same as him – evil.

"He was angry that his own son – the one that he had created to follow him, had became the one that would now fight him. So, he took you and tortured you every day hoping that you would lose faith, causing you to give into him. But you never did, you kept your hope and faith close to your heart and was able to escape his clutches," Angel explains.

"What about the other women?" I ask as I continue to take in everything he is telling me.

"Those were other women his followers had taken to have their children. After they found out what the men truly were, the women tried to run and hide. But he captured them and kept them hostage until their babies were born. Then, to keep them quiet, he would kill them," Angel says as he begins to weep. "They were the women I did not get to in time."

"The room I was brought into was an infirmary?" I ask, sickened by the thought.

"Yes," Angel replies with a weary heart.

I start to think back about the women I had seen that day in the other room of the dungeon. I now know why that one girl was cut from her chest to her pelvic area. They had cut out her baby. What a horrible thing to happen!

"But Samantha wasn't pregnant, nor cut," I say to Angel as I continue thinking back to what she had looked like. "But she did mention something about them saying she was ready to be seeded. Does that mean get pregnant?"

"Yes, for the ones that refuse them, they torture them until their hearts became impure. Then and only then can they 'seed' them."

"What a horrible thing!" I say with sadness in my heart. "They only want the babies, so there will be more of them?"

"Yes," Angel answers.

"The note said it gave him power to kill these women. But you said that they torture the women so that their souls will be impure, and then they could have their baby? I am a little confused." I inquire.

"That is right, you see when he kills a person and that person has an impure soul, their soul goes to him. Now if you look around this world, you will notice that there are a lot of people that are impure. So you would think they will just go after them, but they don't. He is a sick and twisted person and by taking someone who is a good person and tearing them down to the point that they have lost all faith, gives him pleasure. Some of us even think that he gets more power from the ones who are changed, and that is why he is now targeting them. So as far as we can tell, they are now taking women, the ones that refuse to give into them, they hurt them and mangle them until they finally give in, then after they have their baby, they kill them," Angel tries to explain. "That way not only do they get pleasure from torturing them, they also get their souls and their babies."

"What happens to the ones that don't give in?" I ask.

"They became lost souls that are held by him in his world until an Angel can release them," Angel answers.

"Is that what we were seeing that night coming from the house after we saved you?" I ask.

"Yes, those were lost souls. The ones that never gave into them, but were still killed," Angel says with a saddened expression.

"Why does he keep coming back after me even though I escaped?" I ask.

"We are not sure why he is being so persistent. All we can think of is that, you are my soul mate and somehow if he were to have your child, when your love and soul belongs to an archangel, it would make him more powerful than he has ever been," Angel explains. "But we are still uncertain. But we will find out."

"Marrying me and possibly having a child does that make you stronger?" I ask, indicating that maybe that is why he wants to marry me.

Angel begin to chuckle.

"No, sweetie, I get my strength from heaven. I want to marry you because I love you with all my heart," Angel says as he kisses my hand, "You are my one and only true love."

I am relieved to hear that because I love him dearly, but I don't want to marry a man that wants to marry me for power. I smile at Angel and kiss his hand back.

"Can you have a child?" I ask.

"Yes, I am pretty much like you or any other person, except for a few exceptions," Angel explains.

"You mean like you have powers," I ask.

"A few," Angel smiles.

"You are the one that healed me?" I ask.

"Yes I did. However, when I did so, I became weak and had to leave to regenerate my strength. See, that is something that is left to a different type of Angel and by doing what I did, I went against all rules, causing me to become weak. Weaker than I had ever been," says Angel.

"Why did you take me to the hospital, why not take me home and fix me right away?" I ask trying not to sound ungrateful.

"I was not sure that I could help you, and I wanted to make sure that you were taken care of before I tried anything so daring. Your safety comes first. It is a good thing that I did wait because I was powerless and if you weren't at my house when I left, they could have taken you again," Angel explains.

"Why take the chance? You should have left me mutilated," I state.

"I love you and could not bear to watch you suffer anymore than you had," Angel says with a smile.

I want to ask about my parents and why he couldn't do the same thing for them. But I don't; as I know that he would have if he could. Besides, I am grateful for what he already has done, and I can tell that he loves me wholeheartedly and would do anything he could for me and that includes bringing my parents back to me.

"Do you mind if I ask you some more questions?" I ask.

"Sure, ask anything you want," Angel replies.

"How does the necklace and chandelier work?" I continue.

"The necklace is a crystal that is filled with a little bit of heaven. The bigger necklace that John had given you that day to sneak in was filled with the souls of Thrones. When you threw the necklace on the ground, it released them. It was the only way they could get into the realm of the demons. As for the chandelier, the angels that surround it are angels that watch over me. When a demon comes in contact with it, they cannot pass under it, as it puts them into a lot of pain. It lets you know who is good and who is evil at heart, I guess you could say. Unfortunately it only keeps them from entering the front door," Angel explains as he reaches over to the basket of food we had brought with us and takes out two sandwiches.

"The room that John brought me to, what was that?" I ask.

"That is a room we use to go from one place to another in a hurry. I guess you could say it is almost like time travel for us angels." Angel smiles.

"But John took me in there, and I was able to travel like him," I say.

"Yes, another rule we broke," Angel chuckles.

I don't like the idea that he has broken rules for me, as I don't know if that means that he will have to answer to a higher power and possibly be taken back to heaven. That is if that could happen.

"Did you get into trouble?" I ask.

"No," Angel laughs, "I just had to explain myself."

"OK," I say in a stern tone, "I don't want to see you get into trouble over me."

"Don't worry, I won't," Angel says as he tries to open a jar of pickles.

I reach over, take the jar from him, and pop it open.

"Thanks," Angel smiles.

Angel hands me a plate of food. Unconsciously I take it, all the while continuing to go over in my head all that has been said.

I find all of this very strange. Here I am talking to the man that I am going to marry about angels and demons as if it is a common, everyday subject.

"I guess maybe it is to some people," I whisper to myself.

"What?" Angel asks.

"Oh, nothing. Just thinking out, loud," I explain.

"OK," Angel says, swallowing the bit of sandwich he has just taken, "I want you to know you can ask me anything."

"You say you live forever." I say, without any further hesitation.

"Yes," Angel answers.

"What is going to happen when I get older and you stay young?" I ask Angel in a concerned voice.

"I have the choice of growing old with you or continuing to live my life as it is now," Angel replies.

"What happens if you choose to grow old with me?" I ask.

"I will be like you. I will have no more powers. I will be human once again," Angel says in a nonchalant tone of voice.

I don't like the sound of that, as I can't see him being anything else than he is now. I don't want him to notice that I am concerned, so I continue talking without any further hesitation.

I have so many more questions, but I have already taken in so much information that I decide I will ask just one more and save the rest for a later time.

"One more question?" I ask Angel.

"Sure," Angel replies.

"Why now? Why tell me now?" I ask.

"I wanted to make sure you will still love me no matter whom or what I was," Angel says as he winks at me. "It is a stipulation of mine, I guess you would say. I couldn't marry you without you knowing the true me."

"Angel . . . I love you unconditionally. You have done so much for me and taken so many chances for me. How could I not love you?" I say as I wink back, "Besides, look at yourself. You are the most beautiful man I have ever seen, and those kisses of yours are like . . . magic."

Angel stands up and holds his hand out for me to hold onto. I stand up and together we walk closer to the fire. As he lifts his arms, music begins to play, as it had before. The music is amazing in the quiet night air.

Holding me in his arms, Angel begins singing softly, his voice . . . the voice of an Angel, instantly melts my heart.

Laying my head on his shoulder, I listen as he sings the most amazing song. I hold him closely as we begin to dance slowly, both of us enjoying being in each other's arms. I know I would never let him go.

"Lue. You can never tell anyone," Angel whispers.

"OK," I say as I kiss him softly.

CHAPTER 17

A Day of Dreams

IT IS THE day before the wedding and people are busy throughout the house, each doing something different. I am trying to help, but every time I start to help someone, they tell me to just sit down and relax. I feel like I am in the way, so I decide to leave everyone alone and keep to the duties John has assigned me. This pretty much consists of pampering myself the entire day. This does not last long, as after a few hours, I begin getting bored and decide that I will ignore their requests and do something to help. At first it worked, and I was able to sneak downstairs and work on things that I noticed had not been done yet. That is until John catches me and I am sent back to my room with the menial task of folding napkins.

At first I try to be creative and try to fold the napkins so that they look like doves, but after two hours of trying, I give up and set the napkins back into the box for later and lay down on the floor for a moment to rest my neck and back. I must have fallen asleep on the floor, because the next thing I know, Angel is picking me up and laying me on the bed. I look up at him; he has the biggest smile I have ever seen him have.

"Are you happy?" I ask in a tired voice.

"Very," he replies and softly kisses my lips.

Angel had insisted on staying in town for the night. He believes the groom should not see the bride before the wedding, so he doesn't want to take the chance of seeing me. I did not want him to leave, and all the begging and pleading I tried, none of it worked. It isn't the fact that he won't be here in the morning when I wake up or that I won't be able to see him until we meet at the altar that is bothering me. The problem is that I am still a little worried about being here alone – afraid of the demons coming here. Angel understands my worries and has decided to have John stay in the room next door and a few of his friends also would stay. It does make me feel better knowing that there are about fifteen strong men watching over me tonight, but I still won't have my Angel.

"Can you lay with me until I fall back asleep?" I ask.

"For a little bit," he teases.

Angel lies down beside me and puts his arms around me. As soon as I feel his warm body next to mine, I fall asleep.

After Angel leaves, I instantly begin tossing and turning in my sleep, as memories of Kamrin, with his mutilated face, begins haunting my dreams, until I am dreaming of nothing more. The dream becomes so intense that I can no longer tell if it is a dream or if it is reality. It is like I can feel his disgusting fingers as he ties me down to a chair. He is so close and so real that I can reach out and touch his scars, feeling his dry scaly skin beneath my fingers. He is wearing all black like I had seen him last. His eyes become fiery red and then snow-white as he touches my stomach and begins chanting in the same language I had heard the other demons speak the day they invaded my room and took Angel away.

My stomach begins to burn with such intensity that I instantly begin to cry. I want to scream, but my screams seem to be muffled, and the only sounds you can hear are the sounds of his deep heavy breathing as he continues to chant. I try to run, but my arms and feet are bound in barbwire. Every inch I move, feels so real that I can feel the sharp edges of the barbwire as it rips into my skin, making it impossible for me to try anymore. I am his hostage.

I try biting him and spitting on his face. Nothing fazes him, and he never loses focus on what he is doing. He just stays in one place saying the same thing over and over again as his chanting becomes louder and more intense. I look down at my stomach as it starts to feel like it is being ripped in half. My stomach is gone! It is as if someone has cut my entire midsection out of my body and then has lit the emptiness of the hole on fire. I am petrified at the sight and afraid that if I don't wake up soon, I will die in my sleep. But no matter how much I toss and turn, nothing works. The dream continues as he continues in his trance. I can't wake up from this nightmare!

The fire inside me continues to grow and I am desperate. I begin begging myself to wake up. Within seconds, the fiery pit that once was my stomach disappears and my midsection returns. The pain in my stomach becomes overwhelming, and I let out a scream that echoes throughout the house as I watch my stomach grow to the size of a woman's stomach that is nine months pregnant. His face becomes red . . . Red as lava and begins to glow, and his eyes instantly change from snow-white to a fiery red. He lets out the most sinister, skin-crawling laugh and then instantly vanishes within a black haze of fire.

I jump out of bed. I am soaked in sweat and had been crying in my sleep. I take my gown in my hands and start to wipe my sweat and tears away, when I suddenly notice that I have cuts on my wrists.

"It was a dream, right?" I ask myself.

I look around and see a broken glass on the bed and realize that at sometime during my dream, I must have swung my arms around and broke the glass with such intensity that some of the glass landed on the bed and that is where the cuts had come from.

"John!" I scream as my wrist continues to bleed and my head begins to spin.

John comes bursting in and runs to my side.

"What happened?" John asks, as he runs into the bathroom for a towel.

"I must have hit my wrists on the glass while I was sleeping," I explain to John as I bent over in pain.

John is concerned, so he insists that I tell him all about the entire nightmare. I described to him about my dream and what had happened. His expression instantly changes from concern to all-out panic, and he begins asking a bunch of questions. I try to answer as many as I can, but my mind is becoming hazy, and I am feeling sick. I run to the bathroom, close the door, and vomit, almost missing my target.

When I am done, I splash some water on my face and walk back to the bed. I can hear John talking to Angel on the phone. He is explaining to him what has happened and what I had told him about the dream. John hangs up the phone quickly, wraps my wrists back up, and sits with me on the bed.

"Angel's on his way home," says John with concern in his eyes.

"You didn't have to call him. I'll be fine," I reply as I look down at the slices on my wrists.

I don't know if I am totally out of it or what, but it seems like it's only seconds after John had hung up the phone that Angel comes running in the room in a panic. He picks me up and sets me in his lap.

"Lue?" Angel asks.

"I'm fine. John worries too much. I cut my wrists on that glass over there, that is the worst of it . . . Dreams go away," I mumble as my mind feels scrambled.

Angel grabs my wrists and holds them tight. I can feel the warmth of his hands on my wrists, and the pain begins to subdue. My wrists suddenly become cold and the pain is completely gone. Angel releases my wrists and looks down at them.

"I see what you mean, it's no big deal. Only a little scratch," Angel smiles.

I look down, the blood is gone and only a pin size scratch remains. In a daze, I look up. Angel, John, and all the men that are staying in the house are standing around me. They are all talking quietly and staring my way. Angel looks at me, lays my head in his arms, and touches my head. I fall fast asleep.

The next morning when I wake up, I look outside. It is a perfect day, and I am anxious to marry Angel.

As I dance around the room singing, I notice that someone has filled my room with vases of every kind of flower imaginable. It is beautiful. I walk around taking in the different smells each flower has to offer.

This day is going to be amazing, I think to myself in excitement.

John knocks on my door to see if I am awake and to inform me I have two hours to get ready. I look at the clock; I had slept in for a long time. Panic overcomes me. I begin running throughout the room getting my attire ready. I had lost one of my shoes a few days ago and had forgotten to look for it. I search for over a half hour, and I start getting very aggravated.

"Calm down and think of the last place you saw it," I say to myself.

I look around the room.

"That's right, I had it over by my bed," I think to myself.

I run over and look under the bed. After searching for only a few moments, I see the heel of the shoe sticking out from underneath a small towel. I start to move the towel aside when I realize that one of the beads from the shoe is tangled up on a loose string on the towel. I pull the shoe and towel out from underneath the bed. There is blood all over the towel. My mind begins to wonder back to last night and what had happened. I look down at my wrist expecting to see deep gashes, but there are nothing more than just a few minor scars that I had recently gotten from working in the garden. After closely inspecting my wrists for a few seconds more, I decide that everything that had happened last night was nothing more than a nightmare. Besides, I only had a little more than an hour left to get ready, so I don't have the time to remember everything that had happened. I am alive and about to marry the man of my dreams, nothing else matters.

My hair is a mess, and I know it will take an hour to get it perfect, as I have no idea how I want to wear it. I stand in front of the mirror for about ten minutes as I try many different hairstyles. Finally, after about ten different styles and an hour of messing with my hair, I find the perfect style. I put half of it up, leaving curly pieces of hair streaming down my face. It looks perfect with the crown and veil I will be wearing.

Slipping on my dress, I can't help but notice how amazing it is. It is white and covered in hand-sewn beads. The top is sleeveless and fits perfectly around my body. The bottom half is made of tulle and shimmers in the light. The dress is full and hard to walk in, but from the moment I had seen it, I knew it was perfect. I would be a princess for the day, like all brides should be.

Suddenly, memories of the past came back, and I start thinking back of the day I was to marry Kamrin and how on that day I was taken to the dungeon where he tortured me for over three years. I become paranoid and find myself constantly looking over my shoulder and in every corner of the room. I have to finish getting ready. I had to get out of here before it happens again. I am now in a full state of panic!

The clock by the bed starts to play wedding music which means it is time for me to leave. I am relieved, I have made it! I take one more glance at the mirror to ensure I am prefect, or as perfect as I can be. Then, one more glance around the room. I am alone. I am safe.

"Are you ready, Lue?" John yells from outside the door, startling me.

"Come on in," I yell back, as I stand facing the door.

John opens the door and stands in the doorway wearing a white tux with tails. He looks handsome. His mouth drops open as he stares at me, smiling in approval.

"You look like an angel," he says with a smile.

I blush.

"So do you," I smile back.

John puts my arm in his and leads me down the hallway. He has decorated the hallway and stairs in white bows and flowers. It is amazing. We walk downstairs and it is the same. He has decorated the entire house. I look at him, smile, and give him a soft kiss on the cheek.

"Thank you," I whisper as we head outside, "Everything is so stunning."

"It is my pleasure," John blushes.

Leading to the same beautiful carriage that I had been in recently is a red carpet sprinkled in white rose petals. The carriage itself is decorated with the same flowers and bows as the ones inside. It is more breathtaking than before.

John opens the door to the carriage and holds his hand out for me to take. I grab his hand and prepare myself to get in. The dress is so full that it takes both of us to lift it up and keep it out from being in front of me as I walk up the stairs, leading to the inside of the carriage.

I am a nervous wreck and am anxiously waiting to see Angel at the altar, as there is still a part of me that is afraid that at anytime Kamrin will show up and take me away. I know I have to calm myself before I get to the altar, as I am afraid that if I work myself up too much, I will pass out during the ceremony. I sit back in the plush seat and listen to the music that is being played in the background. It is the same music I have heard before. However, a little different as this time it seems to be a little louder and a little more calming. I am able to relax instantly.

What beautiful music! I think to myself.

I look around for speakers but once again never find any. I listen closer and then realize that somehow, it is coming from outside. I shrug my shoulders and enjoy the rest of the ride.

We come to the garden we had to go through to reach the lake. I had expected to walk from there, but now there is a temporary white wooden bridge built over it.

"I didn't want you to get that wonderful dress dirty," John yells from the front of the carriage.

I am amazed at all this man has gone through for me. This is the most beautiful wedding I have ever seen, and he has made it possible. I can't imagine anyone doing anymore than he has done. We drive over the bridge and I know we are only seconds away from where Angel is waiting.

"Where are we going?" I ask as I notice that we are not headed in the direction of the lake.

"There's a note from Angel sitting on the other side, he wants you to read it," John yells back.

Tears fill my eyes as I imagine that Angel has changed his mind and has run as fast as he could, away. Nervously, I pick up the letter that is bound in a red ribbon and unrolled it.

It read:

> *To my love,*
> *I have a wedding present for you, but I must give it to you*
> *before the wedding. It is important that you receive it now. Go with*
> *John and don't worry, I am waiting for you at the altar.*
>
> *Love Always, Your Angel.*

I am confused on what possibly can't wait until after the wedding and find myself excited to see what it is. We drive a while in the opposite direction until we come to a small cabin. I hate cabins and become worried of what awaits me inside.

John stops the carriage by the front door and then comes and helps me out.

I know Angel would never hurt me, so I follow John inside.

Hesitantly, I open the door. The cabin is completely empty. I am now really confused.

Maybe the cabin is the present, I think to myself. *Or maybe this is where we are staying on our honeymoon.*

Both of which I think could have waited until after the wedding.

"Go in, Lue," I hear John say from behind me.

I look back at him; he smiles and gives me a wink. I can tell he knows I am a little concerned because he gives me a little shove pushing me toward the door.

"There's nothing here to hurt you," he assures me.

His voice is that of sincerity, so I trust him.

"Plus, Angel is waiting for you. So, you better hurry before he smartens up," John laughs.

I smack his arm lightly and go further in the room. I look around, still uncertain of why I am there.

"I'll be outside," John says as he closes the door behind him, leaving me alone in the cabin.

I don't understand, I think to myself as I continue to look around the room for any indication as to why I am there.

I can see no significance of why I have to be here – now. I want to be at the altar with Angel. Not here, in an empty cabin by myself. I am out of patience and decide that I can find out later what all this is about, so I walk toward the front door. When I reach for the handle, I hear a voice behind me. It is a soft voice – a familiar voice. I freeze. I am too afraid to turn around.

"Aren't you going to say hi?" I hear the voice say again.

My eyes begin to tear. I want to turn around but every piece of my body is yelling at me, telling me that this cannot be happening. I can't move. I can't breath. My heart is pounding out of my chest. This has to be a sick joke; there is no way this can be true.

Why would someone do this to me? I cry to myself.

Without warning, Kamrin's face flashes in front of my eyes, and I know he has found me and is somehow making all of this happen. I know it! In fact, that probably isn't even John outside the door. It is one of Kamrin's followers, and right now, Angel and John are looking for me. Kamrin has taken me again.

I am just about to scream, when I hear the voice again.

"Now, Lue . . . Don't you ignore your mother!" A stern voice says from behind me.

I turn quickly, expecting to see Kamrin standing there, ready to take me away. It isn't him! There, standing in front of me are my parents. I blink my eyes. They are still there. I run toward them, I have to touch them; I have to know if they are real. I touch my mom's face; it is warm and as soft as I remember. She smiles as tears run down her face.

I touch my dad's face; he needs a shave, but his skin is warm. I begin to cry hysterically.

"How?" I cry, "I saw . . ."

My mom puts her finger on my lips and stops me from talking. I grab her hand and hold it on my face. Her touch feels so nice; it is a thing I never thought I would feel again. I grab my dad's hand and lay it on my other cheek. They both smile at me. I smiled back.

"Is that really you?" I sob.

"Yes, it's us, Lue." They cry.

I grab them both in my arms. I never want to let them go again. We hold each other for the longest time, crying and looking at each other. I have so many questions to ask and so many stories to tell them, and I am sure they do also.

Suddenly, my dad releases me from his hold and pulls my mom away also.

"We have to get you to that altar." He smiles and says, "We promised Angel."

"You met Angel?" I ask.

"Well, yes, silly girl. Who do you think brought us here?" My mom laughs. "And we promised him that we would get you to the altar in time, so that is what we are going to do."

My dad is a strong man, a proud man, and always keeps his promise. So, I know there is no reason to argue with him; I wouldn't win anyway.

My mom and dad each take one of my hands in theirs and walk me to the front door. I can't quit looking at them, and I find myself staring at them the entire time, as I can't believe they are real. I have to stop and hug them one more time before we walk out the door, just in case it is a dream.

John is waiting at the carriage. He is weeping, so it is obvious that he knew why I am here. He holds open the door to the carriage and helps my parents in first. He then takes my hand and starts to help me up also. I stop him, wrap my arms around him, and hold him tight. We both cry for a moment, and then he kisses my forehead.

"Angel's waiting," he says as he helps me in the carriage.

The ride back to the wedding is amazing. My parents and I hold hands the entire way and talk. Each of us interrupting one another with different stories. I am so happy, and I never imagined I could be this happy again. I don't know if I want to laugh or cry, as my emotions are running wild.

"We are here," John announces.

The ride to the lake is faster than I had anticipated it would be, and I wish I had more time to talk with my parents.

As we come to our destination, my mom pulls out a hanky and wipes my eyes.

"We can't have you going out looking like that now, can we?" she states as she hands me a small compact with a mirror.

Opening the mirror, I see that my makeup has become a mess, and I have mascara streaming down my face. Taking the makeup she has just given me, I try to fix myself. However, it is useless, as all the makeup I had applied earlier is now wiped clean by all the tears.

"You look amazing," my dad insists as he kisses my cheek, "I never liked a lot of makeup on you anyway. You're beautiful just the way you are."

My mom exits the carriage first, as she kisses me on the forehead and states how much she loves me. It is so nice to feel her touch again. I reach for her hand as she gets out of the carriage, holding her hand for a brief second more as I enjoy every moment of the feeling.

"I love you," my mom whispers to me, and then kisses my cheek.

"I love you too," I whisper back.

John takes my mom's hand in his; together they walk hand in hand toward where she would be sitting.

"I'll see you in a few minutes," my mom says with a smile as they turn the corner to the aisle.

Next, my father exits the carriage holding out his hand to help me out. I take his hand and hold it tight, never wanting to let it go.

As he walk me to the aisle, a smile larger than life is on my face; I never want this day to end.

I peek around the large floral covered arch and see that everyone is sitting waiting patiently. There aren't very many people, as everyone I know is acquainted with Kamrin, so I could not invite them. There are just my parents and a few close friends of Angel, or at least that is what I thought, until I look again and see that there has to be at least hundred people.

I wonder if they are angels, I think to myself as I become extremely fidgety and nervous.

The music starts to play; it is finally time for Angel and me to be together.

One quick glance around. No Kamrin! I smile, this is really going to happen!

"Are you ready?" my father asks, holding his arms out for me.

"Yes," I smile, wrapping my arm in his.

Walking down the aisle, I can't help but notice the detail that John has put into the wedding. Each podium is draped in white bows, and accentuated with red roses, and every guest is holding a lit, white candle, lighting my way to Angel.

At the end of the aisle, stands Angel. His eyes, a brilliant baby blue, shine within the candlelight. He is wearing a white tux with tails; his blond hair flowing down to his shoulder glistens from the glow of the candles. He is amazing. I am hypnotized by the way the light seems to illuminate around him, almost like a white haze of peace and serenity have taken over his presence. An Angel from heaven is standing in front of me – my Angel, and I can't wait to marry him. Excited to be by his side, I unconsciously pick up my pace until I am now at a slow sprint. My dad laughs and whispers in my ear to slow down. Both of us now laughing, I slow my pace.

When we reach the end of the aisle where Angel awaits, my father kisses my cheek softly and places my hand in Angel's.

"I love you, puddin," my dad whispers, then walks over to take his seat by my mom.

After kissing me gently on the hand, Angel and I turn to the preacher, ready to take our vows. I can't believe the day has finally come, and I am about to marry the most amazing man. I am finally at peace. I have my parents with me and a wonderful man at my side.

I am positive that the preacher is an Angel also, as when he talks, he his voice is calming and sincere. He talks about how Angel has waited for me all his life and how once he found me he knew instantly that he never wanted to let me go. That I am and always will be Angel's one and only true love. I know what he means by that, and I think, so does most of the other people here, that is except for my parents. Or do they know who he is? I forgot to ask.

"Lue," I hear the preacher say.

I look over and realize that I have drifted off into my own little world.

"Yes," I answer.

"Are you ready with your vows?" the preacher asks.

"Yes," I answer with a smile.

We had both written our own vows. I am certain that Angel's vows will be beautiful, but mine? I am not that confident about it. I become nervous, as I am uncertain if mine could express how I truly felt.

First comes Angel. He turns, holds my hand to his heart, and says:

> "Lue, I love you more than words can express. From the moment I saw you and looked into your beautiful eyes, I knew that you were the one I had been waiting for my entire life. You are my best friend and the one I want to spend every moment of my life with. You have made me the happiest I have ever been and await our new beginning."

Kissing my hand, he then places my ring onto my hand.

I am surprisingly calmer than I thought I was going to be when I begin reciting my vows to Angel.

Taking his hand and placing it on my heart I say:

> "Angel, from the first day I met you, the day you saved my life, I knew you were my destiny. You are truly my Angel. My love will continue to grow for you each and every day of our life together. I am yours forever."

I too, then, place a ring on his finger.

We both turn to the preacher as he pronounces us husband and wife. After engaging in a semi passionate kiss, we then turn to our guests.

As we walk back down the aisle, the preacher announces:

> "I would like to be the first to introduce Mr. and Mrs. Angel Richardson."

All the guests all stand up and clap.

I looked over at Angel with a confused expression on my face.

"It is my true last name," Angel explains, "the one I was born with. I want you to have that name, not the name that I use now." He then kisses me gently on the lips.

The wedding reception is amazing and so is the food. John has made a dinner that consists of salmon and prime rib, not to mention all the trimmings that go with it. It is delicious, and I know if I eat one more bite, I will explode out of my dress.

After dinner, it is time for John to say a toast. Now, I had expected him to say an amazing toast, but that is not what happens. John stand and looks at me and Angel, then raises his glass to ours:

"I was told that the best man has to give toast to the bride and groom," he says as he reaches into his pocket and hands us a piece of toast out of his pocket, "so here is your toast."

Everyone at the reception begin laughing so hard that I think the laughter will never end. John sits back down and after a few minutes, the laughter softens to just a few people in the background talking and having a good time.

"I think it is time for some dancing," the DJ announces, "Can we please have the happy couple up here for their first dance."

I had picked out the perfect song for our first dance and can't wait to be in Angel's arms. Angel and I dance that song and every song together, holding each other tightly. People come over and tap Angel on the shoulder, indicating that they would like to dance with me. Angel honors their request, then comes back and takes me away only after a few seconds. I don't mind though, in fact, I am happy that he does, as all I want is to be in his arms.

"You're my angel," I whisper in his ear.

"And you are mine," Angel whispers back.

I can feel the love he has for me every time he looks into my eyes, and I hope that he can feel mine.

The night becomes cold and the reception begins to wind down. I am anticipating the honeymoon, as I know it will be just as magical as everything else has been today. Angel will not tell me where we are going, and he had insisted on packing my bags for me. He insists it would give our destination away if I were to have packed them myself. At first, I tried to figure out where we were going by searching my closet for missing clothing, but Angel had caught me, so he bought me all new clothes just for the trip, that way I would have no idea. I know it will be astonishing, and I can't wait to be alone with him.

"Can I have the last dance with my daughter," My dad asks Angel, ultimately interrupting my dream of where we could be going on our honeymoon.

"Of course," Angel says with a smile. "Only if your lovely wife will honor me with a dance."

Angel winks at me, then walks over to my mother, and asks her to dance.

The four of us twirl around the dance floor to one of the favorite songs. I am enjoying dancing with my father, as it is reminds me of my childhood. Before I know it, the song is over. My dad kisses me gently on the head, walks over to my mom, and then together they sit back down.

After all the guests leave the reception, Angel and I get in the carriage and go home. I tried to get my parents to ride with us, but they insisted that Angel and I should ride alone.

The ride is shorter than before, as angel and I never parted lips the entire ride, making the trip short but yet sweet.

As soon as we get inside, Angel and I both excuse ourselves, then go upstairs to change into something more comfortable for our honeymoon trip. Not wanting to lose the feeling of the wedding, I put on a white lace summer dress, whereas Angel puts on a nice blue suit.

We have a few hours before we have to leave, so we dress as fast as we can, then hurry back downstairs where my parents are waiting patiently. I had found out very little information on the trip to the wedding, about the two miracles that are sitting in front me and hope I can find out more before we leave. However, that does not happen. They want to know about the three years I had lost of my life, and the story about Angel and me. Starting from the day I was taken away, I tell them the story about how I was captured and kept in a small room for three years. I then explain how I escaped and how Angel had found me and brought me back home. Finishing my story, I explain that I had gone to their house and found a note.

They become confused and insist they never left their home; instantly they begin looking at me as if I am insane. I don't understand why they don't remember being taken, tortures, and most of all, dying.

They have to remember that. I look over at Angel, and he gives me a wink, indicating for me to let the subject go. I decide that maybe that would be best, if I can keep that memory from them, they will be better off.

All I know is that, the wonderful man who is sitting next to me, gave me my life back, my family back, and that I love him with all my heart. I look over at him and smile. I know, some day, I will understand completely what he has told me about his life and the magic that makes him who he is.

"I don't mean any disrespect, but what happened with Kamrin?" my dad asks abruptly.

I choke on my saliva and begin coughing so hard that my face turns instantly red. Angel begins tapping me on the back, trying to relieve the coughing-fit I am now in. After a few deep breaths, my cough finally stops.

Glancing over at my mother and father, I don't know how to answer his question. I am uncertain if I am allowed to tell them that he was the one that had kept me captured, as I know that could and probably would raise more questions. So I lie.

"When I came back, I was told that he and Cheyenne had gotten married, so I thought it would be best to leave things the way they were," I explain.

"I think that was best, just look at who you have now. This is the most wonderful man I have ever met," my mom says as she winks at Angel.

"I too think so." I smile as I hold Angel's hand tighter.

We sit and talk a little longer as my dad proceeds to ask Angel about what he does for a living, where his family came from, and just about any question a father would ask. I know that he isn't trying to be rude; he is just being a "dad," and I think Angel knows that also, as every once in a while, he will turn to me and with a smile on his face, gives me a little wink.

"I hate to interrupt everyone, but if you don't leave soon, you will miss your plane," John comes in and tells Angel and me.

We say our good-byes at the front door, as we head for the airport. I hold my mom and dad for so long that Angel had to pry us apart, or we will be late. Angel knows I am ecstatic to see my parents, so he offers to delay the honeymoon for a bit longer.

After a few seconds of debate, I convince him that is not needed. That there will be plenty of time to catch up later. Besides, my parents look tired, and we will be gone for only a few days.

My parents wave good-bye and we are on our way.

I am so excited about being alone with Angel that I can barely contain my excitement. In fact, I have been planning this evening since the day he asked me to marry him. For days, I shopped for the perfect nightgown and had picked out a special attire for the evening of our marriage, which Angel has no idea about. I did not pack it with our other stuff, because Angel would have known. Instead, I had John ship it to the place we are going, as he and Angel are the only ones that know where that is.

The flight is long and gives no hint to where we are headed. It is Angel's own jet, so there is never an announcement of where we are going. I try over and over again to get the destination out of Angel, but he is stubborn and will not say a word. All I know is that we are flying over the ocean. At first, I stare out the window at the beautiful ocean, but the never-ending blue makes me tired and my eyes begin to droop.

"Lue, we are here," I hear Angel say.

"I must have fallen asleep," I yawn.

I look outside the plane, and we are at wonderful white sand beach. As I step outside the plane, I can't help but notice the scent of the fresh sea air. It smells so wonderful and so fresh, that I stand on top of the plane's stairs and took in the scent.

"Doesn't that smell wonderful?" I ask Angel as I take in a deep breath.

"Yes, it does," Angel answers as he joins me and takes in a deep breath also.

I stand there for a while longer as I look around the beach. It looks desolate and seems to possess only a single hut. We will be completely alone. The thought of being alone with Angel for three days is exhilarating. Angel takes my hand and leads me to the waiting hut.

When we reach the front door, he lifts me in his arms and carries me over the threshold. His arms feel so warm and comforting that

I never want him to let me go. I hold onto him tight, as I kiss his neck and cheek, thanking him over and over again for being such a wonderful man. He stands holding me, laughing and kissing me back. Once inside, he reluctantly sets me down on the couch and then walks back outside to get our bags.

"Here, put this on. Let's go to the beach for a while," he says as he hands me a small bikini he takes out of one of my bags he had packed for me.

"I haven't worn one of these in years," I exclaim, "I don't know about this."

Angel laughs and says, "You're beautiful, don't worry about it, besides, all the other guests are on the other side of the island. We have this place to ourselves."

I realize while changing that it is the first time I have seen him without a shirt on. His entire chest and midsection is perfectly toned and his skin, the color of milk, glimmers in the candle light. I continue to stare at his perfection as I notice that each of his muscles are perfectly defined as the illumination of his skin, gives off shadows defining each muscle. He is so captivating that I become embarrassed changing in front of him. He is perfect, and I know I am not. Becoming self-conscious, I change quickly, ensuring that he does not get a glimpse of my body.

After changing, Angel grabs a picnic basket full of food, and a blanket. I pick up a bottle of wine, two glasses, and a couple towels. We are all set to go to the beach and enjoy ourselves.

We play on the beach the entire day. It is warm outside, and it feels good in the cool water. I am not the best of swimmers, so Angel holds me close in his arms while we swim about. He says he will not let anything happen to me, that he will never let me go and I know I never want him to.

The day is like a dream, as dolphins come to our side and let us pet them. Angel seems to be able to communicate with them; when he tells them to give me a kiss, one puts his nose on my cheek. It's amazing.

After swimming for a while, we set out a search of the area, until we find the perfect place to have our dinner. It is an old palm tree that seems to have fallen or maybe it has grown that way, either way it has a perfect shaded area for us to sit and eat at. While eating the gourmet meal that John had prepared for us, we watch as the two dolphins continue to play. It is one of the tastiest meals I have ever had, and I know I have eaten too much. I am afraid to go back into the water, as I have always heard that you can get cramps and possibly drown, if you go swimming after eating a big meal. So, I convince Angel that we should stay on the beach and enjoy the sun on our pale skin.

The air becomes chilly as the day turns into night. We gather our things and walk back to the house.

I want everything to be perfect tonight, so I insist Angel to wait outside the bedroom, while I prepare the room for our wedding night. After taking a shower and fixing my hair, I begin placing candles throughout the room, lighting them as I go along. I had put some red roses in my purse before we left, so I take them out and begin de-petaling them and placing the petals on the bed. When I am finished, I step to the middle of the room and admire my work. The room is perfect.

"Lue," Angel yells from the shower. "There's a box for you in the other room, it just came."

I peek my head out the bedroom door to ensure he is not standing there. I can hear the water running in the other bathroom, so I know it is safe to come out. I have worked hard on my hair and makeup and want to surprise him with the beautiful gown I had bought. I want to look so beautiful that he will never let me go.

I pick up the box from the chair that is set in the living room. It is a big white dress box wrapped with a black bow. I stare at the black bow for a while wondering why John would have put a bow of that color on it. Then excusing it in my mind as one of his pranks, I then walk back into the bedroom and shut the door.

"Very funny, John," I say out loud.

I take the note that is on the box and read it.

It read:

"Good luck – with the marriage. I will see you soon, and remember, I will always love you!"

The note gives me the chills, and I can't understand why John would write such a note. Afraid that the box had not come from John, I yell to Angel in the bathroom to see from where he had got it. He is singing so loudly that he does not hear me. I try again. Still no answer.

"Maybe my parents wrote it," I think to myself.

I can hear the shower stop in the other room, so I know I have to get dressed quickly. I tear the box open. After removing the white tissue paper, I recognize what has been placed in there. It is my old dirty wedding dress that I had sliced into pieces, and it has been sewn back together! I lift it up in disbelief and scream.

The room goes dark!

CHAPTER 18

The Unforeseen

BESIDES THE CANDLES that I had lit earlier, the room is now ultimately dark. I look around the room as it becomes chilly and unsettling. I remember back to the times before, when I had experienced the same situation. I become nervous and scared. I try to call out for Angel, but I am frozen. My lips won't move and no sound will come out of my mouth. I try to run, but it is as if my feet are nailed to the ground. I am quickly reminded of the time in the bathroom when I had experienced something similar, when my body was pinned to the bottom of the bathtub. My heart begins beating faster. Looking over at my old, beat-up wedding dress lying on the bed, I know exactly what is going to happen. I try to brace myself for what will come next, but my mind begins to race. A cold breeze fills the room and the candles begin extinguishing one by one. I can hear someone or something moving about the room. I want to look around but my body is still frozen at the spot I now stand. I can't move an inch. My breathing gets heavy, and I feel as if I am going to hyperventilate and pass out at any time.

A chill rushes through my body as I feel a familiar presence behind me. He has found us! I don't know how he has found us, but I know he is here! I look toward the door expecting Angel to burst in at anytime and save me, but he never does. I listen closely. I can no longer hear Angel singing in the other room and begin wondering if they have already taken him away and what they will do to him this time! What they will do to me! Tears begin to fill my eyes as a force overcomes me, forcing me into a kneeling position on the floor. My head and arms are now being held down by the same force, and I can feel his hot breath on my neck.

"This is the way you are to greet me!" he snarls.

My stomach begins to turn, I feel sick. His long, scaly fingers touch my cheek. I try to escape his cold, slimy touch, but it's of no use, I still can't move. He moves his fingers around my face, outlining my eyes and lips. Every touch is becoming more uneasy. I try to close my eyes, but I am in a trance, and I can do nothing more than sit and continue to look forward. I am helpless! As I feel his lips next to my ear, I cringe and start to imagine the worst. He rubs his rough dry face on mine making it feel as if a million dull razors are being slid across my face.

As he picks me up and lays me on the bed, I can feel his snakelike tongue enter my mouth as he kisses me. Every bit of my heart and soul wishes I could bite it off, but I have to lay there and endure the horror. I begin to scream within myself. I don't want this to happen and not this way. I had been saving myself until I got married, and I had married Angel. Tonight was the night I was going to give myself to the man I love and cherish with all my heart. But now it has turned into a night of terror, as the man I despise is taking that away from me.

Now, feeling his rough hands moving up my thigh raising my gown, I know he is going to get something I have cherished all my life. I try to shut my mind off so I will not have to experience anymore of what is happening. But it is as if he is in my mind also, not allowing me to do so. He begins kissing me again, however, this time with more power and desperation. His hands now wandering around my exposed body, I feel all is lost. I want this man off me. No! I want this man dead!

"It's time to finish what I started, little one," he says as he continues to explore my body with his scaly hands.

I am screaming in my head for him to stop and please leave me be, hoping that if he is somehow in my mind, he will hear my plea and have some kind of compassion for me and let me go.

"I'm sorry," I hear him whisper in my ear, "You should have been mine a long time ago, and I am tired of waiting."

I can hear Angel stirring outside the door, and I know that I have to get his attention, so I try giving into the intruder that is now on top of me, in hopes that he will put his guard down and release some, if not all of his power he has on me. I can't do it, as when I try to kiss him, vomit rises up my throat at the thought of what I am kissing. I know that the only way I will be able to go through with my plan is to imagine that the intruder that I am kissing is the "Kamrin" I once knew and loved. Not the demon I have come to hate and despise. It works and I am able to kiss him back. Kissing him with great intense and passion, I almost forget who I am really kissing. I start to give into him – that is until I open my eyes and look into his glowing, snow-white eyes. Instantly, I close my eyes as vomit rises back up to the top of my throat, causing me to come back to reality.

The intruder doesn't seem to question my motives and begins to kiss me harder. My stomach is hurting and my heart is breaking, but I know I have to do this. It is the only way I will be able to escape from his clutches. I know I can't look into his soulless eyes again, or my fear will overcome me and will become powerless again.

As Kamrin continues to become more passionate, the hold he has on me seems to weaken. My arms come under my control again, and I am able to move them. Not wanting to give away my plan as of yet, I move my arms slowly, wrapping them around his now half-naked body. Feeling his back with my hands, I can feel that he does not have the skin of a man. It is scaly and wet with perspiration and feels disgusting beneath my hands. My body cringes as I can no longer take the horror.

I refuse to give my body to him completely, and I don't want him to get his way. I feel I now have power enough to get Angel's attention, so I slowly remove one of my arms from his back, all the while still kissing him and moving my other hand over his scaly skin, acting like I am enjoying him and what he is doing to me. I then position myself in a way that I feel I will be able to push him off me.

He is so caught up in what he is doing that he is unaware of what I have done. He begins kissing my neck. His hot breath makes me feel as if it is fire melting beneath my skin. I know I have to take action soon, as he is becoming very intense and begins unbuttoning my gown. I feel over to the table on the side of the bed until I can feel something that might help me get away. My fingers instantly come in contact with a large vase that I had placed there when I was decorating the room for our honeymoon night. It is barley at my reach, and I know I have to reposition myself again, so I can get a full grasp of it. Keeping his attention by kissing his disgusting sweat-covered neck, I am able to move a little to the side, which allows me to reach the vase.

The vase now in my hands, I know there is no turning back. I have to move fast so he will not have time to get me back within his power. Taking a deep breath, I lift the vase and slam it as hard as I can onto his head, causing him to let out a loud growl.

Not convinced that has worked, I then kick him with my knee as hard as I can. As he crouches over in pain, giving me enough time to escape from underneath him. My entire body is just about to get off the bed, when all of a sudden I feel a sharp pain overtake my leg as he embeds his long nails into my skin. Ignoring the pain, I am able to rip my leg away from his new-found hold. Moving swiftly, I run toward the door letting out a scream that can be heard throughout the island.

As I grab the handle to open the door to safety, the knob becomes hot as melted metal, causing my hand to experience a substantial burn. Holding my hand in pain, I cower into a corner awaiting the wrath from what I know is coming next. I can hear him coming closer, and I wonder once again why Angel has not come to my rescue.

"Angel!" I scream in my head.

This time not only can I hear myself scream within my head, it can be heard throughout the room.

The room begins to shake as I hear the bedroom door explode around me. Shards of wood fly across the room, busting out the glass to the window overlooking the ocean. The candles around the room begin igniting one by one, as if some unforeseen entity is lighting them.

Angel, now standing in the doorway, is angry and ready to fight. Without hesitation the intruder grabs my hand and pulls me next to him, letting out an ear-piercing growl that makes every hair on my body stand on end. In one leap, the intruder takes me across the room to the newly busted window. I grab the headboard of the bed and try to keep him from taking me any further. I can't let him get me out of the room, as I know what will happen to me then.

Now, angrier than ever, Angel raises his head and lets out a cry, as no other I have ever heard in my lifetime. This angers Kamrin, and he throws me to the other side of the room, causing my body to slam into the unwelcoming wall. In one leap, he is flying through the air in Angel's direction. Simultaneously, Angel takes action and leaps toward Kamrin causing them to collide in midair. The room rattles, as their two bodies slam together, causing a sound of explosion of thunder throughout the room.

My head is now bleeding from the sudden blow. I try to focus myself on what is going on around me. However, the room is dark again, as the candles were extinguished by the percussion from the two men colliding. I am unable to see but two glowing figures moving around the room.

I can't tell what is happening, so I crawl my way over to the light switch on the wall. However, before I can switch it on, a bolt of electricity surges through my fingertips, causing me to back my hand away.

Determined to turn on a light, I fell on the floor, until I find something I can use. Holding a plastic hanger in my hand, I once again reach for the switch and push the hanger up the wall. Bolts of electricity once again begin shooting from the light socket, causing me to endure a sudden shock. I know I have no choice, so I continue enduring the pain as I push the light switch on. The lights come on, and I am able to see around the room. Quietly I work my way back to the corner and crouch down trying to keep a safe distance from the two men fighting. Peeking around the bureau I am hiding beside, I watch the two men as they slam one another into one wall and then another, picking each other up and tossing one another as if they are throwing merely a feather pillow, causing each other extreme pain.

As the fight continues, the men seem to change. I am dumbfounded. Whereas I can partially see through the men, as if they are made of glittered-filled water, but yet, both are letting off a slight glow. I know

Angel is an archangel, but I have never seen him in this form. I blink my eyes to ensure I am really seeing what is in front of me. He is exquisite as his skin seems to sparkle and glow at the same time. It is truly as if I am looking at an angel straight from heaven. I have to smile, as the sight is so heavenly, it is at that moment that I finally come to terms with the idea that he is honestly an angel.

My daydream is ended abruptly when I feel someone hit the wall beside me. I look up in time to see the fiery red eyes of Kamrin as he leaps up from the fall he has just been thrown against. He is livid and in one leap he is back to where Angel awaits him. The two men are fighting once again.

While watching what is unfolding in front of me I can see that the two men fighting look as one. Separating in only brief intervals, it is obvious that Angel is the stronger of the two, as he always seems to have the upper hand.

I know right away which one is Angel as he let offs a light blue, heavenlike glow and moves around with grace and ease. It is hypnotizing watching him, and I find it hard to turn away. The other figure, however, is dark and gloomy, his glow putting off a dark red haze. His movements are more violent and clumsy.

The fight continues as neither man seems to back down. I become frightened as with every violent hit one of the men will endure, a clap of thunder will echo throughout the room, and the one that has suffered the blow will let out a screech. I know they are hurting each other tremendously.

Still cowering in a corner, I feel helpless and know the only thing I can do is to wait for the fight to be over and pray that Angel is the one who will still be standing. However, it never seems to end. The room is being destroyed by the hard blows each man is enduring, causing me to become more concerned. I don't know how much more either of them can take, and I hope that Kamrin will give up soon and leave as I am afraid that the only way this battle will end is by the death of one of them.

Suddenly the room goes silent and the lights begin to flicker. A loud growl echoes, engulfing the room. The lights go out completely. I try to see what is happening, but I can see no one. Working my way over to a table, I reach for a candle and light it with the matches that I have found next to it. The candle lights up the room just enough that I can see faint shadows.

Looking closer, I can see that there is one figure standing over another that is laid out on the floor. I smile, as I know Angel is the one standing and that he has defeated Kamrin. The shadow begins to move in my direction.

"Angel," I smile and ask, "Are you OK?"

"What makes you think I am Angel?" A deep immortal voice answers.

My heart skips a beat as I realize that Angel is the one on the floor. He had been defeated. I begin to cry. I can't believe what has happened. He can't be gone.

Suddenly, I can hear Kamrin's footsteps as he gets closer.

"Leave us alone!" I scream as I lay my head down. "Why can't you just let me live my life with Angel?"

"I told you, you were mine. That you were my special girl," he says with an evil laugh.

I look up and to my surprise Kamrin is no longer the disgusting demon I am used to seeing. He is the handsome man I once knew.

"Are you surprised to see me?" Kamrin hisses.

"No. I knew it was you," I snap.

"It was the passionate kiss that I gave you earlier that gave me away, wasn't it?" Kamrin laughs.

"No, it was the stink of your breath that gave you away," I say as I spit on his face. "Not to mention, I don't know anyone as hideous looking as you."

Standing beside me, Kamrin hisses in my ear, "What's wrong? Your little husband over there couldn't save you this time, and it put you in a bad mood?"

I lift my hand from my side and try to slap his face, but his lightning reflexes stop me. His hands are strong and his grip is stronger as I feel the bones in my arm crushing beneath his grip. I scream in pain as he continues to crush my arm.

"Fun time is over. It's time to go," he says as he slightly releases my arm.

I refuse to walk, but it doesn't seem to bother him; he kicks my feet out from under me and begins pulling me along his side as he walks toward the bedroom door. This is hurting my arms more, so I catch my balance and begin walking beside him. The room begins to change around us as we walk. The walls begin to melt, changing from the beautiful blue floral wall print, to dark moldy concrete walls, and the floor mutating from the polished cherrywood to concrete stairs. The room continues to change until the once-charming bedroom becomes a long, dark, gloomy staircase.

Instantly, I know that he is taking me back to his house – the house of terror. And there is nothing I can do except to go with him.

The staircase is cold and damp, causing me to shiver as I reluctantly walk beside him. He has not spoken in a while, causing the room to become silent with only faint sounds of women crying. I can't see where the cries are coming from, but the further we walk down the stairs, the louder the women's cries get. I look around and see only solid bumpy walls.

Kamrin begins walking faster, causing me to lose my stepping. I trip and fall to the floor, banging up my knees. Lifting myself off the floor, I lay my hand on the wall for support. The wall becomes soft and begins to move under my hand.

Startled, I try to jump back, but someone or something from within the wall grabs my hand and holds it tight. I try to pull away from their grip, but it's too strong. I try again. It's of no use; they are now holding me with both hands. Kamrin begins to growl as the cries from the wall become louder.

I stop pulling away and listen closer. It is a woman, and she is pleading with Kamrin to let me go. I begin feeling the wall with my other hand and realize that the lumps on the wall resemble the outline of women. I close my eyes and then reopen them as I try to focus them in the dark.

As my eyes adjust to the darkness, I can see that the walls are made up of women. They all have mutilated faces and bodies and are crying, causing the walls to look as if they are dripping with water. My heart sinks as I realize that these are the trapped souls of the women that Kamrin has killed. I begin to weep as the thought of how many women have endured his torture floods my mind like a new implanted memory. Kamrin grabs the hand that is holding me and begins to hiss. The woman releases me and starts to cry louder.

My hand, now, back in Kamrin's, he begins pulling me further down the staircase. The walls on both sides of the staircase are completely made up of these women and seem to never end. There has to be thousands of them on the wall, and they all are weeping.

The sounds become louder and more desperate as we walk further down the stairs. I know I have to try to get away; I just don't know how or where to run. Acting like I trip once again, I fall to the floor. Kamrin releases my hand and begins to yell for me to get back up.

Taking a quick glance back up the staircase, I catch my balance and stand up. Kamrin begins to walk down the stairs once again, however, this time forgetting to hold my hand. I turn and run as fast as I can up the stairs.

I have been running for what seems an eternity, never getting any further than where I had begun my escape. I stop and turn back looking for Kamrin. He is not there, and I become excited thinking I have outrun him.

I turn to face the direction I have been running and slam into a hard surface. With great force, I am knocked to the ground, causing me to lose my breath. I look up. It's Kamrin!

He has somehow gotten in front of me. I pick myself up again and begin running back down the stairs; however, not getting far before Kamrin is standing in front of me once again. Slamming his hands in my chest, he thrusts me across the staircase and into the wall.

"That is enough!" he growls, showing me his yellow sharpened teeth.

Lying there, unable to breath, I begin to feel hands surround my body.

Suddenly, I find myself being lifted off the ground. I turn my head to look behind me and see that the women on the wall have me in their arms, and they are lifting me up. They look at peace now, as everyone of them is smiling.

Feeling at peace myself, I close my eyes and give into them, letting them hold me in their comforting arms. Kamrin begins to hiss at the women with his snakelike tongue. They refuse to release me and hang on to me with all the strength they have. Suddenly, his eyes turn from the fiery red that I had seen so many times before to snow-white. He starts screaming at them in the same foreign language I have heard a few times before.

The women's expressions turn to fear, and they once again begin to weep.

"No . . . leave her be," I hear a woman cry next to my ear.

I turn to look at the woman and realize it is Samantha . . . the girl I had helped to die. Tears fill my eyes as I know that she is not at peace as she had hoped. That she too, has become a captured soul. Kamrin hisses again as if it he is giving out his final warning.

The weeping from the women becomes overwhelming, as Samantha defies Kamrin and refuses to release me. Outraged, Kamrin walks over to where she is holding me down and begins to try and pry me from her grasp. She tightens their hold and pulls me in closer to her.

Stepping back away, Kamrin lets out an immortal growl that shakes the walls and floor beneath me. Samantha instantly begins to loosen her grip she has on me, until I am once again free from her arms.

I turn and look, the wall is solid once again, and as the women seem to freeze into the position they once were. The crying ceases, and the room becomes dead silent once again. Angry and out of patience, Kamrin grabs me by the arm and pulls me down the final few steps. I trip once again plummeting to the floor.

"Get up, you clumsy bitch!" Kamrin screams as he grabs my hair and pulls me up off the floor.

With a sudden jerk, I am once again standing.

My head now pounding from the handful of hair he has just pulled out, I try to prepare myself for what may be waiting me behind the closed door. Kamrin lifts his hands into the air and begins chanting in an evil, ireful tone – chanting so quickly that I am unable to understand what he is saying.

The door to the room flies open with such extreme force that it slams into the wall behind it, causing the walls to rattle. I rub my eyes trying to adjust to the bright room that is now in front of me. Taking a glance around, I see that the room seems to be empty except for a single bed that lay in the middle of the floor. As I take a closer look, I can now see that it is some type of hospital bed with restraints on each corner.

My knees begin to buckle under me as my shaking becomes out of control. I know what my fate is now, and I know that Angel will not be able to save me this time. I begin to cry hysterically as I can no longer control my emotions.

"I'm sick of hearing your whining!" Kamrin screams as he lifts me up and launches me over toward the bed.

Missing the bed, I fall onto the floor, slamming my head into the hard concrete. Blood begins gushing down my head from the fresh wound. My ears begin to ring, the room starts to spin, and I know I am going to pass out. I look up and reach for the bed; however, Kamrin is now standing in front of me blocking my way from doing so. Grabbing his pants for support, I try to lift myself from the floor. I lose my grip as my legs slip on the fresh blood and plummet back to the ground.

Finding myself once more on the floor, I look back up at Kamrin, hoping that he will have some kind of compassion and help me to the bed.

He is now holding something in his arms; I rub my eyes and look closer as I can hear a baby crying.

Taking the baby from its blanket, Kamrin holds the baby in front of me. I can now see its face. He is an adorable baby, in fact, one of the cutest babies I have ever seen. I have smile as I watch him move about in Kamrin's arms.

Suddenly, the baby begins to mutate. His face now profusely overcome with scars and his eyes a fiery red, the baby lets out an immortal cry that rattles the walls of the room.

Kamrin walks over and lays the baby in my arms. A sharp pain shoots through my stomach as something inside me begins to move about with extreme power.

Petrified, I am unable to move. I begin to hyperventilate from the pain, or maybe it is from the sight of the mutilated baby. I do not know, but I can no longer control my breathing. My head becomes heavy and the room starts to spin again.

My body goes limp, and the baby falls from my arms. I hit the floor.

Trying to keep focused on all that is around me, I slowly lift my heavy eyes and see that Kamrin is holding the baby once again.

"He will be mine!" Kamrin screeches as he points toward my stomach.

A bright light overtakes the room causing the already bright room to become snow blinding. I pass out.

Here is a sneak peek at "Seeded from Evil"

An irresistible sequel to "Lessons from an Evil Mind"

PREFACE

MY MIND AND body are tired, but more than that my soul is exhausted, and I am unsure how much more I can take before I give in to the evil that haunts me. All I want is to live my life as any other normal person would. But now I have another burden, one that I will not be able to escape. One that "he" is determined to take from me.

I try to move, but once again he is in complete power of me, pulling me further into his wrath of evilness that he is.

I want to wake up. But this is no nightmare; he has taken away something from me that I will never forgive him for. I don't care about my life anymore. I want revenge, and that is something I will get!

CHAPTER 1

Heaven or Hell

DEATH IS THAT of loneliness. I look around. I am alone in the desolation that now surrounds me.

I scream in hopes that someone will hear me, but my words seem to be left unheard, leaving me with only the echoing of my own voice to comfort me.

Laying on my back I continue to scream in desperation. No one comes, leaving me helpless and without another.

I close my eyes. I need to find a memory to comfort me. I try to think of people within my life. But I am finding it hard to concentrate, leaving my memories that of something hidden within me. Within seconds, I can no longer remember anything, anyone, except that of a man named Kamrin.

Within seconds, my sadness disappears and I am at peace, as the man in my memory becomes more clear. His beautiful face now embedded in my mind, I find myself longing for him, wishing that he was here with me.

"Kamrin," I yell into the emptiness that has captured me.

Suddenly I can hear that of footsteps.

My heart begins to beat in excitement as I anticipate his presence.

The footsteps come closer and closer until they sound as if they are right behind me.

I quickly turn. There is no one there. In disappointment, I take a deep breath and lower my head. I am destined to remain alone in this emptiness with the memory of Kamrin.

"Come with me," I hear someone say from within the emptiness.

I look through the darkened mist that occupies the area around me. There is what looks to be a figure of a man standing in the distance.

Instantly, a sense of urgency overtakes my mind and I know I must follow him. The further I walk, the mist begins to lift, until I can see that indeed in front of me is a man, a man that I know must be the only person that I have left in my memories. Kamrin. I am alone and scared as the memory of who I am also begins to disappear. I run towards him. I need to be with him, I have to know who I am, who he is and where we are.

My pace, now that of running, I find myself catching up to him. I reach for him. As my fingers touch his shoulder, the man turns and looks at me. His hair that of brown and his eyes of a bright blue; he is handsome; his smile welcoming, making me want to follow him further. My hand slips from his shoulder and suddenly Kamrin is ten feet in front of me.

"Wait!" I scream.

My voice, that of a fading plea, is ignored.

Kamrin continues to fade in the distance, his beauty being engulfed by the haze that continues to surround us.

Within moments Kamrin is disintegrated into thousands of sparkling crystals. The beauty of the glittering crystals as they continue to change colors, then fade, mesmerizes me.

Kamrin is gone.

Now more desperate then ever I begin running towards the faded crystals, running as fast as I can, but never able to reach the area.

At that moment I have never felt so alone. I needed someone to comfort me, but who. I don't know who I am, so my search is left empty and unfulfilling. All I crave is Kamrin and he is has faded into a unknown force. Instantly I find myself wishing that I could be with him, that maybe if my body disintegrated also, I would once again be with him.

I walk further into the mist, hoping, preying that the force will take me in my entirety, That I too could have the feeling of peace and be with Kamrin once again.

My heart begins to beat faster as the lonesomeness continues to grow within me. Finding myself desperate, I begin to run. My efforts are futile, as my body never seems to leave the immediate area.

I'm tired and out of breath, and although I have an undying need to be with Kamrin, I know I must stop and take a break.

My lungs are burning and I find it hard to take in a deep breath. I bend over, put my hand on my knees and take in shallow breaths until my lungs are finally relaxed enough to take in a deep refreshing breath.

"Lue," I hear in the distance.

Instantly my mind begins to wander, "Am I Lue? Could that be Kamrin calling me?"

Confused I look around. I am the only person in the god-for-saken-place, I must be Lue.

Filled with excitement I begin walking towards the voice. It has to be Kamrin. Although, now uncertain who Kamrin is, the need to be by his side has taken over my body and I know he is the person that can help me.

Walking towards a light that is now illuminating in front of me, I know that I will soon find my destiny.

Within minutes, my stomach begins to turn and my head feel dizzy. The further I walk, the sicker I feel. But, I can't stop, the light has me now in a trance, and my body refuses to stop moving forward. The area is calling to me, wanting me to continue. Pulling me in. My legs begin to feel as if they are floating in air and no longer touching the ground. Concerned about what I am feeling, I look down and realize that where my legs once were, is now like Kamrins was before he completely disintegrated into nothingness. They are now a sparkling see-through haze of colored crystals. Everything within me screams for me to stop and head back to the area I had once been. My entire body fighting against my mind, I try to stop walking, but legs are no longer visible, leaving me powerless to my continued movement. I scream, but my voice is lost within me.

Without warning a sense of overwhelming, serenity and peace overtakes my heart, pulling me further in. The further I glide, the more feeling of weightlessness overcomes my body, and the more at peace I become. The sickness I had felt just moments before fades until I can no longer remember being sick at all.

Stopping for a moment, I watch in amazement as the lower half my body continues to be taken over with the same unknown white haze. It is the strangest, however the most beautiful thing I have ever experienced, as my entire lower body is now sparkling haze of white, crystals. Hypnotized by the beauty, I lift my hands as the unknown force continues to take over the rest of me. Finding it amazing and utmost beautiful, I continue to stare at my hands; turning them in every direction as I admire the beautiful colors of the crystals where skin once laid. I can't run, I don't want to run. I want whatever this is to take me in my entirety, as I have never felt so at peace.

Now completely overtaken by the haze, I am a shinning, ghostly figure. The feeling of compete tranquility I am feeling is indescribable. With my ghostly hand, I reach over and touch my arm. To my surprise, I can still feel the sensation of my touch against my skin. I continue to feel my arms in amazement. I feel soft and cool to the touch, as if my skin is made of silk, but there is nothing there except that of the crystal haze.

My mind begins to wonder as a cool and calming cloud surrounds me, relieves me of all future worries.

I take in a deep, appeasing breath as the remaining dark haze in the distance turns to that of white embracing clouds.

I look up, close my eyes, and take in the feeling. Within seconds, the brightness coming from above warms my ghostly physique. I look up to see what is causing such warmth.

My eyes are drawn to the center of the clouds, where a bright light continues to appear, Instantly pulling me into an unfamiliar place. Now totally engulfed by white fluffy clouds, I continue to stare at the light as it continues to illuminate brighter and more intense, until I find it almost impossible to keep my eyes open.

Unexpectedly, memories of who I am floods my mind and I instantly remember everything.

The man I had recently longed for comes to mind, and I realize that it was Kamrin I had wanted so badly. My stomach sickens at the thought that I could have been left with only the memory of the man I despise; Kamrin and I could have went with him.

Coming back to realization, I begin to wonder where I am and how I got here.

A recent event comes to mind and I remember that of a baby. The baby, instantly turning from one of the cutest babies I have ever seen to that of a mutilated, demon-like baby. The horrible memory of Kamrin, the room and the baby floods my mind.

"I was in a room with Kamrin," I think to myself, "I fell and bumped my head."

Fear overtakes me.

My heart begins to race as I look at my ghostly body.

"It will be okay," A voice from within the light above me says.

Stunned by the sudden voice, I look up.

All of a sudden, I find myself spinning around, starring at the faces of people I had known in my lifetime. They all are holding their arms out inviting me to come further. I want to go, but a sudden wave of panic overcomes me when I realize, they are all family and friends that have passed away, and they are in fact inviting me to what I believe is Heaven.

It is not so much that I realize I am dying and going to heaven, that frightens me, as it is the thought of giving up my life before my time. I still have so much I want to do and I know my parents will be crushed if I am to leave them so soon after all that has happened.

Heartbroken, I want to run back to Angel's waiting arms, but I can't as I know he is already dead. The memory of his dead lifeless body laying on the bedroom floor seems to empower me and I find my legs paralyzed where I stand. Tears filling my eyes as I become lost within the memory.

I lower my head and continue to let my tears fall.

My body instantly weakens to state that I can no longer hold my own weight. I fall to the ground. Now completely enclosed by sadness, I lay alone in my own self-pity.

"Don't cry," I hear someone whisper in my ear. "You are not alone."

Suddenly, memories of my childhood begin to flash in front of my eyes. Faster and faster the memories come, as if my own picture show is being played in front of me. My fears of death fade and I feel at peace again, as I watch myself as a child playing in the sun with my parents. I reach out as I gaze into the memory of my father swinging me around in his arms; but there is nothing but emptiness beyond the pictures.

Without warning, the haze begins to fade and within seconds there is nothing more then a light mist that continues to encircle my body.

The ghostly image of my legs, no longer paralyzed, I begin looking in desperation for the memories that seem to have faded within the haze. My body becomes weak and I can feel my soul weakening, leaving me within my desperation to follow the illumination of the bright light as it continues to fade around me.

Chasing the disappearing haze, I find myself walking further into the mist, searching for something I am unsure of. A sudden burst of light radiates around me, flooding my mind with memories of Angel.

I stop abruptly as my emotions overwhelm me. I once again begin to cry, as I watch Angel helplessly looking for me within emptiness. I had wanted to spend my life with him and have his child, but now I will never have that chance. Uncontrollable tears flood my eyes as I continue to try and come to terms with the fact that I will never see his beautiful face again.

Desperate to feel his warm body one more time, I reach towards where he is standing and try to touch his hand. But once again my efforts are useless and I find myself reaching into the blankness that continues to haunt me.

"No!" I scream as suddenly the haze thickens around him, overtaking his body.

The closer I get, the further away he seems to be, until he is a ghostly figure within the thickening mist. Unwilling to give into the indefinite, I try to run towards him, however never able to reach his side. It is as if he is standing in front of me, but somehow running away from me at the same time. Within seconds, he disappears into the thickened haze. I keep running until I can no longer breathe; finding myself once again alone in a field of emptiness.

I stop within my new found isolation and catch my breath.

The haze and faces have disappeared, desolating me to the unknown that has now enclosed me. An uncomfortable feeling of suffering and sorrow overcomes the hollowness of the field and I know something is not right. Listening closely around me I hear nothing more then a soft whimper. However, the voice is to far away and I can not make out what it is saying. Suddenly, the voice comes closer, as if it is running towards me. Panic-stricken, I look through the mist, but see nothing, but a dark cloud of haze encircling me. A wave of heaviness surrounds my body, as the voice is now only a few feet away. I am able to hear it clearer now, however I am still unable to understand what it the person is saying. Suddenly a chill runs up my spine and I begin to shiver as I realize I have heard this voice before. It is the voice of Samantha! Without warning, her dead, mutilated face manifests in front of me, letting out a bloodcurdling screech, that rips throughout my body.

"RUN!" Samantha screams. "He is coming!"

A feeling of evil overtakes the area, as the sinister mist encloses around me, engulfing me with the desperate cries of different women. I know right away that I am no longer in the same peaceful place as before. Terrified, I glance around quickly looking for a way out, but the darkness refuses to let me see through the dark misted field, leaving me vulnerable with no place to run.

Petrified, I close my eyes and scream into the haze that now has me captured.

"Someone help me," I scream.

I want to go back to where I had been. Back into the ghostly arms of Angel. Back to field of white haze where I know there are beautiful memories awaiting me. Desperation overtakes my fear and I begin to run into the emptiness of the field, hoping to find away out. However, the faster I run, the thicker the blackened haze becomes, until I can no longer see any further then three inches in front of me. Panicked, I stop abruptly. I look around. To my delight, I can see a faint sparkle in front of me. Overjoyed seeing a glimpse of hope within my desolation; I hope it is the gates to Heaven.

My instincts tell me to run as fast as I can towards the sparkling light, but my mind insists differently.

I stop.

Now cautious to what it could be I walk over slowly until the sparkle becomes bright enough to see what is awaiting me. To my dismay standing in front of me is a mirror. I turn to run, however I am now surrounded by hundreds of mirrors in every size and every shape possible. The dark haze that once surrounded me now faded, allowing to see clearly all that is around me. I look into the mirror in front of me. To my horror, I am no longer a shinning glow of white light. I am now, as I had been back in the dungeon, covered in scars and dirty. I scream in disbelief as the horrific image continues to haunt me, mimicking my every move. As I continue to look in the mirror, I begin feeling my face. The image in the mirror does the same. Instantly I realize that it is truly me that I am looking at and not some sort of illusion. The more I touch my skin the more scars I receive, until my face resembles Kamrins; a Demons.

I try to wipe the scars off, but with every desperate attempt my nails dig deep into my skin, causing me horrific pain. Instantly the new wounds turning into scars. Without warning, my white, glowing skin begins to turn to a bright red, overtaking my body until there is not a piece of skin unchanged. I look down at my hands, they are now scaly and look as if they are covered in the skin of a dead snake. As I stare at my disgusting physique, I realize that the scales are now overtaking the rest of me, causing ever piece of my skin to become snakelike. The site sickens me, causing vomit to rise to the top of my throat. I have to remove the scales, as I did not want to die with the body of evil. Peeling the raised scales off, my skin is left with raw, bleeding skin exposed. The site is disturbing and sickness my stomach even more, but I have no choice, it is better then having the skin of a Demon. I continue ripping the scales off my arms until I am sure I have succeeded in removing every inch of it. I look in the mirror again. Within seconds my new bloodied skin is overtaken by the reddened snakelike scales. It is useless, I am putting my body in agonizing pain, and in no way any closer to releasing myself from the Demon body.

I lower my head in disgust, as I can no longer look at my new self.

"Help us!" I hear that of a desperate women whisper to me. Instantly more women join in, all pleading for me to help them. I look up. I can longer see my reflection in the mirrors, as my reflection is now that of the women from the pictures I had found in the cabin. Their faces that of mutilation, makes my heart sink. I look into their soulless eyes, and realize that they are those of lost souls. As they continue to beg for my help they reach for me. Their touch lost within the mirrors, their faces turn to that of desperation and despair. Unable to help them, the sadness in their voice pierces my heart. I can't take it anymore, I have to close my eyes and plug my ears.

Suddenly I feel that of a warm touch against by demon like skin. The touch that of love and sympathy, I open my eyes.

Standing in front of me is Samantha. She is as God had attended her to be, beautiful.

"You have to get out of here," Samantha whispers in my ear. "Go back."

Suddenly the women in the mirrors begin to scream in terror. Instantly they all fade.

"Come back," I scream to Samantha.

Its to late, she is gone.

My body becomes hot and no longer feels cool to the touch. The feeling of being light as air changes and I now feel as if I am falling, falling into a deep hole of emptiness.

"See how beautiful you are," A voice echoes in my ear.

I turn, there is no one, however I know the voice and I know it well.

"You need to get the Hell out of here!" My mind screams.

I turn to run, but I am lost within the mirrors without any way of escape. Unsure where to run or how to get away from all the mirrors I run directly into the biggest one I see, busting it into thousands pieces. Never loosing my stride, I run as fast as I can, turning around only for a second when I see through the corner of my eye a dark shadow.

The shadow instantly disappears. A feeling of triumph shoots through my body, as I know I have gotten away. In desperation to keep my freedom I keep running as fast as I can. The further I get away from the mirrors the more my body changes, until it is once again the beautiful white haze of brilliant crystals.

Suddenly I feel someone tap my shoulder. My heart plummets into my stomach as I look to my side. He is now right besides me, running along with me, laughing as if he thinks of this as a game. Petrified, I run as fast as my legs will allow, ignoring the fact that the dark haze has surrounded me once again. In desperation I change my direction often, hoping to throw him off my path. Within minutes of doing so I realize that I have accomplished nothing more then confusing myself, and that more then likely I am running in circles, back to the area of the mirrors. Back to the despairing cries of the women,

"Where are you going to run?" I hear Kamrin laugh as he runs by my side. "Your in my world now. No place to go, but to Hell from here."

Kamrin leans over, placing his foot in front of mine, he trips me. I instantly fall to the ground. My efforts have been useless, I am certain I have no chance of getting away now. Suddenly, I feel his slimy hands on my neck. I know what is coming next. Without warning I find myself being lifted into the air. My body now floating in the air, I look down at Kamrin. He is holding me in front of him, his hands still wrapped around my neck.

"I'm not done playing yet," He laughs. "Now run!" He says as he sets me gently on the ground beneath me.

The tightness of his hands around my neck has caused me to be short of breath. I start to run but I know with the lack of oxygen I am experiencing I will not get far. Besides, I know that it is inevitable, he has more power then me, and I am alone, I have no one to help me. Stubborn, I stand my ground and refuse to move.

This angers Kamrin more then I have ever seen him. His skin that of fiery red, bursts into flames. His body now that of a silhouette of fire, he screams in such a sinister voice that my body instantly cringes.

"I said run!" He yells; his breath that of a dead, rotting body explodes in my face.

Complete and utter fear overtakes me. I have to get away. I don't want to suffer the pain and anguish I know I will endure if I give into him. I begin to run as fast as I can, running into the emptiness of the dark haze until I no longer hear his laughter in the background. Although I can no linger her him, I now he is somewhere behind me. I have to do something, or it will be seconds before he has me once again. With the sick games he likes to play, it won't be over. He will make me suffer a minimal pain and then make me run again and I don't know how much longer my body can endure the running. Thinking quickly, I suddenly stop. The area is silent with only the sounds of Kamrin footsteps as they continue to come closer. In hopes that he does not trip on me, I lay as flat as I can, letting the dark haze cover my body, ultimately shielding me from any possible visibility. As I listen closely I can hear him. He is right behind me, and coming closer, fast. Hoping that he will continue to run until he has lost me in the darkness, I take in a deep breath and hold it in, laying as still as my fear-stricken body will allow. Within seconds I feel a breeze from his body as he passes by my still body. I listen closely as I can hear him continuing to taunt the emptiness that is now around him.

"Do I run?" I ask myself, a little concerned on what would be the best thing to do.

Without warning a surge of energy rushes through the silhouette that was once my body, almost knocking me to the ground. Petrified, I catch my balance and glance around me; there is nothing except complete blackness. I wait for what may come next, what pain awaits me. The surge of power slams my body again, this time with such power that I am knocked to the ground. My body is tired; I have no fight left within me. Kamrin has one, I will fight no longer.

LaVergne, TN USA
14 June 2010
186019LV00004B/17/P